The Faber Book of

POLITICAL VERSE

Edited by
Tom Paulin

faber and faber
LONDON · BOSTON

First published in 1986
by Faber and Faber Limited
3 Queen Square London WC1N 3AU

Filmset by Wilmaset Birkenhead Wirral
Printed in Great Britain by
Butler and Tanner Ltd, Frome and London
All rights reserved

British Library Cataloguing in Publication Data

Faber book of political verse.
1. Political poetry, English
I. Paulin, Tom
821'.008'0358   PR1195.H5

ISBN 0–571–13947–7
ISBN 0–571–13667–2 (Pbk)

Contents

Preface

During the compilation of this anthology I received much help and encouragement from many friends, colleagues and members of the poetry-reading public. For their advice and heartening of my editorial labours I would like to thank: Jonathan Barker and the staff of the Arts Council Poetry Library, David Young and the staff of Nottingham University Library, Elizabeth Boa, Sidney and Nancy Burris, Robert Cockcroft, Adam Czerniawski, Roy Foster, David Hammond, Christopher Hampton, Seamus and Marie Heaney, Francis Higman, John Hirsch, Keith Howden, Cilla Huggins, Russell King, John Lucas, John McClelland, Pete Messent, Blake Morrison, Dave Murray, Bernard and Heather O'Donoghue, Giles Oakley, George Parfitt, Frank Pike, Bob Reinders, Peter Robinson, Ann Pasternak Slater, Angela Smallwood, Nigel Smith, James Sutherland-Smith, Jeremy Treglown, Thorlac Turville-Petre, Elizabeth Watson, Irving Weinman.

I am most grateful to Jacqueline Marsh who acted as my research assistant and encouraged me throughout, and I want to thank David Williams for giving me the benefit of his learning and wisdom. I am also grateful to Craig Raine who commissioned the anthology, made a number of inspired suggestions and provoked the polemical introduction. I must also acknowledge Adrian Frazier's generous help in giving me a copy of his essay, 'Whose Abbey Theatre?', which discusses Yeats's relationship with Annie Horniman. For Milton's view of the Belfast Presbyterians I am indebted to Marianne Elliott's inspiring, post-revisionist pamphlet, *Watchmen in Sion: the Protestant Idea of Liberty* (Field Day pamphlet no. 8). It is my hope that this anthology will contribute towards the creation of a broad 'canon' of political verse in English.

Introduction

We have been taught, many of us, to believe that art and politics are separated by the thickest and most enduring of partitions. Art is a garden of pure perfect forms which effortlessly 'transcends' that world of compromise, cruelty, dead language and junk cars which Manicheans dismiss as mere politics. Art stands for freedom, while politics is a degrading bondage we must reject and escape from. Indeed, there is an influential school of literary criticism – appropriately, it dominates literary studies in the United States – which argues that the political and historical content of literature must be dismissed as 'extrinsic irrelevance'. The practitioner of close reading agrees with Henry Ford that history is bunk and enforces that belief with a series of fallacies – biographical, intentional, historical, 'personalist', ideological. Like intimidating heresies, these supposedly fallacious ways of reading literature are designed to hinder the reader who believes that there is often a relationship between art and politics, rather than a clear-cut opposition between formal garden and contingent scrapheap.

The poet who elects to write about political reality is no different from the poet who chooses love, landscape or a painting by Cézanne as the subject for a poem. The choice of a political subject entails no necessary or complete commitment to an ideology – Burns, for example, was a radical republican but he nevertheless based 'Charlie He's My Darling' on popular Jacobite songs about the Young Pretender. He could combine a dedicated egalitarianism with a pride in the House of Stuart that was both personal and national. And if Burns had been more extensively cavalier in his sympathies, Arnold might not have dismissed him as a 'Scotch' provincial who speaks in a bogus voice, lacks high seriousness and has mistakenly elected to write about 'a harsh, a sordid, a repulsive world'.

Burns is one of the most notable victims of the aristocratic, hierarchical, conservative tradition which Arnold and T. S. Eliot have floated as the major cultural hegemony in these islands. And although Eliot offered a strategic defence of Burns's verse, his subversion of Milton's reputation was a major act of cultural desecration (the subsequent modification in Eliot's attitude did not repair the damage). Both Arnold and Eliot adopt a romantic, curiously puritan and personal attitude to Milton – Arnold criticizes his 'asperity and acerbity, his want of sweetness of temper', while Eliot confesses 'an antipathy towards Milton the man'. Abetted by Leavis, the *Scrutiny*-group, the New Critics and that reactionary theologian, C. S. Lewis, Eliot was able to rewrite English literary history and almost obliterate the Protestant prophetic tradition. And as David Norbrook has pointed out in his brilliant, pioneering study, *Poetry and Politics in the English Renaissance*, the Renaissance poetic tradition culminated in Milton, a figure whose

> uncompromising republicanism places his views even today outside the conventional framework of political discussion in England. Eliot and Leavis did not flinch from a drastic solution: Milton must be declared to have been a bad poet, and 'dislodged' from the canon.

As Norbrook reminds those of us who still revere Milton as the greatest English poet and the most dedicated servant of English liberty, some of the major Renaissance poets were politicians. But this unsettling historical fact was pushed out of the cultural memory by a group of literary critics dedicated to a 'transcendental' vision which ostensibly depoliticized art.

This orthodoxy has meant that students of English literature have for several generations now been encouraged to believe that Milton's theology is entirely separate from whatever his political beliefs might have happened to be. And in any case, Milton had been smeared by T. S. Eliot as a master of 'a dead language' and was therefore a writer who might be respectably avoided. The ghost of an earlier *entryiste*, Edmund Burke, must have smiled at Eliot's enterprise, and Arnold's eccentric praise of that Irish counter-revolutionary as 'our greatest English prose-writer' is one of his more 'interested' or committed critical judgements, even though Arnold astutely balances it with a criticism of Burke's stylistic extravagance and 'Asiatic' provinciality.

Together, Arnold and Eliot ensured that the magic of monarchy and superstition permeated English literary criticism and education like a syrupy drug. Fortunately, the work of Christopher Hill challenges the bland, unhistorical, insidiously tendentious readings of Milton which have been dominant until recently, and in time it may be generally acknowledged that Milton is no more a non-political writer than Joyce was – or Dante, or Virgil.

One of the dogmas of the ahistorical school of literary criticism is the belief that political commitment necessarily damages a poem. Thus poets tend to be praised for their liberal open-mindedness, their freedom from the constricting dictates of ideology. As Douglas Bush has shown, Cleanth Brooks transforms Marvell's 'Horatian Ode' into an expression of modern 'uncommitted' liberalism. Yet the two greatest political poems in English – *Paradise Lost* and *Absalom and Achitophel* – are works of the committed imagination. Milton was a republican, a regicide, the official propagandist of the English parliament, Dryden became a monarchist and a Tory after the Restoration. Their political beliefs are fundamental to their poems and our reading is enriched by a knowledge of those beliefs and an understanding of the social experience which helped to form them (I say 'helped' because in the end we accede to a political position by an act of faith – Milton's essential faith was love of liberty, Dryden's love of order).

In the Western democracies it is still possible for many readers, students and teachers of literature to share the view that poems exist in a timeless vacuum or a soundproof museum, and that poets are gifted with an ability to hold themselves above history, rather like skylarks or weather satellites. However, in some societies – particularly totalitarian ones – history is a more or less inescapable condition. In those cold, closed societies a liberal belief in the separation of the public from the private life is not possible. Nor is it possible to believe that a poet may take only an occasional interest in politics, or adopt a position which in the West would be termed 'purely aesthetic and non-political'. The ironic gravity and absence of hope in poets such as Zbigniew Herbert, Różewicz, Holub, remind us that in Eastern Europe the poet has a responsibility both to art and to society, and that this responsibility is single and indivisible. The poet, in Joyce's special use of the term, is the 'conscience' of his or her society.

Pasternak on Hamlet, Herbert on Fortinbras, Holub on the illusion that 'Hamlet will be saved and that an extra act will be added', all remind us that in certain societies to write poetry is to act socially, not to turn one's back on contingency. Here, symbols are deployed like ciphers in a secret code – the dissident Hamlet becomes an honorary citizen of the Eastern Bloc. He is the intellectual and poet-figure whose presence in a poem always implies the existence of the usurping tyrant, Claudius, who smuggled poison into the garden and caused the Fall. To initiate the analogy is almost to ghost the rumour that Stalin had Lenin poisoned.

The actor-Hamlet's nervousness is Pasternak's fear that by speaking out directly like Mandelstam he will join him in the Gulag. But in this exposed, public confrontation with the tyrant it is Hamlet alone who will die. And it was partly by adopting an 'antic' disposition that Pasternak survived the great purges and lived to translate *Hamlet*. Like Shakespeare, Pasternak saw 'art tongue-tied by authority' and by pretending to be merely voluble, eccentric, a harmless cloud-treader, he earned Stalin's protection. No one would blame him – Nadezdha Mandelstam never did – for in a sense he made a reality of the illusion 'that Hamlet will be saved'.

To consider Pasternak's career is to understand how completely the personal life can be saturated by political reality, for politics is like a rainstorm that catches us all in its wet noise. Only in a liberal democracy can we hope to dodge it and even there we may be misleading ourselves, or being misled by others – ageing New Critics, or those neo-Christians William Empson so despised.

Although the imagination can be strengthened rather than distorted by ideology, my definition of a political poem does not assume that such poems necessarily make an ideological statement. They can instead embody a general historical awareness – an observation of the rain – rather than offering a specific attitude to state affairs.

And sometimes a political poem does not make an obviously ideological statement – 'To Penshurst', for example, conceals its politics behind a series of apparently innocent and 'natural' images.

Almost invariably, though, a political poem is a public poem, and it often begins in a direct response to a current event, just as a pamphlet or a piece of journalism springs from and addresses a particular historical moment. For example, in March 1681, the Whigs introduced the Third Exclusion Bill which was designed to safeguard liberty by preventing James Stuart, the Duke of York, succeeding Charles II. Charles dissolved parliament (he had already removed it to royalist Oxford), and in July he imprisoned the Whig leader, Shaftesbury, in the Tower on a charge of high treason. Dryden was both historiographer-royal and poet laureate, and he supported Charles in a prose-pamphlet, *His Majesties Declaration Defended*, and then in *Absalom and Achitophel* which was published in mid-November and is said to have been undertaken at the King's request. The poem was published as a pamphlet and it aimed to prejudice Shaftesbury's trial at the end of the month. Like Auden's 'Spain' – also first published as a pamphlet – Dryden's poem was generated by the hurry of contemporary political events. It is in no sense disinterested or transcendental of society – quite the reverse, in fact, for it aimed to bring Shaftesbury to the scaffold. Politically, it is a brilliant dirty trick, an inspired piece of black propaganda; aesthetically, it is a great masterpiece. But no-one should call it 'pure'. The writer who prompts a judge, a jury, and an executioner is necessarily guilty, and although Shaftesbury managed to escape to Holland, that distinguished libertarian is now only a faint presence in the historical memory. He has melted into Dryden's fiction, a fiction that invests him with something of the engaging *élan* of Shakespeare's Richard III – a dramatic character whose historical accuracy Josephine Tey and others have challenged.

Yeats's couplet on the poet's impurity, his responsibility for political violence, is a well-rubbed quotation, though few critics have tried to follow up the question, 'And did that play of mine send out/Certain men the English shot?' by placing the writings in their immediate social context. This is partly because literary history is almost a lost art and partly because many literary critics have no interest in biography or in history proper (for example, it seems likely that Yeats's insistence on art's superiority to politics was partly a ruse designed to mislead Annie

Horniman who funded the Abbey Theatre and was a British patriot). 'Easter 1916' is dated '25 September 1916' and Yeats began writing the poem after the executions of the fifteen rebel leaders which took place between 3 and 12 May, 1916. Curiously, the most famous modern political poem was originally published as a sort of underground pamphlet – it was privately printed in a limited edition of twenty-five copies by Clement Shorter for distribution among Yeats's friends. Yeats waited another four years before publishing the poem, and in his seminal essay, 'Passion and Cunning', Conor Cruise O'Brien argues that:

> By the time when 'Easter 1916' and 'The Rose Tree' were published, in the autumn of 1920, the pot had boiled over. The Black and Tan terror was now at its height throughout Ireland. To publish these poems in this context was a political act, and a bold one: probably the boldest of Yeats's career.

It could be argued that Yeats displayed his characteristic cunning in waiting four years before releasing 'Easter 1916'. He had told Lady Gregory in a letter of 11 May, 1916, that 'I had no idea that any public event could so deeply move me', but he did not hasten to express that emotion in public. However, in the autumn of 1920 an influential British Labour Party commission was inquiring into the conduct of the war, and by publishing his poem in the *New Statesman* Yeats aligned it with Labour's condemnation of British reprisals (it appeared two days before Terence MacSwiney, the mayor of Cork, died on hunger strike). In 1916, he would have had no definite idea what a future Ireland might look like – the Union may well have appeared rock-solid at that time – but the poem's publication on 23 October, 1920, coincided with Lloyd George's first tentative moves towards a truce and a settlement. And, appropriately, that issue of the *New Statesman* was dominated by Irish politics (it contained several articles criticizing the British government's campaign of 'official terrorism' – i.e. the Black and Tan campaign). Yeats's poem is therefore part of a new political climate and like *Absalom and Achitophel* it must also have helped to mould opinion. A statement which might have isolated and exposed Yeats in the autumn of 1916, now helped to consolidate links between British socialists and Irish nationalists.

Yeats was an intensely political writer and his frequent sneers at politicians, journalists and other 'groundlings' are part of his consistent deviousness, his influential habit of first affirming that art and politics are hostile opposites and then managing to slip through the barrier, a naked politician disguised as an aesthete. It is a self-confessed circus-act which appears to have fooled many spectators into believing the poet was somehow above the vulgarities of politics. This element of populism, cruelty and calculated circus-like improvisation is an important characteristic of Yeats's work and I would guess that Samuel Beckett had the great ringmaster in mind when he created Pozzo in *Waiting for Godot*. Yeats belongs, though, to a separate Irish tradition of political verse and in order to consider the concept of the political poem it is necessary to define the various traditions which inform such poetry.

THE POPULAR TRADITION

In England, this type of political verse began long ago in the complaints and rebellions of the common people against those in authority. It shapes itself in anonymous ballads, popular songs, broadsheets, nursery rhymes like 'Gunpowder Plot Day', and its visceral energies can be felt in both Kipling and Yeats. It is the groundbase, the deep tidal pull, which underlies much political verse written in 'higher' or more 'official' modes. Often it can be witty, tough, idealistic, and resolute with a sense of egalitarian integrity:

> I mean the ploughman,
> I mean the plain true man,
> I mean the handcraftman.

This rich proletarian tradition looks to the prelapsarian Adam and Eve as ideal images of a just society, and these primal figures were invoked by John Ball in the text of the revolutionary sermon he preached at Blackheath in 1381. Adam delving, Eve spinning – the image became a radical, republican commonplace and it was invoked frequently during the 1640s. In *Vox Plebis*, a work ascribed to the Leveller, John Lilburne, we read: 'For as

God created every man free in Adam: so by nature are all alike freemen born'. The image of free Adam – an image often used pejoratively by episcopalians – passes from Milton and Marvell in the 17th century to Clough in the 19th, and Clough's ironic, half-admiring reference to 'Democracy upon New Zealand' in *The Bothie of Tober-Na-Vuolich* is a late version of the ideal puritan commonwealth whose failure Milton probes in *Paradise Lost*.

One of the masterpieces in this tradition is John Clare's 'The Fallen Elm', a bitter and tender elegy which speaks for a dying social class – the agricultural labourers who were displaced by the enclosure acts. Like Jonson's 'To Penshurst', Clare's poem is conservative in its sacral sense of the value of tradition, and it gains enormously from Ann Tibble's restoration of Clare's original orthography:

> The common heath became the spoilers prey
> The rabbit had not where to make his den
> & labours only cow was drove away
> No matter – wrong was right & right was wrong
> & freedoms bawl was sanction to the song
> – Such was thy ruin music making elm
> The rights of freedom was to injure thine

Like a Luddite pamphlet, Clare's poem seems to rise up from a vast, anonymous historical experience, and we can see that experience expressing itself actively in this United English oath which E. P. Thompson cites in *The Making of the English Working Class*:

> In a ful Presence of God. I a.b. doo swear not to abey the Cornall but the . . . Peapell. Not the officers but the Committey of United Inglashmen . . . and to assist with arms as fare as lise in my power to astablish a Republican Government in this Country and others and to asist the french on ther Landing to free this Contray.

The Irish accent of the oath is a reminder of the close links between radical movements in these islands, and it is significant that the English Chartist poet, Ebenezer Elliott, should echo Burns in 'Drone v. Worker'.

It seems likely that Browning's 'The Lost Leader' is spoken by a Chartist, and the poem's lithe dactyllic rhythms are shared by many Irish rebel songs. Again, this poem was inspired by a particular occasion – Wordsworth's acceptance of the laureateship on 4 April, 1843. The speaker of the poem voices the feeling that Wordsworth has betrayed 'us' – i.e. the working class. Browning had a nonconformist background and was a convinced Liberal (see, for example, the uncollected sonnet 'Why I am a Liberal'). He was briefly a student at University College and his poems show traces of Bentham's philosophy, and they also manifest a distinctively Protestant fascination with the workings of the individual conscience. It is possible to discern in Browning's numerous portraits of Renaissance egotists both a traditional Protestant and libertarian obsession with the power of Italian Catholicism and a topical criticism of the individualistic ethos of Victorian England. Like Arnold in *Culture and Anarchy*, Browning is voicing – though less directly – an unease with the *laissez-faire* philosophy of 'doing as one likes'. In this he resembles Clough who was deeply interested in political economy and hostile to an unbridled capitalist ethic.

Tragically, the popular verse tradition appears to be almost extinct in England now, though the work of the 'pop' poet, John Cooper Clarke, and that of a number of poets who write in West Indian and reject standard British English, may be aligned with this type of political verse. Linton Kwesi Johnson on the Brixton riots of 'April nineteen eighty-wan' is like an echo of these lines from the early 15th-century 'A Song of Freedom':

> þin ffadere was a bond man,
> þin moder curtesye non can.
> Euery beste þat leuyth now
> Is of more fredam þan þow!

To read these poems with their deep libertarian instincts and demand for social justice is like discovering a hidden, living tap-root which permanently feeds a vigorous eloquence. Clare's lament for his 'music making elm' becomes symbolic of the uprooting of his class and of the loss of certain traditional

English liberties. Anyone who has seen the Stars and Stripes flying over a piece of English common land will understand something of Clare's answer to the 'cant of tyranny'. The student of Ted Hughes's poetry will notice that it draws strongly on a popular vernacular, but his recent acceptance of the laureateship suggests that he has been co-opted by the rival monarchist tradition.

THE MONARCHIST TRADITION

Despite T. S. Eliot's influence on the shape of English literary history, this is not the major tradition of political verse in England. It is important, but not as omnipotent as its supporters would have us believe. Although Spenser is a Protestant prophet, his poetry has been commonly aligned with that mystic patriotism, belief in social hierarchy and reverence for institutions 'sprong out from English race' which characterize monarchism. Spenser served the Earl of Leicester and he shared his patron's extreme Protestantism. Thus when Spenser looks forward to the 'new Hierusalem' and identifies the English as God's 'chosen people', he is expressing radical Protestant beliefs which were later held by Milton and the English republicans. Spenser's historical placing long before the Civil War enables him apparently to span both the Protestant and the monarchist traditions. But for Milton there was no doubt that 'our sage and serious poet Spenser' was fully committed to the puritan cause.

Shakespeare's conservative pessimism belongs to the opposing tradition, though there is a populist anger in Sonnet 66 which is radically disgusted and anarchistic, like much of Swift's writing. This rejection of a corrupt public world is also offered in Ralegh's 'The Lie', and his anti-Spanish stance made him both a popular hero and, like Spenser, an influence on Milton. It would require a large and separate anthology to give a comprehensive account of Shakespeare's political vision and I have therefore included only two excerpts from *Coriolanus*, a play which has had a far-reaching influence on subsequent political verse. Its anti-populism is present in Hopkins's use of the verb 'mammocks'* in 'Tom's Garland' and although Eliot's 'Coriolan' is not one of his better poems, it must be noted that his designation of *Coriolanus* as Shakespeare's 'most assured artistic success' represents more than a disinterested aesthetic judgement. The hostility towards popular education which Eliot expresses in *Notes Towards the Definition of Culture* issues from his deep conservative loathing for democracy and his fear that education – which indeed comes under the influence of politics – will take upon itself the reformation and direction of culture, instead of keeping to its place as one of the activities through which a culture realizes itself.

Hopkins, though he called himself a 'communist' in the early 1870s, is essentially a right-wing patriot who is fascinated, like Kipling, by a vernacular energy and a primitivist vision of life. In a letter to Robert Bridges, he explicated 'Tom's Garland' and spoke of his indignation with 'the fools of Radical Levellers'. He also denounced 'Loafers, Tramps, Cornerboys, Roughs, Socialists and other pests of society', and informed Bridges that the model for his sonnet was Milton's 'caudated' sonnet, 'On the New Forcers of Conscience'. Thus 'Tom's Garland' is a reply-poem which opposes that libertarian tradition of which Milton is the supreme exemplar in England. The working-class speaker in 'The Lost Leader' says 'Milton was for us', and though Milton's writings are often aligned with radical causes he was personally opposed to the Levellers and the Diggers. Hopkins, however, is in no sense a libertarian and he sees the working class as occupying a fixed position in the divine social design – it is a lowly member of the body politic and leads a bestial, mindless existence, careless of the 'lacklevel' or inegalitarian nature of society.

The major figure in this hierarchical tradition is Dryden and like 'Tom's Garland' *Absalom and Achitophel* answers Milton's radical vision, his belief in the free individual conscience. Following Milton, Dryden employs Mosaic imagery drawn from the Book of Exodus and his comparison of David (Charles II) to 'the prince of angels' follows the Miltonic parallel with Satan.

---

*When Coriolanus's son tears a butterfly to pieces, Valeria says 'Oh, I warrant how he mammock'd it' (I,3,71).

The political or topical use of imagery drawn from Exodus and other biblical books was commonplace in the 17th century, and Oliver Cromwell employed it in 1654 when he accused the English clergy of 'a design . . . to bring us again into Egyptian bondage'. Dryden was a civil servant under Cromwell and in the 1680s he inverted traditional puritan readings of the biblical account of the Garden of Eden by transforming Achitophel into Satan tempting the blushing Eve (i.e. Absalom who is the Duke of Monmouth). Dryden aims to bury English republicanism and Whiggery, and he compares the post-Restoration adherents of 'the good old cause' to fallen angels, fiends 'harden'd in impenitence'. Shakespearian drama is a major influence on the poem (it helps shape the subtle, often sympathetic portrait of Achitophel), and Dryden's account of Absalom's temptation is similar to Queen Isabel's defence of royal hierarchy in *Richard II* – a defence which Shakespeare is less than wholly committed to in the play.

Rebuking the gardener for his radical criticism of a corrupt aristocracy, the Queen cries:

> Thou, old Adam's likeness, set to dress this garden,
> How dares thy harsh rude tongue sound this unpleasing news?
> What Eve, what serpent hath suggested thee
> To make a second fall of cursed man?
> Why dost thou say King Richard is deposed?
>
> (III, 4, 73–77)

For the monarchist, the deposition or execution of the lawful anointed king represents a split in society akin to a breach in nature. Ben Jonson, writing from within the social tensions that were ultimately to lead to the Civil War, designs a utopian image of a feudal garden in 'To Penshurst' and like Shakespeare he is hostile to that new type of economic man which Edmund speaks for in *King Lear*. However, in *Richard II* Shakespeare's hostility is muted and offset by his sympathetic portrayal of Bolingbroke, and it is possible to detect a closet republicanism in *Julius Caesar*, a play that cannot be unconnected with fears for the post- Elizabethan future.

Jonson was hostile to republican ideas, acted as a government spy, and was in Frank Kermode's phrase a 'collaborator with Stuart absolutism', though his modern affinities are with the socially cohesive, paternalist strain within English conservatism. This paternalist idea informs 'To Penshurst' which is a classic one-nation poem, hostile to mercantile capitalism and recent money. Such hostility forms part of traditional or 'wet' conservatism, and it is also present in Swift's work. This anarchistic disdain for the cash-nexus also forms the opening section of *Maud* and it is an influential strand in Yeats's social thought. Like Jonson, Dryden, Pope, Yeats has a horror of the destruction of culture by the rough beasts of egalitarianism. Echoing Hobbes, Dryden imagines kings and governments falling to 'nature's state, where all have right to all'. It is no accident that Yeats should echo *Richard II*, as Hopkins does in the terrible sonnets, for he is reacting against that aggressive challenge to numinous hierarchy which Bolingbroke symbolizes. Bolingbroke/Cromwell/Robespierre/Lenin would be the paternalist conservative's thumbnail sketch of the continuity of tyranny, and we can sense in Dryden and Pope a cosmic terror at a levelling mediocrity bent on destroying culture, that 'ceremony of innocence' which Yeats celebrates in 'A Prayer for My Daughter'.

The conservative poet is naturally a pessimist and I would guess that the academic who rendered Ecclesiastes into English was not a member of the reforming puritan party within the Church of England. It is common for conservative historians, and particularly those who write about Irish history, to echo the preacher's statement, 'The thing that hath been, it is that which shall be; and that which is done is that which shall be done: and there is no new thing under the sun.' (Ecclesiastes 1,9) For the conservative pessimist, intellectuals disturb the peace: 'he that increaseth knowledge increaseth sorrow.' This is a hard-line conservative position and it is weary with a quietist distaste for the topical and the new. Like many writers of pastoral, the conservative obscures political realities by professing an envy of the ignorant and by shuffling responsibility for historical suffering onto those who aim to increase knowledge by challenging received ideas. At times, the conservative pessimist echoes Eliot in *After Strange Gods* ('What is still more important is unity of religious background; and reasons of race and religion combine to make any large number of free-thinking Jews undesirable'), and we must note that Yeats, like Eliot and Jung, also believed in a concept of racial memory.

It was Eliot's influential ambition to express a unifying conservative vision in his religious verse and in his social and literary criticism. In 'Little Gidding' he imagines a cultural consensus where the English people are at last united 'in the strife which divided them'. Charles I – the beaten, broken 'king at nightfall' – combines in Eliot's historical memory with 'one who died blind and quiet', and that unnamed figure is the poet whose reputation Eliot did so much to maim. The regicide Milton is here allowed a ghostly presence in the canon as the ancient wounds are healed by Eliot's sacramental vision.*

In these salving lines Eliot appears to echo a consensual, Spenserian combination of the monarchist and puritan traditions, for now that the king and the blind epic poet have become part of the national memory the opposing sides of an old argument can be seen 'folded in a single party'. It is a most poignant vision, and we must remember that it is an experience grounded in the British people's profound sense of national solidarity during the Second World War. Eliot aims to heal or 'associate' a split cultural sensibility, and whatever reservations we may have about his politics it is impossible not to admire his achievement in writing this type of religious and patriotic verse. However, that admiration ought not to make us collude with Eliot's displacement of the major tradition of English political verse and we must be alert to the Burkean or High Anglican conspiracy which has so distorted literary history.

---

* Cp. 'The anniversary of the execution of King Charles I was celebrated as normal on 30 January by the Society of King Charles the Martyr, an esoteric group on the rainbow fringes of high church/right-wing/monarchist/anglo-catholic frontiers who hope and pray for the late King's canonization. An altar was set up in Banqueting House in Whitehall – the scene of his execution supposedly consecrated by his spilled blood. Much gin was drunk. All in all, a funny sort of gathering for Mr John (Selwyn) Gummer to be found addressing, expressing his hope that the spirit of King Charles would enter the heart of the Bishop of Durham.' (Report in the *Guardian* 2 February 1985.)

THE PURITAN–REPUBLICAN TRADITION

The puritan imagination is altogether more complex than its opponents suppose – its essential libertarianism can be ironic, playful, dedicated to the primal lushness of a new beginning, as well as paranoid, self-righteous, aggressive and intransigently committed. The puritan reads the Bible in a directly personal manner and to such an eager imagination this psalm in the Authorized Version is a song of freedom that exults in the litheness of a released vernacular:

> When Israel went out of Egypt, the house of Jacob from a
> > people of strange language;
> Judah was his sanctuary, and Israel his dominion.
> The sea saw it, and fled: Jordan was driven back.
> The mountains skipped like rams, and the little hills like
> > lambs.
> What ailed thee, O thou sea, that thou fleddest? thou Jordan,
> > that thou wast driven back?
> Ye mountains, that ye skipped like rams; and ye little hills,
> > like lambs?
> Tremble, thou earth, at the presence of the Lord, at the
> > presence of the God of Jacob;
> Which turned the rock into a standing water, the flint into a
> > fountain of waters.
> > (Psalm 114)

Milton made a beautiful metrical version of this psalm when he was fifteen years old and ten years later he adapted it into Greek heroic verse. That Stuart absolutism which Jonson helped to beautify, was for Milton a sojourn in Egypt where a 'people of strange language' oppressed God's chosen people, the English. And the parallel is made explicit in *Eikonoklastes* where Milton compares Pharaoh's blindness to that of King Charles.

The true puritan rejects traditional monarchy and the authority of the church, and looks instead to the Bible for sanction and inspiration. Puritan ideology draws often on these verses from St John:

> And ye shall know the truth, and the truth shall make you
> > free.

They answered him, We be Abraham's seed, and were never
in bondage to any man: how sayest thou, Ye shall be made
free?

(8, 32–3)

Milton echoes John in his sonnet defending his divorce treatises
and he does so in order to express his commitment to the free
individual conscience. Like Cromwell, he believed in 'the free
way' not 'the formal'. He is therefore opposed to 'a classic
hierarchy' (the phrase refers in the first instance to the
presbyterian church) and this is an influential libertarian idea.
Yeats drew strongly on this tradition at certain moments in his
career and it informs his famous senate speech on divorce where
he invoked Irish Protestant rights 'won by the labours of John
Milton and other great men.' Bernard Shaw also belongs to this
resolute Anglo-Irish tradition, a tradition which paradoxically
finds its most complete aesthetic summation in Joyce's superbly
'catholic' imagination.

In the closing years of the 20th century we have the histories
of many revolutions to remind us of the crimes committed in the
name of liberty, and there are moments when Milton expresses
that type of radical – not conservative – pessimism which can
take a full look at those crimes. In *Paradise Lost* the forces of
darkness occasionally voice their love of freedom with an
affecting, but troubling sincerity. Thus when Mammon speaks
of preferring 'Hard liberty before the easy yoke/Of servile pomp'
(II, 256–7), it is impossible not to feel that he is expressing a
Miltonic credo. But as Christopher Hill argues, the fallen angels
combine features drawn from both the royalists and those
revolutionaries whom Milton believed had betrayed the republic, and here it is necessary to note that some Leveller leaders
plotted with the royalists. Theology and politics fuse completely
in the Protestant imagination, and it is essential that we read
Milton in that knowledge, hard as Protestant hermeneutics are
to convey in an England which appears to have forgotten its
remarkable history. As Norbrook rightly insists, 'In abstract
theological terms the debate between Calvinists and Arminians
was abstruse and raised enormously complex philosophical
issues. But it aroused deep passions amongst the laity because it

had direct political connotations.' We wrong Milton's epic genius if we split *Paradise Lost* into different 'levels' or 'layers' of meaning and by doing so suggest that the poem's politics are separate from its theological vision. One of the things Milton learnt from Spenser's work was the *ennui* of allegory and we must not insidiously allegorize the greatest poem in the English language.

Adam and Eve in the garden is myth as history or history as myth – the ideal puritan republic is innocent of superstition and monarchy. When Satan enters the garden and sits 'like a cormorant' on the tree of life (IV, 196), Milton is employing an image of greed which had traditional associations with 'hireling' clergy and which also possessed oppressive royalist associations for the poet. As Alastair Fowler notes, Milton must at least have heard the cormorant's cry 'for just across the road from his house in Petty France the king's cormorants were kept in St James's Park'. And we may compare this composite image with the characteristic movement of Milton's mind at the close of *Areopagitica* where he remarks that the Star-Chamber 'is now fallen from the stars with Lucifer'. He wrote *Paradise Lost* after the starry empire had struck back.

Following Spenser, Milton imagines the English people 'Growing into a nation' – a nation that believes in 'free reason'. This rational liberty rejects the fate of Noah's younger son, Canaan, who became a 'Server of servants', and this is echoed in *Ulysses* when Stephen Dedalus casts himself bitterly as a 'server of a servant'. Indeed, the Book of Exodus provides one of the major mythic frameworks for Joyce's epic and we should note how the idea of full republican nationhood is fundamental to both *Paradise Lost* and *Ulysses*. The critic who refuses to face this truth frankly is in danger of adopting a monarchist ideology of hierarchy with its accompanying values of rigid order and deference:

> Wolves shall succeed for teachers, grievous wolves,
> Who all the sacred mysteries of heaven
> To their own vile advantages shall turn
> Of lucre and ambition, and the truth
> With superstitions and traditions taint,

Left only in the written record pure,
Though not but by the Spirit understood.

(XII, 508–14)

The Archangel Michael speaks rather like a New Critic as he
voices the embattled puritan sense of how the written record
can be falsified by the forces of reaction, and he then imagines
the New Jerusalem which will be established by the revolutionary consciousness, or free virtuous reason:

New heavens, new earth, ages of endless date
Founded in righteousness and peace and love
To bring forth fruits joy and eternal bliss.

(449–51)

In these prophetic lines, Michael echoes the Second Epistle of
Peter where earth and heaven melt away: 'Nevertheless we,
according to his promise, look for new heavens and a new earth,
wherein dwelleth righteousness' (2 Peter 3, 13). This prophecy is
echoed in Revelations: 'And I saw a new heaven and a new earth:
for the first heaven and the first earth were passed away; and
there was no more sea' (21, 1). At the end of The Rainbow,
Lawrence evokes this Protestant prophetic tradition when he
rejects industrial society in its entirety and describes Ursula
Brangwen seeing 'in the rainbow the earth's new architecture'.
This manner of interpreting the Bible contains much that is coldly
self-righteous, and it informs 'Hibiscus and Salvia Flowers'
where Lawrence witnesses in a distinctively puritan manner to
his own swaying, contradictory feelings about Italian socialism.
The destructive wish to melt the old social traditions in a
consuming fire is a common Protestant form of political
frustration – it is expressed at the end of Samson Agonistes and at
the conclusion of 'In Memory of Eva Gore-Booth and Con
Markievicz' where Yeats commands, 'Bid me strike a match and
blow'. Intransigence, then a complete purging destruction, are
the last stages of the élitist libertarian consciousness trapped
within an imposed orthodoxy. A subjective individualism ends
by abolishing itself along with the entire social order. At this
point the traditional wisdom of the via media reminds us of the
dangers of breaking the mould and making it all new.

If Milton is an example of the committed imagination, Marvell possesses an eirenic vision which is fluid and only sceptically involved with historical change. In his youth, Marvell appears to have been briefly converted to Catholicism by the Jesuits, and although he was a dedicated member of the anti-court party in the House of Commons his earlier commitment may partly explain the double-minded texture of his verse. His sophisticated ironies, and his warm, green, distinctly vegetarian disposition resemble that form of Hinduism which rejects the world of the meat-eaters who mix sex, politics, war. For this type of mystic it isn't possible to make love instead of war – the two activities are cruelly synonymous. Marvell may therefore be said to embody something of the pacificist strain in English radicalism, but this does not mean that he 'speaks more clearly and unequivocally with the voice of his literary age than does Milton'. Eliot's remark is again part of his effort to taint the 'written record pure' with superstitions and false traditions.

Marvell's Protestant vision of history is evident in his miniature epic 'Upon Appleton House' where he symbolizes the English Church as the Virgin Thwaites trapped in a convent – 'The nun's smooth tongue had sucked her in'. This is an echo of Spenser's papal Archimago who lives in a 'little lowly Hermitage' where he files 'his tongue as smooth as glas' and succeeds in parting the Redcross Knight from Una who is Truth. Both poets offer symbols of the English Church before the Reformation and we may compare their evocations of sinister enclosing houses with Milton's famous puritan refusal in *Areopagitica*, 'I cannot praise a fugitive and cloistered virtue, unexercised and unbreathed'. The rescue of the virgin Thwaites in Marvell's poetic narrative is therefore symbolic of the English Reformation and this is given a local foundation by the fact that the Yorkshire estate of Nun Appleton was originally a Cistercian Priory which the Fairfax family acquired at the dissolution of the monasteries.

There are many echoes of *Richard II* in Marvell's poem* and he

---

*In the play, Bushy, Bagot and their accomplices are called the 'caterpillars of the commonwealth' (II, 3, 165), and Marvell's garden imagery and reference to 'caterpillars' (stanza 74) echoes this. His comparison of the woodpecker or 'hewel' to an executioner and his image of the 'traitor-worm' picks up the gardener's comparison of one of his men to an executioner, and the man's answering seditious question:

fuses these reminiscences of the prelude to Shakespeare's civil-war cycle with the classical Horatian theme of retirement and political apathy. His central concern, though, is to analyse the manner in which the individual consciousness within a polarized society can never be pure, can never make the transcendental exit from history. This is evident in stanza 46 where he looks over at Cawood Castle, the nearby seat of the Archbishop of York, and compares the act of seeing or 'sighting' the castle to the action of a field-gun ('invisible artillery'). Even eyesight is not innocent in a conceit which suggests that Marvell is lobbing cannonballs at the 'ambition of its prelate great'. The prelate is the enemy ('the episcopal arts begin to bud again', Milton warns in *Areopagitica*), and in what is really a metaphor for the political consciousness during a time of revolution, Marvell shows how such a consciousness sees politics everywhere, rather like a sexually obsessive imagination.

Nature is not innocent, and even grasshoppers, in a probable echo of Marvell's royalist friend, Lovelace, become giant cavaliers perilously balanced on 'green spires' (these grasshoppers also echo Numbers 13 where the Children of Israel search for Canaan and hear a report of a land of giants that eats up its inhabitants). This pastoral phantasmagoria is full of strange distortions, like *Alice in Wonderland*, and Marvell shares with Carroll an affection for prepubertal girls. Dreaming of innocence – a prelapsarian innocence before war, sex, history – he suggests a sinister sexuality in the nun's invitation

———————

Why should we, in the compass of a pale,
Keep law and form and due proportion,
Showing, as in a model, our firm estate,
When our sea-walled garden, the whole land,
Is full of weeds, her fairest flowers choked up,
Her fruit trees all unpruned, her hedges ruined,
Her knots disordered, and her wholesome herbs
Swarming with caterpillars?

(III, 4, 40–47)

John of Gaunt's 'This England' speech is also a pervasive influence on the poem.

to the virgin Thwaites:

> Each night among us to your side
> Appoint a fresh and virgin bride;
> Whom if Our Lord at midnight find,
> Yet neither should be left behind.
> Where you may lie as chaste in bed,
> As pearls together billeted,
> All night embracing arm in arm
> Like crystal pure with cotton warm.

The lovely sexual narcissism of Marvell's walk through the woods has something of the ironic self-consciousness of a Hockney painting, and I can never read that line 'Like some great prelate of the grove' without hearing a rich camp accent – Kenneth Williams dressed as a bishop and exuberantly intoning Marvell's words.

In a witty condensation of the Exodus theme, Marvell compares the 'tawny mowers' to the Israelites. The grass which they 'massacre' becomes the Red Sea (or Sea of Reeds as it is more accurately named), and the mowers are then transformed into Levellers. After the Israelites had crossed the Red Sea, 'quails came up, and covered the camp: and in the morning the dew lay round about the host' (Exodus 16,13). Marvell refers to this and to the biblical idea of popular discontent in stanza 51, and by introducing a mower who accidentally 'carves the rail' he offers a 17th-century version of the glib revolutionary adage, 'you can't make an omelette without breaking eggs'. The prophetic symbol of the mower mown suggests that those who execute kings will themselves be executed and it anticipates the fate of the regicides under the Restoration.

Marvell's 'tawny' mowers are versions of the 'yron man' Talus in *The Faerie Queene*:

> But when as overblowen was that brunt,
> Those knights began a fresh them to assayle,
> And all about the fields like Squirrels hunt;
> But chiefly *Talus* with his yron flayle,
> Gainst which no flight nor rescue mote auayle,
> Made cruell hauocke of the baser crew,

And chaced them both ouer hill and dale:
The raskall manie soone they ouerthrew,
But the two knights themselues their captains did subdew.

(V, XI, 59)

Talus accompanies Artegall, Knight of Justice, and his job is to carry out executions. Spenser based Artegall on Lord Grey whom he served as secretary while Grey was lord deputy of Ireland and whose violent measures he supported. It is interesting to note that Talus tends to run amok, rather like an early Black and Tan, and it seems likely that Marvell is drawing out of the Spenserian echo a subliminal image of Cromwell's Irish policy. Spenser based Talus on Talos, the Bronze Man who was guardian of Crete, and the bronzed, sun-tanned mowers in Marvell's poem associate with this metallic image.

The poem's closing vision of the salmon fishers 'like Antipodes in shoes' is a literal embodiment of a popular folk image which was known as 'the World Turned Upside Down'. This phrase, which derives ultimately from St Paul, was applied to an inn-sign illustrating an unnatural state of affairs and alluding to the Antipodes. It often took the form of a man walking at the South Pole. There was a broadside ballad of 1646 entitled 'The World is Turned Upside Down' and the tune is believed to have been played when Cornwallis surrendered at Yorktown in 1781. Although Hill mentions the tune in his fine study *The World Turned Upside Down*, he does not note the popular source of this idea as an antipodean image.

When Queen Isabel in *Richard II* rebukes the gardener for speaking in a 'harsh rude tongue' we note the obvious link between accent and social class. It is a sign of Marvell's playful double-mindedness that he should give his egalitarian mower a polished, aristocratic, classical style in 'The Mower against Gardens'. By couching the mower's criticism of upper-class luxury and art in a language free of all dialect words, Marvell sets up a subversive argument in which the mower is trapped by the highly formal, artificial nature of the poem. This amounts to a reversal of Cromwell's preference for the 'free way' and we may compare it with Walt Whitman's choice of free, vernacular verse to express a populist democratic ethos. Perhaps, though, the mower has appropriated an aristocratic style, prior to occupying both house and gardens?

The mower's reference to the 'gods themselves' who dwell with 'us' aligns the poem with an anti-establishment attitude, and the puritan tradition often crosses over into the popular tradition with its sense of social and economic disadvantage. Bunyan's Valiant-for-Truth straddles both traditions, and as E. P. Thompson has shown *Pilgrim's Progress* is, with Paine's *Rights of Man*, one of the two 'foundation texts of the English working-class movement'. As a further example of the links between these traditions, it should be noted that Bunyan remains a powerful influence within Protestant populism in the north of Ireland. Though upper-class in style and manner, Gray's *Elegy* expresses a compassion for the rural poor which makes it a member of the popular tradition, like Blake's entire canon with its firm biblical foundations and Miltonic vision. The 'dark satanic mills' of 'Jerusalem' echo Samson at the mill with slaves, and although 'The Tiger' is not limited to the sphere of politics, any reading of it must draw on David Erdmann's compelling historical interpretation of the poem which argues that Blake was thinking of Yorktown and also of Valmy (where the French people halted a counter-revolutionary Prussian invasion). The comparison of an awakened revolutionary people to a tiger was commonplace and Erdmann cites a report in *The Times* of 7 January, 1792, which said that the French people were now 'loose from all restraints and . . . more ferocious than wolves and tigers'. Here, it may be remarked that when Eliot criticizes Blake for lacking 'a framework of accepted and traditional ideas which would have prevented him from indulging in a philosophy of his own' he is really saying something like 'what a pity Blake was a radical Protestant prophet'.

In both versions of *The Prelude*, Wordsworth employs the tiger image in an agonized consideration of the September massacres, and although the 1850 version represents a defection from the poet's youthful belief in 'mountain liberty' and 'equal ground' we must respect the honesty of his intentions as he rewrote his early masterpiece. For the most part he strove to be true to his younger self, though his putative admiration for Burke's counter-revolutionary eloquence is notably absent from the 1805

Prelude. Yet in the 1850 version he retains his admiration for the revolution, and a Miltonic echo of the fallen angels is apparent in his description of the royalist counter-revolutionary officers 'bent upon undoing what was done' (IX, 133). This is a direct echo of Adam's cry after Eve has eaten the apple, 'But past who can recall, or done undo?' (IX, 926). For Milton, the eating of the apple historically symbolizes a servile acceptance of conformity, tradition, superstition, but the postlapsarian reference in Wordsworth's memory suggests a subconscious belief that the overthrow of Louis XVI was the primal sin. This feeling pulls against the major statement that the officers were misguided in their attempts to undo the done, or put the historical clock back. That major statement relies for its force partly on the use of 'bent' with its suggestion of a distortion. Wordsworth's mixed feelings about revolution lack the trepid delicacy of Marvell's vision, partly because Wordsworth casts himself so consciously as the inheritor of Milton's republicanism. There is a proleptically Yeatsian and very protestant cadence in that heroic invocation to 'The later Sidney, Marvel, Harrington,/Young Vane, and others who called Milton friend', and Wordsworth presents himself sternly in the line of succession to these 'moralists'.

Time and again, political poets divide on the issue of whether primal nature is a prelapsarian garden republic or a beneficent monarchy, and Clough clearly belongs with those utopians who nourish a belief in the pure republic:

So that the whole great wicked artificial civilized fabric –
All its unfinished houses, lots for sale, and railway
   outworks –
Seems reaccepted, resumed to Primal Nature and Beauty.
              (*The Bothie of Tober-Na-Vuolich*, IX, 105–7)

Clough is a shamefully neglected poet who was closely interested in British, Irish, European and American politics. He undertook a detailed study of economics, and his criticism of *laissez-faire* attitudes are pertinent to the monetarist issues which now exercise Western society. A self-styled republican, socialist and feminist, Clough's nimbly ironic classicism always avoids a disablingly tendentious mode, and his sophisticated integrity unsettled the more devious cultivation of his friend, Matthew Arnold.

In two sonnets composed during that year of revolutions, 1848, Arnold addressed his 'republican friend', saying 'God knows it, I am with you', but concluding that the day of 'liberated man' will not dawn at a 'human nod'. Although both sonnets are flawed by Arnold's lack of a distinctive individual style, they reveal that influential strain of religious pessimism which links him to Burke and Eliot and the later Wordsworth. Arnold, finally, is anti-intellectual because he is against those who seek to increase knowledge,* and one notes with frustration how in his criticism he will often stop himself from following through the implications of the issues he raises.

The intellectual eagerness and freshness of Clough's verse belongs with the Milton who feared that 'this iron yoke of outward conformity hath left a slavish print upon our necks; the ghost of a linen decency yet haunts us'. And although Clough later became an embittered reactionary, his major works were written at the height of his radical commitment during 1848 and 1849. It is an ambition of this anthology to redeem Clough from the neglect which his work has suffered and to suggest his links with Auden in a tradition of upper-middle-class radicalism and sympathy with 'the old democratic fervour'. The 'gaitered gamekeeper' in Auden's 'Who will endure' seems almost a direct echo of the grouse-moor conservatism which is evoked at the beginning of Clough's *Bothie*, while the figure of the thin man 'clad as the Saxon' makes a link between the Scottish radicalism of Burns and Carlyle and the Chartist movement Clough so admired. Lowland Scotland is one of the most influential centres of the British Labour movement, though for Orwell Scotland suggested simply grouse-moors and ghillies, which is why he rejected his surname 'Blair' for the very English name 'Orwell'.

Auden presents himself in 'Letter to Lord Byron' as the inheritor of the republican tradition when he describes the Hobbesian ogre of Security:

---

*For example, in 1882 Arnold recommended this motto to the students of Liverpool: 'Don't think: try and be patient'. Quoted in Chris Baldick, *The Social Mission of English Criticism*.

> Milton beheld him on the English throne,
>   And Bunyan sitting in the Papal chair;
> The hermits fought him in their caves alone,
>   At the first Empire he was also there,
>   Dangling his Pax Romana in the air.

Auden later crossed over to the monarchist or Anglo-Catholic tradition and in the Christian ritualism of his post-war verse he combines this essentially reactionary vision with a Horatian celebration of political apathy and domestic life. This is the theme of 'In Praise of Limestone' where the volcano symbolizes romantic politics (specifically the Byron whom Bertrand Russell regarded as an influence on European fascism). Alluding to Goebbels' threat, 'If we are defeated, we shall slam the doors of history behind us', Auden rejects the politics of heroism, and his civilized vision of man in society is beautifully present in the closing image of the early poem, 'From scars where kestrels hover', which sends the 'leader' or *Führer* to Cape Wrath and shows the host passing 'Alive into the house'.

The puritan–republican tradition ends in England with the early Auden, though some critics would claim that its inheritor is Tony Harrison. The diminution of this tradition is a tragic impoverishment, and so too is the attenuation of the rival monarchist tradition. Geoffrey Hill plaintively exemplifies a conservative Christianity in his lament for the past's 'Weightless magnificence' ruined by the recent concrete of the Welfare State, while Larkin's lament for lost imperial glory is a deliberately drab, formal gesture of futility and resignation. Sadly, it would seem that political verse is virtually a lost art in England now, and it is difficult to admire the conservative vision of Charles Tomlinson and Donald Davie, though Davie's 'Remembering the Thirties' is a terse reply-poem which confusingly identifies that Corolanian virtue 'courage' with the presumably pacifist 'vegetable king'. It is a mystifying conclusion offered by a conservative literary puritan who was later to join the Church of England and support the reactionary Anglicanism of *Poetry Nation Review*.

THE IRISH TRADITION

Curiously, the monarchist tradition within English verse is echoed by 17th- and 18th-century gaelic poetry in Ireland. Egan O'Rahilly's *aisling* or vision poem, 'A Time of Change', is a lament for the downfall of the native Irish aristocracy which followed from the defeat of James II at the Battle of the Boyne. The king who will come over the water in 'Reverie at Dawn' is James's son, the Old Pretender, and the lighting of the three candles symbolizes the restoration of the three kingdoms of Ireland, Scotland and England. The vision is therefore backward-looking and aristocratic, and although this may appear to be nationalistic the poet is in fact an adherent of the Jacobite order and an exponent of a distinctive type of Irish snobbery which we can variously detect in Wilde, Synge and Yeats. As Seamus Deane has argued, the Irish Catholic self-image is often expressed in terms of 'the aristocrat forced into the slum', and this is echoed in the patrician attitudes of many Irish Protestant writers.

The historical memory from which this self-image derives may be seen in Fear Dorcha Ó Mealláin's 'Exodus to Connacht' which is a response to the events that followed from an Act of Parliament which was passed in 1652. The Act ordered that all Catholics and many Protestant royalists above the rank of tradesman and labourer were to remove themselves into Connacht and Clare, where they were given small allotments. Any of those found east of the Shannon after 1 May 1654, might be killed by whoever met them. The move was made mostly during a severe winter and many hundreds died on the way.

The Irish Jacobite and the Irish rebel traditions of political verse are opposed by a populist Orange tradition which believes in hierarchy and deference – a deference to the new Williamite order which can be combined with hostility to England. That hostility is present in the reference to Bond Street dandies in 'The Orange Lily' and it is an expression of that aggressive feeling of cultural inferiority which still afflicts the loyalist imagination. Yeats in his *Autobiographies* mentions that as a child he first discovered 'the pleasure of rhyme' by reading Orange songs in his grandfather's hayloft, and his mature verse combines muscle-flexing protestant

triumphalism with an élitist dedication. His magisterial aristocratic style delights in certain intent cadences drawn from the
ballad traditions of both protestant and catholic culture. And the
more brutal qualities of that stylistic merging of peasant and
aristocrat owe as much to the dark side of the Protestant
imagination as they do to Yeats's reading of Nietzsche.

Yeats's 'The Fisherman' is, as Blake Morrison shrewdly notes,
echoed formally in Seamus Heaney's 'Casualty', and the
cadence of these lines

> They move in equal pace
> With the habitual
> Slow consolation
> Of a dawdling engine,

echo the definite 'They' and use of an adjectival rhyme in 'The
Wild Swans at Coole':

> Unwearied still, lover by lover,
> They paddle in the cold
> Companionable streams or climb the air.

Marvellously, Heaney appropriates Yeats's high ascendancy
rhetoric – a rhetoric that employs the swan-image traditionally
symbolic of royalty – and spiritually repossesses Yeats's concern
in 'The Fisherman' to find an audience of 'my own race'. The
context is changed from the Anglo-Irish country house, Coole
Park, to an Ulster Catholic funeral. The low, constant, diesel
sound of the hearse's 'dawdling engine' becomes the outboard
motor of the fisherman's boat in the succeeding lines, and it is
also reminiscent of the ominously 'ticking' bicycle in 'A
Constable Calls'. Reading these poems, we catch the pulse of a
deterministic sense of history.

An Ulster Protestant poet once told me that Heaney's later
work made him feel 'lonely', and for the Irish poet who does not
espouse a Unionist politics the temptation is to indulge an
exclusive rhetoric of complaint and to offer images drawn from
the jaded repertoire of romantic Irish nationalism. The pressures
of tribal loyalty and 'complicity' are a permanent theme in
Heaney's work and his warmly inclusive vision has always

rejected those nets of class, religion and ethnicity which Stephen Dedalus describes in *A Portrait of the Artist*. As the ghost of Joyce informs the poet in *Station Island*, 'That subject people stuff is a cod's game'. Noting that, we must also recognize the manner in which Heaney's work rises out of the post-partition Ulster Catholic community, out of a rural society which has always felt itself trapped within the modern concrete of the State of Northern Ireland. To oppose the historic legitimacy of that state and at the same time refuse the simplicities of traditional nationalism is to initiate certain imaginative positives and offer a gracious and civil trust.

The revisionist school of Irish history – a school hostile to Irish nationalism – is an influence on Paul Muldoon's 'Anseo', which is a classic critique of the enduring dominance of the heroic idea of Irish history. 'Meeting the British', a later poem, is coded for a nationalist account of that history and throughout Muldoon's work there is a cutting awareness of the long tradition of agrarian violence in his native county, Armagh. Like Marvell, Muldoon ironizes the theme of love and war, sex and politics, and there is a fascination in his poems with the idea of no man's land, the waste ground between the tribal factions or between 'a hole in the hedge/And a room in the Latin Quarter'.

Neither Heaney nor Muldoon write in the direct manner of Swift's 'Ireland':

> While English sharpers take the pay,
> And then stand by to see fair play.

Swift's couplet is still relevant to the circumstances of Irish political life and we may compare his analysis with this sentence from a political thriller by a recent Secretary of State for Northern Ireland:

> The Irish fever, the worst variety known to man. It destroys all gentleness, truth, sensible calculation. When Englishmen catch it they get it worst of all. And Englishwomen.

It must be possible to imagine that there is a vision which lies beyond a self-regarding emotional Irish nationalism and an equally self-regarding British complacency, and in their very different manners both Heaney and Muldoon give that possibility a strict and definite shape. The cadences of Anglican self-esteem – 'all gentleness, truth, sensible calculation' – are as remote for them as they are for any Irish writer, and the rhythms of Irish English have yet to echo Hurd's combination of plainsong and pragmatism. Only nationalists, whether British or Irish, claim a monopoly of 'truth'.

THE SCOTTISH TRADITION

In 1649, Milton rebuked the 'blockish' Presbyterians of Belfast for their support of King Charles and reminded them that John Knox 'taught professedly the doctrine of deposing, and of killing kings'. This Calvinist doctrine is a major intellectual influence on the Scottish tradition of radical verse, and it has obvious affinities with the English puritan tradition. There is also a Jacobite tradition in Scotland which is hostile to English Protestantism, and as I have noted Burns temporarily occupies that tradition in 'Charlie He's My Darling'*. Burns's statement that the Tree of Liberty:

> stands where ance the Bastile stood,
> A prison built by kings, man,
> When Superstition's hellish brood
> Kept France in leading strings, man,

is echoed by his remark in a letter about the executions of Louis XVI and Marie Antoinette: 'What is there in the delivering over of a perjured Blockhead and an unprincipled Prostitute to the hands of the hangman, that it should arrest for a moment, attention, in an eventful hour?'

Burns believes in 'equal rights and equal laws' and in 'For A'That and A'That' he 'slegs' an aristocratic hierarchy:

> Ye see yon birkie ca'd, a lord,
> Wha struts, and stares, and a' that,
> Though hundreds worship at his word,
> He's but a coof for a' that.

---

* It seems likely that Auden's 'The Quarry' draws on the Jacobite tradition though the reference to a 'parson' must mean that these are English red-coats moving through an English village.

> For a' that, and a' that,
> His ribband, star and a' that,
> The man of independant mind,
> He looks and laughs at a' that.

Here Burns is echoing a passage in *The Rights of Man* where Paine says:

> Titles are but nicknames, and every nickname is a title. The thing is perfectly harmless in itself, but it marks a sort of foppery in the human character, which degrades it. It reduces man into the diminutive of man in things which are great, and the counterfeit of woman in things which are little. It talks about its fine blue *ribbon* like a girl, and shows its new *garter* like a child.

Although Paine's sexual stereotyping now seems dated, his internationalist sympathies are enlightened and forward-looking. And Burns, like Paine, imagines that man 'the world o'er/ Shall brothers be for a'that'. We may be nowadays much more sceptical about the realization of internationalist ideals, but that scepticism can too easily become a hardened pessimism which helps to promote an exclusive nationalism.

Hugh MacDiarmid's Marxist internationalism is counterbalanced by a strong anti-English attitude which is the result of his commitment to Scottish nationalism. His hostility to the English tradition of 'sensible calculation' produces the arresting invective of that passage from 'In Memoriam James Joyce' which attacks English amateurism and the Arnoldian doctrine of the balanced 'disinterested' imagination:

> English official criticism has erected
> A stone-heap, a dead load of moral qualities.
> A writer must have optimism, irony,
> A healthy outlook,
> A middle-class standard of morality,
> As much religion as, say, St Paul had,
> As much atheism as Shelley had . . .
> And, finally, on top of an immense load
> Of self-neutralizing moral and social qualities,
> Above all, Circumspection,

> So that, in the end, no English writer
> According to these standards,
> Can possess authenticity.

MacDiarmid brilliantly savages that strain of Anglican whimsy and antiquarian eccentricity in English culture, and his parody of Arnoldian judgement is especially pertinent now that certain schools of literary criticism are being attacked for their blandness and subjectivity. The idea of balanced judgement is a reflection of consensus politics, and in a polarized society with high unemployment such a concept is bound to appear comically irrelevant. MacDiarmid's polemical imagination instinctively polarizes reality and in this he has more in common with a European critical imagination than with English literary practice. The figure of the 'bewildered foreigner' represents that common European exasperation with the very professional English cult of the amateur. Again, MacDiarmid points to that tedious moralism which is such a dominant force in English literary criticism and which is so careless of formal beauty.

Nationalist feelings often inform the political imagination and Douglas Dunn's 'Washing the Coins' also draws subtly on the Scottish socialist tradition:

> I filled the basin to its brim with cold;
> And when the water settled I could see
> Two English kings among their drowned Britannias.

As in MacDiarmid, there is a rigorously Calvinist tendency in Dunn's imagination which expresses itself in his angry, disciplined attack on Sir Walter Scott for turning 'our country round upon its name/And time.' Scott's chivalric, kitsch conservatism is rejected as snobbish, hierarchical and 'mendacious'. Like Christopher Hill, Dunn is concerned with that popular experience which lies beneath the surface of recorded history – what Hill vividly terms 'the vast mass of the population, surviving sometimes in records when they are born, married, accused of crime, or buried, but otherwise leaving no trace'.

This sense of anonymous history is strong in Carlyle's work and it would appear to be a much more powerful manner of thinking and feeling in disadvantaged societies like Scotland

and Ireland. It is connected with those ideas of piety and reverence for the dead which form such a significant part of the imagination those cultures share. Piety, though, can easily shade into sentimentality – it is a conservative, communal habit of mind which can be resistant to social change.

THE AMERICAN TRADITION

There is, sadly, a rather meagre tradition of political verse in the United States. Philip Freneau, who was a close associate of Thomas Jefferson, is the first American political poet and his 'George the Third's Soliloquy' is ironically echoed at the end of Robert Lowell's *Day By Day* where Richard Nixon is compared to that reactionary British King. Freneau's new world republicanism is unfortunately shackled by the old world couplets he employs:

> For late I find the nations are my foes,
> I must submit, and that with bloody nose,
> Or, like our James, fly basely from the state,
> Or share, what still is worse – old *Charles's* fate.

The stylistic failure here demonstrates the difficulties which attend an effort to create a new style in a separate Anglophone culture, and it wasn't until later in the 19th century that American poets were able to break decisively with this distractingly formal, aristocratic idiom.

Whitman's free verse is remarkable for its Jeffersonian, populist confidence in republican democracy:

> Of Life immense in passion, pulse, and power,
> Cheerful, for freest action form'd under the laws divine,
> The Modern Man I sing.

This is a declaration of poetic independence, a dedication to life, liberty and the pursuit of happiness, and it speaks for the pleasure-loving side of the puritan imagination. Whitman's loose-limbed modern vernacular draws strongly on the rhythms of the Authorized Version and on native speech rhythms (modern American speech retains many cadences reminiscent of the early 17th-century speech which shaped the translation of the Bible).

At times, Whitman resembles an aggressive type of customs-officer who is trying to stop the importation of European ideas and attitudes. His suspicious question, 'is the good old cause in it?' ('By Blue Ontario's Shore'), is ambiguously poised between an imperative rejection of an English republican ideology and an affectionate sympathy for that cause.

The United States contains untold millions of blockishly reactionary people and at first sight Robert Frost's 'Mending Wall' appears to express an obdurately conservative vision. It is invisibly dedicated to the Roman god, Terminus, the lord of boundaries and limitations. Thus the neighbour's traditional adage, 'Good fences make good neighbors', is pessimistic and Hobbesian in its definite wisdom. It expresses a belief in good manners, decorum, formality and personal privacy, and this is naturally opposed to the sprawling libertarianism of Whitman. Such a belief is based on that concept of original sin which despite Milton's application of it to kingship remains one of the most powerful conservative arguments. Socialists tend to believe in sin but they usually draw the line at the idea of inheriting it.

Frost's imagination is foxy and he deploys that cunning by transforming the subversive 'something' which doesn't love a wall into his own mischievous wish to trick and subvert his neighbour's dogma. The subversive something can be the force which rules a Hobbesian state of nature but Frost upsets that identification by associating his neighbour with darkness and the primeval past (he is like an 'old-stone savage armed'). Thus this figure becomes primitive, not civil, man, and in making that identification Frost aligns himself with Noah Webster and Whitman in their rejection of the past. The neighbour appears briefly as a bone-headed reactionary so that his repetition of his father's saying is rocked slightly by the reservations Frost has insinuated during our reading of this sly, vernal poem.

If Frost often appears to belong inside the Georgian tradition of English verse, Robinson Jeffers can be placed within a European tradition of élitist criticism of democracy. Like T. E. Hulme, he expresses that rigid conservative belief in man's limitations and this is combined with a certain Corolanian contempt for mass consumer society. Though his verse line is paradoxically based on Whitman's, Jeffers reins in the democratic expansiveness of that style by introducing a consonantal terseness and spartan abruptness which discipline each line by splitting it into brief complete units:

> The quality of these trees, green height; of the sky, shining, of
>   water, a clear flow; of the rock, hardness.

It is a poetry in love with 'hardness and reticence', a vision which is instinct with a prophetic conservative pessimism about the nature of man and the future of the United States. The sober, tight *pietas* of the statement, 'The love of freedom has been the quality of Western man', helps to make Jeffers' prophetic vision of American freedom hooded 'like a kept hawk . . . on the wrist of Caesar' sound with a descriptive urgency. And the spondees in 'Bé gréat, cárve déep your héel-márks' give the line a tense classical texture, rather like the sudden deep jab of a chariot's wheelmarks on a sandy battlefield. Like Hopkins, Jeffers is a sophisticated primitivist and is clearly a major influence on the work of Ted Hughes. This type of spartan conservatism draws inspiration from Aufidius's image of Coriolanus:

> he'll be to Rome
> As is the osprey to the fish, who takes it
> By sovereignty of Nature.
>   (IV, 7, 32–4)

Such a vision is fascinated by the lethal mysteries of power and knows that the misplaced idealism of Woodrow Wilson must fade beside a Leninist marriage of ideology and *realpolitik*.

Jeffers is a critical analyst of American freedom and there is a relatively oblique criticism of that idea in the witty, anecdotal formality of Elizabeth Bishop's evocation of Trollope's visit to Washington during the Civil War. We know that the swampy capital is being mediated through an English conservative consciousness and if we also know that Elizabeth Bishop's maternal ancestors were New York State Tories at the time of the American revolution then we can see that this perfect poem is the work of an ironic conservative patrician. This is Jane Austen incognito in America, silently amused at the vulgarities of democracy and offended by the thuggish, gimcrack recency of the country's neoclassical capital. Here the paleface tradition in American writing indirectly reminds the 'redskin' writers of the fate of the country's indigenous population. Invisibly, and with fastidious grace, several old scores are being settled here. Reading this poem, we shudder like Eugenia in *The Europeans* and understand e.e. cummings' anarchic criticisms of American patriotism. Bishop's sophisticated quietism challenges the democratic Yankee triumphalism of much American verse, and 'Trollope in Washington' is in a sense a reply-poem to Whitman's massive corpus. Like that other patrician, her friend Robert Lowell, Bishop is a social critic who believes in original sin, not primal innocence.

A patriotic critic would judge her verse to be 'unAmerican' and in a sense she is a silent political poet – by not choosing the puritan freeway her delicately formal verse expresses a high, cultured reaction against American optimism. That pessimism is present throughout Lowell's public verse which indicts America's 'savage servility', commercial vulgarity and disposable view of the individual human life. But the injustice which so disfigures American society is most persuasively criticized by Blues singers – they are the most authentic American political poets and their work challenges the more comfortable written tradition.

THE ANTI-POLITICAL TRADITION

Elizabeth Bishop's vision of what Yeats terms a 'measured quietude' makes her also a member of this tradition, and many reply-poems belong here. The Horatian poem of retirement adopts by its very nature an anti-political attitude, and although it can be argued that such poems are essentially conservative since their deliberate apathy must uphold the status quo, such an absolutist reading usually wrongs the sacral moments of being which this type of poetry can offer. Politics, after all, is often relentlessly second-rate in style, language and personality, and the imagination which can derive ideological significance from the fall of a leaf is too earnest to appreciate the mysterious fragrance or mushroom odour of this type of verse.

Derek Mahon's 'A Disused Shed in Co. Wexford' belongs to this tradition and the formal intuitions of *Dasein* which his verse embodies owe much to Elizabeth Bishop's work. Marvell's verse with its voluptuously vegetarian warmth belongs to this tradition, as does Southey's 'The Battle of Blenheim' which is both an anti-war ballad and a humanist vision of historical suffering. This is Mahon's theme in 'A Disused Shed' where the references to the Irish Civil War and to Treblinka implicitly connect the political fantasies of romantic nationalism with European fascism.

Such poems issue from that condition of supremely un-illusioned quietism – the wisest of passivities – which is usually the product of bitter historical experience and which is temperamentally different from disillusion. To be politically disillusioned is often to be cynical; to be politically apathetic is usually to be ignorant, but to possess no illusions is to understand a spiritual reality which is religious in its negativity. Beckett's characters occupy that bare drained landscape, as do many Russian and East European poets. At times their work resembles a type of elegant, ironic, highly sophisticated skrimshandering – this is the art of a prison-camp society, verse produced in a closed world without hope but with an obstinate integrity which simultaneously negates as it creates. These poets acknowledge that what they are doing appears to be a pointless activity, but they go on writing, sometimes visiting the West, perhaps effecting the slightest, most minimal changes in the ruling consciousness of their societies. Like prisoners tapping out messages along the heating pipes in a cell block, they speak to us in cipher from an underground culture we in the West have difficulty in comprehending, or which we can too readily twist to our own smug purposes. As Różewicz says in 'Poem of Pathos'

> A poet buried alive
> is like a subterranean river
> he preserves within
> faces names
> hope
> and homeland

(trans. Adam Czerniawski)

The poet is like Aeneas in the underworld. Invisibly, secretly, his epic imagination draws on a mnemonic compulsion to preserve the past and the dead, and this is contrasted with the 'deceived poet' who relies on external influences and an individual or a lyric credo. Such a poet is woken at dawn like a man being arrested or a prisoner about to be shot.

Finally, there is the lying poet, the laureate whose work is propagandist and ripe for transmission by the Ministry of Culture. The possible self-reference here is a severe irony, like the poem's dismissive title, and this ironic insight into the nature of the committed action is also shared by Różewicz's fellow Pole, Joseph Conrad. The end of the first section of *Under Western Eyes* resembles 'Poem of Pathos' in its tragic sense of complete closure:

> An unhurried voice said –
> 'Kirylo Sidorovitch.'
> Razumov at the door turned his head.
> 'To retire,' he repeated.
> 'Where to?' asked Councillor Mikulin softly.

In this autocratic or totalitarian reality there is no private life, no domestic sanctuary, to retire into. Here, any and every action has a political significance which cannot be evaded and this means that East European poetry is not finally 'anti-political' – it is instead the most advanced type of political verse. In confronting a sealed, utterly fixed reality the East European imagination designs a form of anti-poetry or survivor's art. It proffers a basic ration of the Word, like a piece of bread and chocolate in wartime.

DANTE ALIGHIERI

Ugolino

We had already left him. I walked the ice
And saw two soldered in a frozen hole
On top of other, one's skull capping the other's,
Gnawing at him where the neck and head
Are grafted to the sweet fruit of the brain,
Like a famine victim at a loaf of bread.
So the berserk Tydeus gnashed and fed
Upon the severed head of Menalippus
As if it were some spattered carnal melon.
'You,' I shouted, 'you on top, what hate
Makes you so ravenous and insatiable?
What keeps you so monstrously at rut?
Is there any story I can tell
For you, in the world above, against him?
If my tongue by then's not withered in my throat
I will report the truth and clear your name.'

That sinner eased his mouth up off his meal
To answer me, and wiped it with the hair
Left growing on his victim's ravaged skull,
Then said, 'Even before I speak
The thought of having to relive all that
Desperate time makes my heart sick;
Yet while I weep to say them, I would sow
My words like curses – that they might increase
And multiply upon this head I gnaw.
I know you come from Florence by your accent
But I have no idea who you are
Nor how you ever managed your descent.
Still, you should know my name, for I was Count
Ugolino, this was Archbishop Roger,
And why I act the jockey to his mount
Is surely common knowledge; how my good faith

Was easy prey to his malignancy,
How I was taken, held, and put to death.
But you must hear something you cannot know
If you're to judge him – the cruelty
Of my death at his hands. So listen now.

Others will pine as I pined in that jail
Which is called Hunger after me, and watch
As I watched through a narrow hole
Moon after moon, bright and somnambulant,
Pass overhead, until that night I dreamt
The bad dream and my future's veil was rent.
I saw a wolf-hunt: this man rode the hill
Between Pisa and Lucca, hounding down
The wolf and wolf-cubs. He was lordly and masterful,
His pack in keen condition, his company
Deployed ahead of him, Gualandi
And Sismundi as well, and Lanfranchi,
Who soon wore down wolf-father and wolf-sons
And my hallucination
Was all sharp teeth and bleeding flanks ripped open.
When I awoke before the dawn, my head
Swam with cries of my sons who slept in tears
Beside me there, crying out for bread.
(If your sympathy has not already started
At all that my heart was foresuffering
And if you are not crying, you are hardhearted.)

They were awake now, it was near the time
For food to be brought in as usual,
Each one of them disturbed after his dream,
When I heard the door being nailed and hammered
Shut, far down in the nightmare tower.
I stared in my sons' faces and spoke no word.
My eyes were dry and my heart was stony.
They cried and my little Anselm said,
'What's wrong? Why are you staring, daddy?'

But I shed no tears, I made no reply
All through that day, all through the night that
                                                                    followed
Until another sun blushed in the sky
And sent a small beam probing the distress
Inside those prison walls. Then when I saw
The image of my face in their four faces
I bit on my two hands in desperation
And they, since they thought hunger drove me to it,
Rose up suddenly in agitation
Saying, "Father, it will greatly ease our pain
If you eat us instead, and you who dressed us
In this sad flesh undress us here again."
So then I calmed myself to keep them calm.
We hushed. That day and the next stole past us
And earth seemed hardened against me and them.
For four days we let the silence gather.
Then, throwing himself flat in front of me,
Gaddo said, 'Why don't you help me, father?'
He died like that, and surely as you see
Me here, one by one I saw my three
Drop dead during the fifth day and the sixth day
Until I saw no more. Searching, blinded,
For two days I groped over them and called them.
Then hunger killed where grief had only wounded.'
When he had said all this, his eyes rolled
And his teeth, like a dog's teeth clamping round a bone,
Bit into the skull and again took hold.

Pisa! Pisa, your sounds are like a hiss
Sizzling in our country's grassy language.
And since the neighbour states have been remiss
In your extermination, let a huge
Dyke of islands bar the Arno's mouth, let
Capraia and Gorgona dam and deluge
You and your population. For the sins
Of Ugolino, who betrayed your forts,

Should never have been visited on his sons.
Your atrocity was Theban. They were young
And innocent: Hugh and Brigata
And the other two whose names are in my song.

from Inferno, xxxii *and* xxxiii
trans. Seamus Heaney

The Peasants' Song

When Adam dalf and Eve span
Who was then the gentleman?

When Adam dalf and Eve span,
Spur if thou wilt speed,
Where was then the pride of man
That now mars his meed?

WILLIAM LANGLAND

from Piers Plowman

Rectors and parish priests complained to the bishop
that their parishes were poor since the plague-time,
they begged a licence and leave to live in London
where they could sell themselves for silver, sweet silver.
    Bishops and BAs, Doctors of Divinity,
who're charged under Christ with the care of souls,
who wear the tonsure as sign they should shrive their flocks,
preach to them, pray for them and feed the poor,
they stay all Lent in London and out of Lent too.
Some serve the king by checking figures or by claiming
what's owed him from wardships, waived estates,
vacant houses with no heir, sturgeons washed on the sea
                                           shore.

    Just then a scour of rats, mice by the nimbling hundreds,
bunched quick in a conference for a common purpose,
because a court cat would come when he wanted
and bite their bums or knock them about a bit.
'We daren't go out we're that terrified of him
and if we girn at his games he'll grab us by the neck
till we loathe this life and cry to be rid of it.
But if we use our wits and stand up firm to him
we could live like lords and rest easy.'
    A big powerful rat, famous for miles round,
put forward this policy in a slick speech:
'I've seen men,' he said, 'in the city of London,
going about with spick collars and neat necklaces on them.
They've no leads and can walk where they like – anyplace –
coney warrens, waste ground, common land –
other places too, at certain times I hear tell.
But it strikes me, by Christ, that those boys
had better each have a bell on his collar.
Then we'd know where they were and could run if we wanted.

So it's clear to me we should buy a bell –
a brass or a silver one, chank and shiny –
stick it to a collar and clip it on the cat's neck.
Then we can hear if he's running or resting or chasing
around.
In a good mood is he? – we can come out and play then –
but if he gets nasty we can skip off quick.'
The whole congress of rats agreed this good plan
but when a bell had been bought and clipped to a collar
there wasn't one rat in the whole worried crowd
would dare run out and tie it to the cat's neck.
We're all scared, they sighed, our work's wasted.
A mouse, a most sensible mouse I thought,
pushed up front and fed these words to the rats:
'If we killed the cat another'd come to annoy us,
so I say to our people – best let him alone.
Seven years since, my father said this to me –
'Where the cat's just a kitten the court is in chaos'.
It's there in the scriptures if you'll heed the preacher:
  Vae terri ubi puer rex est, etc.
At night no-one can rest for fear of the rats.
So let's be fair, while he's out after rabbits
we needn't fear for our skins – it's game he feeds on.
Better a little loss than a long sorrow:
though we kicked that tyrant out there'd be worse trouble,
we mice would munch many tons of good malt
and you rats'd rip the clothes off men's backs.
If that cat wasn't there to walk all over you
there'd be a right rat-mess, for you'll never rule yourselves.
Don't cross the cat or the kitten ever – that's my advice.
All this talk about collars is total crap –
let the rat jump where he wants when he wants.
My motto is this: we're all individuals so let's
each one chase his own interests and be done
with this gassing in groups: it's getting us nowhere.'

What this dream of mine means, or what it's message is,
the critics can tell when they lift their eyes from the text.

(from the Prologue, trans. Tom Paulin)

ANON

from Vox Populi, Vox Dei

I pray you, be not wroth
For telling of the troth;
For thus the world it goeth
As God himself knoweth;
And, as all men understand,
Both lordships and lands
Are now in few men's hands;
Both substance and bands
Of all the holy realm
As most men esteem
Are now consumed clean
From the farmer and the poor
To the town and the tower;
Which maketh them to lower,
To see that in their flower
Is neither malt nor meal,
Bacon, beef, nor veal,
Crock, milk, nor keel.
But ready for to steal
For very pure need.
Your commons say indeed
They be not able to feed
In their stable scant a steed,
To bring up nor to breed,
Yea, scant able to bring
To the market anything
Towards their housekeeping:
And scant have a cow,
Nor to keep a poor sow:
Thus the world is now.
And to hear the relation
Of the poor men's communication,
Under what sort and fashion

They make their exclamation,
You would have compassion.
Thus goeth their protestation,
Saying that such and such
That of late are made rich
Have too, too much
By grasping and regrating,
By polling and debating,
By rolling and dating,
By check and checkmating,
So that your Commons say,
They still pay, pay,
Most willingly alway,
But that they see no stay
To this outrageous array.
Vox populi, vox dei.
O most noble king.
Consider well this thing.

ANON

from Vox Populi, Vox Dei

And yet not long ago
Was preachers one or two,
That spake it plain enough
To you, and you, and you,
High time for to repent
This devilish intent.
From Scotland unto Kent
This preaching was besprent,
And from the east front
Unto Saint Michael's Mount,
This saying did surmount
Abroad to all men's ears
And to your grace's peers,
That from pillar unto post
The poor man he was tost;
I mean the labouring man,
I mean the husbandman,
I mean the ploughman,
I mean the plain true man,
I mean the handcraftman,
I mean the victualing man,
Also the good yeoman,
That sometime in this realm
Had plenty of kye and cream,
Butter, eggs, and cheese,
Honey, wax and bees,
But now alack, alack,
All these men go to wrack,
That are the body and stay
Of your grace's realm alway.

SIR THOMAS WYATT

'They flee from me'

They flee from me that sometime did me seek
With naked foot stalking in my chamber.
I have seen them gentle, tame, and meek
That now are wild and do not remember
That sometime they put themselves in danger
To take bread at my hand; and now they range
Busily seeking with a continual change.

Thanked be fortune it hath been otherwise
Twenty times better, but once in special,
In thin array after a pleasant guise,
When her loose gown from her shoulders did fall
And she me caught in her arms long and small,
Therewithal sweetly did me kiss
And softly said, 'Dear heart, how like you this?'

It was no dream: I lay broad waking.
But all is turned thorough my gentleness
Into a strange fashion of forsaking.
And I have leave to go of her goodness
And she also to use newfangleness.
But since that I so kindly am served
I would fain know what she hath deserved.

'Stand whoso list'

Stand whoso list upon the slipper top
Of court's estates, and let me here rejoice
And use me quiet without let or stop,
Unknown in court that hath such brackish joys.
In hidden place so let my days forth pass
That, when my years be done withouten noise,
I may die aged after the common trace.
For him death grip'th right hard by the crop
That is much known of other, and of himself, alas,
Doth die unknown, dazed, with dreadful face.

'The pillar perished is'

The pillar perished is whereto I leant,
The strongest stay of mine unquiet mind;
The like of it no man again can find –
From east to west still seeking though he went –
To mine unhap, for hap away hath rent
Of all my joy the very bark and rind,
And I, alas, by chance am thus assigned
Dearly to mourn till death do it relent.
But since that thus it is by destiny,
What can I more but have a woeful heart,
My pen in plaint, my voice in woeful cry,
My mind in woe, my body full of smart,
And I myself myself always to hate
Till dreadful death do cease my doleful state?

'It may be good'

It may be good, like it who list.
But I do doubt. Who can me blame?
For oft assured yet have I missed
And now again I fear the same.
The windy words, the eyes' quaint game
Of sudden change maketh me aghast.
For dread to fall I stand not fast.

Alas, I tread an endless maze
That seek to accord two contraries;
And hope still, and nothing haze,
Imprisoned in liberties;
As one unheard and still that cries;
Always thirsty yet naught I taste.
For dread to fall I stand not fast.

Assured I doubt I be not sure.
And should I trust to such surety
That oft hath put the proof in ure
And never hath found it trusty?
Nay, sir, in faith it were great folly.
And yet my life thus I do waste:
For dread to fall I stand not fast.

from The Faerie Queene

Faire knight (quoth he) *Hierusalem* that is,
   The new *Hierusalem*, that God has built
   For those to dwell in, that are chosen his,
   His chosen people purg'd from sinfull guilt,
   With pretious bloud, which cruelly was spilt
   On cursed tree, of that vnspotted lam,
   That for the sinnes of all the world was kilt:
   Now are they Saints all in that Citie sam,
More deare vnto their God, then younglings to their dam.

Till now, said then the knight, I weened well,
   That great *Cleopolis*, where I haue beene,
   In which that fairest *Faerie Queene* doth dwell,
   The fairest Citie was, that might be seene;
   And that bright towre all built of christall cleene,
   Panthea, seemd the brightest thing, that was:
   But now by proofe all otherwise I weene;
   For this great Citie that does far surpas,
And this bright Angels towre quite dims that towre of glas.

Most trew, then said the holy aged man;
   Yet is *Cleopolis* for earthly frame,
   The fairest peece, that eye beholden can:
   And well beseemes all knights of noble name,
   That couet in th'immortall booke of fame
   To be eternized, that same to haunt,
   And doen their seruice to that soueraigne Dame,
   That glorie does to them for guerdon graunt:
For she is heauenly borne, and heauen may iustly vaunt.

And thou faire ymp, sprong out from English race,
   How euer now accompted Elfins sonne,
   Well worthy doest thy seruice for her grace,
   To aide a virgin desolate foredonne.
   But when thou famous victorie hast wonne,
   And high emongst all knights hast hong thy shield,
   Thenceforth the suit of earthly conquest shonne,
   And wash thy hands from guilt of bloudy field:
For bloud can nought but sin, and wars but sorrowes yield.

Then seeke this path, that I to thee presage,
   Which after all to heauen shall thee send;
   Then peaceably thy painefull pilgrimage
   To yonder same *Hierusalem* do bend,
   Where is for thee ordaind a blessed end:
   For thou emongst those Saints, whom thou doest see,
   Shalt be a Saint, and thine owne nations frend
   And Patrone: thou Saint *George* shalt called bee,
Saint *George* of mery England, the signe of victoree.

                    (Book I, X, stanzas 57–61)

Sonnet 66

Tired with all these, for restful death I cry,
As, to behold desert a beggar born,
And needy nothing trimmed in jollity,
And purest faith unhappily forsworn,
And gilded honour shamefully misplaced,
And maiden virtue rudely strumpeted,
And right perfection wrongfully disgraced,
And strength by limping sway disabled,
And art made tongue-tied by authority,
And folly (doctorlike) controlling skill,
And simple truth miscalled simplicity,
And captive good attending captain ill.
   Tired with all these, from these would I be gone,
   Save that to die, I leave my love alone.

from Coriolanus

MARTIUS: He that will give good words to thee, will flatter
Beneath abhorring. What would you have, you curs,
That like nor peace, nor war? The one affrights you,
The other makes you proud. He that trusts to you,
Where he should find you lions, finds you hares:
Where foxes, geese you are: no surer, no,
Than is the coal of fire upon the ice,
Or hailstone in the sun. Your virtue is,
To make him worthy, whose offence subdues him,
And curse that Justice did it. Who deserves greatness,
Deserves your hate: and your affections are
A sick man's appetite; who desires most that
Which would increase his evil. He that depends
Upon your favours, swims with fins of lead,
And hews down oaks, with rushes. Hang ye: trust ye?
With every minute you do change a mind,
And call him noble, that was now your hate:
Him vile, that was your garland. What's the matter,
That in these several places of the City,
You cry against the noble Senate, who
(Under the Gods) keep you in awe, which else
Would feed on one another? What's their seeking?
MENENIUS: For corn at their own rates, whereof they say
The City is well stor'd.
MARTIUS: Hang 'em; they say?
They'll sit by th' fire, and presume to know
What's done i' th' Capitol: who's like to rise,
Who thrives, and who declines: side factions, and give out
Conjectural marriages, making parties strong,
And feebling such as stand not in their liking,
Below their cobbled shoes. They say there's grain enough?
Would the Nobility lay aside their ruth,
And let me use my sword, I'd make a quarry
With thousands of these quarter'd slaves, as high
As I could pick my lance.

(I, i, 165–198)

from Coriolanus

BRUTUS: All tongues speak of him, and the bleared sights
    Are spectacled to see him. Your prattling nurse
    Into a rapture lets her baby cry,
    While she chats him: the kitchen malkin pins
    Her richest lockram 'bout her reechy neck,
    Clambering the walls to eye him:
    Stalls, bulks, windows, are smother'd up,
    Leads fill'd, the ridges hors'd
    With variable complexions; all agreeing
    In earnestness to see him: seld-shown Flamens
    Do press among the popular throngs, and puff
    To win a vulgar station: our veil'd dames
    Commit the war of white and damask
    In their nicely gawded cheeks, to th' wanton spoil
    Of Phoebus' burning kisses: such a pother,
    As if that whatsoever God, who leads him,
    Were slily crept into his human powers,
    And gave him graceful posture.

                                        (II, i, 195–211)

LXXXI

Under a throne I saw a virgin sit,
The red, and white rose quarter'd in her face;
Star of the North, and for true guards to it,
Princes, Church, states, all pointing out her grace.
The homage done her was not born of wit,
Wisdom admir'd, zeal took ambition's place,
State in her eyes taught order how to fit,
And fix confusion's unobserving race.
    Fortune can here claim nothing truly great,
    But that this princely creature is her seat.

XC

The Turkish government allows no law,
Men's lives and states depend on his behest;
We think subjection there a servile awe,
Where nature finds both honour, wealth and rest.
Our Christian freedom is, we have a law,
Which even the heathen think no power should wrest;
Yet proves it crooked as power lists to draw,
The rage or grace that lurks in prince's breasts.
    Opinion bodies may to shadows give,
    But no burnt zone it is, where people live.

XCII

Virgula divina, sorcerers call a rod,
Gather'd with vows, and magic sacrifice;
Which borne about, by influence doth nod,
Unto the silver, where it hidden lies;
   Which makes poor men to these black arts devout,
   Rich only in the wealth which hope finds out.

Nobility, this precious treasure is,
Laid up in secret mysteries of state,
King's creature, subjection's gilded bliss,
Where grace, not merit, seems to govern fate.
   Mankind I think to be this rod divine,
   For to the greatest ever they incline.

Eloquence, that is but wisdom speaking well,
(The poets feign) did make the savage tame;
Of ears and hearts chain'd unto tongues they tell;
I think nobility to be the same:
   For be they fools, or speak they without wit,
   We hold them wise, we fools bewonder it.

Invisible there is an art to go,
(They say that study Nature's secret works)
And art there is to make things greater show;
In nobleness I think this secret lurks,
   For place a coronet on whom you will,
   You straight see all great in him, but his ill.

CI

Man's youth it is a field of large desires,
Which pleas'd within, doth all without them please,
For in this love of men live those sweet fires,
That kindle worth and kindness unto praise,
    And where self-love most from her selfness gives,
    Man greatest in himself, and others lives.

Old age again which deems this pleasure vain,
Dull'd with experience of unthankfulness,
Scornful of fame, as but effects of pain,
Folds up that freedom in her narrowness,
    And for it only loves her own dreams best,
    Scorn'd and contemned is of all the rest.

Such working youth there is again in state,
Which at the first with justice, piety,
Fame, and reward, true instruments of fate,
Strive to improve this frail humanity:
    By which as kings enlarge true worth in us,
    So crowns again are well enlarged thus.

But states grow old, when princes turn away
From honour, to take pleasure for their ends;
For that a large is, this a narrow way,
That wins a world, and this a few dark friends;
    The one improving worthiness spreads far,
    Under the other good things prisoners are.

Thus sceptres shadow-like, grow short or long,
As worthy, or unworthy princes reign,
And must contract, cannot be large or strong,
If man's weak humours real power restrain,
    So that when power and nature do oppose,
    All but the worst men are assur'd to lose.

For when respect, which is the strength of states,
Grows to decline by kings' descent within
That power's baby-creatures dare set rates
Of scorn upon worth, honour upon sin;
    Then though kings, player-like, act glory's part,
    Yet all within them is but fear and art.

ANON

Gunpowder Plot Day

Please to remember
The·Fifth of November,
Gunpowder treason and plot;
I see no reason
Why gunpowder treason
Should ever be forgot.

ANON

'Vanity of vanities'

Vanity of vanities, saith the Preacher, vanity of vanities; all is vanity.

What profit hath a man of all his labour which he taketh under the sun?

One generation passeth away, and another generation cometh: but the earth abideth for ever.

The sun also ariseth, and the sun goeth down, and hasteth to his place where he arose,

The wind goeth toward the south, and turneth about unto the north; it whirleth about continually, and the wind returneth again according to his circuits.

All the rivers run into the sea; yet the sea is not full; unto the place from whence the rivers come, thither they return again.

All things are full of labour; man cannot utter it: the eye is not satisfied with seeing, nor the ear filled with hearing.

The thing that hath been, it is that which shall be; and that which is done is that which shall be done: and there is no new thing under the sun.

Is there any thing whereof it may be said, See, this is new? it hath been already of old time, which was before us.

There is no remembrance of former things; neither shall there be any remembrance of things that are to come with those that shall come after.

I the Preacher was king over Israel in Jerusalem.

And I gave my heart to seek and search out by wisdom concerning all things that are done under heaven: this sore travail hath God given to the sons of man to be exercised therewith.

I have seen all the works that are done under the sun; and, behold, all is vanity and vexation of spirit.

That which is crooked cannot be made straight: and that which is wanting cannot be numbered.

I communed with mine own heart, saying, Lo, I am come to great estate, and have gotten more wisdom than all they that have been before me in Jerusalem: yea, my heart had great experience of wisdom and knowledge.

And I gave my heart to know wisdom, and to know madness and folly: I perceived that this also is vexation of spirit.

For in much wisdom is much grief: and he that increaseth knowledge increaseth sorrow.

(Ecclesiastes, Chapter 1, Authorized Version)

BEN JONSON

To Penshurst

Thou art not, Penshurst, built to envious show,
Of touch, or marble; nor canst boast a row
Of polished pillars, or a roof of gold:
Thou hast no lanthern, whereof tales are told;
Or stair, or courts; but stand'st an ancient pile,
And these grudged at, art reverenced the while.
Thou joy'st in better marks, of soil, of air,
Of wood, of water: therein thou art fair.
Thou hast thy walks for health, as well as sport:
Thy Mount, to which the dryads do resort,
Where Pan, and Bacchus their high feasts have made,
Beneath the broad beech, and the chestnut shade;
That taller tree, which of a nut was set,
At his great birth, where all the muses met.
There, in the writhèd bark, are cut the names
Of many a Sylvan, taken with his flames.
And thence, the ruddy satyrs oft provoke
The lighter fauns, to reach thy lady's oak.
Thy copse, too, named of Gamage, thou hast there,
That never fails to serve thee seasoned deer,
When thou would'st feast, or exercise thy friends.
The lower land, that to the river bends,
Thy sheep, thy bullocks, kine, and calves do feed:
The middle grounds thy mares, and horses breed.
Each bank doth yield thee conies; and the tops
Fertile of wood, Ashore, and Sidney's copse,
To crown thy open table, doth provide
The purpled pheasant, with the speckled side:
The painted partridge lies in every field,
And, for thy mess, is willing to be killed.
And if the high-swoll'n Medway fail thy dish,
Thou hast thy ponds, that pay thee tribute fish,
Fat, agèd carps, that run into thy net.

And pikes, now weary their own kind to eat,
As loth, the second draught, or cast to stay,
Officiously, at first, themselves betray.
Bright eels, that emulate them, and leap on land,
Before the fisher, or into his hand.
Then hath thy orchard fruit, thy garden flowers,
Fresh as the air, and new as are the hours.
The early cherry, with the later plum,
Fig, grape, and quince, each in his time doth come:
The blushing apricot, and woolly peach
Hang on thy walls, that every child may reach.
And though thy walls be of the country stone,
They are reared with no man's ruin, no man's groan,
There's none, that dwell about them, wish them down;
But all come in, the farmer, and the clown:
And no one empty-handed, to salute
Thy lord, and lady, though they have no suit.
Some bring a capon, some a rural cake,
Some nuts, some apples; some that think they make
The better cheeses, bring them; or else send
By their ripe daughters, whom they would commend
This way to husbands; and whose baskets bear
An emblem of themselves, in plum, or pear.
But what can this (more than express their love)
Add to thy free provisions, far above
The need of such? Whose liberal board doth flow,
With all, that hospitality doth know!
Where comes no guest, but is allowed to eat,
Without his fear, and of thy lord's own meat:
Where the same beer, and bread, and self-same wine,
That is his lordship's, shall be also mine.
And I not fain to sit (as some, this day,
At great men's tables) and yet dine away.
Here no man tells my cups; nor, standing by,
A waiter, doth my gluttony envy;
But gives me what I call, and lets me eat,
He knows, below, he shall find plenty of meat,

Thy tables hoard not up for the next day,
Nor, when I take my lodging, need I pray
For fire, or lights, or livery: all is there;
As if thou, then, wert mine, or I reigned here:
There's nothing I can wish, for which I stay.
That found King James, when hunting late, this way,
With his brave son, the prince, they saw thy fires
Shine bright on every hearth as the desires
Of thy Penates had been set on flame,
To entertain them; or the country came,
With all their zeal, to warm their welcome here.
What (great, I will not say, but) sudden cheer
Didst thou, then, make them! And what praise was heaped
On thy good lady, then! Who, therein, reaped
The just reward of her high huswifery;
To have her linen, plate, and all things nigh,
When she was far: and not a room, but dressed,
As if it had expected such a guest!
These, Penshurst, are thy praise, and yet not all.
Thy lady's noble, fruitful, chaste withal.
His children thy great lord may call his own:
A fortune, in this age, but rarely known.
They are, and have been taught religion: thence
Their gentler spirits have sucked innocence.
Each morn, and even, they are taught to pray,
With the whole household, and may, every day,
Read, in their virtuous parents' noble parts,
The mysteries of manners, arms, and arts.
Now, Penshurst, they that will proportion thee
With other edifices, when they see
Those proud, ambitious heaps, and nothing else,
May say, their lords have built, but thy lord dwells.

The Lie

Go, Soul, the body's guest,
Upon a thankless arrant:
Fear not to touch the best;
The truth shall be thy warrant:
Go, since I needs must die,
And give the world the lie.

Say to the court, it glows
And shines like rotten wood;
Say to the church, it shows
What's good, and doth no good:
If church and court reply,
Then give them both the lie.

Tell potentates, they live
Acting by others' action;
Not loved unless they give,
Not strong but by a faction:
If potentates reply,
Give potentates the lie.

Tell men of high condition,
That manage the estate,
Their purpose is ambition,
Their practice only hate:
And if they once reply,
Then give them all the lie.

Tell them that brave it most,
They beg for more by spending,
Who, in their greatest cost,
Seek nothing but commending:
And if they make reply,
Then give them all the lie.

Tell zeal it wants devotion;
Tell love it is but lust:
Tell time it is but motion;
Tell flesh it is but dust:
And wish them not reply,
For thou must give the lie.

Tell age it daily wasteth;
Tell honour how it alters;
Tell beauty how she blasteth;
Tell favour how it falters:
And as they shall reply,
Give every one the lie.

Tell wit how much it wrangles
In tickle points of niceness;
Tell wisdom she entangles
Herself in over-wiseness:
And when they do reply,
Straight give them both the lie.

Tell physic of her boldness;
Tell skill it is pretension;
Tell charity of coldness;
Tell law it is contention:
And as they do reply,
So give them still the lie.

Tell fortune of her blindness;
Tell nature of decay;
Tell friendship of unkindness;
Tell justice of delay:
And if they will reply,
Then give them all the lie.

Tell arts they have no soundness,
But vary by esteeming;
Tell schools they want profoundness,
And stand too much on seeming:
If arts and schools reply,
Give arts and schools the lie.

Tell faith it's fled the city;
Tell how the country erreth;
Tell manhood shakes off pity
And virtue least preferreth:
And if they do reply,
Spare not to give the lie.

So when thou hast, as I
Commanded thee, done blabbing
– Although to give the lie
Deserves no less than stabbing –
Stab at thee he that will,
No stab the soul can kill.

The Hock-Cart, or Harvest Home:
To the Right Honourable Mildmay,
Earl of Westmorland

Come, sons of summer, by whose toil
We are the lords of wine and oil;
By whose tough labours and rough hands
We rip up first, then reap our lands;
Crowned with the ears of corn, now come,
And, to the pipe, sing harvest home.
Come forth, my lord, and see the cart
Dressed up with all the country art.
See here a maukin, there a sheet,
As spotless pure as it is sweet;
The horses, mares, and frisking fillies,
Clad all in linen, white as lilies;
The harvest swains and wenches bound
For joy to see the hock-cart crowned.
About the cart, hear how the rout
Of rural younglings raise the shout;
Pressing before, some coming after,
Those with a shout, and these with laughter.
Some bless the cart; some kiss the sheaves;
Some prank them up with oaken leaves;
Some cross the fill-horse; some with great
Devotion stroke the home-borne wheat;
While other rustics, less attent
To prayers than to merriment,
Run after with their breeches rent.
Well, on, brave boys, to your lord's hearth,
Glitt'ring with fire; where, for your mirth,
Ye shall see first the large and chief
Foundation of your feast, fat beef,
With upper stories, mutton, veal,
And bacon, which makes full the meal;

With sev'ral dishes standing by,
As here a custard, there a pie,
And here all-tempting frumenty.
And for to make the merry cheer,
If smirking wine be wanting here,
There's that which drowns all care, stout beer,
Which freely drink to your lord's health;
Then to the plough, the commonwealth,
Next to your flails, your fans, your fats;
Then to the maids with wheaten hats;
To the rough sickle, and crook'd scythe,
Drink, frolic boys, till all be blithe.
Feed, and grow fat; and as ye eat,
Be mindful that the labouring neat,
As you, may have their fill of meat.
And know, besides, ye must revoke
The patient ox unto the yoke,
And all go back unto the plough
And harrow, though they're hanged up now.
And, you must know, your lord's word's true,
Feed him ye must, whose food fills you,
And that this pleasure is like rain,
Not sent ye for to drown your pain,
But for to make it spring again.

Epitaph on the Earl of Strafford

Here lies wise and valiant dust,
Huddled up 'twixt fit and just:
STRAFFORD, who was hurried hence
'Twixt treason and convenience.
He spent his time here in a mist;
A Papist, yet a Calvinist.
His Prince's nearest joy, and grief.
He had, yet wanted all relief.
The prop and ruin of the state;
The people's violent love, and hate:
One in extremes lov'd and abhor'd.
Riddles lie here; or in a word,
Here lies blood; and let it lie
Speechless still, and never cry.

The Character of a Roundhead

What creature's this with his short hairs,
His little band and huge long ears,
    That this new faith hath founded,
The Puritans were never such,
The Saints themselves, had ne'er so much,
    Oh, such a knave's a Roundhead.

What's he that doth the Bishops hate,
And count their calling reprobate,
    Cause by the Pope propounded,
And says a zealous cobbler's better,
Then he that studieth every letter,
    Oh, such a knave's a Roundhead.

What's he that doth high Treason say,
As often as his yea and nay,
    And wish the King confounded,
And dare maintain that Master Pym,
Is fitter for the Crown than him,
    Oh, such a rogue's a Roundhead.

What's he that if he chance to hear,
A piece of London's Common-Prayer,
    Doth think his conscience wounded.
And goes five miles to preach and pray,
And lies with's sister by the way,
    Oh, such a rogue's a Roundhead.

What's he that met a holy Sister,
And in a hay-cock gently kissed her,
    Oh! then his zeal abounded,
Close underneath a shady willow,
Her Bible serv'd her for her pillow,
    And there they got a Roundhead.

JOHN MILTON

On the New Forcers of Conscience
under the Long Parliament

Because you have thrown off your prelate lord,
   And with stiff vows renounced his liturgy
   To seize the widowed whore plurality
   From them whose sin ye envied, not abhorred,
Dare ye for his adjure the civil sword
   To force our consciences that Christ set free,
   And ride us with a classic hierarchy
   Taught ye by mere A. S. and Rutherford?
Men whose life, learning, faith and pure intent
   Would have been held in high esteem with Paul
   Must now be named and printed heretics
By shallow Edwards and Scotch What-d'ye-call:
   But we do hope to find out all your tricks,
   Your plots and packing worse than those of Trent,
      That so the Parliament
May with their wholesome and preventive shears
Clip your phylacteries, though baulk your ears,
      And succour our just fears
When they shall read this clearly in your charge
New *Presbyter* is but old *Priest* writ large.

On the Detraction which followed
upon my
Writing Certain Treatises

I did but prompt the age to quit their clogs
  By the known rules of ancient liberty,
  When straight a barbarous noise environs me
  Of owls and cuckoos, asses, apes and dogs.
As when those hinds that were transformed to frogs
  Railed at Latona's twin-born progeny
  Which after held the sun and moon in fee.
  But this is got by casting pearl to hogs;
That bawl for freedom in their senseless mood,
  And still revolt when truth would set them free.
  Licence they mean when they cry liberty;
For who loves that, must first be wise and good;
  But from that mark how far they rove we see
  For all this waste of wealth, and loss of blood.

To the Lord General Cromwell

Cromwell, our chief of men, who through a cloud
  Not of war only, but detractions rude,
  Guided by faith and matchless fortitude
  To peace and truth thy glorious way hast ploughed,
And on the neck of crowned fortune proud
  Hast reared God's trophies and his work pursued,
  While Darwen stream with blood of Scots imbrued,
  And Dunbar field resounds thy praises loud.
And Worcester's laureate wreath; yet much remains
  To conquer still; peace hath her victories
  No less renowned than war, new foes arise
Threatened to bind our souls with secular chains:
  Help us to save free conscience from the paw
  Of hireling wolves whose gospel is their maw.

from Paradise Lost

Thus Belial with words clothed in reason's garb
Counselled ignoble ease, and peaceful sloth,
Not peace: and after him thus Mammon spake.
  Either to disenthrone the king of heaven
We war, if war be best, or to regain
Our own right lost: him to unthrone we then
May hope when everlasting fate shall yield
To fickle chance, and Chaos judge the strife:
The former vain to hope argues as vain
The latter: for what place can be for us
Within heaven's bound, unless heaven's lord supreme
We overpower? Suppose he should relent
And publish grace to all, on promise made
Of new subjection; with what eyes could we
Stand in his presence humble, and receive
Strict laws imposed, to celebrate his throne
With warbled hymns, and to his Godhead sing
Forced hallelujahs; while he lordly sits
Our envied sovereign, and his altar breathes
Ambrosial odours and ambrosial flowers,
Our servile offerings? This must be our task
In heaven, this our delight; how wearisome
Eternity so spent in worship paid
To whom we hate. Let us not then pursue
By force impossible, by leave obtained
Unacceptable, though in heaven, our state
Of splendid vassalage, but rather seek
Our own good from ourselves, and from our own
Live to ourselves, though in this vast recess,
Free, and to none accountable, preferring
Hard liberty before the easy yoke
Of servile pomp. Our greatness will appear
Then most conspicuous, when great things of small,
Useful of hurtful, prosperous of adverse
We can create, and in what place so e'er

Thrive under evil, and work ease out of pain
Through labour and endurance. This deep world
Of darkness do we dread? How oft amidst
Thick clouds and dark doth heaven's all-ruling sire
Choose to reside, his glory unobscured,
And with the majesty of darkness round
Covers his throne; from whence deep thunders roar
Mustering their rage, and heaven resembles hell?
As he our darkness, cannot we his light
Imitate when we please? This desert soil
Wants not her hidden lustre, gems and gold;
Nor want we skill or art, from whence to raise
Magnificence; and what can heaven show more?
Our torments also may in length of time
Become our elements, these piercing fires
As soft as now severe, our temper changed
Into their temper; which must needs remove
The sensible of pain. All things invite
To peaceful counsels, and the settled state
Of order, how in safety best we may
Compose our present evils, with regard
Of what we are and where, dismissing quite
All thoughts of war: ye have what I advise.
    He scarce had finished, when such murmur filled
The assembly, as when hollow rocks retain
The sound of blustering winds, which all night long
Had roused the sea, now with hoarse cadence lull
Seafaring men o'erwatched, whose bark by chance
Or pinnace anchors in a craggy bay
After the tempest: such applause was heard
As Mammon ended, and his sentence pleased,
Advising peace: for such another field
They dreaded worse than hell: so much the fear
Of thunder and the sword of Michael
Wrought still within them; and no less desire
To found this nether empire, which might rise
By policy, and long process of time,

In emulation opposite to heaven.
Which when Beelzebub perceived, than whom,
Satan except, none higher sat, with grave
Aspect he rose, and in his rising seemed
A pillar of state; deep on his front engraven
Deliberation sat and public care;
And princely counsel in his face yet shone,
Majestic though in ruin: sage he stood
With Atlantean shoulders fit to bear
The weight of mightiest monarchies; his look
Drew audience and attention still as night
Or summer's noontide air, while thus he spake.
   Thrones and imperial powers, offspring of heaven
Ethereal virtues; or these titles now
Must we renounce, and changing style be called
Princes of hell? For so the popular vote
Inclines, here to continue, and build up here
A growing empire; doubtless; while we dream,
And know not that the king of heaven hath doomed
This place our dungeon, not our safe retreat
Beyond his potent arm, to live exempt
From heaven's high jurisdiction, in new league
Banded against his throne, but to remain
In strictest bondage, though thus far removed,
Under the inevitable curb, reserved
His captive multitude: for he, be sure
In highth or depth, still first and last will reign
Sole king, and of his kingdom lose no part
By our revolt, but over hell extend
His empire, and with iron sceptre rule
Us here, as with his golden those in heaven.
What sit we then projecting peace and war?
War hath determined us, and foiled with loss
Irreparable; terms of peace yet none
Vouchsafed or sought; for what peace will be given
To us enslaved, but custody severe,
And stripes, and arbitrary punishment

Inflicted? And what peace can we return,
But to our power hostility and hate,
Untamed reluctance, and revenge though slow,
Yet ever plotting how the conqueror least
May reap his conquest, and may least rejoice
In doing what we most in suffering feel?
Nor will occasion want, nor shall we need
With dangerous expedition to invade
Heaven, whose high walls fear no assault or siege,
Or ambush from the deep. What if we find
Some easier enterprise? There is a place
(If ancient and prophetic fame in heaven
Err not) another world, the happy seat
Of some new race called Man, about this time
To be created like to us, though less
In power and excellence, but favoured more
Of him who rules above; so was his will
Pronounced among the gods, and by an oath,
That shook heaven's whole circumference, confirmed.
Thither let us bend all our thoughts, to learn
What creatures there inhabit, of what mould,
Or substance, how endued, and what their power,
And where their weakness, how attempted best,
By force or subtlety: though heaven be shut,
And heaven's high arbitrator sit secure
In his own strength, this place may lie exposed
The utmost border of his kingdom, left
To their defence who hold it: here perhaps
Some advantageous act may be achieved
By sudden onset, either with hell fire
To waste his whole creation, or possess
All as our own, and drive as we were driven,
The puny habitants, or if not drive,
Seduce them to our party, that their God
May prove their foe, and with repenting hand
Abolish his own works. This would surpass
Common revenge, and interrupt his joy

In our confusion, and our joy upraise
In his disturbance; when his darling sons
Hurled headlong to partake with us, shall curse
Their frail original, and faded bliss,
Faded so soon. Advise if this be worth
Attempting, or to sit in darkness here
Hatching vain empires.

(Book II, lines 226–378)

from Paradise Lost

                    . . . the fiend
Saw undelighted all delight, all kind
Of living creatures new to sight and strange:
Two of far nobler shape erect and tall,
Godlike erect, with native honour clad
In naked majesty seemed lords of all,
And worthy seemed, for in their looks divine
The image of their glorious maker shone,
Truth, wisdom, sanctitude severe and pure,
Severe but in true filial freedom placed;
Whence true authority in men; though both
Not equal, as their sex not equal seemed;
For contemplation he and valour formed,
For softness she and sweet attractive grace,
He for God only, she for God in him:
His fair large front and eye sublime declared
Absolute rule; and hyacinthine locks
Round from his parted forelock manly hung
Clustering, but not beneath his shoulders broad:
She as a veil down to the slender waist
Her unadorned golden tresses wore
Dishevelled, but in wanton ringlets waved
As the vine curls her tendrils, which implied
Subjection, but required with gentle sway,
And by her yielded, by him best received,

Yielded with coy submission, modest pride,
And sweet reluctant amorous delay.
Nor those mysterious parts were then concealed,
Then was not guilty shame, dishonest shame
Of nature's work, honour dishonourable,
Sin-bred, how have ye troubled all mankind
With shows instead, mere shows of seeming pure,
And banished from man's life his happiest life,
Simplicity and spotless innocence.
So passed they naked on, nor shunned the sight
Of God or angel, for they thought no ill:
So hand in hand they passed, the loveliest pair
That ever since in love's embraces met,
Adam the goodliest man of men since born
His sons, the fairest of her daughters Eve.
Under a tuft of shade that on a green
Stood whispering soft, by a fresh fountain side
They sat them down, and after no more toil
Of their sweet gardening labour than sufficed
To recommend cool zephyr, and made ease
More easy, wholesome thirst and appetite
More grateful, to their supper fruits they fell,
Nectarine fruits which the compliant boughs
Yielded them, sidelong as they sat recline
On the soft downy bank damasked with flowers:
The savoury pulp they chew, and in the rind
Still as they thirsted scoop the brimming stream;
Nor gentle purpose, nor endearing smiles
Wanted, nor youthful dalliance as beseems
Fair couple, linked in happy nuptial league,
Alone as they. About them frisking played
All beasts of the earth, since wild, and of all chase
In wood or wilderness, forest or den;
Sporting the lion ramped, and in his paw
Dandled the kid; bears, tigers, ounces, pards,
Gambolled before them, the unwieldly elephant
To make them mirth used all his might, and wreathed

His lithe proboscis; close the serpent sly
Insinuating, wove with Gordian twine
His braided train, and of his fatal guile
Gave proof unheeded; others on the grass
Couched, and now filled with pasture gazing sat,
Or bedward ruminating: for the sun
Declined was hasting now with prone career
To the Ocean Isles, and in the ascending scale
Of heaven the stars that usher evening rose:
When Satan still in gaze, as first he stood,
Scarce thus at length failed speech recovered sad.

(Book IV, lines 285-357)

from Paradise Lost

Half yet remains unsung, but narrower bound
Within the visible diurnal sphere;
Standing on earth, not rapt above the pole,
More safe I sing with mortal voice, unchanged
To hoarse or mute, though fallen on evil days,
On evil days though fallen, and evil tongues;
In darkness, and with dangers compassed round,
And solitude; yet not alone, while thou
Visit'st my slumbers nightly, or when morn
Purples the east: still govern thou my song,
Urania, and fit audience find, though few.
But drive far off the barbarous dissonance
Of Bacchus and his revellers, the race
Of that wild rout that tore the Thracian bard
In Rhodope, where woods and rocks had ears
To rapture, till the savage clamour drowned
Both harp and voice; nor could the Muse defend
Her son. So fail not thou, who thee implores:
For thou art heavenly, she an empty dream.

(Book VII, lines 21-39)

from Paradise Lost

To whom thus Michael. Those whom last thou saw'st
In triumph and luxurious wealth, are they
First seen in acts of prowess eminent
And great exploits, but of true virtue void;
Who having spilt much blood, and done much waste
Subduing nations, and achieved thereby
Fame in the world, high titles, and rich prey,
Shall change their course to pleasure, ease, and sloth,
Surfeit, and lust, till wantonness and pride
Raise out of friendship hostile deeds in peace.
The conquered also, and enslaved by war
Shall with their freedom lost all virtue lose
And fear of God, from whom their piety feigned
In sharp contest of battle found no aid
Against invaders; therefore cooled in zeal
Thenceforth shall practice how to live secure,
Worldly or dissolute, on what their lords
Shall leave them to enjoy; for the earth shall bear
More than enough, that temperance may be tried:
So all shall turn degenerate, all depraved,
Justice and temperance, truth and faith forgot;
One man except, the only son of light
In a dark age, against example good,
Against allurement, custom, and a world
Offended; fearless of reproach and scorn,
Or violence, he of their wicked ways
Shall them admonish, and before them set
The paths of righteousness, how much more safe,
And full of peace, denouncing wrath to come
On their impenitence; and shall return
Of them derided, but of God observed
The one just man alive; by his command
Shall build a wondrous ark, as thou beheld'st,
To save himself and household from amidst
A world devote to universal rack.

No sooner he with them of man and beast
Select for life shall in the ark be lodged,
And sheltered round, but all the cataracts
Of heaven set open on the earth shall pour
Rain day and night, all fountains of the deep
Broke up, shall heave the ocean to usurp
Beyond all bounds, till inundation rise
Above the highest hills: then shall this mount
Of Paradise by might of waves be moved
Out of his place, pushed by the horned flood,
With all his verdure spoiled, and trees adrift
Down the great river to the opening gulf,
And there take root an island salt and bare,
The haunt of seals and orcs, and sea-mews' clang.

(Book XI, lines 787–835)

from Paradise Lost

To whom thus Michael. Justly thou abhorr'st
That son, who on the quiet state of men
Such trouble brought, affecting to subdue
Rational liberty; yet know withal,
Since thy original lapse, true liberty
Is lost, which always with right reason dwells
Twinned, and from her hath no dividual being:
Reason in man obscured, or not obeyed,
Immediately inordinate desires
And upstart passions catch the government
From reason, and to servitude reduce
Man till then free. Therefore since he permits
Within himself unworthy powers to reign
Over free reason, God in judgment just
Subjects him from without to violent lords;
Who oft as undeservedly enthral
His outward freedom: tyranny must be,
Though to the tyrant thereby no excuse.

Yet sometimes nations will decline so low
From virtue, which is reason, that no wrong,
But justice, and some fatal curse annexed
Deprives them of their outward liberty,
Their inward lost: witness the irreverent son
Of him who built the ark, who for the shame
Done to his father, heard this heavy curse,
Servant of servants, on his vicious race.

(Book XII, lines 79–104)

from Paradise Lost

Egypt, divided by the river Nile;
See where it flows, disgorging at seven mouths
Into the sea: to sojourn in that land
He comes invited by a younger son
In time of dearth, a son whose worthy deeds
Raise him to be the second in that realm
Of Pharao: there he dies, and leaves his race
Growing into a nation, and now grown
Suspected to a sequent king, who seeks
To stop their overgrowth, as inmate guests
Too numerous; whence of guests he makes them slaves
Inhospitably, and kills their infant males:
Till by two brethren (those two brethren call
Moses and Aaron) sent from God to claim
His people from enthralment, they return
With glory and spoil back to their promised land.
But first the lawless tyrant, who denies
To know their God, or message to regard,
Must be compelled by signs and judgments dire;
To blood unshed the rivers must be turned,
Frogs, lice and flies must all his palace fill
With loathed intrusion, and fill all the land;
His cattle must of rot and murrain die,
Botches and blains must all his flesh emboss,

And all his people; thunder mixed with hail,
Hail mixed with fire must rend the Egyptian sky
And wheel on the earth, devouring where it rolls;
What it devours not, herb, or fruit, or grain,
A darksome cloud of locusts swarming down
Must eat, and on the ground leave nothing green:
Darkness must overshadow all his bounds,
Palpable darkness, and blot out three days;
Last with one midnight stroke all the first-born
Of Egypt must lie dead. Thus with ten wounds
The river-dragon tamed at length submits
To let his sojourners depart, and oft
Humbles his stubborn heart, but still as ice
More hardened after thaw, till in his rage
Pursuing whom he late dismissed, the sea
Swallows him with his host, but them lets pass
As on dry land between two crystal walls,
Awed by the rod of Moses so to stand
Divided, till his rescued gain their shore:
Such wondrous power God to his saint will lend,
Though present in his angel, who shall go
Before them in a cloud, and pillar of fire,
By day a cloud, by night a pillar of fire,
To guide them in their journey, and remove
Behind them, while the obdurate king pursues:
All night he will pursue, but his approach
Darkness defends between till morning watch;
Then through the fiery pillar and the cloud
God looking forth will trouble all his host
And craze their chariot wheels: when by command
Moses once more his potent rod extends
Over the sea; the sea his rod obeys;
On their embattled ranks the waves return,
And overwhelm their war: the race elect
Safe towards Canaan from the shore advance
Through the wild desert, not the readiest way,
Lest entering on the Canaanite alarmed

War terrify them inexpert, and fear
Return them back to Egypt, choosing rather
Inglorious life with servitude; for life
To noble and ignoble is more sweet
Untrained in arms, where rashness leads not on.
This also shall they gain by their delay
In the wide wilderness, there they shall found
Their government, and their great senate choose
Through the twelve tribes, to rule by laws ordained:
God from the mount of Sinai, whose grey top
Shall tremble, he descending, will himself
In thunder lightning and loud trumpets' sound
Ordain them laws; part such as appertain
To civil justice, part religious rites
Of sacrifice, informing them, by types
And shadows, of that destined seed to bruise
The serpent, by what means he shall achieve
Mankind's deliverance.

(Book XII, lines 157–235)

from Paradise Lost

So spake the archangel Michael, then paused,
As at the world's great period; and our sire
Replete with joy and wonder thus replied.
O goodness infinite, goodness immense!
That all this good of evil shall produce,
And evil turn to good; more wonderful
Than that which by creation first brought forth
Light out of darkness! Full of doubt I stand,
Whether I should repent me now of sin
By me done and occasioned, or rejoice
Much more, that much more good thereof shall spring,
To God more glory, more good will to men
From God, and over wrath grace shall abound.
But say, if our deliverer up to heaven

Must reascend, what will betide the few
His faithful, left among the unfaithful herd,
The enemies of truth; who then shall guide
His people, who defend? Will they not deal
Worse with his followers than with him they dealt?
   Be sure they will, said the angel; but from heaven
He to his own a Comforter will send,
The promise of the Father, who shall dwell
His Spirit within them, and the law of faith
Working through love, upon their hearts shall write,
To guide them in all truth, and also arm
With spiritual armour, able to resist
Satan's assaults, and quench his fiery darts,
What man can do against them, not afraid,
Though to the death, against such cruelties
With inward consolations recompensed,
And oft supported so as shall amaze
Their proudest persecutors: for the Spirit
Poured first on his apostles, whom he sends
To evangelize the nations, then on all
Baptized, shall them with wondrous gifts endue
To speak all tongues, and do all miracles,
As did their Lord before them. Thus they win
Great numbers of each nation to receive
With joy the tidings brought from heaven: at length
Their ministry performed, and race well run,
Their doctrine and their story written left,
They die; but in their room, as they forewarn,
Wolves shall succeed for teachers, grievous wolves,
Who all the sacred mysteries of heaven
To their own vile advantages shall turn
Of lucre and ambition, and the truth
With superstitions and traditions taint,
Left only in those written records pure,
Though not but by the Spirit understood.
Then shall they seek to avail themselves of names,
Places and titles, and with these to join

Secular power, though feigning still to act
By spiritual, to themselves appropriating
The Spirit of God, promised alike and given
To all believers; and from that pretence,
Spiritual laws by carnal power shall force
On every conscience; laws which none shall find
Left them enrolled, or what the Spirit within
Shall on the heart engrave. What will they then
But force the spirit of grace itself, and bind
His consort liberty; what, but unbuild
His living temples, built by faith to stand,
Their own faith not another's: for on earth
Who against faith and conscience can be heard
Infallible? Yet many will presume:
Whence heavy persecution shall arise
On all who in the worship persevere
Of spirit and truth; the rest, far greater part,
Well deem in outward rites and specious forms
Religion satisfied; truth shall retire
Bestuck with slanderous darts, and works of faith
Rarely be found: so shall the world go on,
To good malignant, to bad men benign,
Under her own weight groaning till the day
Appear of respiration to the just,
And vengeance to the wicked, at return
Of him so lately promised to thy aid
The woman's seed, obscurely then foretold,
Now amplier known thy saviour and thy Lord,
Last in the clouds from heaven to be revealed
In glory of the Father, to dissolve
Satan with his perverted world, then raise
From the conflagrant mass, purged and refined,
New heavens, new earth, ages of endless date
Founded in righteousness and peace and love
To bring forth fruits joy and eternal bliss.

(Book XII, lines 466–551)

Samson before the Prison in Gaza

A little onward lend thy guiding hand
To these dark steps, a little further on;
For yonder bank hath choice of sun or shade,
There I am wont to sit, when any chance
Relieves me from my task of servile toil,
Daily in the common prison else enjoined me,
Where I a prisoner chained, scarce freely draw
The air imprisoned also, close and damp,
Unwholesome draught: but here I feel amends,
The breath of heaven fresh blowing, pure and sweet,
With day-spring born; here leave me to respire.
This day a solemn feast the people hold
To Dagon their sea-idol, and forbid
Laborious works, unwillingly this rest
Their superstition yields me; hence with leave
Retiring from the popular noise, I seek
This unfrequented place to find some ease,
Ease to the body some, none to the mind
From restless thoughts, that like a deadly swarm
Of hornets armed, no sooner found alone,
But rush upon me thronging, and present
Times past, what once I was, and what am now.
O wherefore was my birth from heaven foretold
Twice by an angel, who at last in sight
Of both my parents all in flames ascended
From off the altar, where an offering burned,
As in a fiery column charioting
His godlike presence, and from some great act
Or benefit revealed to Abraham's race?
Why was my breeding ordered and prescribed
As of a person separate to God,
Designed for great exploits; if I must die
Betrayed, captivated, and both my eyes put out,
Made of my enemies the scorn and gaze;
To grind in brazen fetters under task

With this heaven-gifted strength? O glorious strength
Put to the labour of a beast, debased
Lower than bond-slave! Promise was that I
Should Israel from Philistian yoke deliver;
Ask for this great deliverer now, and find him
Eyeless in Gaza at the mill with slaves,
Himself in bonds under Philistian yoke;
Yet stay, let me not rashly call in doubt
Divine prediction; what if all foretold
Had been fulfilled but through mine own default,
Whom have I to complain of but myself?
Who this high gift of strength committed to me,
In what part lodged, how easily bereft me,
Under the seal of silence could not keep,
But weakly to a woman must reveal it,
O'ercome with importunity and tears.
O impotence of mind, in body strong!
But what is strength without a double share
Of wisdom, vast, unwieldy, burdensome,
Proudly secure, yet liable to fall
By weakest subtleties, not made to rule,
But to subserve where wisdom bears command.
God, when he gave me strength, to show withal
How slight the gift was, hung it in my hair.
But peace, I must not quarrel with the will
Of highest dispensation, which herein
Haply had ends above my reach to know:
Suffices that to me strength is my bane,
And proves the source of all my miseries;
So many, and so huge, that each apart
Would ask a life to wail, but chief of all,
O loss of sight, of thee I most complain!
Blind among enemies, O worse than chains,
Dungeon, or beggary, or decrepit age!
Light the prime work of God to me is extinct,
And all her various objects of delight
Annulled, which might in part my grief have eased,

Inferior to the vilest now become
Of man or worm; the vilest here excel me,
The creep, yet see, I dark in light exposed
To daily fraud, contempt, abuse and wrong,
Within doors, or without, still as a fool,
In power of others, never in my own;
Scarce half I seem to live, dead more than half.
O dark, dark, dark, amid the blaze of noon,
Irrecoverably dark, total eclipse
Without all hope of day!
O first-created beam, and thou great word,
Let there be light, and light was over all;
Why am I thus bereaved thy prime decree?
The sun to me is dark
And silent as the moon,
When she deserts the night
Hid in her vacant interlunar cave.
Since light so necessary is to life,
And almost life itself, if it be true
That light is in the soul,
She all in every part; why was the sight
To such a tender ball as the eye confined?
So obvious and so easy to be quenched,
And not as feeling through all parts diffused,
That she might look at will through every pore?
Then had I not been thus exiled from light;
As in the land of darkness yet in light,
To live a life half dead, a living death,
And buried; but O yet more miserable!
Myself, my sepulchre, a moving grave,
Buried, yet not exempt
By privilege of death and burial
From worst of other evils, pains and wrongs,
But made hereby obnoxious more
To all the miseries of life,
Life in captivity
Among inhuman foes.

                              (Samson Agonistes, lines 1–109)

RICHARD LOVELACE

The Grasshopper

To my noble friend Mr Charles Cotton

O thou that swing'st upon the waving hair
   Of some well-filled oaten beard,
Drunk ev'ry night with a delicious tear
   Dropt thee from heav'n, where now th' art rear'd:

The joys of earth and air are thine entire,
   That with thy feet and wings dost hop and fly;
And when thy poppy works thou dost retire
   To thy carv'd acorn-bed to lie.

Up with the day, the sun thou welcom'st then,
   Sport'st in the gilt plats of his beams,
And all these merry days mak'st merry men,
   Thyself, and melancholy streams.

But ah the sickle! golden ears are cropt;
   Ceres and Bacchus bid good night;
Sharp frosty fingers all your flow'rs have topt,
   And what scythes spar'd, winds shave off quite.

Poor verdant fool! and now green ice! thy joys,
   Large and as lasting as thy perch of grass,
Bid us lay in 'gainst winter rain, and poise
   Their floods with an o'erflowing glass.

Thou best of men and friends! we will create
   A genuine Summer in each other's breast;
And spite of this cold Time and frozen Fate,
   Thaw us a warm seat to our rest.

Our sacred hearths shall burn eternally
　　As vestal flames; the North-wind, he
Shall strike his frost-stretch'd wings, dissolve and fly
　　This Etna in epitome.

Dropping December shall come weeping in,
　　Bewail th' usurping of his reign;
But when in show'rs of old Greek we begin,
　　Shall cry, he hath his crown again!

Night as clear Hesper shall our tapers whip
　　From the light casements where we play,
And the dark hag from her black mantle strip,
　　And stick there everlasting day.

Thus richer than untempted kings are we,
　　That asking nothing, nothing need:
Though lord of all what seas embrace, yet he
　　That wants himself is poor indeed.

GERRARD WINSTANLEY

The Diggers' Song

'You noble Diggers all, stand up now, stand up now,
  You noble Diggers all, stand up now,
The waste land to maintain, seeing Cavaliers by name
Your digging do disdain and persons all defame.
    Stand up now, stand up now.

Your houses they pull down, stand up now, stand up now,
  Your houses they pull down, stand up now;
Your houses they pull down to fright poor men in town,
But the Gentry must come down, and the poor shall wear the
                                                    crown.
    Stand up now, Diggers all!

With spades and hoes and plowes, stand up now, stand up
                                                    now,
  With spades and hoes and plowes, stand up now;
Your freedom to uphold, seeing Cavaliers are bold
To kill you if they could, and rights from you withhold.
    Stand up now, Diggers all!

Their self-will is their law, stand up now, stand up now,
  Their self-will is their law, stand up now;
Since tyranny came in, they count it now no sin
To make a goal a gin, to starve poor men therein.
    Stand up now, stand up now.

The Gentry are all round, stand up now, stand up now,
  The Gentry are all round, stand up now;
The Gentry are all round, on each side they are found,
Their wisdom's so profound to cheat us of our ground.
    Stand up now, stand up now.

The Lawyers they conjoin, stand up now, stand up now,
  The Lawyers they conjoin, stand up now!
To arrest you they advise, such fury they devise,
The devil in them lies, and hath blinded both their eyes.
    Stand up now, stand up now.

The Clergy they come in, stand up now, stand up now,
  The Clergy they come in, stand up now;
The Clergy they come in, and say it is a sin
That we should now begin our freedom for to win.
    Stand up now, Diggers all!

The tithes they yet will have, stand up now, stand up now,
  The tithes they yet will have, stand up now;
The tithes they yet will have, and Lawyers their fees crave,
And this they say is brave to make the poor their slave.
    Stand up now, Diggers all!

'Gainst Lawyers and 'gainst Priests, stand up now, stand up
                                                    now,
  'Gainst Lawyers and 'gainst Priests, stand up now;
For tyrants they are both, even flat against their oath,
To grant us they are loath, free meat and drink and cloth.
    Stand up now, Diggers all!

The club is all their law, stand up now, stand up now,
  The club is all their law, stand up now;
The club is all their law, to keep poor men in awe;
But they no vision saw to maintain such a law.
    Stand up now, Diggers all!

The Cavaliers are foes, stand up now, stand up now,
  The Cavaliers are foes, stand up now;
The Cavaliers are foes, themselves they do disclose
By verses, not in prose, to please the singing boys.
    Stand up now, Diggers all!

To conquer them by love, come in now, come in now,
  To conquer them by love, come in now;
To conquer them by love, as it does you behove,
For He is King above, no Power is like to Love.
    Glory here, Diggers all!'

Upon Appleton House

To my Lord Fairfax

1

Within this sober frame expect
Work of no foreign architect,
That unto caves the quarries drew,
And forests did to pastures hew,
Who of his great design in pain
Did for a model vault his brain,
Whose columns should so high be raised
To arch the brows that on them gazed.

2

Why should of all things man unruled
Such unproportioned dwellings build?
The beasts are by their dens expressed:
And birds contrive an equal nest;
The low-roofed tortoises do dwell
In cases fit of tortoise shell:
No creature loves an empty space;
Their bodies measure out their place.

3

But he, superfluously spread,
Demands more room alive than dead;
And in his hollow palace goes
Where winds (as he) themselves may lose;
What need of all this marble crust
T'impark the wanton mote of dust,
That thinks by breadth the world t'unite
Though the first builders failed in height?

4

But all things are composèd here
Like Nature, orderly and near:
In which we the dimensions find
Of that more sober age and mind,
When larger-sizèd men did stoop
To enter at a narrow loop;
As practising, in doors so strait,
To strain themselves through heaven's gate.

5

And surely when the after age
Shall hither come in pilgrimage,
These sacred places to adore,
By Vere and Fairfax trod before,
Men will dispute how their extent
Within such dwarfish confines went:
And some will smile at this, as well
As Romulus his bee-like cell.

6

Humility alone designs
Those short but admirable lines,
By which, ungirt and unconstrained,
Things greater are in less contained.
Let others vainly strive t'immure
The circle in the quadrature!
These holy mathematics can
In every figure equal man.

7
Yet thus the laden house does sweat,
And scarce endures the Master great:
But where he comes the swelling hall
Stirs, and the square grows spherical,
More by his magnitude distressed,
Then he is by its straitness pressed:
And too officiously it slights
That in itself which him delights.

8
So honour better lowness bears,
Than that unwonted greatness wears:
Height with a certain grace does bend,
But low things clownishly ascend.
And yet what needs there here excuse,
Where everything does answer use?
Where neatness nothing can condemn,
Nor pride invent what to contemn?

9
A stately frontispiece of poor
Adorns without the open door:
Nor less the rooms within commends
Daily new furniture of friends.
The house was built upon the place
Only as for a mark of grace;
And for an inn to entertain
Its Lord a while, but not remain.

10

Him Bishop's Hill or Denton may,
Or Bilbrough, better hold than they:
But Nature here hath been so free
As if she said, 'Leave this to me.'
Art would more neatly have defaced
What she had laid so sweetly waste,
In fragrant gardens, shady woods,
Deep meadows, and transparent floods.

11

While with slow eyes we these survey,
And on each pleasant footstep stay,
We opportunely may relate
The progress of his house's fate.
A nunnery first gave it birth
(For virgin buildings oft brought forth);
And all that neighbour-ruin shows
The quarries whence this dwelling rose.

12

Near to this gloomy cloister's gates
There dwelt the blooming virgin Thwaites,
Fair beyond measure, and an heir
Which might deformity make fair.
And oft she spent the summer suns
Discoursing with the subtle nuns.
Whence in these words one to her weaved,
(As 'twere by chance) thoughts long conceived.

13
'Within this holy leisure we
Live innocently, as you see.
These walls restrain the world without,
But hedge our liberty about.
These bars inclose that wider den
Of those wild creatures callèd men.
The cloister outward shuts its gates,
And, from us, locks on them the grates.

14
'Here we, in shining armour white,
Like virgin Amazons do fight.
And our chaste lamps we hourly trim,
Lest the great Bridegroom find them dim.
Our orient breaths perfumèd are
With incense of incessant prayer.
And holy-water of our tears
Most strangely our complexion clears.

15
'Not tears of grief; but such as those
With which calm pleasure overflows;
Or pity, when we look on you
That live without this happy vow.
How should we grieve that must be seen
Each one a spouse, and each a queen,
And can in heaven hence behold
Our brighter robes and crowns of gold?

16

'When we have prayèd all our beads,
Someone the holy legend reads;
While all the rest with needles paint
The face and graces of the saint.
But what the linen can't receive
They in their lives do interweave.
This work the saints best represents;
That serves for altar's ornaments.

17

'But much it to our work would add
If here your hand, your face we had:
By it we would Our Lady touch;
Yet thus She you resembles much.
Some of your features, as we sewed,
Through every shrine should be bestowed.
And in one beauty we would take
Enough a thousand saints to make.

18

'And (for I dare not quench the fire
That me does for your good inspire)
'Twere sacrilege a man t'admit
To holy things, for heaven fit.
I see the angels in a crown
On you the lilies showering down:
And around about you glory breaks,
That something more than human speaks.

19
'All beauty, when at such a height,
Is so already consecrate.
Fairfax I know; and long ere this
Have marked the youth, and what he is.
But can he such a rival seem
For whom you heav'n should disesteem?
Ah, no! and 'twould more honour prove
He your *devoto* were than love.

20
'Here live belovèd, and obeyed:
Each one your sister, each your maid.
And, if our rule seem strictly penned,
The rule itself to you shall bend.
Our abbess too, now far in age,
Doth your succession near presage.
How soft the yoke on us would lie,
Might such fair hands as yours it tie!

21
'Your voice, the sweetest of the choir,
Shall draw heaven nearer, raise us higher.
And your example, if our head,
Will soon us to perfection lead.
Those virtues to us all so dear,
Will straight grow sanctity when here:
And that, once sprung, increase so fast
Till miracles it work at last.

22
'Nor is our order yet so nice,
Delight to banish as a vice.
Here pleasure piety doth meet;
One pérfecting the other sweet.
So through the mortal fruit we boil
The sugar's uncorrupting oil:
And that which perished while we pull,
Is thus preservèd clear and full.

23
'For such indeed are all our arts,
Still handling Nature's finest parts.
Flowers dress the altars; for the clothes,
The sea-born amber we compose;
Balms for the grieved we draw; and pastes
We mold, as baits for curious tastes.
What need is here of man? unless
These as sweet sins we should confess.

24
'Each night among us to your side
Appoint a fresh and virgin bride;
Whom if Our Lord at midnight find,
Yet neither should be left behind.
Where you may lie as chaste in bed,
As pearls together billeted,
All night embracing arm in arm
Like crystal pure with cotton warm.

25
'But what is this to all the store
Of joys you see, and may make more!
Try but a while, if you be wise:
The trial neither costs, nor ties.'
Now, Fairfax, seek her promised faith:
Religion that dispensèd hath,
Which she henceforward does begin;
The nun's smooth tongue has sucked her in.

26
Oft, though he knew it was in vain,
Yet would he valiantly complain.
'Is this that sanctity so great,
An art by which you finelier cheat?
Hypocrite witches, hence avaunt,
Who though in prison yet enchant!
Death only can such thieves make fast,
As rob though in the dungeon cast.

27
'Were there but, when this house was made,
One stone that a just hand had laid,
It must have fall'n upon her head
Who first thee from thy faith misled.
And yet, how well soever meant,
With them 'twould soon grow fraudulent:
For like themselves they alter all,
And vice infects the very wall.

28
'But sure those buildings last not long,
Founded by folly, kept by wrong.
I know what fruit their gardens yield,
When they it think by night concealed.
Fly from their vices. 'Tis thy 'state,
Not thee, that they would consecrate.
Fly from their ruin. How I fear,
Though guiltless, lest thou perish there.'

29
What should he do? He would respect
Religion, but no right neglect:
For first religion taught him right,
And dazzled not but cleared his sight.
Sometimes resolved, his sword he draws,
But reverenceth then the laws:
For justice still that courage led;
First from a judge, then soldier bred.

30
Small honour would be in the storm.
The court him grants the lawful form;
Which licensed either peace or force,
To hinder the unjust divorce.
Yet still the nuns his right debarred,
Standing upon their holy guard.
Ill-counselled women, do you know
Whom you resist, or what you do?

31
Is not this he whose offspring fierce
Shall fight through all the universe;
And with successive valour try
France, Poland, either Germany;
Till one, as long since prophesied,
His horse through conquered Britain ride?
Yet, against fate, his spouse they kept,
And the great race would intercept.

32
Some to the breach against their foes
Their wooden saints in vain oppose.
Another bolder stands at push
With their old holy-water brush.
While the disjointed abbess threads
The jingling chain-shot of her beads.
But their loudest cannon were their lungs;
And sharpest weapons were their tongues.

33
But waving these aside like flies,
Young Fairfax through the wall does rise.
Then th' unfrequented vault appeared,
And superstitions vainly feared.
The relics false were set to view;
Only the jewels there were true –
But truly bright and holy Thwaites
That weeping at the altar waits.

34
But the glad youth away her bears,
And to the nuns bequeaths her tears:
Who guiltily their prize bemoan,
Like gypsies that a child had stolen.
Thenceforth (as when the enchantment ends,
The castle vanishes or rends)
The wasting cloister with the rest
Was in one instant dispossessed.

35
At the demolishing, this seat
To Fairfax fell as by escheat.
And what both nuns and founders willed
'Tis likely better thus fulfilled.
For if the virgin proved not theirs,
The cloister yet remainèd hers.
Though many a nun there made her vow,
'Twas no religious house till now.

36
From that blest bed the hero came,
Whom France and Poland yet does fame:
Who, when retirèd here to peace,
His warlike studies could not cease;
But laid these gardens out in sport
In the just figure of a fort;
And with five bastions it did fence,
As aiming one for every sense.

37
When in the east the morning ray
Hangs out the colours of the day,
The bee through these known alleys hums,
Beating the *dian* with its drums.
Then flowers their drowsy eyelids raise,
Their silken ensigns each displays,
And dries its pan yet dank with dew,
And fills its flask with odours new.

38
These, as their Governor goes by,
In fragrant volleys they let fly;
And to salute their Governess
Again as great a charge they press:
None for the virgin Nymph; for she
Seems with the flowers a flower to be.
And think so still! though not compare
With breath so sweet, or cheek so fair.

39
Well shot, ye firemen! O how sweet,
And round your equal fires do meet,
Whose shrill report no ear can tell,
But echoes to the eye and smell.
See how the flowers, as at parade,
Under their colours stand displayed:
Each regiment in order grows,
That of the tulip, pink, and rose.

40

But when the vigilant patrol
Of stars walks round about the Pole,
Their leaves, that to the stalks are curled,
Seem to their staves the ensigns furled.
Then in some flower's belovèd hut
Each bee as sentinel is shut,
And sleeps so too: but, if once stirred,
She runs you through, nor asks the word.

41

Oh thou, that dear and happy isle
The garden of the world ere while,
Thou paradise of four seas,
Which heaven planted us to please,
But, to exclude the world, did guard
With watery if not flaming sword;
What luckless apple did we taste,
To make us mortal, and thee waste?

42

Unhappy! shall we never more
That sweet militia restore,
When gardens only had their towers,
And all the garrisons were flowers,
When rose only arms might bear,
And men did rosy garlands wear?
Tulips, in several colours barred,
Were then the Switzers of our Guard.

43
The gardener had the soldier's place,
And his more gentle forts did trace
The nursery of all things green
Was then the only magazine.
The winter quarters were the stoves,
Where he the tender plants removes.
But war all this doth overgrow;
We ordnance plant and powder sow.

44
And yet there walks one on the sod
Who, had it pleasèd him and God,
Might once have made our gardens spring
Fresh as his own and flourishing.
But he preferred to the Cinque Ports
These five imaginary forts,
And, in those half-dry trenches, spanned
Power which the ocean might command.

45
For he did, with his utmost skill,
Ambition weed, but conscience till –
Conscience, that heaven-nursèd plant,
Which most our earthy gardens want.
A prickling leaf it bears, and such
As that which shrinks at every touch;
But flowers eternal, and divine,
That in the crowns of saints do shine.

46

The sight does from these bastions ply,
The invisible artillery;
And at proud Cawood Castle seems
To point the battery of its beams.
As if it quarrelled in the seat
The ambition of its prelate great.
But o'er the meads below it plays,
Or innocently seems to graze.

47

And now to the abyss I pass
Of that unfathomable grass,
Where men like grasshoppers appear,
But grasshoppers are giants there:
They, in their squeaking laugh, contemn
Us as we walk more low than them:
And, from the precipices tall
Of the green spires, to us do call.

48

To see men through this meadow dive,
We wonder how they rise alive,
As, under water, none does know
Whether he fall through it or go.
But, as the mariners that sound,
And show upon their lead the ground,
They bring up flowers so to be seen,
And prove they've at the bottom been.

49
No scene that turns with engines strange
Does oftener than these meadows change.
For when the sun the grass hath vexed,
The tawny mowers enter next;
Who seem like Israelites to be,
Walking on foot through a green sea.
To them the grassy deeps divide,
And crowd a lane to either side.

50
With whistling scythe, and elbow strong,
These massacre the grass along:
While one, unknowing, carves the rail,
Whose yet unfeathered quills her fail.
The edge all bloody from its breast
He draws, and does his stroke detest,
Fearing the flesh untimely mowed
To him a fate as black forebode.

51
But bloody Thestylis, that waits
To bring the mowing camp their cates,
Greedy as kites, has trussed it up,
And forthwith means on it to sup:
When on another quick she lights,
And cries, 'He called us Israelites;
But now, to make his saying true,
Rails rain for quails, for manna, dew.'

52

Unhappy birds! what does it boot
To build below the grass's root;
When lowness is unsafe as height,
And chance o'ertakes, what 'scapeth spite?
And now your orphan parents' call
Sounds your untimely funeral.
Death-trumpets creak in such a note,
And 'tis the sourdine in their throat.

53

Or sooner hatch or higher build:
The mower now commands the field,
In whose new traverse seemeth wrought
A camp of battle newly fought:
Where, as the meads with hay, the plain
Lies quilted o'er with bodies slain:
The women that with forks it fling,
Do represent the pillaging.

54

And now the careless victors play,
Dancing the triumphs of the hay;
Where every mower's wholesome heat
Smells like an Alexander's sweat.
Their females fragrant as the mead
Which they in fairy circles tread:
When at their dance's end they kiss,
Their new-made hay not sweeter is.

55
When after this 'tis piled in cocks,
Like a calm sea it shows the rocks,
We wondering in the river near
How boats among them safely steer.
Or, like the desert Memphis sand,
Short pyramids of hay do stand.
And such the Roman camps do rise
In hills for soldiers' obsequies.

56
This scene again withdrawing brings
A new and empty face of things,
A levelled space, as smooth and plain
As cloths for Lely stretched to stain.
The world when first created sure
Was such a table rase and pure.
Or rather such is the *toril*
Ere the bulls enter at Madril.

57
For to this naked equal flat,
Which Levellers take pattern at,
The villagers in common chase
Their cattle, which it closer rase;
And what below the scythe increased
Is pinched yet nearer by the beast.
Such, in the painted world, appeared
D'Avenant with the universal herd.

58
They seem within the polished grass
A landskip drawn in looking-glass,
And shrunk in the huge pasture show
As spots, so shaped, on faces do –
Such fleas, ere they approach the eye,
In multiplying glasses lie.
They feed so wide, so slowly move,
As constellations do above.

59
Then, to conclude these pleasant acts,
Denton sets ope its cataracts,
And makes the meadow truly be
(What it but seemed before) a sea.
For, jealous of its Lord's long stay,
It tries t'invite him thus away.
The river in itself is drowned,
And isles the astonished cattle round.

60
Let others tell the paradox,
How eels now bellow in the ox;
How horses at their tails do kick,
Turned as they hang to leeches quick;
How boats can over bridges sail;
And fishes do the stables scale,
How salmons trespassing are found;
And pikes are taken in the pound.

61
But I, retiring from the flood,
Take sanctuary in the wood,
And, while it lasts, myself embark
In this yet green, yet growing ark,
Where the first carpenter might best
Fit timber for his keel have pressed.
And where all creatures might have shares,
Although in armies, not in pairs.

62
The double wood of ancient stocks,
Linked in so thick, an union locks,
It like two pedigrees appears,
On th' one hand Fairfax, th' other Vere's:
Of whom though many fell in war,
Yet more to heaven shooting are:
And, as they Nature's cradle decked,
Will in green age her hearse expect.

63
When first the eye this forest sees
It seems indeed as wood not trees:
As if their neighbourhood so old
To one great trunk them all did mould.
There the huge bulk takes place, as meant
To thrust up a fifth element,
And stretches still so closely wedged
As if the night within were hedged.

64
Dark all without it knits; within
It opens passable and thin;
And in as loose an order grows,
As the Corinthean porticoes.
The arching boughs unite between
The columns of the temple green;
And underneath the wingèd choirs
Echo about their tunèd fires.

65
The nightingale does here make choice
To sing the trials of her voice.
Low shrubs she sits in, and adorns
With music high the squatted thorns.
But highest oaks stoop down to hear,
And listening elders prick the ear.
The thorn, lest it should hurt her, draws
Within the skin its shrunken claws.

66
But I have for my music found
A sadder, yet more pleasing sound:
The stock-doves, whose fair necks are graced
With nuptial rings, their ensigns chaste;
Yet always, for some cause unknown,
Sad pair unto the elms they moan.
O why should such a couple mourn,
That in so equal flames do burn!

67

Then as I careless on the bed
Of gelid strawberries do tread,
And through the hazels thick espy
The hatching throstle's shining eye,
The heron from the ash's top,
The eldest of its young lets drop,
As if it stork-like did pretend
That tribute to its Lord to send.

68

But most the hewel's wonders are,
Who here has the holtfelster's care.
He walks still upright from the root,
Measuring the timber with his foot,
And all the way, to keep it clean,
Doth from the bark the woodmoths glean.
He, with his beak, examines well
Which fit to stand and which to fell.

69

The good he numbers up, and hacks,
As if he marked them with the axe.
But where he, tinkling with his beak,
Does find the hollow oak to speak,
That for his building he designs,
And through the tainted side he mines.
Who could have thought the tallest oak
Should fall by such a feeble stroke!

70
Nor would it, had the tree not fed
A traitor-worm, within it bred,
(As first our flesh corrupt within
Tempts impotent and bashful sin).
And yet that worm triumphs not long,
But serves to feed the hewel's young,
While the oak seems to fall content,
Viewing the treason's punishment.

71
Thus I, easy philosopher,
Among the birds and trees confer.
And little now to make me wants
Or of the fowls, or of the plants:
Give me but wings as they, and I
Straight floating on the air shall fly:
Or turn me but, and you shall see
I was but an inverted tree.

72
Already I begin to call
In their most learn'd original:
And where I language want, my signs
The bird upon the bough divines:
And more attentive there doth sit
Than if she were with lime-twigs knit.
No leaf does tremble in the wind
Which I, returning, cannot find.

73
Out of these scattered sibyl's leaves
Strange prophecies my fancy weaves:
And in one history consumes,
Like Mexique paintings, all the plumes.
What Rome, Greece, Palestine, ere said
I in this light mosaic read.
Thrice happy he who, not mistook,
Hath read in Nature's mystic book.

74
And see how chance's better wit
Could with a mask my studies hit!
The oak leaves me embroider all,
Between which caterpillars crawl:
And ivy, with familiar trails,
Me licks, and clasps, and curls, and hales.
Under this antic cope I move
Like some great prelate of the grove.

75
Then, languishing with ease, I toss
On pallets swoll'n of velvet moss,
While the wind, cooling through the boughs,
Flatters with air my panting brows.
Thanks for my rest, ye mossy banks;
And unto you, cool zephyrs, thanks,
Who, as my hair, my thoughts too shed,
And winnow from the chaff my head.

76
How safe, methinks, and strong, behind
These trees have I encamped my mind:
Where beauty, aiming at the heart,
Bends in some tree its useless dart;
And where the world no certain shot
Can make, or me it toucheth not.
But I on it securely play,
And gall its horsemen all the day.

77
Bind me, ye woodbines, in your twines,
Curl me about, ye gadding vines,
And, oh, so close your circles lace,
That I may never leave this place:
But lest your fetters prove too weak,
Ere I your silken bondage break,
Do you, O brambles, chain me too,
And, courteous briars, nail me through.

78
Here in the morning tie my chain,
Where the two woods have made a lane,
While, like a guard on either side,
The trees before their Lord divide;
This, like a long and equal thread,
Betwixt two labyrinths does lead.
But where the floods did lately drown,
There at the evening stake me down.

79
For now the waves are fall'n and dried,
And now the meadows fresher dyed,
Whose grass, with moister colour dashed,
Seems as green silks but newly washed.
No serpent new nor crocodile
Remains behind our little Nile,
Unless itself you will mistake,
Among these meads the only snake.

80
See in what wanton harmless folds
It everywhere the meadow holds;
And its yet muddy back doth lick,
Till as a crystal mirror slick,
Where all things gaze themselves, and doubt
If they be in it or without.
And for his shade which therein shines,
Narcissus-like, the sun too pines.

81
Oh what a pleasure 'tis to hedge
My temples here with heavy sedge,
Abandoning my lazy side,
Stretched as a bank unto the tide,
Or to suspend my sliding foot
On th' osier's undermined root,
And in its branches tough to hang,
While at my lines the fishes twang!

82
But now away my hooks, my quills,
And angles – idle utensils.
The young Maria walks tonight:
Hide, trifling youth, thy pleasures slight.
'Twere shame that such judicious eyes
Should with such toys a man surprise;
She, that already is the law
Of all her sex, her age's awe.

83
See how loose Nature, in respect
To her, itself doth recollect;
And everything so whisht and fine,
Starts forthwith to its *bonne mine*.
The sun himself, of her aware,
Seems to descend with greater care;
And lest she see him go to bed,
In blushing clouds conceals his head.

84
So when the shadows laid asleep
From underneath these banks do creep,
And on the river as it flows
With eben shuts begin to close;
The modest halcyon comes in sight,
Flying betwixt the day and night;
And such an horror calm and dumb,
Admiring Nature does benumb.

85

The viscous air, wheres'e'er she fly,
Follows and sucks her azure dye;
The jellying stream compacts below,
If it might fix her shadow so;
The stupid fishes hang, as plain
As flies in crystal overta'en;
And men the silent scene assist,
Charmed with the sapphire-wingèd mist.

86

Maria such, and so doth hush
The world, and through the evening rush.
No new-born comet such a train
Draws through the sky, nor star new-slain.
For straight those giddy rockets fail,
Which from the putrid earth exhale,
But by her flames, in heaven tried,
Nature is wholly vitrified.

87

'Tis she that to these gardens gave
That wondrous beauty which they have;
She straightness on the woods bestows;
To her the meadow sweetness owes;
Nothing could make the river be
So crystal pure but only she;
She yet more pure, sweet, straight, and fair,
Than gardens, woods, meads, rivers are.

88

Therefore what first she on them spent,
They gratefully again present:
The meadow, carpets where to tread;
The garden, flow'rs to crown her head;
And for a glass, the limpid brook,
Where she may all her beauties look;
But, since she would not have them seen,
The wood about her draws a screen.

89

For she, to higher beauties raised,
Disdains to be for lesser praised.
She counts her beauty to converse
In all the languages as hers;
Nor yet in those herself employs
But for the wisdom, not the noise;
Nor yet that wisdom would affect,
But as 'tis heaven's dialect.

90

Blest Nymph! that couldst so soon prevent
Those trains by youth against thee meant:
Tears (watery shot that pierce the mind);
And signs (Love's cannon charged with wind);
True praise (that breaks through all defence);
And feigned complying innocence;
But knowing where this ambush lay,
She 'scaped the safe, but roughest way.

91
This 'tis to have been from the first
In a domestic heaven nursed,
Under the discipline severe
Of Fairfax, and the starry Vere;
Where not one object can come nigh
But pure, and spotless as the eye;
And goodness doth itself entail
On females, if there want a male.

92
Go now, fond sex, that on your face
Do all your useless study place,
Nor once at vice your brows dare knit
Lest the smooth forehead wrinkled sit:
Yet your own face shall at you grin,
Thorough the black-bag of your skin,
When knowledge only could have filled
And virtue all those furrows tilled.

93
Hence she with graces more divine
Supplies beyond her sex the line;
And like a sprig of mistletoe
On the Fairfacian oak does grow;
Whence, for some universal good,
The priest shall cut the sacred bud,
While her glad parents most rejoice,
And make their destiny their choice.

94

Meantime, ye fields, springs, bushes, flowers,
Where yet she leads her studious hours,
(Till fate her worthily translates,
And find a Fairfax for our Thwaites),
Employ the means you have by her,
And in your kind yourselves prefer;
That, as all virgins she precedes,
So you all woods, streams, gardens, meads.

95

For you, Thessalian Tempe's seat
Shall now be scorned as obsolete;
Aranjuez, as less, disdained;
The Bel-Retiro as contrained;
But name not the Idalian grove –
For 'twas the seat of wanton love –
Much less the dead's Elysian Fields,
Yet nor to them your beauty yields.

96

'Tis not, what once it was, the world,
But a rude heap together hurled,
All negligently overthrown,
Gulfs, deserts, precipices, stone.
Your lesser world contains the same,
But in more decent order tame;
You, heaven's centre, Nature's lap,
And paradise's only map.

97
But now the salmon-fishers moist
Their leathern boats begin to hoist,
And like Antipodes in shoes,
Have shod their heads in their canoes.
How tortoise-like, but not so slow,
These rational amphibii go!.
Let's in: for the dark hemisphere
Does now like one of them appear.

The Mower against Gardens

Luxurious man, to bring his vice in use,
    Did after him the world seduce,
And from the fields the flowers and plants allure,
    Where nature was most plain and pure.
He first enclosed within the gardens square
    A dead and standing pool of air,
And a more luscious earth for them did knead,
    Which stupefied them while it fed.
The pink grew then as double as his mind;
    The nutriment did change the kind.
With strange perfumes he did the roses taint,
    And flowers themselves were taught to paint.
The tulip, white, did for complexion seek,
    And learned to interline its cheek:
Its onion root they then so high did hold,
    That one was for a meadow sold.
Another world was searched, through oceans new,
    To find the *Marvel of Peru*.
And yet these rarities might be allowed
    To man, that sovereign thing and proud,
Had he not dealt between the bark and tree,
    Forbidden mixtures there to see.
No plant now knew the stock from which it came;
    He grafts upon the wild the tame:

That th' uncertain and adulterate fruit
    Might put the palate in dispute.
His green seraglio has its eunuchs too,
    Lest any tyrant him outdo.
And in the cherry he does nature vex,
    To procreate without a sex.
'Tis all enforced, the fountain and the grot,
    While the sweet fields do lie forgot:
Where willing nature does to all dispense
    A wild and fragrant innocence:
And fauns and fairies do the meadows till,
    More by their presence than their skill.
Their statues, polished by some ancient hand,
    May to adorn the gardens stand:
But howsoe'er the figures do excel,
    The gods themselves with us do dwell.

An Horatian Ode
upon Cromwell's Return
from Ireland

The forward youth that would appear
Must now forsake his muses dear,
    Nor in the shadows sing
    His numbers languishing.
'Tis time to leave the books in dust,
And oil the unusèd armour's rust:
    Removing from the wall
    The corslet of the hall.
So restless Cromwell could not cease
In the inglorious arts of peace,
    But through adventurous war
    Urged his active star.
And, like the three-forked lightning, first
Breaking the clouds where it was nursed,
    Did thorough his own side

His fiery way divide.
(For 'tis all one to courage high
The emulous or enemy:
    And with such to inclose
    Is more than to oppose.)
Then burning through the air he went,
And palaces and temples rent:
    And Caesar's head at last
    Did through his laurels blast.
'Tis madness to resist or blame
The force of angry heaven's flame:
    And, if we would speak true,
    Much to the man is due,
Who, from his private gardens, where
He lived reservèd and austere,
    As if his highest plot
    To plant the bergamot,
Could by industrious valour climb
To ruin the great work of time,
    And cast the kingdoms old
    Into another mould.
Though justice against fate complain,
And plead the ancient rights in vain:
    But those do hold or break
    As men are strong or weak.
Nature, that hateth emptiness,
Allows of penetration less:
    And therefore must make room
    Where greater spirits come.
What field of all the Civil Wars,
Where his were not the deepest scars?
    And Hampton shows what part
    He had of wiser art,
Where, twining subtle fears with hope,
He wove a net of such a scope,
    That Charles himself might chase
    To Carisbrooke's narrow case:

That thence the royal actor born
The tragic scaffold might adorn:
   While round the armèd bands
   Did clap their bloody hands.
He nothing common did or mean
Upon that memorable scene:
   But with his keener eye
   The axe's edge did try:
Nor called the gods with vulgar spite
To vindicate his helpless right,
   But bowed his comely head,
   Down, as upon a bed.
This was that memorable hour
Which first assured the forcèd power.
   So when they did design
   The Capitol's first line,
A bleeding head where they begun,
Did fright the architects to run;
   And yet in that the State
   Foresaw its happy fate.
And now the Irish are ashamed
To see themselves in one year tamed:
   So much one man can do,
   That does both act and know.
They can affirm his praises best,
And have, though overcome, confessed
   How good he is, how just,
   And fit for highest trust:
Nor yet grown stiffer with command,
But still in the Republic's hand:
   How fit he is to sway
   That can so well obey.
He to the Commons' feet presents
A kingdom, for his first year's rents:
   And, what he may, forbears
   His fame, to make it theirs:
And has his sword and spoils ungirt,

To lay them at the public's skirt.
  So when the falcon high
  Falls heavy from the sky,
She, having killed, no more does search
But on the next green bough to perch,
  Where, when he first does lure,
  The falc'ner has her sure.
What may not then our isle presume
While Victory his crest does plume?
  What may not others fear
  If thus he crowns each year?
A Caesar, he, ere long to Gaul,
To Italy an Hannibal,
  And to all states not free
  Shall climactéric be.
The Pict no shelter now shall find
Within his parti-coloured mind,
  But from this valour sad
  Shrink underneath the plaid:
Happy, if in the tufted brake
The English hunter him mistake,
  Nor lay his hounds in near
  The Caledonian deer.
But thou, the Wars' and Fortune's son,
March indefatigably on,
  And for the last effect
  Still keep thy sword erect:
Besides the force it has to fright
The spirits of the shady night,
  The same arts that did gain
  A power, must it maintain.

FEAR DORCHA Ó MEALLÁIN

Exodus To Connacht

In the name of the Father full of virtue,
  in the name of the Son Who suffered pain,
in the name of the Holy Ghost in power,
  Mary and her Son be with us.

Our sole possessions: Michael of miracles,
  the virgin Mary, the twelve apostles,
Brigid, Patrick and Saint John
  – and fine rations: faith in God.

Sweet Colm Cille of miracles too,
  and Colmán Mac Aoidh, poets' patron,
will all be with us on our way.
  Do not bewail our journey West.

Brothers mine, do you not see
  the ways of the world a while now?
However much we may possess
  we'll go with little into the grave.

Consider a parable of this:
  Israel's people, God's own,
although they were in bonds in Egypt,
  found in time a prompt release.

Through the mighty sea they passed,
  an ample road was made for them,
then the grey-green ocean rose
  out there above them like a rock.

When they came to dry land
  the King of Heaven minded them
– relief, succour and nourishment
  from the God Who ever was and is.

Food from Heaven they received:
  great wheat, in no small measure,
honey settling like a mist,
  abundant water out of rock.

Likewise it shall be done to you:
  all good things shall first be yours.
Heaven is your inheritance.
  Be not faint-hearted in your faith.

People of my heart, stand steady,
  don't complain of your distress.
Moses got what he requested,
  religious freedom – and from Pharaoh.

Identical their God and ours.
  One God there was and still remains.
Here or Westward God is one,
  one God ever and shall be.

If they call you 'Papishes'
  accept it gladly for a title.
Patience, for the High King's sake.
  Deo Gratias, good the name!

God Who art generous, O Prince of Blessings,
behold the Gael, stripped of authority.
Now as we journey Westward into Connacht
old friends we'll leave behind us in their grief.

                              trans. Thomas Kinsella

JOHN BUNYAN

Valiant-for-Truth's Song

Who would true Valour see
Let him come hither;
One here will Constant be,
Come Wind, come Weather.
There's no *Discouragement*
Shall make him once *Relent*,
His first avow'd *Intent*,
To be a Pilgrim.

Who so beset him round,
With dismal *Storys*,
Do but themselves Confound;
His Strength the *more is*.
No *Lyon* can him fright,
He'l with a *Gyant* Fight,
But he will have a right,
To be a Pilgrim.

Hobgoblin, nor foul *Fiend*,
Can *daunt* his Spirit:
He knows, he *at the end*,
Shall Life Inherit.
Then Fancies fly away,
He'l fear not what men say,
He'l labour Night and Day,
To be a Pilgrim.

Absalom and Achitophel

In pious times ere priestcraft did begin,
Before polygamy was made a sin;
When man on many multiplied his kind,
Ere one to one was cursedly confined;
When nature prompted, and no law denied   5
Promiscuous use of concubine and bride;
Then Israel's monarch after heaven's own heart,
His vigorous warmth did variously impart
To wives and slaves; and wide as his command,
Scatter'd his Maker's image through the land.   10
Michal, of royal blood, the crown did wear;
A soil ungrateful to the tiller's care:
Not so the rest; for several mothers bore
To god-like David several sons before.
But since like slaves his bed they did ascend,   15
No true succession could their seed attend.
Of all this numerous progeny was none
So beautiful, so brave, as Absalon:
Whether inspir'd by some diviner lust,
His father got him with a greater gust: 20
Or that his conscious destiny made way,
By manly beauty to imperial sway.
Early in foreign fields he won renown,
With kings and states allied to Israel's crown:
In peace the thoughts of war he could remove,   25
And seem'd as he were only born for love.
Whate'er he did, was done with so much ease,
In him alone 'twas natural to please:
His motions all accompanied with grace;
And paradise was open'd in his face.   30
With secret joy indulgent David view'd
His youthful image in his son renew'd:
To all his wishes nothing he denied;

And made the charming Annabel his bride.
What faults he had, (for who from faults is free?)   35
His father could not, or he would not see.
Some warm excesses which the law forbore,
Were constru'd youth that purg'd by boiling o'er,
And Amnon's murder by a specious name,
Was call'd a just revenge for injur'd fame.   40
Thus prais'd and lov'd, the noble youth remain'd,
While David, undisturb'd, in Sion reign'd.
But life can never be sincerely blest;
Heaven punishes the bad, and proves the best.
The Jews, a headstrong, moody, murmuring race,   45
As ever tried the extent and stretch of grace;
God's pamper'd people, whom debauch'd with ease,
No king could govern, nor no God could please;
(Gods they had tried of every shape and size,
That godsmiths could produce, or priests devise:)   50
These Adam-wits, too fortunately free,
Began to dream they wanted liberty;
And when no rule, no precedent was found,
Of men, by laws less circumscrib'd and bound;
They led their wild desires to woods and caves,   55
And thought that all but savages were slaves.
They who, when Saul was dead, without a blow,
Made foolish Ishbosheth the crown forego;
Who banish'd David did from Hebron bring,
And with a general shout proclaim'd him king: 60
Those very Jews, who, at their very best,
Their humour more than loyalty exprest,
Now wonder'd why so long they had obey'd
An idol monarch, which their hands had made;
Thought they might ruin him they could create,   65
Or melt him to that golden calf a state.
But these were random bolts: no form'd design,
Nor interest made the factious crowd to join:
The sober part of Israel, free from stain,
Well knew the value of a peaceful reign;   70

And, looking backward with a wise affright,
Saw seams of wounds dishonest to the sight:
In contemplation of whose ugly scars
They curst the memory of civil wars.
The moderate sort of men thus qualified,   75
Inclined the balance to the better side;
And David's mildness managed it so well,
The bad found no occasion to rebel.
But when to sin our bias'd nature leans,
The careful devil is still at hand with means;   80
And providently pimps for ill desires:
The good old cause revived a plot requires.
Plots, true or false, are necessary things,
To raise up commonwealths, and ruin kings.
   The inhabitants of old Jerusalem   85
Were Jebusites; the town so call'd from them;
And theirs the native right —
But when the chosen people grew more strong,
The rightful cause at length became the wrong;
And every loss the men of Jebus bore,   90
They still were thought God's enemies the more.
Thus worn or weaken'd, well or ill content,
Submit they must to David's government:
Impoverish'd and deprived of all command,
Their taxes doubled as they lost their land;   95
And what was harder yet to flesh and blood,
Their gods disgraced, and burnt like common wood.
This set the heathen priesthood in a flame;
For priests of all religions are the same.
Of whatsoe'er descent their godhead be,   100
Stock, stone, or other homely pedigree,
In his defence his servants are as bold,
As if he had been born of beaten gold.
The Jewish rabbins, though their enemies,
In this conclude them honest men and wise;   105
For 'twas their duty all the learned think,
T' espouse his cause, by whom they eat and drink.

From hence began that plot, the nation's curse,
Bad in itself, but represented worse;
Rais'd in extremes, and in extremes decried;   110
With oaths affirm'd, with dying vows denied;
Not weigh'd nor winnow'd by the multitude;
But swallow'd in the mass, unchew'd and crude.
Some truth there was, but dash'd and brew'd with lies,
To please the fools, and puzzle all the wise.   115
Succeeding times did equal folly call,
Believing nothing, or believing all.
Th' Egyptian rites the Jebusites embrac'd;
Where gods were recommended by their taste.
Such savoury deities must needs be good,   120
As served at once for worship and for food.
By force they could not introduce these gods;
For ten to one in former days was odds.
So fraud was used, the sacrificer's trade:
Fools are more hard to conquer than persuade.   125
Their busy teachers mingled with the Jews,   .
And rak'd for converts even the court and stews:
Which Hebrew priests the more unkindly took,
Because the fleece accompanies the flock.
Some thought they God's anointed meant to slay   130
By guns, invented since full many a day:
Our author swears it not; but who can know
How far the devil and Jebusites may go?
This plot, which fail'd for want of common sense,
Had yet a deep and dangerous consequence: 135
For as when raging fevers boil the blood,
The standing lake soon floats into a flood,
And every hostile humour, which before
Slept quiet in its channels, bubbles o'er;
So several factions from his first ferment   140
Work up to foam, and threat the government.
Some by their friends, more by themselves thought wise,
Oppos'd the power to which they could not rise.
Some had in courts been great, and thrown from thence,

Like fiends were harden'd in impenitence.   145
Some, by their monarch's fatal mercy, grown
From pardon'd rebels kinsmen to the throne,
Were rais'd in power and public office high;
Strong bands, if bands ungrateful men could tie.
  Of these the false Achitophel was first;   150
A name to all succeeding ages curst:
For close designs, and crooked councils fit;
Sagacious, bold, and turbulent of wit;
Restless, unfix'd in principles and place;
In power unpleas'd, impatient of disgrace: 155
A fiery soul, which, working out its way,
Fretted the pigmy-body to decay,
And o'er inform'd the tenement of clay.
A daring pilot in extremity;
Pleas'd with the danger, when the waves went high   160
He sought the storms; but for a calm unfit,
Would steer too nigh the sands to boast his wit.
Great wits are sure to madness near allied,
And thin partitions do their bounds divide;
Else why should he, with wealth and honour blest,   165
Refuse his age the needful hours of rest?
Punish a body which he could not please;
Bankrupt of life, yet prodigal of ease?
And all to leave what with his toil he won,
To that unfeather'd two-legg'd thing, a son;   170
Got, while his soul did huddled notions try;
And born a shapeless lump, like anarchy.
In friendship false, implacable in hate;
Resolv'd to ruin or to rule the state.
To compass this the triple bond he broke;   175
The pillars of the public safety shook;
And fitted Israel for a foreign yoke:
Then seiz'd with fear, yet still affecting fame,
Usurp'd a patriot's all-atoning name.
So easy still it proves in factious times   180
With public zeal to cancel private crimes.

How safe is treason, and how sacred ill,
Where none can sin against the people's will?
Where crowds can wink, and no offence be known,
Since in another's guilt they find their own?   185
Yet fame deserv'd no enemy can grudge;
The statesman we abhor, but praise the judge.
In Israel's courts ne'er sat an Abethdin
With more discerning eyes, or hands more clean,
Unbrib'd, unsought, the wretched to redress;   190
Swift of dispatch, and easy of access.
Oh! had he been content to serve the crown,
With virtues only proper to the gown;
Or had the rankness of the soil been freed
From cockle, that oppress'd the noble seed;   195
David for him his tuneful harp had strung,
And heaven had wanted one immortal song.
But wild Ambition loves to slide, not stand,
And Fortune's ice prefers to Virtue's land.
Achitophel, grown weary to possess   200
A lawful fame, and lazy happiness,
Disdain'd the golden fruit to gather free,
And lent the crowd his arm to shake the tree.
Now, manifest of crimes contriv'd long since,
He stood at bold defiance with his prince;   205
Held up the buckler of the people's cause
Against the crown, and skulk'd behind the laws.
The wish'd occasion of the plot he takes;
Some circumstances finds, but more he makes.
By buzzing emissaries fill the ears   210
Of listening crowds with jealousies and fears
Of arbitrary counsels brought to light,
And proves the king himself a Jebusite.
Weak arguments! which yet he knew full well
Were strong with people easy to rebel.   215
For, govern'd by the moon, the giddy Jews
Tread the same track when she the prime renews;
And once in twenty years, their scribes record,

By natural instinct they change their lord.
Achitophel still wants a chief, and none   220
Was found so fit as warlike Absalom.
Not that he wish'd his greatness to create,
For politicians neither love nor hate:
But, for he knew his title not allow'd,
Would keep him still depending on the crowd: 225
That kingly power, thus ebbing out, might be
Drawn to the dregs of a democracy.
Him he attempts with studied arts to please,
And sheds his venom in such words as these.
    Auspicious prince, at whose nativity   230
Some royal planet rul'd the southern sky;
Thy longing country's darling and desire;
Their cloudy pillar and their guardian fire:
Their second Moses, whose extended wand
Divides the seas, and shows the promis'd land: 235
Whose dawning day in every distant age
Has exercis'd the sacred prophet's rage:
The people's prayer, the glad diviner's theme,
The young men's vision, and the old men's dream!
Thee, Saviour, thee the nation's vows confess,   240
And, never satisfied with seeing, bless:
Swift unbespoken pomps thy steps proclaim,
And stammering babes are taught to lisp thy name.
How long wilt thou the general joy detain,
Starve and defraud the people of thy reign!   245
Content ingloriously to pass thy days
Like one of virtue's fools that feed on praise;
Till thy fresh glories, which now shine so bright,
Grow stale, and tarnish with our daily sight!
Believe me, royal youth, thy fruit must be   250
Or gather'd ripe, or rot upon the tree.
Heaven has to all allotted, soon or late,
Some lucky revolution of their fate:
Whose motions if we watch and guide with skill,
(For human good depends on human will,)   255

Our fortune rolls as from a smooth descent,
And from the first impression takes the bent:
But, if unseiz'd, she glides away like wind,
And leaves repenting folly far behind.
Now, now she meets you with a glorious prize,   260
And spreads her locks before her as she flies.
Had thus old David, from whose loins you spring,
Not dar'd when fortune call'd him to be king,
At Gath an exile he might still remain,
And heaven's anointing oil had been in vain.   265
Let his successful youth your hopes engage;
But shun the example of declining age:
Behold him setting in his western skies,
The shadows lengthening as the vapours rise.
He is not now, as when on Jordan's sand   270
The joyful people throng'd to see him land,
Covering the beach, and blackening all the strand;
But, like the prince of angels, from his height
Comes tumbling downward with diminish'd light:
Betray'd by one poor plot to public scorn: 275
(Our only blessing since his curst return):
Those heaps of people which one sheaf did bind,
Blown off and scatter'd by a puff of wind.
What strength can he to your designs oppose,
Naked of friends and round beset with foes?   280
If Pharaoh's doubtful succour he should use,
A foreign aid would more incense the Jews:
Proud Egypt would dissembled friendship bring;
Foment the war, but not support the king:
Nor would the royal party e'er unite   285
With Pharaoh's arms to assist the Jebusite;
Or if they should, their interest soon would break,
And with such odious aid make David weak.
All sorts of men by my successful arts,
Abhorring kings, estrange their alter'd hearts   290
From David's rule: and 'tis the general cry,
Religion, commonwealth, and liberty.

If you, as champion of the public good,
Add to their arms a chief of royal blood,
What may not Israel hope, and what applause   295
Might such a general gain by such a cause?
Not barren praise alone, that gaudy flower
Fair only to the sight, but solid power:
And nobler is a limited command,
Given by the love of all your native land,   300
Than a successive title, long and dark,
Drawn from the mouldy rolls of Noah's ark.
   What cannot praise effect in mighty minds,
When flattery soothes, and when ambition blinds?
Desire of power, on earth a vicious weed,   305
Yet sprung from high is of celestial seed:
In God 'tis glory; and when men aspire,
'Tis but a spark too much of heavenly fire.
The ambitious youth too covetous of fame,
Too full of angel's metal in his frame,   310
Unwarily was led from virtue's ways,
Made drunk with honour, and debauch'd with praise.
Half loath, and half consenting to the ill,
For loyal blood within him struggled still,
He thus replied. – And what pretence have I   315
To take up arms for public liberty?
My father governs with unquestion'd right;
The faith's defender, and mankind's delight;
Good, gracious, just, observant of the laws;
And heaven by wonders has espous'd his cause.   320
Whom has he wrong'd in all his peaceful reign?
Who sues for justice to his throne in vain?
What millions has he pardon'd of his foes,
Whom just revenge did to his wrath expose!
Mild, easy, humble, studious of our good;   325
Inclin'd to mercy, and averse from blood,
If mildness ill with stubborn Israel suit,
His crime is God's beloved attribute.
What could he gain his people to betray,

Or change his right for arbitrary sway?   330
Let haughty Pharaoh curse with such a reign
His fruitful Nile, and yoke a servile train.
If David's rule Jerusalem displease,
The dogstar heats their brains to this disease.
Why then should I, encouraging the bad,   335
Turn rebel and run popularly mad?
Were he a tyrant, who, by lawless might,
Oppress'd the Jews, and rais'd the Jebusite,
Well might I mourn; but nature's holy bands
Would curb my spirits and restrain my hands: 340
The people might assert their liberty;
But what was right in them were crime in me.
His favour leaves me nothing to require,
Prevents my wishes, and outruns desire;
What more can I expect while David lives?   345
All but his kingly diadem he gives:
And that – But there he paus'd; then sighing, said –
Is justly destin'd for a worthier head.
For when my father from his toils shall rest,
And late augment the number of the blest,   350
His lawful issue shall the throne ascend,
Or the collateral line, where that shall end.
His brother, though oppress'd with vulgar spite,
Yet dauntless, and secure of native right,
Of every royal virtue stands possest;   355
Still dear to all the bravest and the best.
His courage foes, his friends his truth proclaim;
His loyalty the king, the world his fame.
His mercy even th'offending crowd will find;
For sure he comes of a forgiving kind.   360
Why should I then repine at heaven's decree,
Which gives me no pretence to royalty?
Yet oh that fate propitiously inclin'd,
Had rais'd my birth, or had debas'd my mind;
To my large soul not all her treasure lent,   365
And then betray'd it to a mean descent!

I find, I find my mounting spirits bold,
And David's part disdains my mother's mould.
Why am I scanted by a niggard birth?
My soul disclaims the kindred of her earth;   370
And, made for empire, whispers me within,
Desire of greatness is a godlike sin.
  Him staggering so, when hell's dire agent found,
While fainting virtue scarce maintain'd her ground,
He pours fresh forces in, and thus replies: 375
  The eternal God, supremely good and wise,
Imparts not these prodigious gifts in vain:
What wonders are reserv'd to bless your reign,
Against your will your arguments have shown
Such virtue's only given to guide a throne.   380
Not that your father's mildness I contemn;
But manly force becomes the diadem.
'Tis true he grants the people all they crave;
And more, perhaps, than subjects ought to have:
For lavish grants suppose a monarch tame,   385
And more his goodness than his wit proclaim.
But when should people strive their bonds to break,
If not when kings are negligent or weak?
Let him give on till he can give no more,
The thrifty Sanhedrin shall keep him poor;   390
And every shekel which he can receive,
Shall cost a limb of his prerogative.
To ply him with new plots shall be my care;
Or plunge him deep in some expensive war;
Which when his treasure can no more supply,   395
He must, with the remains of kingship, buy.
His faithful friends, our jealousies and fears
Call Jebusites, and Pharaoh's pensioners;
Whom when our fury from his aid has torn,
He shall be naked left to public scorn.   400
The next successor, whom I fear and hate,
My arts have made obnoxious to the state;
Turn'd all his virtues to his overthrow,

And gain'd our elders to pronounce a foe.
His right, for sums of necessary gold, 405
Shall first be pawn'd, and afterwards be sold;
Till time shall ever-wanting David draw,
To pass your doubtful title into law:
If not, the people have a right supreme
To make their kings; for kings are made for them. 410
All empire is no more than power in trust,
Which, when resum'd, can be no longer just.
Succession, for the general good design'd,
In its own wrong a nation cannot bind;
If altering that the people can relieve, 415
Better one suffer than a nation grieve.
The Jews well know their power: ere Saul they chose,
God was their king, and God they durst depose.
Urge now your piety, your filial name,
A father's right, and fear of future fame; 420
The public good, that universal call,
To which even heav'n submitted, answers all.
Nor let his love enchant your generous mind;
'Tis nature's trick to propagate her kind.
Our fond begetters, who would never die, 425
Love but themselves in their posterity.
Or let his kindness by the effects be tried,
Or let him lay his vain pretence aside.
God said, he lov'd your father; could he bring
A better proof, than to anoint him king? 430
It surely show'd he lov'd the shepherd well,
Who gave so fair a flock as Israel.
Would David have you thought his darling son?
What means he then to alienate the crown?
The name of godly he may blush to bear: 435
Is't after God's own heart to cheat his heir?
He to his brother gives supreme command,
To you a legacy of barren land:
Perhaps the old harp, on which he thrums his lays,
Or some dull Hebrew ballad in your praise. 440

Then the next heir, a prince severe and wise,
Already looks on you with jealous eyes;
Sees through the thin disguises of your arts,
And marks your progress in the people's hearts;
Though now his mighty soul its grief contains: 445
He meditates revenge who least complains;
And like a lion, slumbering in the way,
Or sleep dissembling, while he waits his prey,
His fearless foes within his distance draws,
Constrains his roaring, and contracts his paws;   450
Till at the last, his time for fury found,
He shoots with sudden vengeance from the ground;
The prostrate vulgar passes o'er and spares,
But with a lordly rage his hunters tears.
Your case no tame expedients will afford: 455
Resolve on death, or conquest by the sword,
Which for no less a stake than life you draw;
And self-defence is nature's eldest law.
Leave the warm people no considering time:
For then rebellion may be thought a crime.   460
Avail yourself of what occasion gives,
But try your title while your father lives:
And that your arms may have a fair pretence,
Proclaim you take them in the king's defence;
Whose sacred life each minute would expose   465
To plots, from seeming friends, and secret foes.
And who can sound the depth of David's soul?
Perhaps his fear his kindness may control.
He fears his brother, though he loves his son,
For plighted vows too late to be undone.   470
If so, by force he wishes to be gain'd:
Like women's lechery to seem constrain'd.
Doubt not, but when he most affects the frown,
Commit a pleasing rape upon the crown.
Secure his person to secure your cause: 475
They who possess the prince possess the laws.
    He said, and his advice above the rest,

With Absalom's mild nature suited best;
Unblam'd of life (ambition set aside),
Not stain'd with cruelty, nor puft with pride,   480
How happy had he been, if destiny
Had higher plac'd his birth, or not so high!
His kingly virtues might have claim'd a throne,
And blest all other countries but his own.
But charming greatness since so few refuse,   485
'Tis juster to lament him than accuse.
Strong were his hopes a rival to remove,
With blandishments to gain the public love:
To head the faction while their zeal was hot,
And popularly prosecute the plot.   490
To further this, Achitophel unites
The malcontents of all the Israelites:
Whose differing parties he could wisely join,
For several ends, to serve the same design.
The best, and of the princes some were such,   495
Who thought the power of monarchy too much;
Mistaken men, and patriots in their hearts,
Not wicked, but seduc'd by impious arts.
By these the springs of property were bent,
And wound so high, they crack'd the government.   500
The next for interest sought to embroil the state,
To sell their duty at a dearer rate;
And make their Jewish markets of the throne;
Pretending public good to serve their own.
Others thought kings a useless heavy load,   505
Who cost too much, and did too little good.
These were for laying honest David by,
On principles of pure good husbandry.
With them join'd all the haranguers of the throng,
That thought to get preferment by the tongue.   510
Who follow next a double danger bring,
Not only hating David, but the king;
The Solymæan rout, well vers'd of old,
In godly faction, and in treason bold;

Cowering and quaking at a conqueror's sword;   515
But lofty to a lawful prince restor'd;
Saw with disdain an Ethnic plot begun,
And scorn'd by Jebusites to be outdone.
Hot Levites headed these, who pull'd before
From the ark, which in the Judges' days they bore,   520
Resum'd their cant, and with a zealous cry
Pursued their old beloved Theocracy:
Where Sanhedrin and priest enslav'd the nation,
And justified their spoils by inspiration:
For who so fit to reign as Aaron's race,   525
If once dominion they could found in grace?
These led the pack, though not of surest scent,
Yet deepest mouth'd against the government.
A numerous host of dreaming saints succeed,
Of the true old enthusiastic breed: 530
'Gainst form and order they their power employ,
Nothing to build, and all things to destroy.
But far more numerous was the herd of such,
Who think too little, and who talk too much.
These out of mere instinct, they knew not why,   535
Ador'd their fathers' God and property;
And by the same blind benefit of fate
The devil and the Jebusite did hate:
Born to be sav'd, even in their own despite,
Because they could not help believing right.   540
Such were the tools: but a whole Hydra more
Remains of sprouting heads too long to score.
   Some of their chiefs were princes of the land;
In the first rank of these did Zimri stand;
A man so various, that he seem'd to be   545
Not one, but all mankind's epitome:
Stiff in opinions, always in the wrong,
Was every thing by starts, and nothing long;
But, in the course of one revolving moon,
Was chymist, fiddler, statesman, and buffoon: 550
Then all for women, painting, rhyming, drinking,

Besides ten thousands freaks that died in thinking.
Blest madman, who could every hour employ,
With something new to wish, or to enjoy!
Railing and praising were his usual themes;   555
And both, to show his judgment, in extremes:
So over violent, or over civil,
That every man with him was God or Devil.
In squandering wealth was his peculiar art:
Nothing went unrewarded but desert.   560
Beggar'd by fools, whom still he found too late;
He had his jest, and they had his estate.
He laugh'd himself from court, then sought relief
By forming parties, but could ne'er be chief:
For, spite of him, the weight of business fell   565
On Absalom and wise Achitophel:
Thus, wicked but in will, of means bereft,
He left not faction, but of that was left.
    Titles and names 'twere tedious to rehearse
Of lords, below the dignity of verse.   570
Wits, warriors, commonwealth's-men, were the best:
Kind husbands, and mere nobles, all the rest.
And therefore, in the name of dulness, be
The well hung Balaam and cold Caleb free:
And canting Nadab let oblivion damn,   575
Who made new porridge for the paschal lamb.
Let friendship's holy band some names assure;
Some their own worth, and some let scorn secure.
Nor shall the rascal rabble here have place,
Whom kings no titles gave, and God no grace:
Not bull-fac'd Jonas, who could statues draw
To mean rebellion, and make treason law.
But he, though bad, is follow'd by a worse,
The wretch who heaven's anointed dar'd to curse;
Shimei, whose youth did early promise bring   585
Of zeal to God and hatred to his king;
Did wisely from expensive sins refrain,
And never broke the sabbath, but for gain:

Nor ever was he known an oath to vent,
Or curse, unless against the government.   590
Thus heaping wealth, by the most ready way
Among the Jews, which was to cheat and pray:
The city, to reward his pious hate
Against his master, chose him magistrate.
His hand a vare of justice did uphold;   595
His neck was loaded with a chain of gold.
During his office treason was no crime;
The sons of Belial had a glorious time:
For Shimei, though not prodigal of pelf,
Yet lov'd his wicked neighbour as himself.   600
When two or three were gather'd to declaim
Against the monarch of Jerusalem,
Shimei was always in the midst of them:
And if they curs'd the king when he was by,
Would rather curse than break good company.   605
If any durst his factious friends accuse,
He pack'd a jury of dissenting Jews,
Whose fellow-feeling in the godly cause
Would free the suffering saint from human laws.
For laws are only made to punish those   610
Who serve the king, and to protect his foes.
If any leisure time he had from power,
(Because 'tis sin to misemploy an hour,)
His business was, by writing to persuade,
That kings were useless, and a clog to trade: 615
And, that his noble style he might refine,
No Rechabite more shunn'd the fumes of wine.
Chaste were his cellars, and his shrieval board
The grossness of a city feast abhorr'd:
His cooks with long disuse their trade forgot;   600
Cool was his kitchen, though his brains were hot.
Such frugal virtue malice may accuse,
But sure 'twas necessary to the Jews:
For towns, once burnt, such magistrates require
As dare not tempt God's providence by fire.   625

With spiritual food he fed his servants well,
But free from flesh that made the Jews rebel:
And Moses' laws he held in more account,
For forty days of fasting in the mount.
  To speak the rest who better are forgot,   630
Would tire a well-breath'd witness of the plot.
Yet, Corah, thou shalt from oblivion pass;
Erect thyself, thou monumental brass,
High as the serpent of thy metal made,
While nations stand secure beneath thy shade.   635
What, though his birth were base, yet comets rise
From earthly vapours ere they shine in skies.
Prodigious actions may as well be done
By weaver's issue, as by prince's son.
This arch-attestor for the public good   640
By that one deed ennobles all his blood.
Who ever ask'd the witnesses' high race,
Whose oath with martyrdom did Stephen grace?
Ours was a Levite, and as times went then,
His tribe were God Almighty's gentlemen.   645
Sunk were his eyes, his voice was harsh and loud,
Sure signs he neither choleric was nor proud:
His long chin prov'd his wit; his saint-like grace
A church vermilion, and a Moses' face.
His memory, miraculously great,   650
Could plots, exceeding man's belief, repeat;
Which therefore cannot be accounted lies,
For human wit could never such devise.
Some future truths are mingled in his book;
But where the witness fail'd, the prophet spoke: 655
Some things like visionary flights appear;
The spirit caught him up the Lord knows where;
And gave him his rabbinical degree,
Unknown to foreign university.
His judgment yet his memory did excel,   660
Which piec'd his wondrous evidence so well,
And suited to the temper of the times,

Then groaning under Jebusitic crimes.
Let Israel's foes suspect his heavenly call,
And rashly judge his writ apocryphal;   665
Our laws for such affronts have forfeits made:
He takes his life who takes away his trade.
Were I myself in witness Corah's place,
The wretch who did me such a dire disgrace,
Should whet my memory, though once forgot,   670
To make him an appendix of my plot.
His zeal to heaven made him his prince despise,
And load his person with indignities.
But zeal peculiar privilege affords,
Indulging latitude to deeds and words: 675
And Corah might for Agag's murder call,
In terms as coarse as Samuel us'd to Saul.
What others in his evidence did join,
The best that could be had for love or coin,
In Corah's own predicament will fall;   680
For witness is a common name to all.
   Surrounded thus with friends of every sort,
Deluded Absalom forsakes the court:
Impatient of high hopes, urg'd with renown,
And fir'd with near possession of a crown.   685
The admiring crowd are dazzled with surprise,
And on his goodly person feed their eyes.
His joy conceal'd, he sets himself to show;
On each side bowing popularly low:
His looks, his gestures, and his words he frames,   690
And with familiar ease repeats their names.
Thus form'd by nature, furnish'd out with arts,
He glides unfelt into their secret hearts.
Then, with a kind compassionating look,
And sighs, bespeaking pity ere he spoke,   695
Few words he said, but easy those and fit,
More slow than Hybla-drops, and far more sweet.
   I mourn, my countrymen, your lost estate;
Though far unable to prevent your fate:

Behold a banish'd man for your dear cause   700
Expos'd a prey to arbitrary laws!
Yet oh! that I alone could be undone,
Cut off from empire, and no more a son!
Now all your liberties a spoil are made;
Egypt and Tyrus intercept your trade,   705
And Jebusites your sacred rites invade.
My father, whom with reverence yet I name,
Charm'd into ease, is careless of his fame;
And, brib'd with petty sums of foreign gold,
Is grown in Bathsheba's embraces old;   710
Exalts his enemies, his friends destroys;
And all his power against himself employs.
He gives, and let him give, my right away:
But why should he his own and yours betray?
He, only he, can make the nation bleed,   715
And he alone from my revenge is freed.
Take then my tears (with that he wip'd his eyes)
'Tis all the aid my present power supplies:
No court-informer can these arms accuse;
These arms may sons against their fathers use: 720
And 'tis my wish, the next successor's reign
May make no other Israelite complain.
    Youth, beauty, graceful action seldom fail;
But common interest always will prevail:
And pity never ceases to be shown   725
To him who makes the people's wrongs his own.
The crowd, that still believe their kings oppress,
With lifted hands their young Messiah bless:
Who now begins his progress to ordain
With chariots, horsemen, and a numerous train: 730
From east to west his glories he displays,
And, like the sun, the promis'd land surveys.
Fame runs before him as the morning-star,
And shouts of joy salute him from afar:
Each house receives him as a guardian god,   735
And consecrates the place of his abode.

But hospitable treats did most commend
Wise Issachar, his wealthy western friend.
This moving court, that caught the people's eyes,
And seem'd but pomp, did other ends disguise: 740
Achitophel had form'd it, with intent
To sound the depths, and fathom where it went,
The people's hearts, distinguish friends from foes;
And try their strength, before they came to blows.
Yet all was colour'd with a smooth pretence   745
Of specious love, and duty to their prince.
Religion, and redress of grievances,
Two names that always cheat, and always please,
Are often urg'd; and good king David's life
Endanger'd by a brother and a wife.   750
Thus in a pageant show a plot is made,
And peace itself is war in masquerade.
Oh foolish Israel! never warn'd by ill,
Still the same bait, and circumvented still!
Did ever men forsake their present ease,   755
In midst of health imagine a disease;
Take pains contingent mischiefs to foresee,
Make heirs for monarchs, and for God decree?
What shall we think? Can people give away,
Both for themselves and sons their native sway?   760
Then they are left defenceless to the sword
Of each unbounded, arbitrary lord:
And laws are vain, by which we right enjoy,
If king's unquestion'd can those laws destroy.
Yet if the crowd be judge of fit and just,   765
And kings are only officers in trust,
Then this resuming covenant was declar'd
When kings were made, or is for ever barr'd.
If those who gave the sceptre could not tie
By their own deed their own posterity,   770
How then could Adam bind his future race?
How could his forfeit on mankind take place?
Or how could heavenly justice damn us all,

Who ne'er consented to our father's fall?
Then kings are slaves to those whom they command 775
And tenants to their people's pleasure stand.
Add, that the power for property allow'd
Is mischievously seated in the crowd:
For who can be secure of private right,
If sovereign sway may be dissolv'd by might? 780
Nor is the people's judgment always true:
The most may err as grossly as the few?
And faultless kings run down by common cry,
For vice, oppression, and for tyranny.
What standard is there in a fickle rout, 785
Which, flowing to the mark, runs faster out?
Nor only crowds but Sanhedrims may be
Infected with this public lunacy,
And share the madness of rebellious times,
To murder monarchs for imagin'd crimes. 790
If they may give and take whene'er they please,
Not kings alone (the Godhead's images,)
But government itself at length must fall
To nature's state, where all have right to all.
Yet grant our lords the people kings can make, 795
What prudent men a settled throne would shake?
For whatsoe'er their sufferings were before.
That change they covet makes them suffer more.
All other errors but disturb a state;
But innovation is the blow of fate. 800
If ancient fabrics nod, and threat to fall,
To patch their flaws, and buttress up the wall,
Thus far 'tis duty; but here fix the mark:
For all beyond it is to touch our ark.
To change foundations, cast the frame anew, 805
Is work for rebels, who base ends pursue;
At once divine and human laws control,
And mend the parts by ruin of the whole.
The tampering world is subject to this curse,
To physic their disease into a worse. 810

Now what relief can righteous David bring?
How fatal 'tis to be too good a king!
Friends he has few, so high the madness grows,
Who dare be such must be the people's foes.
Yet some there were, e'en in the worst of days;   815
Some let me name, and naming is to praise.
  In this short file Barzillai first appears;
Barzillai, crown'd with honour and with years.
Long since, the rising rebels he withstood
In regions waste beyond the Jordan's flood: 820
Unfortunately brave to buoy the state,
But sinking underneath his master's fate,
In exile with his godlike prince he mourn'd;
For him he suffer'd, and with him return'd.
The court he practis'd, not the courtier's art: 825
Large was his wealth, but larger was his heart;
Which well the noblest objects knew to choose,
The fighting warrior, and recording muse.
His bed could once a fruitful issue boast;
Now more than half a father's name is lost.   830
His eldest hope, with every grace adorn'd,
By me, so heaven will have it, always mourn'd,
And always honour'd, snatch'd in manhood's prime
By unequal fates, and providence's crime;
Yet not before the goal of honour won,   835
All parts fulfill'd of subject and of son:
Swift was the race, but short the time to run.
Oh narrow circle, but of power divine,
Scanted in space, but perfect in thy line!
By sea, by land, thy matchless worth was known,   840
Arms thy delight, and war was all thy own:
Thy force, infus'd, the fainting Tyrians propp'd:
And haughty Pharaoh found his fortune stopp'd.
Oh ancient honour! Oh unconquer'd hand,
Whom foes unpunish'd never could withstand!   845
But Israel was unworthy of thy name;
Short is the date of all immoderate fame.

It looks as heaven our ruin had design'd,
And durst not trust thy fortune and thy mind.
Now, free from earth, thy disencumber'd soul   850
Mounts up, and leaves behind the clouds and starry pole:
From thence thy kindred legions mayst thou bring,
To aid the guardian angel of thy king.
Here stop, my muse, here cease thy painful flight;
No pinions can pursue immortal height.   855
Tell good Barzillai thou canst sing no more,
And tell thy soul she should have fled before;
Or fled she with his life, and left this verse
To hang on her departed patron's hearse?
Now take thy steepy flight from heaven, and see   860
If thou canst find on earth another he:
Another he would be too hard to find;
See then whom thou canst see not far behind.
Zadoc the priest, whom, shunning power and place,
His lowly mind advanc'd to David's grace.   865
With him the Sagan of Jerusalem,
Of hospitable soul, and noble stem;
Him of the western dome, whose weighty sense
Flows in fit words and heavenly eloquence.
The prophets' sons, by such example led,   870
To learning and to loyalty were bred:
For colleges on bounteous kings depend,
And never rebel was to arts a friend.
To these succeed the pillars of the laws,
Who best can plead, and best can judge a cause.   875
Next them a train of loyal peers ascend;
Sharp-judging Adriel, the muses' friend.
Himself a muse – in Sanhedrin's debate
True to his prince, but not a slave of state –
Whom David's love with honours did adorn,   880
That from his disobedient son were torn.
Jotham of piercing wit, and pregnant thought,
Endued by nature, and by learning taught,
To move assemblies, who but only tried

The worse awhile, then chose the better side: 885
Nor chose alone, but turn'd the balance too,
So much the weight of one brave man can do.
Hushai, the friend of David in distress,
In public storms of manly steadfastness:
By foreign treaties he inform'd his youth,   890
And join'd experience to his native truth.
His frugal care supplied the wanting throne;
Frugal for that, but bounteous of his own:
'Tis easy conduct when exchequers flow,
But hard the task to manage well the low: 895
For sovereign power is too depress'd or high,
When kings are forc'd to sell, or crowds to buy.
Indulge one labour more my weary muse,
For Amiel, who can Amiel's praise refuse?
Of ancient race by birth, but nobler yet   900
In his own worth, and without title great:
The Sanhedrin long time as chief he rul'd,
Their reason guided and their passion cool'd:
So dexterous was he in the crown's defence,
So form'd to speak a loyal nation's sense,   905
That, as their band was Israel's tribes in small,
So fit was he to represent them all.
Now rasher charioteers the seat ascend,
Whose loose careers his steady skill commend:
They, like the unequal ruler of the day,   910
Misguide the seasons, and mistake the way;
While he withdrawn at their mad labours smiles,
And safe enjoys the sabbath of his toils.
    These were the chief, a small but faithful band
Of worthies, in the breach who dar'd to stand,   915
And tempt the united fury of the land,
With grief they view'd such powerful engines bent,
To batter down the lawful government.
A numerous faction, with pretended frights,
In Sanhedrins to plume the regal rights,   920
The true successor from the court remov'd;

The plot, by hireling witnesses, improv'd.
These ills they saw, and, as their duty bound,
They show'd the king the danger of the wound;
That no concessions from the throne would please,   925
But lenitives fomented the disease:
That Absalom, ambitious of the crown,
Was made the lure to draw the people down:
That false Achitophel's pernicious hate
Had turn'd the plot to ruin church and state: 930
The council violent, the rabble worse
That Shimei taught Jerusalem to curse.
    With all these loads of injuries opprest,
And long revolving in his careful breast
The events of things, at last his patience tir'd,   935
Thus, from his royal throne, by heaven inspir'd,
The god-like David spoke; with awful fear
His train their Maker in their master hear.
    Thus long have I, by native mercy sway'd,
My wrongs dissembled, my revenge delay'd: 940
So willing to forgive the offending age,
So much the father did the king assuage.
But now so far my clemency they slight,
The offenders question my forgiving right.
That one was made for many, they contend;   945
But 'tis to rule, for that's a monarch's end.
They call my tenderness of blood my fear:
Though manly tempers can the longest bear.
Yet, since they will divert my native course,
'Tis time to show I am not good by force.   950
Those heap'd affronts that haughty subjects bring,
Are burdens for a camel, not a king.
Kings are the public pillars of the state,
Born to sustain and prop the nation's weight:
If my young Samson will pretend a call   955
To shake the column, let him share the fall:
But oh, that yet he would repent and live!
How easy 'tis for parents to forgive!

With how few tears a pardon might be won
From nature, pleading for a darling son!   960
Poor pitied youth, by my paternal care,
Rais'd up to all the height his frame could bear!
Had God ordain'd his fate for empire born,
He would have given his soul another turn:
Gull'd with a patriot's name, whose modern sense   965
Is one that would by law supplant his prince;
The people's brave, the politician's tool,
Never was patriot yet, but was a fool.
Whence comes it that religion and the laws
Should more be Absalom's than David's cause?   970
His old instructor, ere he lost his place,
Was never thought indued with so much grace.
Good heavens, how faction can a patriot paint!
My rebel ever proves my people's saint.
Would they impose an heir upon the throne!   975
Let Sanhedrins be taught to give their own.
A king's at least a part of government,
And mine as requisite as their consent;
Without my leave a future king to choose,
Infers a right the present to depose.   980
True, they petition me to approve their choice,
But Esau's hands suit ill with Jacob's voice.
My pious subjects for my safety pray;
Which to secure, they take my power away.
From plots and treasons heaven preserve my years   985
But save me most from my petitioners!
Unsatiate as the barren womb or grave,
God cannot grant so much as they can crave.
What then is left, but with a jealous eye
To guard the small remains of royalty!   900
The law shall still direct my peaceful sway,
And the same law teach rebels to obey:
Votes shall no more establish'd power control,
Such votes as make a part exceed the whole.
No groundless clamours shall my friends remove,   995

Nor crowds have power to punish ere they prove;
For Gods and godlike kings their care express,
Still to defend their servants in distress.
Oh, that my power to saving were confined!
Why am I forc'd, like heaven, against my mind,　　1000
To make examples of another kind!
Must I at length the sword of justice draw?
Oh curst effects of necessary law!
How ill my fear they by my mercy scan!
Beware the fury of a patient man.　　1005
Law they require, let law then show her face;
They could not be content to look on Grace,
Her hinder parts, but with a daring eye
To tempt the terrors of her front and die.
By their own arts 'tis righteously decreed,　　1010
Those dire artificers of death shall bleed.
Against themselves their witnesses will swear,
'Till viper-like their mother plot they tear
And suck for nutriment that bloody gore,
Which was their principle of life before.　　1015
Their Belial with their Beelzebub will fight;
Thus on my foes, my foes shall do me right.
Nor doubt the event, for factious crowds engage
In their first onset, all their brutal rage.
Then let 'em take an unresisted course,　　1020
Retire, and traverse, and delude their force:
But, when they stand all breathless, urge the fight,
And rise upon them with redoubled might:
For lawful power is still superior found;
When long driven back at length it stands the ground.　1025
　　He said. The Almighty nodding gave consent
And peals of thunder shook the firmament.
Henceforth a series of new time began,
The mighty years in long procession ran:
Once more the godlike David was restor'd,　　1030
And willing nations knew their lawful lord.

A Time of Change

Without flocks or cattle or the curved horns
Of cattle, in a drenching night without sleep
My five wits on the famous uproar
Of the wave toss like ships
And I cry for boyhood, long before
Winkle and dogfish had defiled my lips.

O if he lived, the prince who sheltered me
And his company who gave me entry
On the river of the Laune,
Whose royalty stood sentry
Over intricate harbours, I and my own
Would not be desolate in Dermot's country.

Fierce McCarthy Mor whose friends were welcome,
McCarthy of the Lee a slave of late,
McCarthy of Kenturk whose blood
Has dried underfoot:
Of all my princes not a single word –
Irrevocable silence ails my heart.

My heart shrinks in me, my heart ails
That every hawk and royal hawk is lost;
From Cashel to the far sea
Their birthright is dispersed
Far and near, night and day, by robbery
And ransack, every town oppressed.

Take warning, wave, take warning, crown of the sea
I, O'Rahilly – witless from your discords –
Were Spanish sails again afloat
And rescue on our tides,
Would force this outcry down your wild throat,
Would make you swallow these Atlantic words.

trans. Eavan Boland

Reverie at Dawn

One morning before Titan thought of stirring his feet
  I climbed alone to a hill where the air was kind,
And saw a throng of magical girls go by
  Who had lived to the north in Croghan time out of mind.

All over the land from Galway to Cork of the ships
  It seemed a bright enchanted mist came down,
Acorns on oaks and clear cold honey on stones,
  Fruit upon every tree from root to crown.

They lit three candles that shone in the mist like stars
  On a high hill top in Connello and then were gone,
I followed through Thomond the track of the hooded queens
  And asked them the cause of the zeal of their office at
                                                    dawn.

The tall queen Eevul so bright of countenance said
  'The reason we light three candles on every strand
Is to guide the king who will come to us over the sea
  And make us happy and reign in a fortunate land.'

And then so suddenly did I start from my sleep
  They seemed to be true, the words that had been so sweet –
It was just that my soul was sick and spent with grief
  One morning before Titan thought of stirring his feet.

trans. Frank O'Connor

A Grey Eye Weeping

That my old bitter heart was pierced in this black doom,
That foreign devils have made our land a tomb,
That the sun that was Munster's glory has gone down
Has made me a beggar before you, Valentine Brown.

That royal Cashel is bare of house and guest,
That Brian's turreted home is the otter's nest,
That the kings of the land have neither land nor crown
Has made me a beggar before you, Valentine Brown.

Garnish away in the west with its master banned,
Hamburg the refuge of him who has lost his land,
An old grey eye, weeping for lost renown,
Have made me a beggar before you, Valentine Brown.

                                        trans. Frank O'Connor

Prometheus

On Wood the Patentee's Irish Halfpence

As, when the squire and tinker, Wood,
Gravely consulting Ireland's good,
Together mingled in a mass
Smith's dust, and copper, lead and brass;
The mixture thus by chemic art,
United close in every part,
In fillets rolled, or cut in pieces,
Appeared like one continuous species,
And by the forming engine struck,
On all the same *impression* stuck.

So, to confound this hated coin,
All parties and religions join;
Whigs, Tories, trimmers, Hanoverians,
Quakers, conformists, presbyterians,
Scotch, Irish, English, French unite
With equal interest, equal spite,
Together mingled in a lump,
Do all in one opinion jump;
And everyone begins to find
The same impression on his *mind*.

A strange event! whom gold incites,
To blood and quarrels, brass unites:
So goldsmiths say, the coarsest stuff
Will serve for solder well enough;
So, by the kettle's loud alarm,
The bees are gathered to a swarm:
So by the brazen trumpet's bluster,
Troops of all tongues and nations muster:
And so the harp of Ireland brings,
Whole crowds about its brazen strings.

There is a chain let down from Jove,
But fastened to his throne above;
So strong, that from the lower end,
They say, all human things depend:
This chain, as ancient poets hold,
When Jove was young, was made of gold.
Prometheus once this chain purloined,
Dissolved, and into money coined;
Then whips me on a chain of brass,
(Venus was bribed to let it pass.)

Now while this brazen chain prevailed,
Jove saw that all devotion failed;
No temple to his godship raised;
No sacrifice on altars blazed:
In short, such dire confusions followed,
Earth must have been in chaos swallowed.
Jove stood amazed, but looking round,
With much ado the cheat he found;
'Twas plain he could no longer hold
The world in any chain but gold;
And to the god of wealth his brother,
Sent Mercury to get another.

Prometheus on a rock was laid,
Tied with the chain himself had made;
On icy Caucasus to shiver,
While vultures eat his growing liver.

Ye powers of Grub Street, make me able,
Discreetly to apply this fable.
Say, who is to be understood
By that old thief Prometheus? Wood.
For Jove, it is not hard to guess him,
I mean His Majesty, God bless him.
This thief and blacksmith was so bold,
He strove to steal that chain of gold,

Which links the subject to the king:
And change it for a brazen string.
But sure, if nothing else must pass
Between the King and us but brass,
Although the chain will never crack,
Yet our devotion may grow slack.

But Jove will soon convert I hope,
This brazen chain into a rope;
With which Prometheus shall be tied,
And high in air for ever ride;
Where, if we find his liver grows,
For want of vultures, we have crows.

Ireland

Remove me from this land of slaves,
Where all are fools, and all are knaves;
Where every knave and fool is bought,
Yet kindly sells himself for naught;
Where Whig and Tory fiercely fight
Who's in the wrong, who in the right;
And when their country lies at stake
They only fight for fighting's sake,
While English sharpers take the pay,
And then stand by to see fair play;
Meantime the Whig is always winner
And for his courage gets a dinner.
His Excellency too perhaps
Spits in his mouth and strokes his chaps.
The humble whelp gives every vote:
To put the question strains his throat.
His Excellency's condescension
Will serve instead of place or pension,
When to the window he's trepanned,
When my Lord shakes him by the hand,

Or in the presence of beholders,
His arms upon the booby's shoulders,
You quickly see the gudgeon bite.
He tells his brother fools at night
How well the Governor's inclined,
So just, so gentle and so kind:
'He heard I kept a pack of hounds,
And longed to hunt upon my grounds;
He said our ladies were so fair,
The court had nothing to compare;
But that indeed which pleased me most,
He called my Doll a perfect toast.
He whispered public things at last,
Asked me how our elections passed.
Some augmentation, sir, you know
Would make at least a handsome show.
New kings a compliment expect;
I shall not offer to direct –
There are some prating fools in town,
But, sir, we must support the crown.
Our letters say a Jesuit boasts
Of some invasion on your coasts;
The King is ready, when you will,
To pass another popery bill;
And for dissenters he intends
To use them as his truest friends:
I think they justly ought to share
In all employments we can spare.
Next for encouragement of spinning,
A duty might be laid on linen;
An act for laying down the plough,
England will send you corn enough.
Another act that absentees
For licences shall pay no fees.
If England's friendship you would keep,
Feed nothing in your hands but sheep;
But make an act secure and full

To hang up all who smuggle wool.
And then he kindly gives me hints
That all our wives should go in chintz.
Tomorrow I shall tell you more,
For I'm to dine with him at four.'

This was the speech, and here's the jest:
His arguments convinced the rest.
Away he runs with zealous hotness
Exceeding all the fools of Totnes,
To move that all the nation round
Should pay a guinea in the pound:
Yet should this blockhead beg a place
Either from Excellence or Grace,
'Tis pre-engaged and in his room
Townshend's cast page or Walpole's groom.

ALEXANDER POPE

from An Essay on Man

What if the foot, ordain'd the dust to tread,
Or hand to toil, aspir'd to be the head?
What if the head, the eye, or ear repin'd
To serve mere engines to the ruling Mind?
Just as absurd for any part to claim
To be another, in this gen'ral frame:
Just as absurd, to mourn the tasks or pains
The great directing MIND of ALL ordains.
    All are but parts of one stupendous whole,
Whose body, Nature is, and God the soul;
That, chang'd thro' all, and yet in all the same,
Great in the earth, as in th' æthereal frame,
Warms in the sun, refreshes in the breeze,
Glows in the stars, and blossoms in the trees,
Lives thro' all life, extends thro' all extent,
Spreads undivided, operates unspent,
Breathes in our soul, informs our mortal part,
As full, as perfect, in a hair as heart;
As full, as perfect, in vile Man that mourns,
As the rapt Seraph that adores and burns;
To him no high, no low, no great, no small;
He fills, he bounds, connects, and equals all.

    Cease then, nor ORDER Imperfection name:
Our proper bliss depends on what we blame.
Know thy own point: This kind, this due degree
Of blindness, weakness, Heav'n bestows on thee.
Submit – In this, or any other sphere,
Secure to be as blest as thou canst bear:
Safe in the hand of one disposing Pow'r,
Or in the natal, or the mortal hour.

All Nature is but Art, unknown to thee;
All Chance, Direction, which thou canst not see;
All Discord, Harmony, not understood;
All partial Evil, universal Good:
And, spite of Pride, in erring Reason's spite,
One truth is clear, 'Whatever IS, is RIGHT.'

(First Epistle, lines 259–294)

from The Dunciad

In vain, in vain, – the all-composing Hour
Resistless falls: The Muse obeys the Pow'r.
She comes! she comes! the sable Throne behold
Of *Night* Primæval, and of *Chaos* old!
Before her, *Fancy*'s gilded clouds decay,
And all its varying Rain-bows die away.
Wit shoots in vain its momentary fires,
The meteor drops, and in a flash expires.
As one by one, at dread Medea's strain,
The sick'ning stars fade off th' ethereal plain;
As Argus' eyes by Hermes' wand opprest,
Clos'd one by one to everlasting rest;
Thus at her felt approach, and secret might,
Art after *Art* goes out, and all is Night.
See skulking *Truth* to her old Cavern fled,
Mountains of Casuistry heap'd o'er her head!
Philosophy, that lean'd on Heav'n before,
Shrinks to her second cause, and is no more.
Physic of *Metaphysic* begs defence,
And *Metaphysic* calls for aid on *Sense!*
See *Mystery* to *Mathematics* fly!
In vain! they gaze, turn giddy, rave, and die.
Religion blushing veils her sacred fires,
And unawares *Morality* expires.
Nor *public* Flame, nor *private*, dares to shine;
Nor *human* Spark is left, nor Glimpse *divine!*
Lo! thy dread Empire, CHAOS! is restor'd;
Light dies before thy uncreating word;
Thy hand, great Anarch! lets the curtain fall;
And Universal Darkness buries All.

(Book IV, lines 627–656)

The Vicar of Bray

In good King Charles's golden days,
  When loyalty no harm meant,
A zealous High-Churchman I was,
  And so I got preferment;
Unto my flock I daily preached
  Kings were by God appointed,
And damned was he that durst resist
  Or touch the Lord's anointed.
    And this is law, I will maintain,
      Until my dying day, Sir,
    That whatsoever king shall reign,
      I'll be the Vicar of Bray, Sir.

When royal James obtained the crown,
  And Popery came in fashion,
The penal laws I hooted down,
  And read the declaration:
The Church of Rome I found would fit
  Full well my constitution,
And had become a Jesuit,
  But for the Revolution.
    And this is law, I will maintain,
      Until my dying day, Sir,
    That whatsoever king shall reign,
      I'll be the Vicar of Bray, Sir.

When William was our king declared
  To ease the nation's grievance,
With this new wind about I steered,
  And swore to him allegiance;
Old principles I did revoke,
  Set conscience at a distance;
Passive obedience was a joke,
  A jest was non-resistance.
    And this is law, I will maintain,
      Until my dying day, Sir,
    That whatsoever king shall reign,
      I'll be the Vicar of Bray, Sir.

When gracious Anne became our queen,
  The Church of England's glory,
Another face of things was seen –
  And I became a Tory:
Occasional Conformists base,
  I scorned their moderation,
And swore the church in danger was
  By such prevarication.
    And this is law, I will maintain,
      Until my dying day, Sir,
    That whatsoever king shall reign,
      I'll be the Vicar of Bray, Sir.

When George in pudding-time came o'er,
  And moderate men looked big, Sir,
I turned a cat-in-pan once more –
  And so became a Whig, Sir:
And this preferment I procured
  From our new faith's defender,
And almost every day abjured
  The Pope and the Pretender.
    And this is law, I will maintain,
      Until my dying day, Sir,
    That whatsoever king shall reign,
      I'll be the Vicar of Bray, Sir.

The illustrious house of Hanover,
  And Protestant succession,
To these I do allegiance swear –
  While they can keep possession:
For in my faith and loyalty
  I never more will falter,
And George my lawful King shall be –
  Until the times do alter.
    And this is law, I will maintain,
      Until my dying day, Sir,
    That whatsoever king shall reign,
      I'll be the Vicar of Bray, Sir.

Elegy Written in a Country Churchyard

1

The curfew tolls the knell of parting day,
The lowing herd wind slowly o'er the lea,
The ploughman homeward plods his weary way,
And leaves the world to darkness and to me.

2

Now fades the glimmering landscape on the sight,
And all the air a solemn stillness holds,
Save where the beetle wheels his droning flight,
And drowsy tinklings lull the distant folds;

3

Save that from yonder ivy-mantled tower,
The moping owl does to the moon complain
Of such, as wandering near her secret bower,
Molest her ancient solitary reign.

4

Beneath those rugged elms, that yew-tree's shade,
Where heaves the turf in many a mould'ring heap,
Each in his narrow cell for ever laid,
The rude forefathers of the hamlet sleep.

5

The breezy call of incense-breathing Morn,
The swallow twitt'ring from the straw-built shed,
The cock's shrill clarion, or the echoing horn,
No more shall rouse them from their lowly bed.

6

For them no more the blazing hearth shall burn,
Or busy housewife ply her evening care:
No children run to lisp their sire's return,
Or climb his knees the envied kiss to share.

7

Oft did the harvest to their sickle yield,
Their furrow oft the stubborn glebe has broke;
How jocund did they drive their team afield!
How bowed the woods beneath their sturdy stroke!

8

Let not Ambition mock their useful toil,
Their homely joys, and destiny obscure;
Nor Grandeur hear with a disdainful smile,
The short and simple annals of the poor.

9

The boast of heraldry, the pomp of power,
And all that beauty, all that wealth e'er gave,
Await alike th' inevitable hour:
The paths of glory lead but to the grave.

10

Nor you, ye proud, impute to these the fault,
If Memory o'er their tomb no trophies raise,
Where thro' the long-drawn aisle and fretted vault
The pealing anthem swells the note of praise.

11

Can storied urn or animated bust
Back to its mansion call the fleeting breath?
Can Honour's voice provoke the silent dust,
Or Flatt'ry soothe the dull cold ear of death?

12

Perhaps in this neglected spot is laid
Some heart once pregnant with celestial fire;
Hands, that the rod of empire might have sway'd,
Or waked to extasy the living lyre.

13

But Knowledge to their eyes her ample page
Rich with the spoils of time did ne'er unroll;
Chill Penury repress'd their noble rage,
And froze the genial current of the soul.

14

Full many a gem of purest ray serene,
The dark unfathom'd caves of ocean bear:
Full many a flower is born to blush unseen,
And waste its sweetness on the desert air.

15

Some village-Hampden, that with dauntless breast
The little tyrant of his fields withstood;
Some mute inglorious Milton here may rest,
Some Cromwell, guiltless of his country's blood.

16

Th' applause of listening senates to command,
The threats of pain and ruin to despise,
To scatter plenty o'er a smiling land,
And read their history in a nation's eyes,

17

Their lot forbad: nor circumscribed alone
Their growing virtues, but their crimes confined;
Forbad to wade through slaughter to a throne,
And shut the gates of mercy on mankind;

18

The struggling pangs of conscious truth to hide,
To quench the blushes of ingenuous shame,
Or heap the shrine of Luxury and Pride
With incense kindled at the Muse's flame.

19

Far from the madding crowd's ignoble strife,
Their sober wishes never learn'd to stray;
Along the cool sequester'd vale of life
They kept the noiseless tenour of their way.

20

Yet ev'n these bones from insult to protect
Some frail memorial still erected nigh,
With uncouth rhymes and shapeless sculpture decked,
Implores the passing tribute of a sigh.

21

Their name, their years, spelt by th' unletter'd Muse,
The place of fame and elegy supply:
And many a holy text around she strews,
That teach the rustic moralist to die.

22

For who, to dumb Forgetfulness a prey,
This pleasing anxious being e'er resign'd,
Left the warm precincts of the cheerful day,
Nor cast one longing lingering look behind?

23

On some fond breast the parting soul relies,
Some pious drops the closing eye requires;
E'en from the tomb the voice of Nature cries,
E'en in our Ashes live their wonted fires.

24

For thee, who, mindful of th' unhonour'd dead,
Dost in these lines their artless tale relate;
If chance, by lonely contemplation led,
Some kindred spirit shall inquire thy fate, –

25

Haply some hoary-headed Swain may say,
'Oft have we seen him at the peep of dawn
Brushing with hasty steps the dews away
To meet the sun upon the upland lawn.

26

'There at the foot of yonder nodding beech
That wreathes its old fantastic roots so high
His listless length at noontide would he stretch,
And pore upon the brook that babbles by.

27

'Hard by yon wood, now smiling as in scorn
Muttering his wayward fancies he would rove;
Now drooping, woeful wan, like one forlorn,
Or crazed with care, or cross'd in hopeless love.

28

'One morn I missed him on the custom'd hill,
Along the heath and near his favourite tree;
Another came; nor yet beside the rill,
Nor up the lawn, nor at the wood was he;

29

'The next, with dirges due in sad array
Slow thro' the church-way path we saw him borne; –
Approach and read (for thou canst read) the lay,
Graved on the stone beneath yon aged thorn.'

The Epitaph

30

Here rests his head upon the lap of Earth,
A Youth, to Fortune and to Fame unknown:
Fair Science frown'd not on his humble birth,
And Melancholy mark'd him for her own.

31

Large was his bounty, and his soul sincere,
Heav'n did a recompense as largely send:
He gave to Misery (all he had), a tear,
He gained from Heav'n ('twas all he wish'd) a friend.

32

No farther seek his merits to disclose,
Or draw his frailties from their dread abode,
(There they alike in trembling hope repose,)
The bosom of his Father and his God.

OLIVER GOLDSMITH

from Retaliation

[Edmund Burke]

Here lies our good Edmund, whose genius was such,
We scarcely can praise it or blame it too much;
Who, born for the universe, narrowed his mind,
And to party gave up what was meant for mankind;
Though fraught with all learning, kept straining his throat
To persuade Tommy Townshend to lend him a vote;
Who, too deep for his hearers, still went on refining,
And thought of convincing, while they thought of dining;
Though equal to all things, for all things unfit;
Too nice for a statesman, too proud for a wit;
For a patriot, too cool; for a drudge, disobedient;
And too fond of the *right* to pursue the *expedient*.
In short, 'twas his fate, unemployed or in place, sir,
To eat mutton cold and cut blocks with a razor.

ROBERT BURNS

The Tree of Liberty

Heard ye o' the tree o' France,
   I watna what's the name o't;
Around it a' the patriots dance,
   Weel Europe kens the fame o't.
It stands where ance the Bastile stood,
   A prison built by kings, man,
When Superstition's hellish brood
   Kept France in leading strings, man.

Upo' this tree there grows sic fruit,
   Its virtues a' can tell, man;
It raises man aboon the brute,
   It maks him ken himsel, man.
Gif ance the peasant taste a bit,
   He's greater than a lord, man,
An' wi' the beggar shares a mite
   O' a' he can afford, man.

This fruit is worth a' Afric's wealth,
   To comfort us 'twas sent, man:
To gie the sweetest blush o' health,
   An' mak us a' content, man.
It clears the een, it cheers the heart,
   Maks high and low gude friends, man;
And he wha acts the traitor's part
   It to perdition sends, man.

My blessings aye attend the chiel
  Wha pitied Gallia's slaves, man,
And staw a branch, spite o' the deil,
  Frae yont the western waves, man.
Fair Virtue water'd it wi' care,
  And now she sees wi' pride, man,
How weel it buds and blossoms there,
  Its branches spreading wide, man.

But vicious folks aye hate to see
  The works o' Virtue thrive, man;
The courtly vermin's banned the tree,
  And grat to see it thrive, man;
King Loui' thought to cut it down,
  When it was unco sma', man;
For this the watchman cracked his crown,
  Cut aff his head and a', man.

A wicked crew syne, on a time,
  Did tak a solemn aith, man,
It ne'er should flourish to its prime,
  I wat they pledged their faith, man.
Awa' they gaed wi' mock parade,
  Like beagles hunting game, man,
But soon grew weary o' the trade
  And wished they'd been at hame, man.

For Freedom, standing by the tree,
  Her sons did loudly ca', man;
She sang a sang o' liberty,
  Which pleased them ane and a', man.
By her inspired, the new-born race
  Soon drew the avenging steel, man;
The hirelings ran – her foes gied chase,
  And banged the despot weel, man.

Let Britain boast her hardy oak,
  Her poplar and her pine, man,
Auld Britain ance could crack her joke,
  And o'er her neighbours shine, man.
But seek the forest round and round,
  And soon 'twill be agreed, man,
That sic a tree can not be found,
  'Twixt London and the Tweed, man.

Without this tree, alake this life
  Is but a vale o'woe, man;
A scene o' sorrow mixed wi' strife,
  Nae real joys we know, man.
We labour soon, we labour late,
  To feed the titled knave, man;
And a' the comfort we're to get
  Is that ayont the grave, man.

Wi' plenty o' sic trees, I trow,
  The warld would live in peace, man;
The sword would help to mak a plough,
  The din o'war wad cease, man.
Like brethren in a common cause,
  We'd on each other smile, man;
And equal rights and equal laws
  Wad gladden every isle, man.

Wae worth the loon wha wadna eat
  Sic halesome dainty cheer, man;
I'd gie my shoon frae aff my feet,
  To taste sic fruit, I swear, man.
Syne let us pray, auld England may
  Sure plant this far-famed tree, man;
And blythe we'll sing, and hail the day
  That gave us liberty, man.

For A' That and A' That

Is there, for honest Poverty
    That hings his head, and a' that;
The coward-slave, we pass him by,
    We dare be poor for a' that!
  For a' that, and a' that,
    Our toils obscure, and a' that,
  The rank is but the guinea's stamp,
    The Man's the gowd of a' that. –

What though on hamely fare we dine,
    Wear hoddin grey, and a' that.
Gie fools their silks, and knaves their wine,
    A Man's a Man for a' that.
  For a' that, and a' that,
    Their tinsel show, and a' that;
  The honest man, though e'er sae poor,
    Is king o' men for a' that. –

Ye see yon birkie ca'd, a lord,
    Wha struts, and stares, and a' that,
Though hundreds worship at his word,
    He's but a coof for a' that.
  For a' that, and a' that,
    His ribband, star and a' that,
  The man of independent mind,
    He looks and laughs at a' that. –

A prince can mak a belted knight,
    A marquis, duke, and a' that;
But an honest man's aboon his might,
    Gude faith he mauna fa' that!
  For a' that, and a' that,
    Their dignities, and a' that,
  The pith o' Sense, and price o' Worth,
    Are higher ranks than a' that. –

Then let us pray that come it may,
   As come it will for a' that,
That Sense and Worth, o'er a' the earth
   Shall bear the gree, and a' that.
  For a' that, and a' that,
   Its comin yet for a' that,
That Man to Man the warld o'er,
   Shall brothers be for a' that. –

Charlie He's My Darling

'Twas on a Monday morning,
   Right early in the year,
That Charlie cam to our town,
   The young Chevalier. –

Chorus
An' Charlie he's my darling, my darling, my darling,
Charlie he's my darling, the young Chevalier. –

As he was walking up the street,
   The city for to view,
O there he spied a bonie lass
   The window looking thro'. –
An Charlie &c.

Sae light's he jimped up the stair,
   And tirled at the pin;
And wha sae ready as hersel
   To let the laddie in. –
   An Charlie &c.

He set his Jenny on his knee,
  All in his Highland dress;
For brawlie weel he ken'd the way
  To please a bonie lass. –
    An Charlie &c.

Its up yon hethery mountain,
  And down yon scroggy glen,
We daur na gang a milking,
  For Charlie and his men. –
    An Charlie &c.

JOHN LEARMONT

from An Address to the Plebeians

Poor crawlin' bodies, sair neglectit,
Trampled on an' disrespeckit,
Seem born for greater fock to geck at,
      To toil an' slave,
An' rest o'body hae nae feck o't
      Till i' the grave.

Your raggit claies an' ghastly features'
Mak ye be lookit on by betters
As some outlandish half'lin creatures
      Nae o' God's mak;
An' born to thole their buffs an' blatters
      Upo' your back.

Though Liberty may shaw her face
An' a' ye're betters roun' embrace,
Ye still maun bend wi' hum'le face
      Beneath her wand;
An' scarcely get an hour's solace
      In ony land.

There maun subordination be;
But O! it maks ane wae to see
The grit fock jamph an' jeer at ye,
      Wha bake their bread;
An' scarce'll lat ye taste their brie
      Whan ye're i' need.

They gang by ye wi' sic a huff,
An' pridfu' caper, snirt an' snuff,
As gif Death ne'er meant them a cuff
            Upo' the head,
To let them ken they're the same stuff
            O' which ye're made.

Ye're sair the wyte, ye stupit bodies!
Ye have nae mair sense i' your nodies
Than serves to work amang the clodies,
            An' do na see
Man's dignity, whilk his ain God has
            Him buskit wi'.

Ye still micht delve i' kailyards green,
Or maw down grass upo' the fen,
Yet mak your reason shaw ye men
            Ful bauld an' slee;
An' lat them see ye brawlie ken
            Man's dignity . . .

A king cries war! but for what end
Ye never speer, but to it stend,
An' at the cannon's mou' ye bend
            I' mony a thrave,
Syne laurels dipped wi' bluid do send
            Ye to the grave.

Yet ye're the sceptre o' the land,
Wha put kings, lairds, unto a stand;
Gif ye but gather on the strand
            Unto a head,
Ye'll either hae yeu're boon i' hand,
            Or ding them dead.

An' some o' you are nae that ill,
An' hae enough o' ruth at will
For ony ane wham Fortune's wheel
   Has crushed wi' wae;
An' will gie pity, or him fill
   Wi' what ye hae.

Arouse ye up then ane an' a',
An' busk yoursels wi' wisdom braw;
An' though ye wade owr hills o' snaw,
   Or plew the field,
Mak ay true honesty your law
   An' safest shield.

The File-Hewer's Lamentation

Ordained I was a beggar,
And have no cause to swagger;
It pierces like a dagger,
   To think I'm thus forlorn.
My trade or occupation
Was ground for lamentation,
Which makes me curse my station,
   And wish I'd ne'er been born.

Of slaving I am weary,
From June to January;
To nature it's contrary,
   This, I presume, is fact.
Although, without a stammer,
Our Nell exclaims I clam her,
I've wield my six-pound hammer
   Till I am grown round-backed.

I'm debtor to a many,
But cannot pay one penny;
Sure I've worse luck than any,
   My sticks are marked for sale.
My creditors may sue me,
And curse the day they knew me;
The bailiffs may pursue me,
   And lock me up in jail.

As negroes in Virginia,
In Maryland or Guinea,
Like them I must continue
  To be both bought and sold.
While negro-ships are filling
I ne'er can save one shilling,
And must, which is more killing,
  A pauper die when old.

My troubles never ceased,
While Nell's bairn-time increased;
While hundreds I've rehearsed,
  Ten thousand more remain;
My income for me, Nelly,
Bob, Tom, Poll, Bet and Sally,
Could hardly fill each belly,
  Should we eat salt and grains.

At every week's conclusion
New wants bring fresh confusion,
It is but mere delusion
  To hope for better days;
While knaves with power invested,
Until by death arrested,
Oppress us unmolested
  By their infernal ways.

An hanging day is wanted;
Was it by justice granted,
Poor men distressed and daunted
  Would then have cause to sing:
To see in active motion
Rich knaves in full proportion,
For their unjust extortion
  And vile offences, swing.

God Save Great Thomas Paine

God save great Thomas Paine,
His 'Rights of Man' explain
      To every soul.
He makes the blind to see
What dupes and slaves they be,
And points out liberty,
      From pole to pole.

Thousands cry 'Church and King'
That well deserve to swing,
      All must allow:
Birmingham blush for shame,
Manchester do the same,
Infamous is your name,
      Patriots vow.

Pull proud oppressors down,
Knock off each tyrant's crown,
      And break his sword;
Down aristocracy,
Set up democracy,
And from hypocrisy
      Save us good Lord.

Why should despotic pride
Usurp on every side?
      Let us be free:
Grant Freedom's arms success,
And all her efforts bless,
Plant through the universe
      Liberty's Tree.

Facts are seditious things
When they touch courts and kings,
   Armies are raised,
Barracks and bastilles built,
Innocence charged with guilt,
Blood most unjustly spilt,
   Gods stand amazed.

Despots may howl and yell,
Though they're in league with hell
   They'll not reign long;
Satan may lead the van,
And do the worst he can,
Paine and his 'Rights of Man'
   Shall be my song.

The Chimney Sweeper

When my mother died I was very young,
And my father sold me while yet my tongue
Could scarcely cry *'weep 'weep, 'weep 'weep*!
So your chimneys I sweep, and in soot I sleep.

There's little Tom Dacre, who cried when his head,
That curled like a lamb's back, was shaved; so I said,
'Hush Tom, never mind it, for when your head's bare,
You know that the soot cannot spoil your white hair.'

And so he was quiet, and that very night,
As Tom was asleeping he had such a sight –
That thousands of sweepers, Dick, Joe, Ned, and Jack,
Were all of them locked up in coffins of black;

And by came an angel, who had a bright key,
And he opened the coffins and set them all free;
Then down a green plain leaping, laughing they run,
And wash in a river and shine in the sun.

Then naked and white, all their bags left behind,
They rise upon clouds and sport in the wind.
And the angel told Tom, if he'd be a good boy,
He'd have God for his father and never want joy.

And so Tom awoke, and we rose in the dark,
And got with our bags and our brushes to work.
Though the morning was cold, Tom was happy and warm;
So if all do their duty, they need not fear harm.

The Tiger

Tiger, tiger, burning bright
In the forests of the night,
What immortal hand or eye
Could frame thy fearful symmetry?

In what distant deeps or skies
Burnt the fire of thine eyes?
On what wings dare he aspire?
What the hand dare seize the fire?

And what shoulder and what art
Could twist the sinews of thy heart?
And when thy heart began to beat,
What dread hand? And what dread feet?

What the hammer? What the chain?
In what furnace was thy brain?
What the anvil? What dread grasp
Dare its deadly terrors clasp?

When the stars threw down their spears
And watered Heaven with their tears,
Did he smile his work to see?
Did he who made the Lamb make thee?

Tiger, tiger, burning bright
In the forests of the night,
What immortal hand or eye
Dare frame thy fearful symmetry?

London

I wander through each chartered street
Near where the chartered Thames does flow,
And mark in every face I meet
Marks of weakness, marks of woe.

In every cry of every man,
In every infant's cry of fear,
In every voice, in every ban,
The mind-forged manacles I hear –

How the chimney-sweeper's cry
Every blackened church appals,
And the hapless soldier's sigh
Runs in blood down palace walls;

But most through midnight streets I hear
How the youthful harlot's curse
Blasts the new-born infant's tear
And blights with plagues the marriage hearse.

'And did those feet in ancient time?'

And did those feet in ancient time
Walk upon England's mountains green?
And was the holy Lamb of God
On England's pleasant pastures seen?

And did the Countenance Divine
Shine forth upon our clouded hills?
And was Jerusalem builded here
Among these dark Satanic mills?

Bring me my bow of burning gold;
Bring me my arrows of desire;
Bring me my spear – O clouds, unfold!
Bring me my chariot of fire!

I will not cease from mental fight,
Nor shall my sword sleep in my hand,
Till we have built Jerusalem,
In England's green and pleasant land.

(*from* Milton, lines 21–36)

'The fields from Islington to Marybone'

The fields from Islington to Marybone,
To Primrose Hill and Saint John's Wood,
    Were builded over with pillars of gold,
And there Jerusalem's pillars stood.

Her little ones ran on the fields,
The Lamb of God among them seen
    And fair Jerusalem his bride,
Among the little meadows green.

Pancras & Kentish Town repose
Among her golden pillars high,
    Among her golden arches which
Shine upon the starry sky.

The Jews-Harp House & the Green Man,
The ponds where boys to bathe delight,
    The fields of cows by Willan's farm,
Shine in Jerusalem's pleasant sight.

She walks upon our meadows green,
The Lamb of God walks by her side,
    And every English child is seen
Children of Jesus & his Bride,

    Forgiving trespasses and sins,
Lest Babylon with cruel Og,
    With moral & self-righteous law
Should crucify in Satan's synagogue!

    What are those golden builders doing
Near mournful ever-weeping Paddington,
    Standing above that mighty ruin
Where Satan the first victory won,

    Where Albion slept beneath the fatal tree
And the druid's golden knife
    Rioted in human gore,
In offerings of human life?

    They groaned aloud on London Stone,
They groaned aloud on Tyburn's brook;
    Albion gave his deadly groan,
And all the Atlantic mountains shook.

    Albion's spectre from his loins
Tore forth in all the pomp of war,
    Satan his name; in flames of fire
He stretched his druid pillars far.

    Jerusalem fell from Lambeth's Vale,
Down through Poplar & Old Bow,
    Through Maldon & across the sea,
In war & howling, death & woe.

The Rhine was red with human blood,
The Danube rolled a purple tide;
   On the Euphrates Satan stood
And over Asia stretched his pride.

   He withered up sweet Zion's hill,
From every nation of the earth;
   He withered up Jerusalem's gates
And in a dark land gave her birth.

   He withered up the human form
By laws of sacrifice for sin
   Till it became a mortal worm
(But oh, translucent all within!).

   The Divine Vision still was seen,
Still was the human form divine
   Weeping in weak & mortal clay;
O Jesus, still the form was thine!

   And thine the human face & thine
The human hands & feet & breath,
   Entering through the gates of birth
And passing through the gates of death.

   And, O thou Lamb of God, whom I
Slew in my dark self-righteous pride,
   Art thou returned to Albion's land,
And is Jerusalem thy Bride?

   Come to my arms & never more
Depart, but dwell for ever here.
   Create my spirit to thy love,
Subdue my spectre to thy fear.

Spectre of Albion, warlike fiend,
In clouds of blood & ruin rolled,
    I here reclaim thee as my own,
My selfhood, Satan, armed in gold.

    Is this thy soft family love,
Thy cruel patriarchal pride
    Planting thy family alone,
Destroying all the world beside?

    A man's worst enemies are those
Of his own house & family;
    And he who makes his law a curse,
By his own law shall surely die.

    In my exchanges every land
Shall walk, & mine in every land
    Mutual shall build Jerusalem:
Both heart in heart & hand in hand.

                    (*from* Jerusalem Chapter 2, lines 19–104)

ANDRÉ CHÉNIER

Iambes VIII

We live: – dishonoured, in the shit. So what? it had to be.
  This is the pits and yet we feed and sleep.
Even here – penned in, watered and waiting for the chop
  (just place your bets) – affairs take off,
there's gossip, bitching and a pecking-order.
  Songs, jokes, card-schools; she lifts her skirts; someone
bops a tight balloon against the window-panes.
  It's like the speeches of those seven hundred eejits
(Barrère's the shiftiest of the lot) – a comic fart
  we whoop and cheer and then forget.
One jumps, another skips; that greasy pack
  of gut and gullet politicians raps and hoots
until, dead quick, the door scrakes open
  and our tiger-masters' wee pimp struts in.
Who's getting it today? We freeze and listen,
  then all but one of us knows it isn't him . . .

trans. Tom Paulin

The Shan Van Vocht

O the French are on the sea,
  Says the Shan Van Vocht,
The French are on the sea,
  Says the Shan Van Vocht.
O the French are in the bay,
They'll be here without delay,
And the Orange will decay,
  Says the Shan Van Vocht.
    O the French are in the bay,
    They'll be here by break of day,
    And the Orange will decay,
      Says the Shan Van Vocht.

And their camp it shall be where?
  Says the Shan Van Vocht,
Their camp it shall be where?
  Says the Shan Van Vocht.
On the Currach of Kildare,
The boys they will be there,
With their pikes in good repair,
  Says the Shan Van Vocht.
    To the Currach of Kildare
    The boys they will repair,
    And Lord Edward will be there,
      Says the Shan Van Vocht.

Then what will the yeomen do?
  Says the Shan Van Vocht,
What will the yeoman do?
  Says the Shan Van Vocht.
What should the yeomen do
But throw off the red and blue
And swear that they'll be true

To the Shan Van Vocht.
What should the yeomen do
But throw off the red and blue,
And swear that they'll be true
To the Shan Van Vocht?

And what colour will they wear?
Says the Shan Van Vocht,
What colour will they wear?
Says the Shan Van Vocht.
What colour should be seen
Where our fathers' homes have been,
But our own immortal green?
Says the Shan Van Vocht.
What colour should be seen
Where our fathers' homes have been,
But our own immortal green?
Says the Shan Van Vocht.

And shall Ireland then be free?
Says the Shan Van Vocht,
Shall Ireland then be free?
Says the Shan Van Vocht.
Yes, Ireland shall be free,
From the centre to the sea.
Then hurrah for liberty!
Says the Shan Van Vocht.
Yes, Ireland shall be free,
From the centre to the sea.
Then hurrah for liberty,
Says the Shan Van Vocht.

The Battle of Blenheim

1

It was a summer evening,
  Old Kaspar's work was done,
And he before his cottage door
  Was sitting in the sun,
And by him sported on the green
His little grandchild Wilhelmine.

2

She saw her brother Peterkin
  Roll something large and round,
Which he beside the rivulet
  In playing there had found;
He came to ask what he had found,
That was so large, and smooth, and round.

3

Old Kaspar took it from the boy,
  Who stood expectant by;
And then the old man shook his head
  And with a natural sigh,
''Tis some poor fellow's skull', said he,
'Who fell in the great victory.

4

'I find them in the garden,
  For there's many here about;
And often when I go to plough,
  The ploughshare turns them out!
For many thousand men', said he,
'Were slain in that great victory.'

5

'Now tell us what 't was all about,'
    Young Peterkin, he cries;
And little Wilhelmine looks up
    With wonder-waiting eyes;
'Now tell us all about the war,
And what they fought each other for.'

6

'It was the English', Kaspar cried,
    'Who put the French to rout;
But what they fought each other for,
    I could not well make out;
But everybody said', quoth he,
'That 't was a famous victory.

7

'My father lived at Blenheim then,
    Yon little stream hard by;
They burnt his dwelling to the ground,
    And he was forced to fly;
So with his wife and child he fled,
Nor had he where to rest his head.

8

'With fire and sword the country round
    Was wasted far and wide,
And many a childing mother then,
    And new-born baby died;
But things like that, you know, must be
At every famous victory.

9

'They say it was a shocking sight
  After the field was won;
For many thousand bodies here
  Lay rotting in the sun;
But things like that, you know, must be
After a famous victory.

10

'Great praise the Duke of Marlbro' won,
  And our good Prince Eugene.'
'Why 't was a very wicked thing!'
  Said little Wilhelmine.
'Nay . . nay . . my little girl', quoth he,
'It was a famous victory.

11

'And everybody praised the Duke
  Who this great fight did win.'
'But what good came of it at last?'
  Quoth little Peterkin.
'Why that I cannot tell,' said he,
'But 't was a famous victory.'

Westbury, 1798.

WILLIAM WORDSWORTH

London, 1802

Milton! thou should'st be living at this hour:
England hath need of thee: she is a fen
Of stagnant waters: altar, sword, and pen,
Fireside, the heroic wealth of hall and bower,
Have forfeited their ancient English dower
Of inward happiness. We are selfish men;
Oh! raise us up, return to us again;
And give us manners, virtue, freedom, power,
Thy soul was like a Star, and dwelt apart:
Thou hadst a voice whose sound was like the sea:
Pure as the naked heavens, majestic, free,
So didst thou travel on life's common way,
In cheerful godliness; and yet thy heart
The lowliest duties on herself did lay.

Composed Near Calais,
On the Road Leading to Ardres,
August 7, 1802

Jones! as from Calais soutward you and I
Went pacing side by side, this public Way
Streamed with the pomp of a too-credulous day.
When faith was pledged to new-born Liberty:
A homeless sound of joy was in the sky:
From hour to hour the antiquated Earth
Beat like the heart of Man: songs, garlands, mirth,
Banners, and happy faces, far and nigh!
And now, sole register that these things were,
Two solitary greetings have I heard,
'Good morrow, Citizen!' a hollow word,
As if a dead man spake it! Yet despair
Touches me not, though pensive as a bird
Whose vernal coverts winter hath laid bare.

Written in London, September, 1802

O Friend! I know not which way I must look
For comfort, being, as I am, opprest,
To think that now our life is only drest
For show; mean handy-work of craftsman, cook,
Or groom! – We must run glittering like a brook
In the open sunshine, or we are unblest:
The wealthiest man among us is the best:
No grandeur now in nature or in book
Delights us. Rapine, avarice, expense,
This is idolatry; and these we adore:
Plain living and high thinking are no more:
The homely beauty of the good old cause
Is gone; our peace, our fearful innocence,
And pure religion breathing household laws.

'Great men have been among us'

Great men have been among us; hands that penned
And tongues that uttered wisdom – better none:
The later Sidney, Marvel, Harrington,
Young Vane, and others who called Milton friend.
These moralists could act and comprehend:
They knew how genuine glory was put on;
Taught us how rightfully a nation shone
In splendour: what strength was, that would not bend
But in magnanimous meekness. France, 'tis strange,
Hath brought forth no such souls as we had then.
Perpetual emptiness! unceasing change!
No single volume paramount, no code,
No master spirit, no determined road;
But equally a want of books and men!

To Toussaint L'Ouverture

Toussaint, the most unhappy man of men!
Whether the whistling Rustic tend his plough
Within thy hearing, or thy head be now
Pillowed in some deep dungeon's earless den; –
O miserable Chieftain! where and when
Wilt thou find patience! Yet die not; do thou
Wear rather in thy bonds a cheerful brow:
Though fallen thyself, never to rise again,
Live, and take comfort. Thou hast left behind
Powers that will work for thee; air, earth, and skies;
There's not a breathing of the common wind
That will forget thee; thou has great allies;
Thy friends are exultations, agonies,
And love, and man's unconquerable mind.

from The Prelude

But 'twas a time when Europe was rejoiced,
France standing on the top of golden hours,
And human nature seeming born again.
Bound, as I said, to the Alps, it was our lot
To land at Calais on the very eve
Of that great federal day; and there we saw,
In a mean city, and among a few,
How bright a face is worn when joy of one
Is joy of tens of millions. Southward thence
We took our way, direct through hamlets, towns,
Gaudy with reliques of that festival,
Flowers left to wither on triumphal arcs,
And window-garlands. On the public roads,
And, once, three days successively, through paths
By which our toilsome journey was abridged,
Among sequestered villages we walked
And found benevolence and blessedness

Spread like a fragrance everywhere, like spring
That leaves no corner of the land untouched:
Where elms for many and many a league in files,
With their thin umbrage, on the stately roads
Of that great kingdom, rustled o'er our heads,
For ever near us as we paced along:
'Twas sweet at such a time, with such delights
On every side, in prime of youthful strength,
To feed a Poet's tender melancholy
And fond conceit of sadness, to the noise
And gentle undulations which they made.
Unhoused, beneath the evening star we saw
Dances of liberty, and, in late hours
Of darkness, dances in the open air.

(1805, Book VI, lines 352–382)

from The Prelude

Genius of Burke! forgive the pen seduced
By specious wonders, and too slow to tell
Of what the ingenious, what bewildered men,
Beginning to mistrust their boastful guides,
And wise men, willing to grow wiser, caught
Rapt auditors! from thy most eloquent tongue –
Now mute, for ever mute in the cold grave.
I see him, – old, but vigorous in age, –
Stand like an oak whose stag-horn branches start
Out of its leafy brow, the more to awe
The younger brethren of the grove. But some –
While he forewarns, denounces, launches forth,
Against all systems built on abstract rights,
Keen ridicule; the majesty proclaims
Of Institutes and Laws, hallowed by time;
Declares the vital power of social ties
Endeared by Custom; and with high disdain,
Exploding upstart Theory, insists

Upon the allegiance to which men are born –
Some – say at once a froward multitude –
Murmur (for truth is hated, where not loved)
As the winds fret within the Aeolian cave,
Galled by their monarch's chain. The times were big
With ominous change, which, night by night, provoked
Keen struggles, and black clouds of passion raised;
But memorable moments intervened,
When Wisdom, like the Goddess from Jove's brain,
Broke forth in armour of resplendent words,
Startling the Synod. Could a youth, and one
In ancient story versed, whose breast had heaved
Under the weight of classic eloquence,
Sit, see, and hear, unthankful, uninspired?

(1850, Book VII, lines 512–543)

from The Prelude

France lured me forth; the realm that I had crossed
So lately, journeying toward the snow-clad Alps.
But now, relinquishing the scrip and staff,
And all enjoyment which the summer sun
Sheds round the steps of those who meet the day
With motion constant as his own, I went
Prepared to sojourn in a pleasant town,
Washed by the current of the stately Loire.

Through Paris lay my readiest course, and there
Sojourning a few days, I visited
In haste, each spot of old or recent fame,
The latter chiefly; from the field of Mars
Down to the suburbs of St Antony,
And from Mont Martyr southward to the Dome
Of Geneviève. In both her clamorous Halls,
The National Synod and the Jacobins,
I saw the Revolutionary Power

Toss like a ship at anchor, rocked by storms;
The Arcades I traversed, in the Palace huge
Of Orleans; coasted round and round the line
Of Tavern, Brothel, Gaming-house and Shop,
Great rendezvous of worst and best, the walk
Of all who had a purpose, or had not;
I stared and listened, with a stranger's ears,
To Hawkers and Haranguers, hubbub wild!
And hissing Factionists with ardent eyes,
In knots, or pairs, or single. Not a look
Hope takes, or Doubt or Fear are forced to wear,
But seemed there present; and I scanned them all,
Watched every gesture uncontrollable,
Of anger, and vexation, and despite,
All side by side, and struggling face to face,
With gaiety and dissolute idleness.

Where silent zephyrs sported with the dust
Of the Bastille, I sate in the open sun,
And from the rubbish gathered up a stone,
And pocketed the relic, in the guise
Of an enthusiast; yet, in honest truth,
I looked for something that I could not find,
Affecting more emotion than I felt;
For 'tis most certain, that these various sights,
However potent their first shock, with me
Appeared to recompense the traveller's pains
Less than the painted Magdalene of Le Brun,
A beauty exquisitely wrought, with hair
Dishevelled, gleaming eyes, and rueful cheek
Pale and bedropped with everflowing tears.

But hence to my more permanent abode
I hasten; there, by novelties in speech,
Domestic manners, customs, gestures, looks,
And all the attire of ordinary life,
Attention was engrossed; and, thus amused,

I stood, 'mid those concussions, unconcerned,
Tranquil almost, and careless as a flower
Glassed in a greenhouse, or a parlour shrub
That spreads its leaves in unmolested peace,
While every bush and tree, the country through,
Is shaking to the roots: indifference this
Which may seem strange: but I was unprepared
With needful knowledge, had abruptly passed
Into a theatre, whose stage was filled
And busy with an action far advanced.
Like others, I had skimmed, and sometimes read
With care, the master pamphlets of the day;
Nor wanted such half-insight as grew wild
Upon that meagre soil, helped out by talk
And public news; but having never seen
A chronicle that might suffice to show
Whence the main organs of the public power
Had sprung, their transmigrations, when and how
Accomplished, giving thus unto events
A form and body; all things were to me
Loose and disjointed, and the affections left
Without a vital interest. At that time,
Moreover, the first storm was overblown,
And the strong hand of outward violence
Locked up in quiet. For myself, I fear
Now in connection with so great a theme
To speak (as I must be compelled to do)
Of one so unimportant; night by night
Did I frequent the formal haunts of men,
Whom, in the city, privilege of birth
Sequestered from the rest, societies
Polished in arts, and in punctilio versed;
Whence, and from deeper causes, all discourse
Of good and evil of the time was shunned
With scrupulous care; but these restrictions soon
Proved tedious, and I gradually withdrew
Into a noiser world, and thus ere long

Became a patriot; and my heart was all
Given to the people, and my love was theirs.

  A band of military Officers,
Then stationed in the city, were the chief
Of my associates: some of these wore swords
That had been seasoned in the wars, and all
Were men well-born; the chivalry of France.
In age and temper differing, they had yet
One spirit ruling in each heart; alike
(Save only one, hereafter to be named)
Were bent upon undoing what was done:
This was their rest and only hope; therewith
No fear had they of bad becoming worse,
For worst to them was come; nor would have stirred,
Or deemed it worth a moment's thought to stir,
In any thing, save only as the act
Looked thitherward. One, reckoning by years,
Was in the prime of manhood, and erewhile
He had sate lord in many tender hearts;
Though heedless of such honours now, and changed:
His temper was quite mastered by the times,
And they had blighted him, had eat away
The beauty of his person, doing wrong
Alike to body and to mind: his port,
Which once had been erect and open, now
Was stooping and contracted, and a face,
Endowed by Nature with her fairest gifts
Of symmetry and light and bloom, expressed,
As much as any that was ever seen,
A ravage out of season, made by thoughts
Unhealthy and vexatious. With the hour,
That from the press of Paris duly brought
Its freight of public news, the fever came,
A punctual visitant, to shake this man,
Disarmed his voice and fanned his yellow cheek
Into a thousand colours; while he read,

Or mused, his sword was haunted by his touch
Continually, like an uneasy place
In his own body. 'Twas in truth an hour
Of universal ferment; mildest men
Were agitated; and commotions, strife
Of passions and opinions, filled the walls
Of peaceful houses with unquiet sounds.
The soil of common life, was, at that time,
Too hot to tread upon. Oft said I then,
And not then only, 'What a mockery this
Of history, the past and that to come!
Now do I feel how all men are deceived,
Reading of nations and their works, in faith,
Faith given to vanity and emptiness;
Oh! laughter for the page that would reflect
To future times the face of what now is!'
The land all swarmed with passion, like a plain
Devoured by locusts, – Carra, Gorsas, – add
A hundred other names, forgotten now,
Nor to be heard of more; yet, they were powers,
Like earthquakes, shocks repeated day by day,
And felt through every nook of town and field.

     Such was the state of things. Meanwhile the chief
Of my associates stood prepared for flight
To augment the band of emigrants in arms
Upon the borders of the Rhine, and leagued
With foreign foes mustered for instant war.
This was their undisguised intent, and they
Were waiting with the whole of their desires
The moment to depart.
                         An Englishman,
Born in a land whose very name appeared
To license some unruliness of mind;
A stranger, with youth's further privilege,
And the indulgence that a half-learnt speech
Wins from the courteous; I, who had been else

Shunned and not tolerated, freely lived
With these defenders of the Crown, and talked,
And heard their notions; nor did they disdain
The wish to bring me over to their cause.

But though untaught by thinking or by books
To reason well of polity or law,
And nice distinctions, then on every tongue,
Of natural rights and civil; and to acts
Of nations and their passing interests,
(If with unworldly ends and aims compared)
Almost indifferent, even the historian's tale
Prizing but little otherwise than I prized
Tales of the poets, as it made the heart
Beat high, and filled the fancy with fair forms,
Old heroes and their sufferings and their deeds;
Yet in the regal sceptre, and the pomp
Of orders and degrees, I nothing found
Then, or had ever, even in crudest youth,
That dazzled me, but rather what I mourned
And ill could brook, beholding that the best
Ruled not, and feeling that they ought to rule.

For, born in a poor district, and which yet
Retaineth more of ancient homeliness,
Than any other nook of English ground,
It was my fortune scarcely to have seen,
Through the whole tenor of my school-day time,
The face of one, who, whether boy or man,
Was vested with attention or respect
Through claims of wealth or blood; nor was it least
Of many benefits, in later years
Derived from academic institutes
And rules, that they held something up to view
Of a Republic, where all stood thus far
Upon equal ground; that we were brothers all
In honour, as in one community,

Scholars and gentlemen; where, furthermore,
Distinction lay open to all that came,
And wealth and titles were in less esteem
Than talents, worth, and prosperous industry.
Add unto this, subservience from the first
To presences of God's mysterious power
Made manifest in Nature's sovereignty,
And fellowship with venerable books,
To sanction the proud workings of the soul,
And mountain liberty. It could not be
But that one tutored thus should look with awe
Upon the faculties of man, receive
Gladly the highest promises, and hail,
As best, the government of equal rights
And individual worth. And hence, O Friend!
If at the first great outbreak I rejoiced
Less than might well befit my youth, the cause
In part lay here, that unto me the events
Seemed nothing out of nature's certain course,
A gift that was rather come late than soon.
No wonder, then, if advocates like these,
Inflamed by passion, blind with prejudice,
And stung with injury, at this riper day,
Were impotent to make my hopes put on
The shape of theirs, my understanding bend
In honour to their honour: zeal, which yet
Had slumbered, now in opposition burst
Forth like a Polar summer: every word
They uttered was a dart, by counter-winds
Blown back upon themselves; their reason seemed
Confusion-stricken by a higher power
Than human understanding, their discourse
Maimed, spiritless; and, in their weakness strong,
I triumphed.
   Meantime, day by day, the roads
Were crowded with the bravest youth of France,
And all the promptest of her spirits, linked

In gallant soldiership, and posting on
To meet the war upon her frontier bounds.
Yet at this very moment do tears start
Into mine eyes: I do not say I weep –
I wept not then, – but tears have dimmed my sight,
In memory of the farewells of that time,
Domestic severings, female fortitude
At dearest separation, patriot love
And self-devotion, and terrestrial hope,
Encouraged with a martyr's confidence;
Even files of strangers merely, seen but once,
And for a moment, men from far with sound
Of music, martial tunes, and banners spread,
Entering the city, here and there a face,
Or person singled out among the rest,
Yet still a stranger and beloved as such;
Even by these passing spectacles my heart
Was oftentimes uplifted, and they seemed
Arguments sent from Heaven to prove the cause
Good, pure, which no one could stand up against,
Who was not lost, abandoned, selfish, proud,
Mean, miserable, wilfully depraved,
Haters perverse of equity and truth.

Among that band of Officers was one,
Already hinted at, of other mould –
A patriot, thence rejected by the rest,
And with an oriental loathing spurned,
As of a different caste. A meeker man
Than this lived never, nor a more benign,
Meek though enthusiastic. Injuries
Made *him* more gracious, and his nature then
Did breathe its sweetness out most sensibly,
As aromatic flowers on Alpine turf,
When foot hath crushed them. He through the events
Of that great change wandered in perfect faith,
As through a book, an old romance, or tale

Of Fairy, or some dream of actions wrought
Behind the summer clouds. By birth he ranked
With the most noble, but unto the poor
Among mankind he was in service bound,
As by some tie invisible, oaths professed
To a religious order. Man he loved
As man; and, to the mean and the obscure,
And all the homely in their homely works,
Transferred a courtesy which had no air
Of condescension; but did rather seem
A passion and a gallantry, like that
Which he, a soldier, in his idler day
Had paid to woman: somewhat vain he was,
Or seemed so, yet it was not vanity,
But fondness, and a kind of radiant joy
Diffused around him, while he was intent
On works of love or freedom, or revolved
Complacently the progress of a cause,
Whereof he was a part: yet this was meek
And placid, and took nothing from the man
That was delightful. Oft in solitude
With him did I discourse about the end
Of civil government, and its wisest forms;
Of ancient loyalty, and chartered rights,
Custom and habit, novelty and change;
Of self-respect, and virtue in the few
For patrimonial honour set apart,
And ignorance in the labouring multitude.
For he, to all intolerance indisposed,
Balanced these contemplations in his mind;
And I, who at that time was scarcely dipped
Into the turmoil, bore a sounder judgement
Than later days allowed; carried about me,
With less alloy to its integrity,
The experience of past ages, as, through help
Of books and common life, it makes sure way
To youthful minds, by objects over near

Not pressed upon, nor dazzled or misled
By struggling with the crowd for present ends.

But though not deaf, nor obstinate to find
Error without excuse upon the side
Of them who strove against us, more delight
We took, and let this freely be confessed,
In painting to ourselves the miseries
Of royal courts, and that voluptuous life
Unfeeling, where the man who is of soul
The meanest thrives the most; where dignity,
True personal dignity, abideth not;
A light, a cruel, and vain world cut off
From the natural inlets of just sentiment,
From lowly sympathy and chastening truth;
Where good and evil interchange their names,
And thirst for bloody spoils abroad is paired
With vice at home. We added dearest themes –
Man and his noble nature, as it is
The gift which God has placed within his power,
His blind desires and steady faculties
Capable of clear truth, the one to break
Bondage, the other to build liberty
On firm foundations, making social life,
Through knowledge spreading and imperishable,
As just in regulation, and as pure
As individual in the wise and good.

We summoned up the honourable deeds
Of ancient Story, thought of each bright spot,
That could be found in all recorded time,
Of truth preserved and error passed away;
Of single spirits that catch the flame from Heaven,
And how the multitudes of men will feed
And fan each other; thought of sects, how keen
They are to put the appropriate nature on,
Triumphant over every obstacle

Of custom, language, country, love, or hate,
And what they do and suffer for their creed;
How far they travel, and how long endure;
How quickly mighty Nations have been formed,
From least beginnings; how, together locked
By new opinions, scattered tribes have made
One body, spreading wide as clouds in heaven.
To aspirations then of our own minds
Did we appeal; and, finally, beheld
A living confirmation of the whole
Before us, in a people from the depth
Of shameful imbecility uprisen,
Fresh as the morning star. Elate we looked
Upon their virtues; saw, in rudest men,
Self-sacrifice the firmest; generous love,
And continence of mind, and sense of right,
Uppermost in the midst of fiercest strife.

                              (1850, Book IX, lines 35–389)

from The Prelude

The State, as if to stamp the final seal
On her security, and to the world
Show what she was, a high and fearless soul,
Exulting in defiance, or heart-stung
By sharp resentment, or belike to taunt
With spiteful gratitude the baffled League,
That had stirred up her slackening faculties
To a new transition, when the King was crushed,
Spared not the empty throne, and in proud haste
Assumed the body and venerable name
Of a Republic. Lamentable crimes,
'Tis true, had gone before this hour, dire work
Of massacre, in which the senseless sword
Was prayed to as a judge; but these were past,
Earth free from them for ever, as was thought, –

Ephemeral monsters, to be seen but once!
Things that could only show themselves and die.

Cheered with this hope, to Paris I returned,
And ranged, with ardour heretofore unfelt,
The spacious city, and in progress passed
The prison where the unhappy Monarch lay,
Associate with his children and his wife
In bondage; and the palace, lately stormed
With roar of cannon by a furious host.
I crossed the square (an empty area then!)
Of the Carrousel, where so late had lain
The dead, upon the dying heaped, and gazed
On this and other spots, as doth a man
Upon a volume whose contents he knows
Are memorable, but from him locked up,
Being written in a tongue he cannot read,
So that he questions the mute leaves with pain,
And half upbraids their silence. But that night
I felt most deeply in what world I was,
What ground I trod on, and what air I breathed.
High was my room and lonely, near the roof
Of a large mansion or hotel, a lodge
That would have pleased me in more quiet times;
Nor was it wholly without pleasure then.
With unextinguished taper I kept watch,
Reading at intervals; the fear gone by
Pressed on me almost like a fear to come.
I thought of those September massacres,
Divided from me by one little month,
Saw them and touched: the rest was conjured up
From tragic fictions or true history,
Remembrances and dim admonishments.
The horse is taught his manage, and no star
Of wildest course but treads back his own steps;
For the spent hurricane the air provides
As fierce a successor; the tide retreats

But to return out of its hiding-place
In the great deep; all things have second birth;
The earthquake is not satisfied at once;
And in this way I wrought upon myself,
Until I seemed to hear a voice that cried,
To the whole city, 'Sleep no more.' The trance
Fled with the voice to which it had given birth;
But vainly comments of a calmer mind
Promised soft peace and sweet forgetfulness.
The place, all hushed and silent as it was,
Appeared unfit for the repose of night,
Defenceless as a wood where tigers roam.

With early morning towards the Palace-walk
Of Orleans eagerly I turned; as yet
The streets were still; not so those long Arcades;
There, 'mid a peal of ill-matched sounds and cries,
That greeted me on entering, I could hear
Shrill voices from the hawkers in the throng,
Bawling, 'Denunciation of the Crimes
Of Maximilian Robespierre'; the hand,
Prompt as the voice, held forth a printed speech,
The same that had been recently pronounced,
When Robespierre, not ignorant for what mark
Some words of indirect reproof had been
Intended, rose in hardihood, and dared
The man who had an ill surmise of him
To bring his charge in openness; whereat,
When a dead pause ensued, and no one stirred,
In silence of all present, from his seat
Louvet walked single through the avenue,
And took his station in the Tribune, saying,
'I, Robespierre, accuse thee!' Well is known
The inglorious issue of that charge, and how
He, who had launched the startling thunderbolt,
The one bold man, whose voice the attack had sounded,
Was left without a follower to discharge

His perilous duty, and retire lamenting
That Heaven's best aid is wasted upon men
Who to themselves are false.
                              But these are things
Of which I speak, only as they were storm
Or sunshine to my individual mind,
No further. Let me then relate that now –
In some sort seeing with my proper eyes
That Liberty, and Life, and Death would soon
To the remotest corners of the land
Lie in the arbitrement of those who ruled
The capital City; what was struggled for,
And by what combatants victory must be won;
The indecision on their part whose aim
Seemed best, and the straightforward path of those
Who in attack or in defence were strong
Through their impiety – my inmost soul
Was agitated; yea, I could almost
Have prayed that throughout earth upon all men,
By patient exercise of reason made
Worthy of liberty, all spirits filled
With zeal expanding in Truth's holy light,
The gift of tongues might fall, and power arrive
From the four quarters of the winds to do
For France, what without help she could not do,
A work of honour; think not that to this
I added, work of safety: from all doubt
Or trepidation for the end of things
Far was I, far as angels are from guilt.

(1850, Book X, lines 31–145)

from The Prelude

When the proud fleet that bears the red-cross flag
In that unworthy service was prepared
To mingle, I beheld the vessels lie,
A brood of gallant creatures, on the deep
I saw them in their rest, a sojourner
Through a whole month of calm and glassy days
In that delightful island which protects
Their place of convocation – there I heard,
Each evening, pacing by the still seashore,
A monitory sound that never failed, –
The sunset cannon. While the orb went down
In the tranquillity of Nature, came
That voice, ill requiem! seldom heard by me
Without a spirit overcast by dark
Imaginations, sense of woes to come,
Sorrow for human kind, and pain of heart.

In France, the men, who, for their desperate ends,
Had plucked up mercy by the roots, were glad
Of this new enemy. Tyrants, strong before
In wicked pleas, were strong as demons now;
And thus, on every side beset with foes,
The goaded land waxed mad; the crimes of few
Spread into madness of the many; blasts
From hell came sanctified like airs from heaven,
The sternness of the just, the faith of those
Who doubted not that Providence had times
Of vengeful retribution, theirs who throned
The human understanding paramount
And made of that their God, the hopes of men
Who were content to barter short-lived pangs
For a paradise of ages, the blind rage
Of insolent tempers, the light vanity
Of intermeddlers, steady purposes
Of the suspicious, slips of the indiscreet,

And all the accidents of life were pressed
Into one service, busy with one work.
The Senate stood aghast, her prudence quenched,
Her wisdom stifled, and her justice scared,
Her frenzy only active to extol
Past outrages, and shape the way for new,
Which no one dared to oppose or mitigate.

(1850, Book X, 315–355)

JOHANN WOLFGANG VON GOETHE

Symbolum

The mason lives
in this or that street
and all his actions
are like yours or mine.
He makes us equal.

He sees loose clouds
like a bishop's jowls
and the furred stars
that should be even –
king superstitions.

But he'll go out
with spirit-level,
square and trowel
to plant a ladder
on this earth.

The sun shines
on his foundations –
a pentagram
cut in packed soil,
the bricks stacked ready.

trans. Tom Paulin

Simile for Two Political Characters of 1819

I

As from an ancestral oak
  Two empty ravens sound their clarion,
Yell by yell, and croak by croak,
When they scent the noonday smoke
  Of fresh human carrion: –

II

As two gibbering night-birds flit
  From their bowers of deadly yew
Through the night to frighten it,
When the moon is in a fit,
  And the stars are none, or few: –

III

As a shark and dog-fish wait
  Under an Atlantic isle,
For the negro-ship, whose freight
Is the theme of their debate,
  Wrinkling their red gills the while –

IV

Are ye, two vultures sick for battle,
  Two scorpions under one wet stone,
Two bloodless wolves whose dry throats rattle,
Two crows perched on the murrained cattle,
  Two vipers tangled into one.

England in 1819

An old, mad, blind, despised, and dying king, –
Princes, the dregs of their dull race, who flow
Through public scorn, – mud from a muddy spring, –
Rulers who neither see, nor feel, nor know,
But leech-like to their fainting country cling,
Till they drop, blind in blood, without a blow, –
A people starved and stabbed in the untilled field, –
An army, which liberticide and prey
Makes as a two-edged sword to all who wield, –
Golden and sanguine laws which tempt and slay;
Religion Christless, Godless – a book sealed;
A Senate, – Time's worst statute unrepealed, –
Are graves, from which a glorious Phantom may
Burst, to illumine our tempestuous day.

GEORGE GORDON, LORD BYRON

from Don Juan

'Tis thus with people in an open boat;
  They live upon the love of life and bear
More than can be believed or even thought,
  And stand like rocks the tempest's wear and tear.
And hardship still has been the sailor's lot,
  Since Noah's ark went cruising here and there.
She had a curious crew as well as cargo,
Like the first old Greek privateer, the *Argo*.

But man is a carnivorous production
  And must have meals, at least one meal a day.
He cannot live like woodcocks upon suction,
  But like the shark and tiger must have prey.
Although his anatomical construction
  Bears vegetables in a grumbling way,
Your labouring people think beyond all question,
Beef, veal, and mutton better for digestion.

And thus it was with this our hapless crew,
  For on the third day there came on a calm,
And though at first their strength it might renew,
  And lying on their weariness like balm,
Lulled them like turtles sleeping on the blue
  Of ocean, when they woke they felt a qualm
And fell all ravenously on their provision,
Instead of hoarding it with due precision.

The consequence was easily foreseen:
  They ate up all they had and drank their wine
In spite of all remonstrances, and then
  On what in fact next day were they to dine?
They hoped the wind would rise, these foolish men,
  And carry them to shore. These hopes were fine,
But as they had but one oar, and that brittle,
It would have been more wise to save their victual.

The fourth day came, but not a breath of air,
  And ocean slumbered like an unweaned child.
The fifth day, and their boat lay floating there,
  The sea and sky were blue and clear and mild.
With their one oar (I wish they had had a pair)
  What could they do? And hunger's rage grew wild,
So Juan's spaniel, spite of his entreating,
Was killed and portioned out for present eating.

On the sixth day they fed upon his hide,
  And Juan, who had still refused, because
The creature was his father's dog that died,
  Now feeling all the vulture in his jaws,
With some remorse received (though first denied)
  As a great favour one of the forepaws,
Which he divided with Pedrillo, who
Devoured it, longing for the other too.

The seventh day and no wind. The burning sun
  Blistered and scorched, and stagnant on the sea
They lay like carcasses, and hope was none,
  Save in the breeze that came not. Savagely
They glared upon each other. All was done,
  Water and wine and food, and you might see
The longings of the cannibal arise
(Although they spoke not) in their wolfish eyes.

At length one whispered his companion, who
  Whispered another, and thus it went round,
And then into a hoarser murmur grew,
  An ominous and wild and desperate sound,
And when his comrade's thought each sufferer knew,
  'Twas but his own, suppressed till now, he found.
And out they spoke of lots for flesh and blood,
And who should die to be his fellow's food.

But ere they came to this, they that day shared
  Some leathern caps and what remained of shoes;
And then they looked around them and despaired,
  And none to be the sacrifice would choose.
At length the lots were torn up and prepared,
  But of materials that much shock the Muse.
Having no paper, for the want of better,
They took by force from Juan Julia's letter.

The lots were made and marked and mixed and handed
  In silent horror, and their distribution
Lulled even the savage hunger which demanded,
  Like the Promethean vulture, this pollution.
None in particular had sought or planned it;
  'Twas nature gnawed them to this resolution,
By which none were permitted to be neuter,
And the lot fell on Juan's luckless tutor.

He but requested to be bled to death.
  The surgeon had his instruments and bled
Pedrillo, and so gently ebbed his breath
  You hardly could perceive when he was dead.
He died as born, a Catholic in faith,
  Like most in the belief in which they're bred,
And first a little crucifix he kissed,
And then held out his jugular and wrist.

The surgeon, as there was no other fee,
  Had his first choice of morsels for his pains,
But being thirstiest at the moment, he
  Preferred a draught from the fast-flowing veins.
Part was divided, part thrown in the sea,
  And such things as the entrails and the brains
Regaled two sharks who followed o'er the billow.
The sailors ate the rest of poor Pedrillo.

The sailors ate him, all save three or four,
  Who were not quite so fond of animal food.
To these was added Juan, who, before
  Refusing his own spaniel, hardly could
Feel now his appetite increased much more.
  'Twas not to be expected that he should,
Even in extremity of their disaster,
Dine with them on his pastor and his master.

'Twas better that he did not, for in fact
  The consequence was awful in the extreme.
For they who were most ravenous in the act
  Went raging mad. Lord! how they did blaspheme
And foam and roll, with strange convulsions racked,
  Drinking salt water like a mountain stream,
Tearing and grinning, howling, screeching, swearing,
And with hyena laughter died despairing.

Their numbers were much thinned by this infliction,
  And all the rest were thin enough, heaven knows,
And some of them had lost their recollection,
  Happier than they who still perceived their woes,
But others pondered on a new dissection,
  As if not warned sufficiently by those
Who had already perished, suffering madly,
For having used their appetites so sadly.

And next they thought upon the master's mate
  As fattest, but he saved himself, because,
Besides being much averse from such a fate,
  There were some other reasons: the first was
He had been rather indisposed of late,
  And that which chiefly proved his saving clause
Was a small present made to him at Cadiz,
By general subscription of the ladies.

Of poor Pedrillo something still remained,
  But was used sparingly. Some were afraid,
And others still their appetites constrained,
  Or but at times a little supper made;
All except Juan, who throughout abstained,
  Chewing a piece of bamboo and some lead.
At length they caught two boobies and a noddy,
And then they left off eating the dead body.

And if Pedrillo's fate should shocking be,
  Remember Ugolino condescends
To eat the head of his archenemy,
  The moment after he politely ends
His tale. If foes be food in hell, at sea
  'Tis surely fair to dine upon our friends
When shipwreck's short allowance grows too scanty,
Without being much more horrible than Dante.

                              (Canto II, stanzas 66–83)

from Don Juan

'Where is the world?' cries Young at eighty. 'Where
  The world in which a man was born?' Alas!
Where is the world of eight years past? 'Twas there –
  I look for it – 'tis gone, a globe of glass,
Cracked, shivered, vanished, scarcely gazed on, ere
  A silent change dissolves the glittering mass.
Statesmen, chiefs, orators, queens, patriots, kings,
And dandies, all are gone on the wind's wings.

Where is Napoleon the Grand? God knows.
  Where little Castlereagh? The devil can tell.
Where Grattan, Curran, Sheridan, all those
  Who bound the bar or senate in their spell?
Where is the unhappy Queen with all her woes?
  And where the daughter, whom the isles loved well?
Where are those martyred saints the five per cents?
And where, oh where the devil are the rents?

Where's Brummell? Dished. Where's Long Pole Wellesley?
                                              Diddled.
  Where's Whitbread? Romilly? Where's George the Third?
Where is his will? That's not so soon unriddled.
  And where is 'Fum' the Fourth, our 'royal bird'?
Gone down it seems to Scotland to be fiddled
  Unto by Sawney's violin, we have heard.
'Caw me, caw thee.' For six months hath been hatching
This scene of royal itch and loyal scratching.

Where is Lord This? And where is my Lady That?
  The Honourable Mistresses and Misses?
Some laid aside like an old opera hat,
  Married, unmarried, and remarried (this is
An evolution oft performed of late).
  Where are the Dublin shouts and London hisses?
Where are the Grenvilles? Turned as usual. Where
My friends the Whigs? Exactly where they were.

Where are the Lady Carolines and Franceses?
  Divorced or doing thereanent. Ye annals
So brilliant, where the list of routs and dances is,
  Thou *Morning Post*, sole record of the panels
Broken in carriages and all the phantasies
  Of fashion, say what streams now fill those channels?
Some die, some fly, some languish on the Continent,
Because the times have hardly left them one tenant.

Some who once set their caps at cautious dukes
  Have taken up at length with younger brothers.
Some heiresses have bit at sharpers' hooks;
  Some maids have been made wives, some merely mothers;
Others have lost their fresh and fairy looks.
  In short, the list of alterations bothers.
There's little strange in this, but something strange is
The unusual quickness of these common changes.

Talk not of seventy years of age. In seven
  I have seen more changes, down from monarchs to
The humblest individual under heaven,
  Than might suffice a moderate century through.
I knew that nought was lasting, but now even
  Change grows too changeable without being new.
Nought's permanent among the human race,
Except the Whigs *not* getting into place.

I have seen Napoleon, who seemed quite a Jupiter,
  Shrink to a Saturn. I have seen a duke
(No matter which) turn politician stupider,
  If that can well be, than his wooden look.
But it is time that I should hoist my blue peter
  And sail for a new theme. I have seen – and shook
To see it – the King hissed and then carest,
But don't pretend to settle which was best.

I have seen the landholders without a rap,
  I have seen Johanna Southcote. I have seen
The House of Commons turned to a tax-trap.
  I have seen that sad affair of the late Queen.
I have seen crowns worn instead of a fool's cap.
  I have seen a congress doing all that's mean.
I have seen some nations like o'erloaded asses
Kick off their burdens – meaning the high classes.

I have seen small poets and great prosers and
  Interminable, not eternal, speakers.
I have seen the Funds at war with house and land.
  I've seen the country gentlemen turn squeakers.
I've seen the people ridden o'er like sand
  By slaves on horseback. I have seen malt liquors
Exchanged for 'thin potations' by John Bull.
I have seen John half detect himself a fool.

But *carpe diem*, Juan, *carpe, carpe*!
  Tomorrow sees another race as gay
And transient and devoured by the same harpy.
  'Life's a poor player.' Then 'play out the play,
Ye villains!' And above all keep a sharp eye
  Much less on what you do than what you say.
Be hypocritical, be cautious, be
Not what you seem, but always what you see.

                    (Canto XI, stanzas 76–86)

The Fallen Elm

Old elm that murmured in our chimney top
The sweetest anthem autumn ever made
& into mellow whispering calms would drop
When showers fell on thy many coloured shade
& when dark tempests mimic thunder made
While darkness came as it would strangle light
With the black tempest of a winter night
That rocked thee like a cradle to thy root
How did I love to hear the winds upbraid
Thy strength without – while all within was mute
It seasoned comfort to our hearts desire
We felt thy kind protection like a friend
& edged our chairs up closer to the fire
Enjoying comforts that was never penned
Old favourite tree thoust seen times changes lower
Though change till now did never injure thee
For time beheld thee as her sacred dower
& nature claimed thee her domestic tree
Storms came & shook thee many a weary hour
Yet stedfast to thy home thy roots hath been
Summers of thirst parched round thy homely bower
Till earth grew iron – still thy leaves was green
The childern sought thee in thy summer shade
& made their play house rings of sticks & stone
The mavis sang & felt himself alone
While in thy leaves his early nest was made
& I did feel his happiness mine own
Nought heeding that our friendship was betrayed
Friend not inanimate – though stocks & stones
There are & many formed of flesh & bones
Thou owned a language by which hearts are stirred
Deeper then by a feeling cloathed in words
& speakest now whats known of every tongue

Language of pity & the force of wrong
What cant assumes what hypocrites will dare
Speaks home to truth & shows it what they are
I see a picture which thy fate displays
& learn a lesson from thy destiny
Self interest saw thee stand in freedoms ways
So thy old shadow must a tyrant be
Thoust heard the knave abusing those in power
Bawl freedom loud & then opress the free
Thoust sheltered hypocrites in many a shower
That when in power would never shelter thee
Thoust heard the knave supply his canting powers
With wrongs illusions when he wanted friends
That bawled for shelter when he lived in showers
& when clouds vanished made thy shade amends
With axe at root he felled thee to the ground
& barked of freedom – O I hate the sound
Time hears its visions speak & age sublime
Had made thee a deciple unto time
– It grows the cant term of enslaving tools
To wrong another by the name of right
It grows the liscence of oerbearing fools
To cheat plain honesty by force of might
Thus came enclosure – ruin was its guide
But freedoms clapping hands enjoyed the sight
Though comforts cottage soon was thrust aside
& workhouse prisons raised upon the scite
Een natures dwellings far away from men
The common heath became the spoilers prey
The rabbit had not where to make his den
& labours only cow was drove away
No matter – wrong was right & right was wrong
& freedoms bawl was sanction to the song
– Such was thy ruin music making elm
The rights of freedom was to injure thine
As thou wert served so would they overwhelm
In freedoms name the little that is mine

& there are knaves that brawl for better laws
& cant of tyranny in stronger powers
Who glue their vile unsatiated maws
& freedoms birthright from the weak devours

The Flitting

Ive left mine own old home of homes
Green fields & every pleasant place
The summer like a stranger comes
I pause & hardly know her face
I miss the hazels happy green
The bluebells quiet hanging blooms
Where envys sneer was never seen
Where staring malice never comes

I miss the heath its yellow furze
Molehills & rabbit tracts that lead
Through beesom ling & teazle burrs
That spread a wilderness indeed
The woodland oaks & all below
That their white powdered branches shield
The mossy paths – the very crow
Croaks music in my native field

I sit me in my corner chair
That seems to feel itself from home
& hear bird-music here & there
From awthorn hedge & orchard come
I hear but all is strange & new
– I sat on my old bench in June
The sailing puddocks shrill 'peelew'
Oer royce wood seemed a sweeter tune

I walk adown the narrow lane
The nightingale is singing now
But like to me she seems at loss
For royce wood & its shielding bough
I lean upon the window sill
The trees & summer happy seem
Green sunny green they shine – but still
My heart goes far away to dream

Of happiness & thoughts arise
With home bred pictures many a one
Green lanes that shut out burning skies
& old crooked stiles to rest upon
Above them hangs the maple tree
Below grass swells a velvet hill
& little footpaths sweet to see
Goes seeking sweeter places still

With bye & bye a brook to cross
Oer which a little arch is thrown
No brook is here I feel the loss
From home & friends & all alone
– The stone pit with its shelvy sides
Seemed hanging rocks in my esteem
I miss the prospect far & wide
From Langley bush & so I seem

Alone & in a stranger scene
Far far from spots my heart esteems
The closen with their ancient green
Heaths woods & pastures sunny streams
The awthorns here were hung with may
But still they seem in deader green
The sun een seems to loose its way
Nor knows the quarter it is in

I dwell on trifles like a child
I feel as ill becomes a man
& still my thoughts like weedlings wild
Grow up to blossom where they can
They turn to places known so long
& feel that joy was dwelling there
So home fed pleasures fill the song
That has no present joys to heir

I read in books for happiness
But books are like the sea to joy
They change – as well give age the glass
To hunt its visage when a boy
For books they follow fashions new
& throw all old esteems away
In crowded streets flowers never grew
But many there hath died away

Some sing the pomps of chivalry
As legends of the ancient time
Where gold & pearls & mystery
Are shadows painted for sublime
But passions of sublimity
Belong to plain & simpler things
& David underneath a tree
Sought when a shepherd Salems springs

Where moss did into cushions spring
Forming a seat of velvet hue
A small unnoticed trifling thing
To all but heavens hailing dew
& Davids crown hath passed away
Yet poesy breaths his shepherd skill
His palace lost – & to this day
The little moss is blooming still

Strange scenes mere shadows are to me
Vague unpersonifying things
I love with my old home to be
By quiet woods & gravel springs
Where little pebbles wear as smooth
As hermits beads by gentle floods
Whose noises doth my spirits sooth
& warms them into singing moods

Here every tree is strange to me
All foreign things were eer I go
There's none where boyhood made a swee
Or clambered up to rob a crow
No hollow tree or woodland bower
Well known when joy was beating high
Where beauty ran to shun a shower
& love took pains to keep her dry

& laid the shoaf upon the ground
To keep her from the dripping grass
& ran for stowks & set them round
Till scarce a drop of rain could pass
Through – where the maidens they reclined
& sung sweet ballads now forgot
Which brought sweet memorys to the mind
But here no memory knows them not

There have I sat by many a tree
& leaned oer many a rural stile
& conned my thoughts as joys to me
Nought heeding who might frown or smile
Twas natures beauty that inspired
My heart with raptures not its own
& shes a fame that never tires
How could I feel myself alone

No – pasture molehills used to lie
& talk to me of sunny days
& then the glad sheep resting bye
All still in ruminating praise
Of summer & the pleasant place
& every weed & blossom too
Was looking upward in my face
With friendship welcome 'how do ye do'

All tennants of an ancient place
& heirs of noble heritage
Coeval they with adams race
& blest with more substantial age
For when the world first saw the sun
There little flowers beheld him too
& when his love for earth begun
They were the first his smiles to woo

There little lambtoe bunches springs
In red tinged & begolden dye
For ever & like china kings
They come but never seem to die
There may-blooms with its little threads
Still comes upon the thorny bowers
& neer forgets those pinky threads
Like fairy pins amid the flowers

& still they bloom as on the day
They first crowned wilderness & rock
When abel haply crowned with may
The firstlings of his little flock
& Eve might from the matted thorn
To deck her lone & lovely brow
Reach that same rose the heedless scorn
Misnames as the dog rosey now

Give me no highflown fangled things
No haughty pomp in marching chime
Where muses play on golden strings
& splendour passes for sublime
Where citys stretch as far as fame
& fancys straining eye can go
& piled untill the sky for shame
Is stooping far away below

I love the verse that mild & bland
Breaths of green fields & open sky
I love the muse that in her hand
Bears wreaths of native poesy
Who walks nor skips the pasture brook
In scorn – but by the drinking horse
Leans oer its little brig to look
How far the sallows lean accross

& feels a rapture in her breast
Upon their root-fringed grains to mark
A hermit morehens sedgy nest
Just like a naiads summer bark
She counts the eggs she cannot reach
Admires the spot & loves it well
& yearns so natures lessons teach
Amid such neighbourhoods to dwell

I love the muse who sits her down
Upon the molehills little lap
Who feels no fear to stain her gown
& pauses by the hedgrow gap
Not with that affectation praise
Of song to sing & never see
A field flower grow in all her days
Or een a forests aged tree

Een here my simple feelings nurse
A love for every simple weed
& een this little 'shepherds purse'
Grieves me to cut it up – Indeed
I feel at times a love & joy
For every weed & every thing
A feeling kindred from a boy
A feeling brought with every spring

& why – this 'shepherds purse' that grows
In this strange spot – In days gone bye
Grew in the little garden rows
Of my old home now left – And I
Feel what I never felt before
This weed an ancient neighbour here
& though I own the spot no more
Its every trifle makes it dear

The Ivy at the parlour end
The woodbine at the garden gate
Are all & each affections friend
That rendered parting desolate
But times will change & friends must part
& nature still can make amends
Their memory lingers round the heart
Like life whose essence is its friends

Time looks on pomp with careless moods
Or killing apathys disdain
– So where old marble citys stood
Poor persecuted weeds remain
She feels a love for little things
That very few can feel beside
& still the grass eternal springs
Where castles stood & grandeur died

To the Snipe

Lover of swamps
The quagmire over grown
With hassock tufts of sedge – where fear encamps
Around thy home alone

The trembling grass
Quakes from the human foot
Nor bears the weight of man to let him pass
Where thou alone and mute

Sittest at rest
In safety neath the clump
Of hugh flag forrest that thy haunts invest
Or some old sallow stump

Thriving on seams
That tiney island swell
Just hilling from the mud and rancid streams
Suiting thy nature well

For here thy bill
Suited by wisdom good
Of rude unseemly length doth delve and drill
The gelid mass for food

And here mayhap
When summer suns hath drest
The moors rude desolate and spungy lap
May hide thy mystic nest

Mystic indeed
For isles that ocean make
Are scarcely more secure for birds to build
Then this flag hidden lake

Boys thread the woods
To their remotest shades
But in these marshy flats these stagnant floods
Security pervades

From year to year
Places untrodden lie
Where man nor boy nor stock hath ventured near
– Nought gazed on but the sky

And fowl that dread
The very breath of man
Hiding in spots that never knew his tread
A wild and timid clan

Wigeon and teal
And wild duck – restless lot
That from mans dreaded sight will ever steal
To the most dreary spot

Here tempests howl
Around each flaggy plot
Where they who dread mans sight the water fowl
Hide and are frighted not

Tis power divine
That heartens them to brave
The roughest tempest and at ease recline
On marshes or the wave

Yet instinct knows
Not safetys bounds – to shun
The firmer ground where sculking fowler goes
With searching dogs and gun

By tepid springs
Scarcely one stride accross
Though brambles from its edge a shelter flings
Thy safety is at loss

And never chuse
The little sinky foss
Streaking the moores whence spa-red waters spews
From pudges fringed with moss

Free booters there
Intent to kill and slay
Startle with cracking guns the trepid air
And dogs thy haunts betray

From dangers reach
Here thou art safe to roam
Far as these washy flag grown marshes stretch
A still and quiet home

In these thy haunts
Ive gleaned habitual love
From the vague world where pride and folly taunts
I muse and look above

Thy solitudes
The unbounded heaven esteems
And here my heart warms into higher moods
And dignifying dreams

I see the sky
Smile on the meanest spot
Giving to all that creep or walk or flye
A calm and cordial lot

Thine teaches me
Right feelings to employ
That in the dreariest places peace will be
A dweller and a joy

Drone v. Worker

How God speeds the tax-bribed plough,
   Fen and moor declare, man;
Where once fed the poor man's cow,
   ACRES drives his share, man.
But, he did not *steal* the fen,
   Did not *steal* the moor, man;
If he feeds on starving men,
   Still he loves the poor, man.
Hush! he bullies state and throne,
   Quids them in his jaw, man;
Thine and mine, he calls *his own*,
   Acres' lie is law, man.
Acres eats his tax on bread,
   Acres loves the plough, man;
Acres' dogs are better fed,
   Beggar's slave! than thou, man.
Acres' feeder pays his debts,
   Waxes thin and pale, man,
Harder works and poorer gets,
   Pays his debts in jail, man.
Acres in a palace lives,
   While his feeder pines, man;
Palaced beggar ne'er forgives
   Dog on whom he dines, man.
Acres' feeder, beggared, begs,
   Treadmill'd rogue is he, man;
Scamp! he deals in pheasants' eggs, –
   Hangs on gallows-tree, man!
Who would be a useful man?
   Who sell cloth, or hats, man?
Who make boiler, or mend pan?
   Who keep Acres' brats, man?
Better ride, and represent –

Better borough tools, man;
Better sit in pauperment –
Better Corn-Law fools, man.
Why not right the plundered poor?
Why not use our *own*, man?
Plough the seas, and *not* the moor?
Why not pick a bone, man?
Lo, the merchant builds huge mills, –
Bread-taxed thinks, and sighs, man!
Thousand mouths and bellies fills, –
Bread-taxed breaks, and dies, man!
Thousand mouths and bellies, then,
Bread-taxed, writhe and swear, man:
England once bred honest men,
Bread-taxed, Burke and Hare, man!
Hark ye! millions soon may pine,
Starving millions curse, man!
Desperate millions long to dine
A-la-Burke, and worse, man!
What will then remain to eat?
Who be eaten then, man?
'Few may part, though many meet,'
At Famine's Feast, ye ken, man.

HEINRICH HEINE

To a Political Poet

Your baggy lyrics,
they're like a cushion
stuffed with smooth grudges
and hairy heroes.

'Me Mam's Cremation',
'Me Rotten Grammar School',
'Ode to the Toffee-Nosed Gits
Who Mocked My Accent'.

Now your whinges
get taught in class
and the kids feel righteous –
righteous but cosy.

trans. Tom Paulin

The Italian in England

That second time they hunted me
From hill to plain, from shore to sea,
And Austria, hounding far and wide
Her blood-hounds thro' the country-side,
Breathed hot and instant on my trace, –
I made six days a hiding-place
Of that dry green old aqueduct
Where I and Charles, when boys, have plucked
The fire-flies from the roof above,
Bright creeping thro' the moss they love:
– How long it seems since Charles was lost!
Six days the soldiers crossed and crossed
The country in my very sight;
And when that peril ceased at night,
The sky broke out in red dismay
With signal fires; well, there I lay
Close covered o'er in my recess,
Up to the neck in ferns and cress,
Thinking on Metternich our friend,
And Charles's miserable end,
And much beside, two days; the third,
Hunger o'ercame me when I heard
The peasants from the village go
To work among the maize; you know,
With us in Lombardy, they bring
Provisions packed on mules, a string
With little bells that cheer their task,
And casks, and boughs on every cask
To keep the sun's heat from the wine;
These I let pass in jingling line,
And, close on them, dear noisy crew,
The peasants from the village, too;
For at the very rear would troop

Their wives and sisters in a group
To help, I knew. When these had passed,
I threw my glove to strike the last,
Taking the chance: she did not start,
Much less cry out, but stooped apart,
One instant rapidly glanced round,
And saw me beckon from the ground.
A wild bush grows and hides my crypt;
She picked my glove up while she stripped
A branch off, then rejoined the rest
With that; my glove lay in her breast.
Then I drew breath; they disappeared:
It was for Italy I feared.

An hour, and she returned alone
Exactly where my glove was thrown.
Meanwhile came many thoughts: on me
Rested the hopes of Italy.
I had devised a certain tale
Which, when 't was told her, could not fail
Persuade a peasant of its truth;
I meant to call a freak of youth
This hiding, and give hopes of pay,
And no temptation to betray.
But when I saw that woman's face,
Its calm simplicity of grace,
Our Italy's own attitude
In which she walked thus far, and stood,
Planting each naked foot so firm,
To crush the snake and spare the worm –
At first sight of her eyes, I said,
'I am that man upon whose head
'They fix the price, because I hate
'The Austrians over us: the State
'Will give you gold – oh, gold so much! –
'If you betray me to their clutch,
'And be your death, for aught I know,

'If once they find you saved their foe.
'Now, you must bring me food and drink,
'And also paper, pen and ink,
'And carry safe what I shall write
'To Padua, which you'll reach at night
'Before the duomo shuts; go in,
'And wait till Tenebræ begin;
'Walk to the third confessional,
'Between the pillar and the wall,
'And kneeling whisper, *Whence comes peace?*
'Say it a second time, then cease;
'And if the voice inside returns,
'*From Christ and Freedom; what concerns*
'*The cause of Peace?* – for answer, slip
'My letter where you placed your lip;
'Then come back happy we have done
'Our mother service – I, the son,
'As you the daughter of our land!'

Three mornings more, she took her stand
In the same place, with the same eyes:
I was no surer of sun-rise
Than of her coming. We conferred
Of her own prospects, and I heard
She had a lover – stout and tall,
She said – then let her eyelids fall,
'He could do much' – as if some doubt
Entered her heart, – then, passing out,
'She could not speak for others, who
'Had other thoughts; herself she knew:'
And so she brought me drink and food.
After four days, the scouts pursued
Another path; at last arrived
The help my Paduan friends contrived
To furnish me: she brought the news.
For the first time I could not choose
But kiss her hand, and lay my own

Upon her head – 'This faith was shown
'To Italy, our mother; she
'Uses my hand and blesses thee.'
She followed down to the sea-shore;
I left and never saw her more.

How very long since I have thought
Concerning – much less wished for – aught
Beside the good of Italy,
For which I live and mean to die!
I never was in love; and since
Charles proved false, what shall now convince
My inmost heart I have a friend?
However, if I pleased to spend
Real wishes on myself – say, three –
I know at least what one should be.
I would grasp Metternich until
I felt his red wet throat distil
In blood thro' these two hands. And next,
– Nor much for that am I perplexed –
Charles, perjured traitor, for his part,
Should die slow of a broken heart
Under his new employers. Last
– Ah, there, what should I wish? For fast
Do I grow old and out of strength.
If I resolved to seek at length
My father's house again, how scared
They all would look, and unprepared!
My brothers live in Austria's pay
– Disowned me long ago, men say;
And all my early mates who used
To praise me so – perhaps induced
More than one early step of mine –
Are turning wise: while some opine
'Freedom grows license,' some suspect
'Haste breeds delay,' and recollect
They always said, such premature
Beginnings never could endure!

So, with a sullen 'All's for best,'
The land seems settling to its rest.
I think then, I should wish to stand
This evening in that dear, lost land,
Over the sea the thousand miles,
And know if yet that woman smiles
With the calm smile; some little farm
She lives in there, no doubt: what harm
If I sat on the door-side bench,
And, while her spindle made a trench
Fantastically in the dust,
Inquired of all her fortunes – just
Her children's ages and their names,
And what may be the husband's aims
For each of them. I'd talk this out,
And sit there, for an hour about,
Then kiss her hand once more, and lay
Mine on her head, and go my way.

So much for idle wishing – how
It steals the time! To business now.

The Lost Leader

I

Just for a handful of silver he left us,
  Just for a riband to stick in his coat –
Found the one gift of which fortune bereft us,
  Lost all the others she lets us devote;
They, with the gold to give, doled him out silver,
  So much was theirs who so little allowed:
How all our copper had gone for his service!
  Rags – were they purple, his heart had been proud!
We that had loved him so, followed him, honoured him,
  Lived in his mild and magnificent eye,
Learned his great language, caught his clear accents,
  Made him our pattern to live and to die!
Shakespeare was of us, Milton was for us,
  Burns, Shelley, were with us, – they watch from their
                                                    graves!
He alone breaks from the van and the freemen,
  – He alone sinks to the rear and the slaves!

II

We shall march prospering, – not thro' his presence;
  Songs may inspirit us, – not from his lyre;
Deeds will be done, – while he boasts his quiescence,
  Still bidding crouch whom the rest bade aspire:
Blot out his name, then, record one lost soul more,
  One task more declined, one more footpath untrod,
One more devils'-triumph and sorrow for angels,
  One wrong more to man, one more insult to God!
Life's night begins: let him never come back to us!
  There would be doubt, hesitation and pain,
Forced praise on our part – the glimmer of twilight,
  Never glad confident morning again!
Best fight on well, for we taught him – strike gallantly,
  Menace our heart ere we master his own;
Then let him receive the new knowledge and wait us,
  Pardoned in heaven, the first by the throne!

How it Strikes a Contemporary

I only knew one poet in my life:
And this, or something like it, was his way.

   You saw go up and down Valladolid,
A man of mark, to know next time you saw.
His very serviceable suit of black
Was courtly once and conscientious still,
And many might have worn it, though none did:
The cloak, that somewhat shone and showed the threads,
Had purpose, and the ruff, significance.
He walked and tapped the pavement with his cane,
Scenting the world, looking it full in face,
An old dog, bald and blindish, at his heels.
They turned up, now, the alley by the church,
That leads nowhither; now, they breathed themselves
On the main promenade just at the wrong time:
You'd come upon his scrutinizing hat,
Making a peaked shade blacker than itself
Against the single window spared some house
Intact yet with its mouldered Moorish work, –
Or else surprise the ferrel of his stick
Trying the mortar's temper 'tween the chinks
Of some new shop a-building, French and fine.
He stood and watched the cobbler at his trade,
The man who slices lemons into drink,
The coffee-roaster's brazier, and the boys
That volunteer to help him turn its winch.
He glanced o'er books on stalls with half an eye,
And fly-leaf ballads on the vendor's string,
And broad-edge bold-print posters by the wall.
He took such cognizance of men and things,
If any beat a horse, you felt he saw;
If any cursed a woman, he took note;
Yet stared at nobody, – you stared at him,
And found, less to your pleasure than surprise,

He seemed to know you and expect as much.
So, next time that a neighbour's tongue was loosed,
It marked the shameful and notorious fact,
We had among us, not so much a spy,
As a recording chief-inquisitor,
The town's true master if the town but knew!
We merely kept a governor for form,
While this man walked about and took account
Of all thought, said and acted, then went home,
And wrote it fully to our Lord the King
Who has an itch to know things, he knows why,
And reads them in his bedroom of a night.
Oh, you might smile! there wanted not a touch,
A tang of . . . well, it was not wholly ease
As back into your mind the man's look came.
Stricken in years a little, – such a brow
His eyes had to live under! – clear as flint
On either side the formidable nose
Curved, cut and coloured like an eagle's claw.
Had he to do with A's surprising fate?
When altogether old B disappeared
And young C got his mistress, – was 't our friend,
His letter to the King that did it all?
What paid the bloodless man for so much pains?
Our Lord the King has favourites manifold,
And shifts his ministry some once a month;
Our city gets new governors at whiles, –
But never word or sign, that I could hear,
Notified to this man about the streets
The King's approval of those letters conned
The last thing duly at the dead of night.
Did the man love his office? Frowned our Lord,
Exhorting when none heard – 'Beseech me not!
'Too far above my people, – beneath me!
'I set the watch, – how should the people know?
'Forget them, keep me all the more in mind!'
Was some such understanding 'twixt the two?

I found no truth in one report at least –
That if you tracked him to his home, down lanes
Beyond the Jewry, and as clean to pace,
You found he ate his supper in a room
Blazing with lights, four Titians on the wall,
And twenty naked girls to change his plate!
Poor man, he lived another kind of life
In that new stuccoed third house by the bridge,
Fresh-painted, rather smart than otherwise!
The whole street might o'erlook him as he sat,
Leg crossing leg, one foot on the dog's back,
Playing a decent cribbage with his maid
(Jacynth, you're sure her name was) o'er the cheese
And fruit, three red halves of starved winter-pears,
Or treat of radishes in April. Nine,
Ten, struck the church clock, straight to bed went he.

My father, like the man of sense he was,
Would point him out to me a dozen times;
''St—'St,' he'd whisper, 'the Corregidor!'
I had been used to think that personage
Was one with lacquered breeches, lustrous belt,
And feathers like a forest in his hat,
Who blew a trumpet and proclaimed the news,
Announced the bull-fights, gave each church its turn,
And memorized the miracle in vogue!
He had a great observance from us boys;
We were in error; that was not the man.

I'd like now, yet had haply been afraid,
To have just looked, when this man came to die,
And seen who lined the clean gay garret-sides
And stood about the neat low truckle-bed,
With the heavenly manner of relieving guard.
Here had been, mark, the general-in-chief,
Thro' a whole campaign of the world's life and death,
Doing the King's work all the dim day long,

In his old coat and up to knees in mud,
Smoked like a herring, dining on a crust, –
And, now the day was won, relieved at once!
No further show or need for that old coat,
You are sure, for one thing! Bless us, all the while
How sprucely we are dressed out, you and I!
A second, and the angels alter that.
Well, I could never write a verse, – could you?
Let's to the Prado and make the most of time.

My Last Duchess

FERRARA

That's my last Duchess painted on the wall,
Looking as if she were alive. I call
That piece a wonder, now: Frà Pandolf's hands
Worked busily a day, and there she stands.
Will't please you sit and look at her? I said
'Frà Pandolf' by design, for never read
Strangers like you that pictured countenance,
The depth and passion of its earnest glance,
But to myself they turned (since none puts by
The curtain I have drawn for you, but I)
And seemed as they would ask me, if they durst,
How such a glance came there; so, not the first
Are you to turn and ask thus. Sir, 't was not
Her husband's presence only, called that spot
Of joy into the Duchess' cheek: perhaps
Frà Pandolf chanced to say 'Her mantle laps
'Over my lady's wrist too much,' or 'Paint
'Must never hope to reproduce the faint
'Half-flush that dies along her throat:' such stuff
Was courtesy, she thought, and cause enough
For calling up that spot of joy. She had
A heart – how shall I say? – too soon made glad,
Too easily impressed; she liked whate'er

She looked on, and her looks went everywhere.
Sir, 't was all one! My favour at her breast,
The dropping of the daylight in the West,
The bough of cherries some officious fool
Broke in the orchard for her, the white mule
She rode with round the terrace – all and each
Would draw from her alike the approving speech,
Or blush, at least. She thanked men, – good! but thanked
Somehow – I know not how – as if she ranked
My gift of a nine-hundred-years-old name
With anybody's gift. Who'd stoop to blame
This sort of trifling? Even had you skill
In speech – (which I have not) – to make your will
Quite clear to such an one, and say, 'Just this
'Or that in you disgusts me; here you miss,
'Or there exceed the mark' – and if she let
Herself be lessoned so, nor plainly set
Her wits to yours, forsooth, and made excuse,
– E'en then would be some stooping; and I choose
Never to stoop. Oh sir, she smiled, no doubt,
Whene'er I passed her; but who passed without
Much the same smile? This grew; I gave commands;
Then all smiles stopped together. There she stands
As if alive. Will 't please you rise? We'll meet
The company below, then. I repeat,
The Count your master's known munificence
Is ample warrant that no just pretence
Of mine for dowry will be disallowed;
Though his fair daughter's self, as I avowed
At starting, is my object. Nay, we'll go
Together down, sir. Notice Neptune, though,
Taming a sea-horse, thought a rarity,
Which Claus of Innsbruck cast in bronze for me!

ARTHUR HUGH CLOUGH

from The Bothie of Tober-Na-Vuolich

Nodding and beckoning across, observed of Attaché and
                              Guardsman:
Adam wouldn't speak, – indeed it was certain he couldn't;
Hewson could, and would if they wished; Philip Hewson a
                              poet,
Hewson a radical hot, hating lords and scorning ladies,
Silent mostly, but often reviling in fire and fury
Feudal tenures, mercantile lords, competition and bishops,
Liveries, armorial bearings, amongst other matters the
                              Game-laws:
He could speak, and was asked-to by Adam, but Lindsay
                              aloud cried
(Whisky was hot in his brain), Confound it, no, not Hewson,
A'nt he cock-sure to bring in his eternal political humbug?
However, so it must be, and after due pause of silence,
Waving his hand to Lindsay, and smiling oddly to Adam,
Up to them rose and spoke the poet and radical Hewson.
   I am, I think, perhaps the most perfect stranger present.
I have not, as have some of my friends, in my veins some
                              tincture,
Some few ounces of Scottish blood; no, nothing like it.
I am therefore perhaps the fittest to answer and thank you.
So I thank you, sir, for myself and for my companions,
Heartily thank you all for this unexpected greeting,
All the more welcome, as showing you do not account us
                              intruders,
Are not unwilling to see the north and the south forgather.
And, surely, seldom have Scotch and English more
                            thoroughly mingled;
Scarcely with warmer hearts, and clearer feeling of manhood
Even in tourney, and foray, and fray, and regular battle,
Where the life and the strength came out in the tug and
                              tussle,

Scarcely, where man met man, and soul encountered with
                                                soul, as
Close as do the bodies and twining limbs of the wrestlers,
When for a final bout are a day's two champions mated, –
In the grand old times of bows, and bills, and claymores,
At the old Flodden-field – or Bannockburn – or Culloden.
– (And he paused a moment, for breath, and because of some
                                                cheering,)
We are the better friends, I fancy, for that old fighting,
Better friends, inasmuch as we know each other the better,
We can now shake hands without pretending or shuffling.
     On this passage followed a great tornado of cheering,
Tables were rapped, feet stamped, a glass or two got broken:
He, ere the cheers died wholly away, and while still there
                                                was stamping,
Added, in altered voice, with a smile, his doubtful
                                                conclusion.
     I have, however, less claim than others perhaps to this
                                                honour,
For, let me say, I am neither game-keeper, nor
                                                game-preserver.
     So he said, and sat down, but his satire had not been
                                                taken.
Only the *men*, who were all on their legs as concerned in the
                                                thanking,
Were a trifle confused, but mostly sat down without
                                                laughing;
Lindsay alone, close-facing the chair, shook his fist at the
                                                speaker.
Only a Liberal member, away at the end of the table,
Started, remembering sadly the cry of a coming election,
Only the Attaché glanced at the Guardsman, who twirled his
                                                moustachio,
Only the Marquis faced round, but, not quite clear of the
                                                meaning,
Joined with the joyous Sir Hector, who lustily beat on the
                                                table.

And soon after the chairman arose, and the feast was over:
Now should the barn be cleared and forthwith adorned for
the dancing,
And, to make way for this purpose, the tutor and pupils
retiring
Were by the chieftain addressed and invited to come to the
castle.
But ere the door-way they quitted, a thin man clad as the
Saxon,
Trouser and cap and jacket of homespun blue, hand-woven,
Singled out, and said with determined accent to Hewson,
Touching his arm: Young man, if ye pass through the Braes
o' Lochaber,
See by the loch-side ye come to the Bothie of Tober-na-
vuolich.

(I, lines 122–179)

from The Bothie of Tober-Na-Vuolich

Ah, you have much to learn, we can't know all things at
twenty.
Partly you rest on truth, old truth, the duty of Duty,
Partly on error, you long for equality.
Ay, cried the Piper,
That's what it is, that confounded *égalité*, French
manufacture,
He is the same as the Chartist who spoke at a meeting in
Ireland,
What, and is not one man, fellow-men, as good as another?
Faith, replied Pat, *and a deal better too!*
So rattled the Piper:
But undisturbed in his tenor, the Tutor.
Partly in error
Seeking equality, *is not one woman as good as another?*
I with the Irishman answer, *Yes, better too*; the poorer
Better full oft than richer, than loftier better the lower.

Irrespective of wealth and of poverty, pain and enjoyment,
Women all have their duties, the one as well as the other;
Are all duties alike? Do all alike fulfil them?
However noble the dream of equality, mark you, Philip,
Nowhere equality reigns in all the world of creation,
Star is not equal to star, nor blossom the same as blossom;
Herb is not equal to herb, any more than planet to planet.
There is a glory of daisies, a glory again of carnations;
Were the carnation wise, in gay parterre by greenhouse,
Should it decline to accept the nurture the gardener gives it,
Should it refuse to expand to sun and genial summer,
Simply because the field-daisy, that grows in the grass-plat
                                                    beside it,
Cannot, for some cause or other, develope and be a
                                                    carnation?
Would not the daisy itself petition its scrupulous neighbour?
Up, grow, bloom, and forget me; be beautiful even to
                                                    proudness,
E'en for the sake of myself and other poor daisies like me.
Education and manners, accomplishments and refinements,
Waltz, peradventure, and polka, the knowledge of music
                                                    and drawing,
All these things are Nature's, to Nature dear and precious.
We have all something to do, man, woman alike, I own it;
We have all something to do, and in my judgement should
                                                    do it
In our station; not thinking about it, but not disregarding;
Holding it, not for enjoyment, but simply because we are in
                                                    it.

                                        (II, lines 168–201)

from The Bothie of Tober-Na-Vuolich

As at return of tide the total weight of ocean,
Drawn by moon and sun from Labrador and Greenland,
Sets-in amain, in the open space betwixt Mull and Scarba,
Heaving, swelling, spreading, the might of the mighty
                                                    Atlantic;
There into cranny and slit of the rocky, cavernous bottom
Settles down, and with dimples huge the smooth sea-surface
Eddies, coils, and whirls; by dangerous Corryvreckan:
So in my soul of souls through its cells and secret recesses,
Comes back, swelling and spreading, the old democratic
                                                    fervour.
But as the light of day enters some populous city,
Shaming away, ere it come, by the chilly day-streak signal,
High and low, the misusers of night, shaming out the gas
                                                    lamps –
All the great empty streets are flooded with broadening
                                                    clearness,
Which, withal, by inscrutable simultaneous access
Permeates far and pierces to the very cellars lying in
Narrow high back-lane, and court, and alley of alleys: –
He that goes forth to his walks, while speeding to the
                                                    suburb,
Sees sights only peaceful and pure; as labourers settling
Slowly to work, in their limbs the lingering sweetness of
                                                    slumber;
Humble market-carts, coming-in, bringing-in, not only
Flower, fruit, farm-store, but sounds and sights of the
                                                    country
Dwelling yet on the sense of the dreamy drivers; soon after
Half-awake servant-maids unfastening drowsy shutters
Up at the windows, or down, letting-in the air by the
                                                    doorway;
School-boys, school-girls soon, with slate, portfolio, satchel,
Hampered as they haste, those running, these others
                                                    maidenly tripping;

Early clerk anon turning out to stroll, or it may be
Meet his sweetheart – waiting behind the garden gate there;
Merchant on his grass-plat haply, bare-headed; and now by
                                                    this time
Little child bringing breakfast to 'father' that sits on the timber
There by the scaffolding; see, she waits for the can beside him;
Meantime above purer air untarnished of new-lit fires:
So that the whole great wicked artificial civilized fabric –
All its unfinished houses, lots for sale, and railway outworks –
Seems reaccepted, resumed to Primal Nature and Beauty: –
– Such – in me, and to me, and on me the love of Elspie!

                                            (IX, lines 73–108)

from The Bothie of Tober-Na-Vuolich

This is the letter of Hobbes the kilted and corpulent hero.
    So the last speech and confession is made, O my eloquent
                                                    speaker!
So *the good time* is *coming*, or come is it? O my chartist!
So the Cathedral is finished at last, O my Pugin of Women;
Finished, and now, is it true? to be taken out whole to New
                                                    Zealand!
Well, go forth to thy field, to thy barley, with Ruth, O Boaz,
Ruth, who for thee hath deserted her people, her gods, her
                                                    mountains.
Go, as in Ephrath of old, in the gate of Bethlehem said they,
Go, be the wife in thy house both Rachel and Leah unto thee!
Be thy wedding of silver, albeit of iron thy bedstead!
Yea, to the full golden fifty renewed be! and fair memoranda
Happily fill the fly-leaves duly left in the Family Bible.
Live, and when Hobbes is forgotten, may'st thou, an
                                            unroasted Grandsire,
See thy children's children, and Democracy upon New
                                                    Zealand!

                                            (IX, lines 149–162)

from Amours De Voyage

CLAUDE TO EUSTACE

What do the people say, and what does the government do?
                                        – you
Ask, and I know not at all. Yet fortune will favour your
                                        hopes; and
I, who avoided it all, am fated, it seems, to describe it.
I, who nor meddle nor make in politics, – I who sincerely
Put not my trust in leagues nor any suffrage by ballot,
Never predicted Parisian millenniums, never beheld a
New Jerusalem coming down dressed like a bride out of
                                        heaven
Right on the Place de la Concorde, – I, nevertheless, let me
                                        say it,
Could in my soul of souls, this day, with the Gaul at the
                                        gates, shed
One true tear for thee, thou poor little Roman Republic!
What, with the German restored, with Sicily safe to the
                                        Bourbon,
Not leave one poor corner for native Italian exertion?
France, it is fouly done! and you, poor foolish England, –
You, who a twelvemonth ago said nations must choose for
                                        themselves, you
Could not, of course, interfere, – you, now, when a nation
                                        has chosen—
Pardon this folly! *The Times* will, of course, have announced
                                        the occasion,
Told you the news of to-day; and although it was slightly in
                                        error
When it proclaimed as a fact the Apollo was sold to a Yankee,
You may believe when it tells you the French are at Civita
                                        Vecchia.

                                        (Canto II, 1)

from Amours De Voyage

CLAUDE TO EUSTACE

Dulce it is, and *decorum*, no doubt, for the country to fall, – to
Offer one's blood an oblation to Freedom, and die for the
                                                    Cause; yet
Still, individual culture is also something, and no man
Finds quite distinct the assurance that he of all others is
                                                    called on,
Or would be justified, even, in taking away from the world
                                                    that
Precious creature, himself. Nature sent him here to abide
                                                    here,
Else why sent him at all? Nature wants him still, it is likely.
On the whole, we are meant to look after ourselves; it is
                                                    certain
Each has to eat for himself, digest for himself, and in general
Care for his own dear life, and see to his own preservation;
Nature's intentions, in most things uncertain, in this are
                                                    decisive;
Which, on the whole, I conjecture the Romans will follow,
                                                    and I shall.
  So we cling to our rocks like limpets; Ocean may bluster,
Over and under and round us; we open our shells to imbibe
                                                    our
Nourishment, close them again, and are safe, fulfilling the
                                                    purpose
Nature intended, – a wise one, of course, and a noble, we
                                                    doubt not.
Sweet it may be and decorous, perhaps, for the country to
                                                    die; but,
On the whole, we conclude the Romans won't do it, and I
                                                    shan't.

                                                (Canto II, 2)

from Amours De Voyage

CLAUDE TO EUSTACE

Will they fight? They say so. And will the French? I can
                                                    hardly,
Hardly think so; and yet—He is come, they say, to Palo,
He is passed from Monterone, at Santa Severa
He hath laid up his guns. But the Virgin, the Daughter of
                                                    Roma,
She hath despised thee and laughed thee to scorn, – the
                                        Daughter of Tiber,
She hath shaken her head and built barricades against thee!
Will they fight? I believe it. Alas! 'tis ephemeral folly,
Vain and ephemeral folly, of course, compared with pictures,
Statues, and antique gems! – Indeed: and yet indeed too,
Yet, methought, in broad day did I dream, – tell it not in St.
                                                    James's,
Whisper it not in thy courts, O Christ Church! – yet did I,
                                                    waking,
Dream of a cadence that sings, *Si tombent nos jeunes héros, la*
Terre en produit de nouveaux contre vous tous prêts à se battre;
Dreamt of great indignations and angers transcendental,
Dreamt of a sword at my side and a battle-horse underneath
                                                    me.

(Canto II, 3)

from Amours De Voyage

VIII. GEORGINA TREVELLYN TO LOUISA —
Only think, dearest Louisa, what fearful scenes we have
                                        witnessed! –
*   *   *   *   *   *   *   *
George has just seen Garibaldi, dressed up in a long white
                                        cloak, on
Horseback, riding by, with his mounted negro behind him:
This is a man, you know, who came from America with him,
Out of the woods, I suppose, and uses a *lasso* in fighting,
Which is, I don't quite know, but a sort of noose, I imagine;
This he throws on the heads of the enemy's men in a battle,
Pulls them into his reach, and then most cruelly kills them:
Mary does not believe, but we heard it from an Italian.
Mary allows she was wrong about Mr Claude *being selfish*;
He was *most* useful and kind on the terrible thirtieth of April.
Do not write here any more; we are starting directly for
                                        Florence:
We should be off to-morrow, if only Papa could get horses;
All have been seized everywhere for the use of this dreadful
                                        Mazzini.

                            (Canto II, 8, lines 219–232)

from Amours De Voyage

CLAUDE TO EUSTACE

Farewell, Politics, utterly! What can I do? I cannot
Fight, you know; and to talk I am wholly ashamed. And
                                                    although I
Gnash my teeth when I look in your French or your English
                                                    papers,
What is the good of that? Will swearing, I wonder, mend
                                                    matters?
Cursing and scolding repel the assailants? No, it is idle;
No, whatever befalls, I will hide, will ignore or forget it.
Let the tail shift for itself; I will bury my head. And what's
                                                    the
Roman Republic to me, or I to the Roman Republic?
  Why not fight? – In the first place, I haven't so much as a
                                                    musket;
In the next, if I had, I shouldn't know how I should use it;
In the third, just at present I'm studying ancient marbles;
In the fourth, I consider I owe my life to my country;
In the fifth, – I forget, but four good reasons are ample.
Meantime, pray, let 'em fight, and be killed. I delight in
                                                    devotion.
So that I 'list not, hurrah for the glorious army of martyrs!
Sanguis martyrum semen Ecclesia; though it would seem this
Church is indeed of the purely Invisible, Kingdom-come
                                                    kind:
Militant here on earth! Triumphant, of course, then,
                                                    elsewhere!
Ah, good Heaven, but I would I were out far away from the
                                                    pother!

                                                    (Canto III, 3)

from Dipsychus

Spirit

As I sat at the café, I said to myself,
They may talk as they please about what they call pelf,
They may sneer as they like about eating and drinking,
But help it I cannot, I cannot help thinking
   How pleasant it is to have money, heigh ho!
   How pleasant it is to have money.

I sit at my table *en grand seigneur,*
And when I have done, throw a crust to the poor;
Not only the pleasure, one's self, of good living,
But also the pleasure of now and then giving.
   So pleasant it is to have money, heigh ho!
   So pleasant it is to have money.

It was but last winter I came up to Town,
But already I'm getting a little renown;
I make new acquaintance where'er I appear;
I am not too shy, and have nothing to fear.
   So pleasant it is to have money, heigh ho!
   So pleasant it is to have money.

I drive through the streets, and I care not a d—mn;
The people they stare, and they ask who I am;
And if I should chance to run over a cad,
I can pay for the damage if ever so bad.
   So pleasant it is to have money, heigh ho!
   So pleasant it is to have money.

We stroll to our box and look down on the pit,
And if it weren't low should be tempted to spit;
We loll and we talk until people look up,
And when it's half over we go out and sup.
   So pleasant it is to have money, heigh ho!
   So pleasant it is to have money.

The best of the tables and best of the fare –
And as for the others, the devil may care;
It isn't our fault if they dare not afford
To sup like a prince and be drunk as a lord.
    So pleasant it is to have money, heigh ho!
    So pleasant it is to have money.

We sit at our tables and tipple champagne;
Ere one bottle goes, comes another again;
The waiters they skip and they scuttle about,
And the landlord attends us so civilly out.
    So pleasant it is to have money, heigh ho!
    So pleasant it is to have money.

It was but last winter I came up to town,
But already I'm getting a little renown;
I get to good houses without much ado,
Am beginning to see the nobility too.
    So pleasant it is to have money, heigh ho!
    So pleasant it is to have money.

O dear! what a pity they ever should lose it!
For they are the gentry that know how to use it;
So grand and so graceful, such manners, such dinners,
But yet, after all, it is we are the winners.
    So pleasant it is to have money, heigh ho!
    So pleasant it is to have money.

Thus I sat at my table *en grand seigneur*,
And when I had done threw a crust to the poor;
Not only the pleasure, one's self, of good eating,
But also the pleasure of now and then treating.
    So pleasant it is to have money, heigh ho!
    So pleasant it is to have money.

                                    (Scene V, lines 130–189)

The Orange Lily

Oh, did you go to see the show,
  Each rose and pink and lily O,
To feast your eyes upon the prize
  Won by the Orange Lily O?

The Viceroy there so debonair,
  Just like a daffydilly O,
And Lady Clarke, blithe as a lark,
  Approached the Orange Lily O.

Then heigh-ho the Lily O,
  The royal loyal Lily O,
Beneath the sky what flow'r can vie
  With Ireland's Orange Lily O.

The elated muse, to hear the news,
  Jumped like a Connacht filly O,
As gossip fame did loud proclaim
  The triumph of the Lily O.

The lowland field may roses yield,
  Gay heaths the highlands hilly O,
But high or low, no flower can show
  Like the glorious Orange Lily O.

Let dandies fine in Bond Street shine,
  Gay nymphs in Piccadilly,
But fine or gay will yield the day
  To Erin's Orange Lily O.

Then heigh-ho the Lily O,
　The royal, loyal Lily O,
There's not a flower in Erin's bower,
　Can match the Orange Lily O.

So come brave boys and share her joys
　And drink a health to Willy O,
Who bravely wore on Boyne's red shore
　The royal loyal Lily O.

ALFRED, LORD TENNYSON

from Maud; A Monodrama

I hate the dreadful hollow behind the little wood,
Its lips in the field above are dabbled with blood-red heath,
The red-ribbed ledges drip with a silent horror of blood,
And Echo there, whatever is asked her, answers 'Death'.

For there in the ghastly pit long since a body was found,
His who had given me life – O father! O God! was it well? –
Mangled, and flattened, and crushed, and dinted into the
        ground:
There yet lies the rock that fell with him when he fell.

Did he fling himself down? who knows? for a vast
        speculation had failed,
And ever he muttered and maddened, and ever wanned
        with despair,
And out he walked when the wind like a broken worldling
        wailed,
And the flying gold of the ruined woodlands drove through
        the air.

I remember the time, for the roots of my hair were stirred
By a shuffled step, by a dead weight trailed, by a whispered
        fright,
And my pulses closed their gates with a shock on my heart as
        I heard
The shrill-edged shriek of a mother divide the shuddering
        night.

Villainy somewhere! whose? One says, we are villains all.
Not he: his honest fame should at least by me be maintained:
But that old man, now lord of the broad estate and the Hall,
Dropt off gorged from a scheme that had left us flaccid and
        drained.

Why do they prate of the blessings of Peace? we have made
them a curse,
Pickpockets, each hand lusting for all that is not its own;
And lust of gain, in the spirit of Cain, is it better or worse
Than the heart of the citizen hissing in war on his own
hearthstone?

But these are the days of advance, the works of the men of
mind,
When who but a fool would have faith in a tradesman's ware
or his word?
Is it peace of war? Civil war, as I think, and that of a kind
The viler, as underhand, not openly bearing the sword.

Sooner or later I too may passively take the print
Of the golden age – why not? I have neither hope nor trust;
May make my heart as a millstone, set my face as a flint,
Cheat and be cheated, and die: who knows? we are ashes
and dust.

Peace sitting under her olive, and slurring the day gone by,
When the poor are hovelled and hustled together, each sex,
like swine,
When only the ledger lives, and when only not all men lie;
Peace in her vineyard – yes! – but a company forges the wine.

And the vitriol madness flushes up in the ruffian's head,
Till the filthy by-lane rings to the yell of the trampled wife,
And chalk and alum and plaster are sold to the poor for bread
And the spirit of murder works in the very means of life,

And Sleep must lie down armed, for the villainous centre-bits
Grind on the wakeful ear in the hush of the moonless nights,
While another is cheating the sick of a few last gasps, as he
sits
To pestle a poisoned chalice behind his crimson lights.

When a Mammonite mother kills her babe for a burial fee,
And Timour-Mammon grins on a pile of children's bones,
Is it peace or war? better, war! loud war by land and by sea,
War with a thousand battles, and shaking a hundred
                                                    thrones.

(Part I, 1–12)

WALT WHITMAN

'One's-Self I Sing'

One's-Self I sing, a simple separate person,
Yet utter the word Democratic, the word En-Masse.

Of physiology from top to toe I sing,
Not physiognomy alone nor brain alone is worthy for the
   Muse, I say the Form complete is worthier far,
The Female equally with the Male I sing.

Of Life immense in passion, pulse, and power,
Cheerful, for freest action form'd under the laws divine,
The Modern Man I sing.

from By Blue Ontario's Shore

Are you he who would assume a place to teach or be a poet
   here in the States?
The place is august, the terms obdurate.

Who would assume to teach here may well prepare himself
   body and mind,
He may well survey, ponder, arm, fortify, harden, make lithe
   himself,
He shall surely be question'd beforehand by me with many
   and stern questions.

Who are you indeed who would talk or sing to America?
Have you studied out the land, its idioms and men?
Have you learn'd the physiology, phrenology, politics,
   geography, pride, freedom, friendship of the land? its
   substratums and objects?

Have you consider'd the organic compact of the first day of
    the first year of Independence, sign'd by the
    Commissioners, ratified by the States, and read by
    Washington at the head of the army?
Have you possess'd yourself of the Federal Constitution?
Do you see who have left all feudal processes and poems
    behind them, and assumed the poems and processes of
    Democracy?
Are you faithful to things? do you teach what the land and
    sea, the bodies of men, womanhood, amativeness, heroic
    angers, teach?
Have you sped through fleeting customs, popularities?
Can you hold your hand against all seductions, follies,
    whirls, fierce contentions? are you very strong? are you
    really of the whole People?
Are you not of some coterie? some school or mere religion?
Are you done with reviews and criticisms of life? animating
    now to life itself?
Have you vivified yourself from the maternity of these
    States?
Have you too the old ever-fresh forbearance and impartiality?
Do you hold the like love for those hardening to maturity? for
    the last-born? little and big? and for the errant?

What is this you bring my America?
Is it uniform with my country?
Is it not something that has been better told or done before?
Have you not imported this or the spirit of it in some ship?
Is it not a mere tale? a rhyme? a prettiness? – is the good old
    cause in it?
Has it not dangled long at the heels of the poets, politicians,
    literats, of enemies' lands?
Does it not assume that what is notoriously gone is still here?
Does it answer universal needs? will it improve manners?
Does it sound with trumpet-voice the proud victory of the
    Union in that secession war?
Can your performance face the open fields and the seaside?

Will it absorb into me as I absorb food, air, to appear again in
my strength, gait, face?
Have real employments contributed to it? original makers,
not mere amanuenses?
Does it meet modern discoveries, calibres, facts, face to face?
What does it mean to American persons, progresses, cities?
Chicago, Kanada, Arkansas?
Does it see behind the apparent custodians the real
custodians standing, menacing, silent, the mechanics,
Manhattanese, Western men, Southerners, significant
alike in their apathy, and in the promptness of their love?
Does it see what finally befalls, and has always finally
befallen, each temporizer, patcher, outsider, partialist,
alarmist, infidel, who has ever ask'd any thing of America?
What mocking and scornful negligence?
The track strew'd with the dust of skeletons,
By the roadside others disdainfully toss'd.

Rhymes and rhymers, pass away, poems distill'd from
poems pass away,
The swarms of reflectors and the polite pass, and leave ashes
Admirers, importers, obedient persons, make but the soil of
literature,
America justifies itself, give it time, no disguise can deceive it
or conceal from it, it is impassive enough,
Only toward the likes of itself will it advance to meet them,
If its poets appear it will in due time advance to meet them,
there is no fear of mistake,
(The proof of a poet shall be sternly deferr'd till his country
absorbs him as affectionately as he has absorb'd it.)

He masters whose spirit masters, he tastes sweetest who
results sweetest in the long run,
The blood of the brawn beloved of time is unconstraint;
In the need of songs, philosophy, and appropriate native
grand-opera, shipcraft, any craft,
He or she is greatest who contributes the greatest original
practical example.

Already a nonchalant breed, silently emerging, appears on
the streets,
People's lips salute only doers, lovers, satisfiers, positive
knowers,
There will shortly be no more priests, I say their work is
done,
Death is without emergencies here, but life is perpetual
emergencies here,
Are your body, days, manners, superb? after death you shall
be superb,
Justice, health, self-esteem, clear the way with irresistible
power;
How dare you place any thing before a man?

(Sections 12 and 13)

'When Lilacs Last in the Dooryard Bloom'd'

1

When lilacs last in the dooryard bloom'd,
And the great star early droop'd in the western sky in the
night,
I mourn'd, and yet shall mourn with ever-returning spring.

Ever-returning spring, trinity sure to me you bring,
Lilac blooming perennial and drooping star in the west,
And thought of him I love.

2

O powerful western fallen star!
O shades of night – O moody, tearful night!
O great star disappear'd – O the black murk that hides the
star!
O cruel hands that hold me powerless – O helpless soul of
me!
O harsh surrounding cloud that will not free my soul.

3

In the dooryard fronting an old farm-house near the white-
    wash'd palings,
Stands the lilac-bush tall-growing with heart-shaped leaves
    of rich green,
With many a pointed blossom rising delicate, with the
    perfume strong I love,
With every leaf a miracle – and from this bush in the
    dooryard,
With delicate-color'd blossoms and heart-shaped leaves of
    rich green,
A sprig with its flower I break.

4

In the swamp in secluded recesses,
A shy and hidden bird is warbling a song.

Solitary the thrush,
The hermit withdrawn to himself, avoiding the settlements,
Sings by himself a song.

Song of the bleeding throat,
Death's outlet song of life, (for well dear brother I know,
If thou wast not granted to sing thou would'st surely die.)

5

Over the breast of the spring, the land, amid cities,
Amid lanes and through old woods, where lately the violets
    peep'd from the ground, spotting the gray debris,
Amid the grass in the fields each side of the lanes, passing
    the endless grass,
Passing the yellow-spear'd wheat, every grain from its
    shroud in the dark-brown fields uprisen,
Passing the apple-tree blows of white and pink in the
    orchards,
Carrying a corpse to where it shall rest in the grave,
Night and day journeys a coffin.

6

Coffin that passes through lanes and streets,
Through day and night with the great cloud darkening the
    land,
With the pomp of the inloop'd flags with the cities draped in
    black,
With the show of the States themselves as of crape-veil'd
    women standing,
With processions long and winding and the flambeaus of the
    night,
With the countless torches lit, with the silent sea of faces and
    the unbared heads,
With the waiting depot, the arriving coffin, and the sombre
    faces,
With dirges through the night, with the thousand voices
    rising strong and solemn,
With all the mournful voices of the dirges pour'd around the
    coffin,
The dim-lit churches and the shuddering organs – where
    amid these you journey,
With the tolling tolling bells' perpetual clang,
Here, coffin that slowly passes,
I give you my sprig of lilac.

7

(Nor for you, for one alone,
Blossoms and branches green to coffins all I bring,
For fresh as the morning, thus would I chant a song for you
    O sane and sacred death.

All over bouquets of roses,
O death, I cover you over with roses and early lilies,
But mostly and now the lilac that blooms the first,
Copious I break, I break the sprigs from the bushes,
With loaded arms I come, pouring for you,
For you and the coffins all of you O death.)

8

O western orb sailing the heaven,
Now I know what you must have meant as a month since I
    walk'd,
As I walk'd in silence the transparent shadowy night,
As I saw you had something to tell as you bent to me night
    after night,
As you droop'd from the sky low down as if to my side,
    (while the other stars all look'd on,)
As we wander'd together the solemn night, (for something I
    know not what kept me from sleep,)
As the night advanced, and I saw on the rim of the west how
    full you were of woe,
As I stood on the rising ground in the breeze in the cool
    transparent night,
As I watch'd where you pass'd and was lost in the
    netherward black of the night,
As my soul in its trouble dissatisfied sank, as where you sad
    orb,
Concluded, dropt in the night, and was gone.

9

Sing on there in the swamp,
O singer bashful and tender, I hear your notes, I hear your
    call,
I hear, I come presently, I understand you,
But a moment I linger, for the lustrous star has detain'd me,
The star my departing comrade holds and detains me.

10

O how shall I warble myself for the dead one there I loved?
And how shall I deck my song for the large sweet soul that
    has gone?
And what shall my perfume be for the grave of him I love?

Sea-winds blown from east and west,
Blown from the Eastern sea and blown from the Western sea,
   till there on the prairies meeting,
These and with these and the breath of my chant,
I'll perfume the grave of him I love.

11

O what shall I hang on the chamber walls?
And what shall the pictures be that I hang on the walls,
To adorn the burial-house of him I love?

Pictures of growing spring and farms and homes,
With the Fourth-month eve at sundown, and the gray smoke
   lucid and bright,
With floods of the yellow gold of the gorgeous, indolent,
   sinking sun, burning, expanding the air,
With the fresh sweet herbage under foot, and the pale green
   leaves of the trees prolific,
In the distance the flowing glaze, the breast of the river, with
   a wind-dapple here and there,
With ranging hills on the banks, with many a line against the
   sky, and shadows,
And the city at hand with dwellings so dense, and stacks of
   chimneys,
And all the scenes of life and the workshops, and the
   workmen homeward returning.

12

Lo, body and soul – this land,
My own Manhattan with spires, and the sparkling and
   hurrying tides, and the ships,
The varied and ample land, the South and the North in the
   light, Ohio's shores and flashing Missouri,
And ever the far-spreading prairies cover'd with grass and
   corn.

Lo, the most excellent sun so calm and haughty,
The violet and purple morn with just-felt breezes,
The gentle soft-born measureless light,
The miracle spreading bathing all, the fulfill'd noon,
The coming eve delicious, the welcome night and the stars,
Over my cities shining all, enveloping man and land.

13

Sing on, sing on you gray-brown bird,
Sing from the swamps, the recesses, pour your chant from
    the bushes,
Limitless out of the dusk, out of the cedars and pines.

Sing on dearest brother, warble your reedy song,
Loud human song, with voice of uttermost woe.

O liquid and free and tender!
O wild and loose to my soul – O wondrous singer!
You only I hear – yet the star holds me, (but will soon depart,)
4,6,14Yet the lilac with mastering odor holds me.

14

Now while I sat in the day and look'd forth,
In the close of the day with its light and the fields of spring,
    and the farmers preparing their crops,
In the large unconscious scenery of my land with its lakes
    and forests,
In the heavenly aerial beauty, (after the perturb'd winds and
    the storms,)
Under the arching heavens of the afternoon swift passing,
    and the voices of children and women,
The many-moving sea-tides, and I saw the ships how they
    sail'd,
And the summer approaching with richness, and the fields
    all busy with labor,
And the infinite separate houses, how they all went on, each
    with its meals and minutia of daily usages,

And the streets how their throbbings throbb'd, and the cities
    pent – lo, then and there,
Falling upon them all and among them all, enveloping me
    with the rest,
Appear'd the cloud, appear'd the long black trail,
And I knew death, its thought, and the sacred knowledge of
    death.
Then with the knowledge of death as walking one side of me,
And the thought of death close-walking the other side of me,
And I in the middle as the companions, and as holding the
    hands of companions,
I fled forth to the hiding receiving night that talks not,
Down to the shores of the water, the path by the swamp in
    the dimness,
To the solemn shadowy cedars and ghostly pines so still.

And the singer so shy to the rest receiv'd me,
The gray-brown bird I know receiv'd us comrades three,
And he sang the carol of death, and a verse for him I love.

From deep secluded recesses,
From the fragrant cedars and the ghostly pines so still,
Came the carol of the bird.

And the charm of the carol rapt me,
As I held as if by their hands my comrades in the night,
And the voice of my spirit tallied the song of the bird.
Come lovely and soothing death,
Undulate round the world, serenely arriving, arriving,
In the day, in the night, to all, to each,
Sooner or later delicate death.

Prais'd be the fathomless universe,
For life and joy, and for objects and knowledge curious,
And for love, sweet love – but praise! praise! praise!
For the sure-enwinding arms of cool-enfolding death.

Dark mother always gliding near with soft feet,
Have none chanted for thee a chant of fullest welcome?
Then I chant it for thee, I glorify thee above all,
I bring thee a song that when thou must indeed come, come
  unfalteringly.

Approach strong deliveress,
When it is so, when thou hast taken them I joyously sing the dead,
Lost in the loving floating ocean of thee,
Laved in the flood of thy bliss O death.

From me to thee glad serenades,
Dances for thee I propose saluting thee, adornments and feastings
  for thee,
And the sights of the open landscape and the high-spread sky are
  fitting,
And life and the fields, and the huge and thoughtful night.

The night in silence under many a star,
The ocean shore and the husky whispering wave whose voice I know,
And the soul turning to thee O vast and well-veil'd death,
And the body gratefully nestling close to thee.

Over the tree-tops I float thee a song,
Over the rising and sinking waves, over the myriad fields and the
  prairies wide,
Over the dense-pack'd cities all and the teeming wharves and ways,
I float this carol with joy, with joy to thee O death.

15

To the tally of my soul,
Loud and strong kept up the gray-brown bird,
With pure deliberate notes spreading filling the night.

Loud in the pines and cedars dim,
Clear in the freshness moist and the swamp-perfume,
And I with my comrades there in the night.

While my sight that was bound in my eyes unclosed,
As to long panoramas of visions.

And I saw askant the armies,
I saw as in noiseless dreams hundreds of battle-flags,
Borne through the smoke of the battles and pierc'd with
    missiles I saw them,
And carried hither and yon through the smoke, and torn and
    bloody,
And at last but a few shreds left on the staffs, (and all in
    silence,)
And the staffs all splinter'd and broken.

I saw battle-corpses, myriads of them,
And the white skeletons of young men, I saw them,
I saw the debris and debris of all the slain soldiers of the war,
But I saw they were not as was thought,
They themselves were fully at rest, they suffer'd not,
The living remain'd and suffer'd, the mother suffer'd,
And the wife and the child and the musing comrade suffer'd,
And the armies that remain'd suffer'd.

16

Passing the visions, passing the night,
Passing, unloosing the hold of my comrades' hands,
Passing the song of the hermit bird and the tallying song of
    my soul,
Victorious song, death's outlet song, yet varying ever-
    altering song,
As low and wailing, yet clear the notes, rising and falling,
    flooding the night,
Sadly sinking and fainting, as warning and warning, and yet
    again bursting with joy,
Covering the earth and filling the spread of the heaven,
As that powerful psalm in the night I heard from recesses,
Passing, I leave thee lilac with heart-shaped leaves,

I leave thee there in the door-yard, blooming, returning with
    spring.
I cease from my song for thee,
From my gaze on thee in the west, fronting the west,
    communing with thee,
O comrade lustrous with silver face in the night.

Yet each to keep and all, retrievements out of the night,
The song, the wondrous chant of the gray-brown bird,
And the tallying chant, the echo arous'd in my soul,
With the lustrous and drooping star with the countenance
    full of woe,
With the holders holding my hand nearing the call of the
    bird,
Comrades mine and I in the midst, and their memory ever to
    keep, for the dead I loved so well,
For the sweetest, wisest soul of all my days and lands – and
    this for his dear sake,
Lilac and star and bird twined with the chant of my soul,
There in the fragrant pines and the cedars dusk and dim.

ARTHUR RIMBAUD

from Eighteen-Seventy

I

A POSTER OF OUR DAZZLING VICTORY AT SAARBRUCKEN

In the centre of the poster, Napoleon
rides in apotheosis, sallow, medalled, a ramrod
perched on a merrygoround horse. He sees life
through rosy glasses, terrible as God,

and sentimental as a bourgeois papa.
Four little conscripts take their nap below
on scarlet guns and drums. One, unbuckling, cheers
Napoleon – he's stunned by the big name!

Another lounges on the butt of his Chassepot,
another feels his hair rise on his neck.
A bearskin shako bounds like a black sun:

VIVE L'EMPEREUR! They're holding back their breath.
And last, some moron, struggling to his knees,
presents a blue and scarlet ass – to what?

II

NAPOLEON AFTER SEDAN

The man waxy – he jogs along the fields
in flower, black, a cigar between his teeth.
The wax man thinks about the Tuilleries
in flower. At times his mossy eye takes fire.

Twenty years of orgy have made him drunk:
he'd said: 'My hand will snuff out Liberty,
politely, gently, as I snuff my stogie.'
Liberty lives; the Emperor is out –

he's captured. Oh what name is shaking on
his lips? What plebescites? Napoleon
cannot tell you. His shark's eye is dead.

An opera glass on the horses at Compere . . .
he watches his cigar fume off in smoke . . .
soirées at Saint Cloud . . . a bluish vapour.

III
TO THE FRENCH OF THE SECOND EMPIRE

You, dead in '92 and '93,
still pale from the great kiss of Liberty –
when tyrants trampled on humanity,
you broke them underneath your wooden shoes.

You were reborn and great by agony,
your hearts in rage still beat for our salvation –
Oh soldiers, sown by death, your noble lover,
in our old furrows you regenerate!

You, whose life-blood washed our soiled standards red,
the dead of Valmy, Italy, Fleurus,
thousands of Christs, red-bonneted . . . we

have let you die with our Republic, we
who lick the boots of our bored kings like dogs –
men of the Second Empire, I mean you!

                                    trans. Robert Lowell

GERARD MANLEY HOPKINS

Tom's Garland

upon the Unemployed

Tom – garlanded with squat and surly steel
Tom; then Tom's fallowbootfellow piles pick
By him and rips out rockfire homeforth – sturdy Dick;
Tom Heart-at-ease, Tom Navvy: he is all for his meal
Sure, 's bed now. Low be it: lustily he his low lot (feel
That ne'er need hunger, Tom; Tom seldom sick,
Seldomer heartsore; that treads through, prickproof, thick
Thousands of thorns, thoughts) swings though.
                                        Commonweal
Little I reck ho! lacklevel in, if all had bread:
What! Country is honour enough in all us – lordly head,
With heaven's lights high hung round, or, mother-ground
That mammocks, mighty foot. But nó way sped,
Nor mind nor mainstrength; gold go garlanded
With, perilous, O nó; nor yet plod safe shod sound;
                        Undenizened, beyond bound
Of earth's glory, earth's ease, all; no one, nowhere,
In wide the world's weal; rare gold, bold steel, bare
                In both; care, but share care –
This, by Despair, bred Hangdog dull; by Rage,
Manwolf, worse; and their packs infest the age.

JOHN DAVIDSON

Thirty Bob a Week

I couldn't touch a stop and turn a screw,
   And set the blooming world a-work for me,
Like such as cut their teeth – I hope, like you –
   On the handle of a skeleton gold key;
I cut mine on a leek, which I eat it every week:
   I'm a clerk at thirty bob as you can see.

But I don't allow it's luck and all a toss;
   There's no such thing as being starred and crossed;
It's just the power of some to be a boss;
   And the bally power of others to be bossed:
I face the music, sir; you bet I ain't a cur;
   Strike me lucky if I don't believe I'm lost!

For like a mole I journey in the dark,
   A-travelling along the underground
From my Pillar'd Halls and broad Suburbean Park,
   To come the daily dull official round;
And home again at night with my pipe all alight,
   A-scheming how to count ten bob a pound.

And it's often very cold and very wet,
   And my missis stitches towels for a hunks;
And the Pillar'd Halls is half of it to let –
   Three rooms about the size of travelling trunks.
And we cough, my wife and I, to dislocate a sigh,
   When the noisy little kids are in their bunks.

But you never hear her do a growl or whine,
   For she's made of flint and roses, very odd;
And I've got to cut my meaning rather fine,
   Or I'd blubber, for I'm made of greens and sod:
So p'r'aps we are in Hell for all that I can tell,
   And lost and damn'd and served up hot to God.

I ain't blaspheming, Mr Silver-tongue;
   I'm saying things a bit beyond your art:
Of all the rummy starts you ever sprung,
   Thirty bob a week's the rummiest start!
With your science and your books and your the'ries about
                              spooks,
   Did you ever hear of looking in your heart?

I didn't mean your pocket, Mr, no:
   I mean that having children and a wife,
With thirty bob on which to come and go,
   Isn't dancing to the tabor and the fife:
When it doesn't make you drink, by Heaven! it makes you
                              think,
   And notice curious items about life.

I step into my heart and there I meet
   A god-almighty devil singing small,
Who would like to shout and whistle in the street,
   And squelch the passers flat against the wall;
If the whole world was a cake he had the power to take,
   He would take it, ask for more, and eat it all.

And I meet a sort of simpleton beside,
   The kind that life is always giving beans;
With thirty bob a week to keep a bride
   He fell in love and married in his teens:
At thirty bob he stuck; but he knows it isn't luck:
   He knows the seas are deeper than tureens.

And the god-almighty devil and the fool
  That meet me in the High Street on the strike,
When I walk about my heart a-gathering wool,
  Are my good and evil angels if you like.
And both of them together in every kind of weather
  Ride me like a double-seated bike.

That's rough a bit and needs its meaning curled.
  But I have a high old hot un in my mind –
A most engrugious notion of the world,
  That leaves your lightning 'rithmetic behind:
I give it at a glance when I say 'There ain't no chance,
  Nor nothing of the lucky-lottery kind.'

And it's this way that I make it out to be:
  No fathers, mothers, countries, climates – none;
Not Adam was responsible for me,
  Nor society, nor systems, nary one:
A little sleeping seed, I woke – I did, indeed –
  A million years before the blooming sun.

I woke because I thought the time had come;
  Beyond my will there was no other cause;
And everywhere I found myself at home,
  Because I chose to be the thing I was;
And in whatever shape of mollusc or of ape
  I always went according to the laws.

I was the love that chose my mother out;
  I joined two lives and from the union burst;
My weakness and my strength without a doubt
  Are mine alone for ever from the first:
It's just the very same with a difference in the name
  As 'Thy will be done.' You say it if you durst!

They say it daily up and down the land
  As easy as you take a drink, it's true;
But the difficultest go to understand,
  And the difficultest job a man can do,
Is to come it brave and meek with thirty bob a week,
  And feel that that's the proper thing for you.

It's naked child against a hungry wolf;
  It's playing bowls upon a splitting wreck;
It's walking on a string across a gulf
  With millstones fore-and-aft about your neck;
But the thing is daily done by many and many a one;
  And we fall, face forward, fighting, on the deck.

Recessional

1897

God of our fathers, known of old,
  Lord of our far-flung battle-line,
Beneath whose awful Hand we hold
  Dominion over palm and pine –
Lord God of Hosts, be with us yet,
Lest we forget – lest we forget!

The tumult and the shouting dies;
  The Captains and the Kings depart:
Still stands Thine ancient sacrifice,
  An humble and a contrite heart.
Lord God of Hosts, be with us yet,
Lest we forget – lest we forget!

Far-called, our navies melt away;
  On dune and headland sinks the fire:
Lo, all our pomp of yesterday
  Is one with Nineveh and Tyre!
Judge of the Nations, spare us yet,
Lest we forget – lest we forget!

If, drunk with sight of power, we loose
  Wild tongues that have not Thee in awe,
Such boastings as the Gentiles use,
  Or lesser breeds without the Law –
Lord God of Hosts, be with us yet,
Lest we forget – lest we forget!

For heathen heart that puts her trust
  In reeking tube and iron shard,
All valiant dust that builds on dust,
  And guarding, calls not Thee to guard.
For frantic boast and foolish word –
Thy mercy on Thy People, Lord!

The White Man's Burden

1899
(The United States and the Philippine Islands)

Take up the White Man's burden –
  Send forth the best ye breed –
Go bind your sons to exile
  To serve your captives' need;
To wait in heavy harness
  On fluttered folk and wild –
Your new-caught, sullen peoples,
  Half devil and half child.

Take up the White Man's Burden –
  In patience to abide,
To veil the threat of terror
  And check the show of pride;
By open speech and simple,
  An hundred times made plain,
To seek another's profit,
  And work another's gain.

Take up the White Man's burden –
  The savage wars of peace –
Fill full the mouth of Famine
  And bid the sickness cease;
And when your goal is nearest
  The end for others sought,
Watch Sloth and heathen Folly
  Bring all your hope to nought.

Take up the White Man's burden –
  No tawdry rule of kings,
But toil of serf and sweeper –
  The tale of common things.
The ports ye shall not enter,
  The roads ye shall not tread,
Go make them with your living,
  And mark them with your dead!

Take up the White Man's burden –
  And reap his old reward:
The blame of those ye better,
  The hate of those ye guard –
The cry of hosts ye humour
  (Ah, slowly!) toward the light: –
'Why brought ye us from bondage,
  Our loved Egyptian night?'

Take up the White Man's burden –
  Ye dare not stoop to less –
Nor call too loud on Freedom
  To cloak your weariness;
By all ye cry or whisper,
  By all ye leave or do,
The silent, sullen peoples
  Shall weigh your Gods and you.

Take up the White Man's burden –
  Have done with childish days –
The lightly proffered laurel,
  The easy, ungrudged praise,
Comes now, to search your manhood
  Through all the thankless years,
Cold-edged with dear-bought wisdom,
  The judgment of your peers!

Chant-Pagan

(English Irregular, discharged)

Me that 'ave been what I've been –
Me that 'ave gone where I've gone –
Me that 'ave seen what I've seen –
  'Ow can I ever take on
With awful old England again,
An' 'ouses both sides of the street,
And 'edges two sides of the lane,
And the parson an' gentry between,
An' touchin' my 'at when we meet –
  Me that 'ave been what I've been?

Me that 'ave watched 'arf a world
'Eave up all shiny with dew,
Kopje on kop to the sun,
An' as soon as the mist let 'em through
Our 'elios winkin' like fun –
Three sides of a ninety-mile square,
Over valleys as big as a shire –
'Are ye there? Are ye there? Are ye there?'
An' then the blind drum of our fire . . .
An' I'm rollin' 'is lawns for the Squire,
                                    Me!

Me that 'ave rode through the dark
Forty mile, often, on end,
Along the Ma'ollisberg Range,
With only the stars for my mark
An' only the night for my friend,
An' things runnin' off as you pass,
An' things jumpin' up in the grass,
An' the silence, the shine an' the size
Of the 'igh, unexpressible skies –
I am takin' some letters almost
As much as a mile to the post,
An' 'mind you come back with the change!'
                                        Me!

Me that saw Barberton took
When we dropped through the clouds on their 'ead,
An' they 'ove the guns over and fled –
Me that was through Di'mond 'Ill,
An' Pieters an' Springs an' Belfast –
From Dundee to Vereeniging all –
Me that stuck out to the last
(An' five bloomin' bars on my chest) –
I am doin' my Sunday-school best,
By the 'elp of the Squire and 'is wife
(Not to mention the 'ousemaid an' cook),
To come in an' 'ands up an' be still,
An' honestly work for my bread,
My livin' in that state of life
To which it shall please God to call
                                        Me!

Me that 'ave followed my trade
In the place where the Lightnin's are made;
'Twixt the Rains and the Sun and the Moon –
Me that lay down an' got up
Three years with the sky for my roof –
That 'ave ridden my 'unger an' thirst
Six thousand raw mile on the hoof,
With the Vaal and the Orange for cup,
An' the Brandwater Basin for dish, –
Oh! it's 'ard to be'ave as they wish
(Too 'ard, an' a little too soon),
I'll 'ave to think over it first –
                              Me!

I will arise an' get 'ence –
I will trek South and make sure
If it's only my fancy or not
That the sunshine of England is pale,
And the breezes of England are stale,
An' there's somethin' gone small with the lot.
For *I* know of a sun an' a wind,
An' some plains and a mountain be'ind,
An' some graves by a barb-wire fence,
An' a Dutchman I've fought 'oo might give
Me a job were I ever inclined
To look in an' offsaddle an' live
Where there's neither a road nor a tree –
But only my Maker an' me,
And I think it will kill me or cure,
So I think I will go there an' see.
                              Me!

Ulster

1912

'Their webs shall not become garments, neither
shall they cover themselves with their works:
their works are works of iniquity, and the act of
violence is in their hands.'—ISAIAH lix. 6.

The dark eleventh hour
Draws on and sees us sold
To every evil power
We fought against of old.
Rebellion, rapine, hate,
Oppression, wrong and greed
Are loosed to rule our fate,
By England's act and deed.

The Faith in which we stand,
The laws we made and guard –
Our honour, lives, and land –
Are given for reward
To Murder done by night,
To Treason taught by day,
To folly, sloth, and spite,
And we are thrust away.

The blood our fathers spilt,
Our love, our toils, our pains,
Are counted us for guilt,
And only bind our chains.
Before an Empire's eyes
The traitor claims his price.
What need of further lies?
We are the sacrifice.

We asked no more than leave
To reap where we had sown,
Through good and ill to cleave
To our own flag and throne.
Now England's shot and steel
Beneath that flag must show
How loyal hearts should kneel
To England's oldest foe.

We know the wars prepared
On every peaceful home,
We know the hells declared
For such as serve not Rome –
The terror, threats, and dread
In market, hearth, and field –
We know, when all is said,
We perish if we yield.

Believe, we dare not boast,
Believe, we do not fear –
We stand to pay the cost
In all that men hold dear.
What answer from the North?
One Law, one Land, one Throne.
If England drive us forth
We shall not fall alone!

Gehazi

1915

Whence comest thou, Gehazi,
So reverend to behold,
In scarlet and in ermines
   And chain of England's gold?
'From following after Naaman
   To tell him all is well,
Whereby my zeal hath made me
   A Judge in Israel.'

Well done, well done, Gehazi!
   Stretch forth thy ready hand.
Thou barely 'scaped from judgment,
   Take oath to judge the land
Unswayed by gift of money
   Or privy bribe, more base,
Of knowledge which is profit
   In any market-place.

Search out and probe, Gehazi,
   As thou of all canst try,
The truthful, well-weighed answer
   That tells the blacker lie –
The loud, uneasy virtue,
   The anger feigned at will,
To overbear a witness
   And make the Court keep still.

Take order now, Gehazi,
  That no man talk aside
In secret with his judges
  The while his case is tried.
Lest he should show them – reason
  To keep a matter hid,
And subtly lead the questions
  Away from what he did.

Thou mirror of uprightness,
  What ails thee at thy vows?
What means the risen whiteness
  Of the skin between thy brows?
The boils that shine and burrow,
  The sores that slough and bleed –
The leprosy of Naaman
  On thee and all thy seed?
    Stand up, stand up, Gehazi,
      Draw close thy robe and go,
    Gehazi, Judge in Israel,
      A leper white as snow!

Mending Wall

Something there is that doesn't love a wall,
That sends the frozen-ground-swell under it
And spills the upper boulders in the sun,
And makes gaps even two can pass abreast.
The work of hunters is another thing:
I have come after them and made repair
Where they have left not one stone on a stone,
But they would have the rabbit out of hiding,
To please the yelping dogs. The gaps I mean,
No one has seen them made or heard them made,
But at spring mending-time we find them there.
I let my neighbor know beyond the hill;
And on a day we meet to walk the line
And set the wall between us once again.
We keep the wall between us as we go.
To each the boulders that have fallen to each.
And some are loaves and some so nearly balls
We have to use a spell to make them balance:
'Stay where you are until our backs are turned!'
We wear our fingers rough with handling them.
Oh, just another kind of outdoor game,
One on a side. It comes to little more:
There where it is we do not need the wall:
He is all pine and I am apple orchard.
My apple trees will never get across
And eat the cones under his pines, I tell him.
He only says, 'Good fences make good neighbors.'
Spring is the mischief in me, and I wonder
If I could put a notion in his head:
'Why do they make good neighbors? Isn't it
Where there are cows? But here there are no cows.
Before I built a wall I'd ask to know
What I was walling in or walling out,

And to whom I was like to give offense.
Something there is that doesn't love a wall,
That wants it down.' I could say 'Elves' to him,
But it's not elves exactly, and I'd rather
He said it for himself. I see him there,
Bringing a stone grasped firmly by the top
In each hand, like an old-stone savage armed.
He moves in darkness as it seems to me,
Not of woods only and the shade of trees.
He will not go behind his father's saying,
And he likes having thought of it so well
He says again, 'Good fences make good neighbors.'

W. B. YEATS

September 1913

What need you, being come to sense,
But fumble in a greasy till
And add the halfpence to the pence
And prayer to shivering prayer, until
You have dried the marrow from the bone?
For men were born to pray and save:
Romantic Ireland's dead and gone,
It's with O'Leary in the grave.

Yet they were of a different kind,
The names that stilled your childish play,
They have gone about the world like wind,
But little time had they to pray
For whom the hangman's rope was spun,
And what, God help us, could they save?
Romantic Ireland's dead and gone,
It's with O'Leary in the grave.

Was it for this the wild geese spread
The grey wing upon every tide;
For this that all that blood was shed,
For this Edward Fitzgerald died,
And Robert Emmet and Wolfe Tone,
All that delirium of the brave?
Romantic Ireland's dead and gone,
It's with O'Leary in the grave.

Yet could we turn the years again,
And call those exiles as they were
In all their loneliness and pain,
You'd cry, 'Some woman's yellow hair
Has maddened every mother's son':
They weighed so lightly what they gave.
But let them be, they're dead and gone,
They're with O'Leary in the grave.

Easter 1916

I have met them at close of day
Coming with vivid faces
From counter or desk among grey
Eighteenth-century houses.
I have passed with a nod of the head
Or polite meaningless words,
Or have lingered awhile and said
Polite meaningless words,
And thought before I had done
Of a mocking tale or a gibe
To please a companion
Around the fire at the club,
Being certain that they and I
But lived where motley is worn:
All changed, changed utterly:
A terrible beauty is born.

That woman's days were spent
In ignorant good-will,
Her nights in argument
Until her voice grew shrill.
What voice more sweet than hers
When, young and beautiful,
She rode to harriers?
This man had kept a school

And rode our wingèd horse;
This other his helper and friend
Was coming into his force;
He might have won fame in the end,
So sensitive his nature seemed,
So daring and sweet his thought.
This other man I had dreamed
A drunken, vainglorious lout.
He had done most bitter wrong
To some who are near my heart,
Yet I number him in the song;
He, too, has resigned his part
In the casual comedy;
He, too, has been changed in his turn,
Transformed utterly:
A terrible beauty is born.

Hearts with one purpose alone
Through summer and winter seem
Enchanted to a stone
To trouble the living stream.
The horse that comes from the road,
The rider, the birds that range
From cloud to tumbling cloud,
Minute by minute they change;
A shadow of cloud on the stream
Changes minute by minute;
A horse-hoof slides on the brim,
And a horse plashes within it;
The long-legged moor-hens dive,
And hens to moor-cocks call;
Minute by minute they live:
The stone's in the midst of all.

Too long a sacrifice
Can make a stone of the heart.
O when may it suffice?

That is Heaven's part, our part
To murmur name upon name,
As a mother names her child
When sleep at last has come
On limbs that had run wild.
What is it but nightfall?
No, no, not night but death;
Was it needless death after all?
For England may keep faith
For all that is done and said.
We know their dream; enough
To know they dreamed and are dead;
And what if excess of love
Bewildered them till they died?
I write it out in a verse –
MacDonagh and MacBride
And Connolly and Pearse
Now and in time to be,
Wherever green is worn,
Are changed, changed utterly:
A terrible beauty is born.

September 25, 1916

Sixteen Dead Men

O but we talked at large before
The sixteen men were shot,
But who can talk of give and take,
What should be and what not
While those dead men are loitering there
To stir the boiling pot?

You say that we should still the land
Till Germany's overcome;
But who is there to argue that
Now Pearse is deaf and dumb?
And is their logic to outweigh
MacDonagh's bony thumb?

How could you dream they'd listen
That have an ear alone
For those new comrades they have found,
Lord Edward and Wolfe Tone,
Or meddle with our give and take
That converse bone to bone?

The Rose Tree

'O words are lightly spoken,'
Said Pearse to Connolly,
'Maybe a breath of politic words
Has withered our Rose Tree;
Or maybe but a wind that blows
Across the bitter sea.'

'It needs to be but watered,'
James Connolly replied,
'To make the green come out again
And spread on every side,
And shake the blossom from the bud
To be the garden's pride.'

'But where can we draw water,'
Said Pearse to Connolly,
'When all the wells are parched away?
O plain as plain can be
There's nothing but our own red blood
Can make a right Rose Tree.'

On a Political Prisoner

She that but little patience knew,
From childhood on, had now so much
A grey gull lost its fears and flew
Down to her cell and there alit,
And there endured her fingers' touch
And from her fingers ate its bit.

Did she in touching that lone wing
Recall the years before her mind
Became a bitter, an abstract thing,
Her thought some popular enmity:
Blind and leader of the blind
Drinking the foul ditch where they lie?

When long ago I saw her ride
Under Ben Bulben to the meet,
The beauty of her country-side
With all youth's lonely wildness stirred,
She seemed to have grown clean and sweet
Like any rock-bred, sea-borne bird:

Sea-borne, or balanced on the air
When first it sprang out of the nest
Upon some lofty rock to stare
Upon the cloudy canopy,
While under its storm-beaten breast
Cried out the hollows of the sea.

The Second Coming

Turning and turning in the widening gyre
The falcon cannot hear the falconer;
Things fall apart; the centre cannot hold;
Mere anarchy is loosed upon the world,
The blood-dimmed tide is loosed, and everywhere
The ceremony of innocence is drowned;
The best lack all conviction, while the worst
Are full of passionate intensity.

Surely some revelation is at hand;
Surely the Second Coming is at hand.
The Second Coming! Hardly are those words out
When a vast image out of *Spiritus Mundi*
Troubles my sight: somewhere in sands of the desert
A shape with lion body and the head of a man,
A gaze blank and pitiless as the sun,
Is moving its slow thighs, while all about it
Reel shadows of the indignant desert birds.
The darkness drops again; but now I know
That twenty centuries of stony sleep
Were vexed to nightmare by a rocking cradle,
And what rough beast, its hour come round at last,
Slouches towards Bethlehem to be born?

The Stare's Nest by My Window

The bees build in the crevices
Of loosening masonry, and there
The mother birds bring grubs and flies.
My wall is loosening; honey-bees,
Come build in the empty house of the stare.

We are closed in, and the key is turned
On our uncertainty; somewhere
A man is killed, or a house burned,
Yet no clear fact to be discerned:
Come build in the empty house of the stare.

A barricade of stone or of wood;
Some fourteen days of civil war;
Last night they trundled down the road
That dead young soldier in his blood:
Come build in the empty house of the stare.

We had fed the heart on fantasies,
The heart's grown brutal from the fare;
More substance in our enmities
Than in our love; O honey-bees,
Come build in the empty house of the stare.

from 'Meditations In Time of Civil War'

In Memory of Eva Gore-Booth and Con Markiewicz

The light of evening, Lissadell,
Great windows open to the south,
Two girls in silk kimonos, both
Beautiful, one a gazelle.
But a raving autumn shears
Blossom from the summer's wreath;
The older is condemned to death,
Pardoned, drags out lonely years
Conspiring among the ignorant.
I know not what the younger dreams –
Some vague Utopia – and she seems,
When withered old and skeleton-gaunt,
An image of such politics.
Many a time I think to seek

One or the other out and speak
Of that old Georgian mansion, mix
Pictures of the mind, recall
That table and the talk of youth,
Two girls in silk kimonos, both
Beautiful, one a gazelle.

Dear shadows, now you know it all,
All the folly of a fight
With a common wrong or right.
The innocent and the beautiful
Have no enemy but time;
Arise and bid me strike a match
And strike another till time catch;
Should the conflagration climb,
Run till all the sages know.
We the great gazebo built,
They convicted us of guilt;
Bid me strike a match and blow.

October 1927

WILFRED OWEN

Dulce Et Decorum Est

Bent double, like old beggars under sacks,
Knock-kneed, coughing like hags, we cursed through
sludge,
Till on the haunting flares we turned our backs,
And towards our distant rest began to trudge.
Men marched asleep. Many had lost their boots,
But limped on, blood-shod. All went lame, all blind;
Drunk with fatigue; deaf even to the hoots
Of gas-shells dropping softly behind.

Gas! GAS! Quick, boys! – An ecstasy of fumbling,
Fitting the clumsy helmets just in time,
But someone still was yelling out and stumbling
And floundering like a man in fire or lime. –
Dim through the misty panes and thick green light,
As under a green sea, I saw him drowning.

In all my dreams before my helpless sight
He plunges at me, guttering, choking, drowning.

If in some smothering dreams, you too could pace
Behind the wagon that we flung him in,
And watch the white eyes writhing in his face,
His hanging face, like a devil's sick of sin;
If you could hear, at every jolt, the blood
Come gargling from the froth-corrupted lungs,
Bitter as the cud
Of vile, incurable sores on innocent tongues, –
My friend, you would not tell with such high zest
To children ardent for some desperate glory,
The old Lie: Dulce et decorum est
Pro patria mori.

André Chénier

André Chénier climbed up the ladder.
Just breathing makes me guilty now.
Iron, iron and cordite, these days,
And a burnt tenor.

What father would cut the collar
From his son's shirt?
There are times the daylight's a quick terror
And no one living looks quite human.

4–20 April, 1918
trans. Tom Paulin

The Right Heart in the Wrong Place

Of spinach and gammon
Bull's full to the crupper
White lice and black famine
Are the mayor of Cork's supper
But the pride of old Ireland
Must be damnably humbled
If a Joyce is found cleaning
The boots of a Rumbold.

'I hate the mention of politics'

. . . the last concert I sang at where its over a year ago when
was it St Teresas hall Clarendon St little chits of missies they
have now singing Kathleen Kearney and her like on account
of father being in the army and my singing the absentminded
beggar and wearing a brooch for lord Roberts when I had the
map of it all and Poldy not Irish enough was it him managed
it this time I wouldnt put it past him like he got me on to sing
in the *Stabat Mater* by going around saying he was putting
Lead Kindly Light to music I put him up to that till the jesuits
found out he was a freemason thumping the piano lead Thou
me on copied from some old opera yes and he was going
about with some of them Sinner Fein lately or whatever they
call themselves talking his usual trash and nonsense he says
that little man he showed me without the neck is very
intelligent the coming man Griffith is he well he doesnt look
it thats all I can say still it must have been him he knew there
was a boycott I hate the mention of politics after the war that
Pretoria and Ladysmith and Bloemfontein where Gardner
Lieut Stanley G 8th Bn 2nd East Lancs Rgt of enteric fever he
was a lovely fellow in khaki and just the right height over me
Im sure he was brave too he said I was lovely the evening we

kissed goodbye at the canal lock my Irish beauty he was pale with excitement about going away or wed be seen from the road he couldnt stand properly and I so hot as I never felt they could have made their peace in the beginning or old oom Paul and the rest of the old Krugers go and fight it out between them instead of dragging on for years killing any finelooking men there were with their fever if he was even decently shot it wouldnt have been so bad I love to see a regiment pass in review the first time I saw the Spanish cavalry at La Roque it was lovely after looking across the bay from Algeciras all the lights of the rock like fireflies or those sham battles on the 15 acres the Black Watch with their kilts in time at the march past the 10th hussars the prince of Wales own or the lancers O the lancers theyre grand or the Dublins that won Tugela his father made his money over selling the horses for the cavalry well he could buy me a nice present up in Belfast after what I gave theyve lovely linen up there or one of those nice kimono things I must buy a mothball like I had before to keep in the drawer with them it would be exciting going around with him shopping buying those things in a new city better leave this ring behind want to keep turning and turning to get it over the knuckle there or they might bell it round the town in their papers or tell the police on me but theyd think were married O let them all go and smother themselves for the fat lot I care he has plenty of money and hes not a marrying man so somebody better get it out of him . . .

(from Ulysses)

'I was washing outside in the darkness'

I was washing outside in the darkness,
the sky burning with rough stars,
and the starlight, salt on an axe-blade.
The cold overflows the barrel.

The gate's locked,
the land's grim as its conscience.
I don't think they'll find the new weaving,
finer than truth, anywhere.

Star-salt is melting in the barrel,
icy water is turning blacker,
death's growing purer, misfortune saltier,
the earth's moving nearer to truth and to dread.

1921
trans. W. S. Merwin and Clarence Brown

Leningrad

I've come back to my city. These are my own old tears,
my own little veins, the swollen glands of my childhood.

So you're back. Open wide. Swallow
the fish-oil from the river lamps of Leningrad.

Open your eyes. Do you know this December day,
the egg-yolk with the deadly tar beaten into it?

Petersburg! I don't want to die yet!
You know my telephone numbers.

Petersburg! I've still got the addresses:
I can look up dead voices.

I live on back stairs, and the bell,
torn out nerves and all, jangles in my temples.

And I wait till morning for guests that I love,
and rattle the door in its chains.

Leningrad. December 1930
trans. W. S. Merwin and Clarence Brown

The Stalin Epigram

Our lives no longer feel ground under them.
At ten paces you can't hear our words.

But whenever there's a snatch of talk
it turns to the Kremlin mountaineer,

the ten thick worms his fingers,
his words like measures of weight,

the huge laughing cockroaches on his top lip,
the glitter of his boot-rims.

Ringed with a scum of chicken-necked bosses
he toys with the tributes of half-men.

One whistles, another meouws, a third snivels.
He pokes out his finger and he alone goes boom.

He forges decrees in a line like horseshoes,
One for the groin, one the forehead, temple, eye.

He rolls the executions on his tongue like berries.
He wishes he could hug them like big friends from home.

trans. W. S. Merwin and Clarence Brown

'Mounds of human heads
are wandering into the distance'

Mounds of human heads are wandering into the distance.
I dwindle among them. Nobody sees me. But in books
much loved, and in children's games I shall rise
from the dead to say the sun is shining.

trans. W. S. Merwin and Clarence Brown

ANNA AKHMATOVA

Voronezh

You walk on permafrost
in these streets.
The town's silly and heavy
like a glass paperweight
stuck on a desk –
a wide steel one
glib as this pavement.
I trimp on ice,
the sledges skitter and slip.
Crows are crowding the poplars,
and St Peter's of Voronezh
is an acidgreen dome
fizzing in the flecked light.
The earth's stout as a bell –
it hums like that battle
on the Field of Snipes.
Lord let each poplar
take the shape of a wine-glass
and I'll make it ring
as though the priest's wed us.
But that tin lamp
on the poet's table
was watched last night.
Judas and the Word
are stalking each other
through this scroggy town
where every line has three stresses
and only the one word, *dark*.

trans. Tom Paulin

D. H. LAWRENCE

Hibiscus and Salvia Flowers

Hark! Hark!
The dogs do bark!
It's the socialists come to town,
None in rags and none in tags,
Swaggering up and down.

Sunday morning,
And from the Sicilian townlets skirting Etna
The socialists have gathered upon us, to look at us.

How shall we know them when we see them?
How shall we know them now they've come?

Not by their rags and not by their tags,
Nor by any distinctive gown;
The same unremarkable Sunday suit
And hats cocked up and down.

Yet there they are, youths, loutishly
Strolling in gangs and staring along the Corso
With the gang-stare
And a half-threatening envy
At every *forestière*,
Every lordly tuppenny foreigner from the hotels, fattening
                                        on the exchange.

Hark! Hark!
The dogs do bark!
It's the socialists in the town.
Sans rags, sans tags,
Sans beards, sans bags,
Sans any distinction at all except loutish commonness.

How do we know then, that they are they?
Bolshevists.
Leninists.
Communists.
Socialists.
-Ists! -Ists!

Alas, salvia and hibiscus flowers.
Salvia and hibiscus flowers.

Listen again.
Salvia and hibiscus flowers.
Is it not so?
Salvia and hibiscus flowers.

Hark! Hark!
The dogs do bark!
Salvia and hibiscus flowers.

Who smeared their doors with blood?
Who on their breasts
Put salvias and hibiscus

Rosy, rosy scarlet,
And flame-rage, golden-throated
Bloom along the Corso on the living, perambulating bush.

Who said they might assume these blossoms?
What god did they consult?

Rose-red, princess hibiscus, rolling her pointed Chinese
                                                    petals!
Azalea and camellia, single peony
And pomegranate bloom and scarlet mallow-flower
And all the eastern, exquisite royal plants
That noble blood has brought us down the ages!
Gently nurtured, frail and splendid

Hibiscus flower –
Alas, the Sunday coats of Sicilian bolshevists!
Pure blood, and noble blood, in the fine and rose-red veins;
Small, interspersed with jewels of white gold
Frail-filigreed among the rest;
Rose of the oldest races of princesses, Polynesian
Hibiscus.

Eve, in her happy moments,
Put hibiscus in her hair,
Before she humbled herself, and knocked her knees with
                                        repentance.

Sicilian bolshevists,
With hibiscus flowers in the buttonholes of your Sunday suits,
Come now, speaking of rights, what right have you to this
                                        flower?

The exquisite and ageless aristocracy
Of a peerless soul,
Blessed are the pure in heart and the fathomless in bright
                                        pride;
The loveliness that knows *noblesse oblige*;
The native royalty of red hibiscus flowers;
The exquisite assertion of new delicate life
Risen from the roots:
Is this how you'll have it, red-decked socialists,
Hibiscus-breasted?
If it be so, I fly to join you,
And if it be not so, brutes to pull down hibiscus flowers!
Or salvia!
Or dragon-mouthed salvia with gold throat of wrath!
Flame-flushed, enraged, splendid salvia,
Cock-crested, crowing your orange scarlet like a tocsin
Along the Corso all this Sunday morning.

Is your wrath red as salvias,

You socialists?
You with your grudging, envious, furtive rage,
In Sunday suits and yellow boots along the Corso.
You look well with your salvia flowers, I must say.
Warrior-like, dawn-cock's-comb flaring flower
Shouting forth flame to set the world on fire,
The dust-heap of man's filthy world on fire,
And burn it down, the glutted, stuffy world,
And feed the young new fields of life with ash,
With ash I say,
Bolshevists,
Your ashes even, my friends,
Among much other ash.

If there were salvia-savage bolshevists
To burn the world back to manure-good ash,
Wouldn't I stick the salvia in my coat!
But these themselves must burn, these louts!
The dragon-faced,
The anger-reddened, golden-throated salvia
With its long antennæ of rage put out
Upon the frightened air.
Ugh, how I love its fangs of perfect rage
That gnash the air;
The molten gold of its intolerable rage
Hot in the throat.

I long to be a bolshevist
And set the stinking rubbish-heap of this foul world
Afire at a myriad scarlet points,
A bolshevist, a salvia-face
To lick the world with flame that licks it clean.
I long to see its chock-full crowdedness
And glutted squirming populousness on fire
Like a field of filthy weeds
Burnt back to ash,
And then to see the new, real souls sprout up.

Not this vast rotting cabbage patch we call the world;
But from the ash-scarred fallow
New wild souls.
Nettles, and a rose sprout,
Hibiscus, and mere grass,
Salvia still in a rage
And almond honey-still,
And fig-wort stinking for the carrion wasp;
All the lot of them, and let them fight it out.

But not a trace of foul equality,
Nor sound of still more foul human perfection.
You need not clear the world like a cabbage patch for me;
Leave me my nettles,
Let me fight the wicked, obstreperous weeds myself, and put
                              them in their place,
Severely in their place.
I don't at all want to annihilate them,
I like a row with them,
But I won't be put on a cabbage-idealistic level of equality
                              with them.

What rot, to see the cabbage and hibiscus-tree
As equals!
What rot, to say the louts along the Corso
In Sunday suits and yellow shoes
Are my equals!
I am their superior, saluting the hibiscus flower, not them.
The same I say to the profiteers from the hotels, the money-
                              fat-ones,
Profiteers here being called dog-fish, stinking dog-fish,
                              sharks.
The same I say to the pale and elegant persons,
Pale-face authorities loitering tepidly:
That I salute the red hibiscus flowers
And send mankind to its inferior blazes.

Mankind's inferior blazes,
And these along with it, all the inferior lot –
These bolshevists,
These dog-fish,
These precious and ideal ones,
All rubbish ready for fire.
And I salute hibiscus and the salvia flower
Upon the breasts of loutish bolshevists,
Damned loutish bolshevists,
Who perhaps will do the business after all,
In the long run, in spite of themselves.

Meanwhile, alas
For me no fellow-men,
No salvia-frenzied comrades, antennæ
Of yellow-red, outreaching, living wrath
Upon the smouldering air,
And throat of brimstone-molten angry gold.
Red, angry men are a race extinct, alas!

Never
To be a bolshevist
With a hibiscus flower behind my ear
In sign of life, of lovely, dangerous life
And passionate disquality of men;
In sign of dauntless, silent violets,
And impudent nettles grabbing the under-earth,
And cabbages born to be cut and eat,
And salvia fierce to crow and shout for fight,
And rosy-red hibiscus wincingly
Unfolding all her coiled and lovely self
In a doubtful world.

Never, bolshevistically
To be able to stand for all these!
Alas, alas, I have got to leave it all
To the youths in Sunday suits and yellow shoes

Who have pulled down the salvia flowers
And rosy delicate hibiscus flowers
And everything else to their disgusting level,
Never, of course, to put anything up again.

But yet
If they pull all the world down,
The process will amount to the same in the end.
Instead of flame and flame-clean ash,
Slow watery rotting back to level muck
And final humus,
Whence the re-start.

And still I cannot bear it
That they take hibiscus and the salvia flower.

                                        Taormina.

VLADIMIR VLADIMIROVICH MAYAKOVSKY

Last Statement

It's after one,
you're in the sack, I guess.
The stars are echoed
in the Volga's darkness
and I'm not fussed
or urgent anymore.
I won't be wiring you
my slogans and my kisses
in daft capitals:
we bit green chillies
and we're through.
We were like lovers
leaning from a ferry
on the White Canal –
our arguments, statistics,
our fucks and cries
notched on the calculus.
Ah, the night has jammed
each signal from the stars,
and this, this is my last
stittering, grief-splintered
call-sign to the future.
Christ, I want to wow
both history and technology . . .
I could tell it to the world right now.

trans. Tom Paulin

The Dead Liebknecht
after the German of Rudolf Leonhardt

His corpse owre a' the city lies
In ilka square and ilka street
His spilt bluid floods the vera skies
And nae hoose but is darkened wi't.

The factory horns begin to blaw
Thro' a' the city, blare on blare,
The lowsin' time o' workers a',
Like emmits skailin' everywhere.

And wi' his white teeth shinin' yet
The corpse lies smilin' underfit.

from In Memoriam James Joyce

It was Landor who first said
That every Frenchman takes a personal share
In the glory of his poets
Whereas every Englishman resents
The achievements of his poets
Because they detract
From the success of his own 'poetry';
And the remark was extraordinarily profound.
So the English literary world
Is an immense arena
Where every spectator is intent
On the deaths of those awaiting judgment
And every gladiator is intent
On causing the death of his fellow-combatant
By smiting him with the corpses
Of other predeceased.

The method, the mania, the typical
'Fair-play' of 'the sporting English'
Is really extraordinary in its operation.

Supposing, having no pet author of your own
Out of whose entrails
You hope to make a living,
No political bias,
No interest in a firm of publishers
Who make dividends out of other 'classics'
You timidly venture to remark
That Trollope, Jane Austen,
And the Mrs Gaskell of Mary Barton,
Are English Authors
Authentic in their methods.

'*But*' you hear the professional reviewers
All protesting at once
'Trollope has not the humour of Dickens,
The irony of Thackeray,
The skill with a plot of Wilkie Collins.
Jane Austen has not the wit of Meredith,
The reforming energy of Charles Reade,
The imperial sense of Charles Kingsley,
The tender pathos of the author of *Cranford*.
And as for Mrs Gaskell who wrote *Cranford*,
Well, she has not the aloofness of Jane Austen,
And Christina Rossetti had not
The manly optimism of Browning,
And Browning lacked the religious confidence
Of Christina Rossetti, or the serenity
Of Matthew Arnold. And who was Matthew Arnold?
Landor could not write about whist and old playbills
Like Charles Lamb.
(*Saint Charles, Thackeray murmured softly!*)

No one who has paid any attention at all
To official-critical appraisements of English writers
Can gainsay the moral to be drawn
From these instances of depreciation
Or the truth of the projection itself.
Literary figures should, of course,
As is said of race-horses, be 'tried high,'
But to attach a Derby winner to a stone cart,
And then condemn it as a horse
Because it does not make so much progress
As a Clydesdale or a Percheron
Is to try the animal
Altogether too high.
And not fairly.
English official criticism has erected
A stone-heap, a dead load of moral qualities.
A writer must have optimism, irony,
A healthy outlook,
A middle-class standard of morality,
As much religion as, say, St Paul had,
As much atheism as Shelley had . . .
And, finally, on top of an immense load
Of self-neutralizing moral and social qualities,
Above all, Circumspection,
So that, in the end, no English writer
According to these standards,
Can possess authenticity.
The formula is this: Thackeray is not Dickens,
So Thackeray does not represent English literature.
Dickens is not Thackeray, so *he*
Does not represent English literature.
In the end literature itself is given up
And you have the singular dictum
Of the doyen of English official literary criticism.
This gentleman writes . . . but always rather uncomfortably . . .
Of Dryden as divine, of Pope as divine,
Of Swift as so filthy

As to intimidate the self-respecting critic.
But when he comes to Pepys of course
His enthusiasm is unbounded.
He salutes the little pawky diarist
With an affection, an enthusiasm,
For his industry, his pawkiness,
His thumb-nail sketches.
Then he asserts amazingly:
'This is scarcely literature'
And continues with panegyrics that leave no doubt
That the critic considers the Diary
To be something very much better.
The judgment is typically English.
The bewildered foreigner can only say:
'But if the Diary is all you assert of it,
It must be literature, or, if it is not literature,
It cannot be all you assert of it.'
And obviously . . .

W. H. AUDEN

'From scars where kestrels hover'

From scars where kestrels hover,
The leader looking over
Into the happy valley,
Orchard and curving river,
May turn away to see
The slow fastidious line
That disciplines the fell,
Hear curlew's creaking call
From angles unforseen,
The drumming of a snipe
Surprise where driven sleet
Had scalded to the bone
And streams are acrid yet
To an unaccustomed lip.
The tall unwounded leader
Of doomed companions, all
Whose voices in the rock
Are now perpetual,
Fighters for no one's sake,
Who died beyond the border.

Heroes are buried who
Did not believe in death
And bravery is now
Not in the dying breath
But resisting the temptations
To skyline operations.
Yet glory is not new;
The summer visitors
Still come from far and wide,
Choosing their spots to view
The prize competitors
Each thinking that he will

Find heroes in the wood,
Far from the capital
Where lights and wine are set
For supper by the lake,
But leaders must migrate:
'Leave for Cape Wrath to-night',
And the host after waiting
Must quench the lamps and pass
Alive into the house.

'Who will endure'

Who will endure
Heat of day and winter danger,
Journey from one place to another,
Nor be content to lie
Till evening upon headland over bay,
Between the land and sea;
Or smoking wait till hour of food,
Leaning on chained-up gate
At edge of wood?

Metals run
Burnished or rusty in the sun
From town to town,
And signals all along are down;
Yet nothing passes
But envelopes between these places,
Snatched at the gate and panting read indoors,
And first spring flowers arriving smashed,
Disaster stammered over wires,
And pity flashed.
For should professional traveller come,
Asked at the fireside he is dumb,
Declining with a small mad smile,
And all the while

Conjectures on the maps that lie
About in ships long high and dry
Grow stranger and stranger.

There is no change of place
But shifting of the head
To keep off glare of lamp from face,
Or climbing over to wall-side of bed;
No one will ever know
For what conversion brilliant capital is waiting,
What ugly feast may village band be celebrating;
For no one goes
Further than railhead or the ends of piers,
Will neither go nor send his son
Further through foothills than the rotting stack
Where gaitered gamekeeper with dog and gun
Will shout 'Turn back'.

'O what is that sound'

O what is that sound which so thrills the ear
  Down in the valley drumming, drumming?
Only the scarlet soldiers, dear,
    The soldiers coming.

O what is that light I see flashing so clear
  Over the distance brightly, brightly?
Only the sun on their weapons, dear,
    As they step lightly.

O what are they doing with all that gear;
  What are they doing this morning, this morning?
Only the usual manœuvres, dear,
    Or perhaps a warning.

O why have they left the road down there;
   Why are they suddenly wheeling, wheeling?
Perhaps a change in the orders, dear;
      Why are you kneeling?

O haven't they stopped for the doctor's care;
   Haven't they reined their horses, their horses?
Why, they are none of them wounded, dear,
      None of these forces.

O is it the parson they want with white hair;
   Is it the parson, is it, is it?
No, they are passing his gateway, dear,
      Without a visit.

O it must be the farmer who lives so near;
   It must be the farmer so cunning, so cunning?
They have passed the farm already, dear,
      And now they are running.

O where are you going? stay with me here!
   Were the vows you swore me deceiving, deceiving?
No, I promised to love you, dear,
      But I must be leaving.

O it's broken the lock and splintered the door,
   O it's the gate where they're turning, turning;
Their feet are heavy on the floor
      And their eyes are burning.

from Letter to Lord Byron

Now for the spirit of the people. Here
    I know I'm treading on more dangerous ground:
I know there're many changes in the air,
    But know my data too slight to be sound.
    I know, too, I'm inviting the renowned
Retort of all who love the Status Quo:
'You can't change human nature, don't you know!'

We've still, it's true, the same shape and appearance,
    We haven't changed the way that kissing's done;
The average man still hates all interference,
    Is just as proud still of his new-born son:
    Still, like a hen, he likes his private run,
Scratches for self-esteem, and slyly pecks
A good deal in the neighbourhood of sex.

But he's another man in many ways:
    Ask the cartoonist first, for he knows best.
Where is the John Bull of the good old days,
    The swaggering bully with the clumsy jest?
    His meaty neck has long been laid to rest,
His acres of self-confidence for sale;
He passed away at Ypres and Passchendaele.

Turn to the work of Disney or of Strube;
  There stands our hero in his threadbare seams;
The bowler hat who straphangs in the tube,
  And kicks the tyrant only in his dreams,
  Trading on pathos, dreading all extremes;
The little Mickey with the hidden grudge;
Which is the better, I leave you to judge.

Begot on Hire-Purchase by Insurance,
  Forms at his christening worshipped and adored;
A season ticket schooled him in endurance,
  A tax collector and a waterboard
  Admonished him. In boyhood he was awed
By a matric, and complex apparatuses
Keep his heart conscious of Divine Afflatuses.

'I am like you', he says, 'and you, and you,
  I love my life, I love the home-fires, have
To keep them burning. Heroes never do.
  Heroes are sent by ogres to the grave.
  I may not be courageous, but I save.
I am the one who somehow turns the corner,
I may perhaps be fortunate Jack Horner.

'I am the ogre's private secretary;
  I've felt his stature and his powers, learned
To give his ogreship the raspberry
  Only when his gigantic back is turned.
  One day, who knows, I'll do as I have yearned.
The short man, all his fingers on the door,
With repartee shall send him to the floor.'

One day, which day? O any other day,
    But not to-day. The ogre knows his man.
To kill the ogre – that would take away
    The fear in which his happy dreams began,
    And with his life he'll guard dreams while he can.
Those who would really kill his dream's contentment
He hates with real implacable resentment.

He dreads the ogre, but he dreads yet more
    Those who conceivably might set him free,
Those the cartoonist has no time to draw.
    Without his bondage he'd be all at sea;
    The ogre need but shout 'Security',
To make this man, so lovable, so mild,
As madly cruel as a frightened child.

Byron, thou should'st be living at this hour!
    What would you do, I wonder, if you were?
Britannia's lost prestige and cash and power,
    Her middle classes show some wear and tear,
    We've learned to bomb each other from the air;
I can't imagine what the Duke of Wellington
Would say about the music of Duke Ellington.

Suggestions have been made that the Teutonic
    Führer-Prinzip would have appealed to you
As being the true heir to the Byronic –
    In keeping with your social status too
    (It has its English converts, fit and few),
That you would, hearing honest Oswald's call,
Be gleichgeschaltet in the Albert Hall.

'Lord Byron at the head of his storm-troopers!'
    Nothing, says science, is impossible:
The Pope may quit to join the Oxford Groupers,
    Nuffield may leave one farthing in his Will,
    There may be someone who trusts Baldwin still,
Someone may think that Empire wines are nice,
There may be people who hear Tauber twice.

You liked to be the centre of attention,
    The gay Prince Charming of the fairy story,
Who tamed the Dragon by his intervention.
    In modern warfare, though it's just as gory,
    There isn't any individual glory;
The Prince must be anonymous, observant,
A kind of lab-boy, or a civil servant.

You never were an Isolationist;
    Injustice you had always hatred for,
And we can hardly blame you, if you missed
    Injustice just outside your lordship's door:
    Nearer than Greece were cotton and the poor.
To-day you might have seen them, might indeed
Have walked in the United Front with Gide,

Against the ogre, dragon, what you will;
    His many shapes and names all turn us pale,
For he's immortal, and to-day he still
    Swinges the horror of his scaly tail.
    Sometimes he seems to sleep, but will not fail
In every age to rear up to defend
Each dying force of history to the end.

Milton beheld him on the English throne,
    And Bunyan sitting in the Papal chair;
The hermits fought him in their caves alone,
        At the first Empire he was also there,
        Dangling his Pax Romana in the air:
He comes in dreams at puberty to man,
To scare him back to childhood if he can.

Banker or landlord, booking-clerk or Pope,
        Whenever he's lost faith in choice and thought,
When a man sees the future without hope,
        Whenever he endorses Hobbes' report
        'The life of man is nasty, brutish, short',
The dragon rises from his garden border
And promises to set up law and order.

He that in Athens murdered Socrates,
        And Plato then seduced, prepares to make
A desolation and to call it peace
        To-day for dying magnates, for the sake
        Of generals who can scarcely keep awake,
And for that doughy mass in great and small
That doesn't want to stir itself at all.

Forgive me for inflicting all this on you,
        For asking you to hold the baby for us;
It's easy to forget that where you've gone, you
        May only want to chat with Set and Horus,
        Bored to extinction with our earthly chorus:
Perhaps it sounds to you like a trunk-call,
Urgent, it seems, but quite inaudible.

Yet though the choice of what is to be done
    Remains with the alive, the rigid nation
Is supple still within the breathing one;
    Its sentinels yet keep their sleepless station,
    And every man in every generation,
Tossing in his dilemma on his bed,
Cries to the shadows of the noble dead.

We're out at sea now, and I wish we weren't;
    The sea is rough, I don't care if it's blue;
I'd like to have a quick one, but I daren't.
    And I must interrupt this screed to you,
    For I've some other little jobs to do;
I must write home or mother will be vexed,
So this must be continued in our next.

                          (Part 2, stanzas 27–47)

Spain 1937

Yesterday all the past. The language of size
Spreading to China along the trade-routes; the diffusion
        Of the counting-frame and the cromlech;
Yesterday the shadow-reckoning in the sunny climates.

Yesterday the assessment of insurance by cards,
The divination of water; yesterday the invention
        Of cart-wheels and clocks, the taming of
Horses; yesterday the bustling world of the navigators.

Yesterday the abolition of fairies and giants;
The fortress like a motionless eagle eyeing the valley,
        The chapel built in the forest;
Yesterday the carving of angels and of frightening gargoyles;

The trial of heretics among the columns of stone;
Yesterday the theological feuds in the taverns
            And the miraculous cure at the fountain;
Yesterday the Sabbath of Witches. But to-day the struggle.

Yesterday the installation of dynamos and turbines;
The construction of railways in the colonial desert;
            Yesterday the classic lecture
On the origin of Mankind. But to-day the struggle

Yesterday the belief in the absolute value of Greek;
The fall of the curtain upon the death of a hero;
            Yesterday the prayer to the sunset,
And the adoration of madmen. But to-day the struggle.

As the poet whispers, startling among the pines
Or, where the loose waterfall sings, compact, or upright
            On the crag by the leaning tower:
'O my vision. O send me the luck of the sailor.'

And the investigator peers through his instruments
At the inhuman provinces, the virile bacillus
            Or enormous Jupiter finished:
'But the lives of my friends. I inquire, I inquire.'

And the poor in their fireless lodgings dropping the sheets
Of the evening paper: 'Our day is our loss. O show us
            History the operator, the
Organizer, Time the refreshing river.'

And the nations combine each cry, invoking the life
That shapes the individual belly and orders
            The private nocturnal terror:
'Did you not found once the city state of the sponge,

'Raise the vast military empires of the shark
And the tiger, establish the robin's plucky canton?
            Intervene. O descend as a dove or
A furious papa or a mild engineer: but descend.'

And the life, if it answers at all, replies from the heart
And the eyes and the lungs, from the shops and squares of
                                                    the city:
            'O no, I am not the Mover,
Not to-day, not to you. To you I'm the

'Yes-man, the bar-companion, the easily-duped:
I am whatever you do; I am your vow to be
            Good, your humorous story;
I am your business voice; I am your marriage.

'What's your proposal? To build the Just City? I will.
I agree. Or is it the suicide pact, the romantic
            Death? Very well, I accept, for
I am your choice, your decision: yes, I am Spain.'

Many have heard it on remote peninsulas,
On sleepy plains, in the aberrant fishermen's islands,
            In the corrupt heart of the city;
Have heard and migrated like gulls or the seeds of a flower.

They clung like burrs to the long expresses that lurch
Through the unjust lands, through the night, through the
                                                    alpine tunnel;
            They floated over the oceans;
They walked the passes: they came to present their lives.

On that arid square, that fragment nipped off from hot
Africa, soldered so crudely to inventive Europe,
            On that tableland scored by rivers,
Our fever's menacing shapes are precise and alive.

To-morrow, perhaps, the future: the research on fatigue
And the movements of packers; the gradual exploring of all
                                                        the
            Octaves of radiation;
To-morrow the enlarging of consciousness by diet and
                                            breathing.

To-morrow the rediscovery of romantic love;
The photographing of ravens; all the fun under
            Liberty's masterful shadow;
To-morrow the hour of the pageant-master and the musician.

To-morrow for the young the poets exploding like bombs,
The walks by the lake, the winter of perfect communion;
            To-morrow the bicycle races
Through the suburbs on summer evenings: but to-day the
                                            struggle.

To-day the inevitable increase in the chances of death;
The conscious acceptance of guilt in the fact of murder;
            To-day the expending of powers
On the flat ephemeral pamphlet and the boring meeting.

To-day the makeshift consolations; the shared cigarette;
The cards in the candle-lit barn and the scraping concert,
            The masculine jokes; to-day the
Fumbled and unsatisfactory embrace before hurting.

The stars are dead; the animals will not look:
We are left alone with our day, and the time is short and
            History to the defeated
May say Alas but cannot help or pardon.

In Praise of Limestone

If it form the one landscape that we, the inconstant ones,
    Are consistently homesick for, this is chiefly
Because it dissolves in water. Mark these rounded slopes
    With their surface fragrance of thyme and, beneath,
A secret system of caves and conduits; hear the springs
    That spurt out everywhere with a chuckle,
Each filling a private pool for its fish and carving
    Its own little ravine whose cliffs entertain
The butterfly and the lizard; examine this region
    Of short distances and definite places:
What could be more like Mother or a fitter background
    For her son, the flirtatious male who lounges
Against a rock in the sunlight, never doubting
    That for all his faults he is loved; whose works are but
Extensions of his power to charm? From weathered outcrop
    To hill-top temple, from appearing waters to
Conspicuous fountains, from a wild to a formal vineyard,
    Are ingenious but short steps that a child's wish
To receive more attention than his brothers, whether
    By pleasing or teasing, can easily take.

Watch, then, the band of rivals as they climb up and down
    Their steep stone gennels in twos and threes, at times
Arm in arm, but never, thank God, in step; or engaged
    On the shady side of a square at midday in
Voluble discourse, knowing each other too well to think
    There are any important secrets, unable
To conceive a god whose temper-tantrums are moral
    And not to be pacified by a clever line
Or a good lay: for, accustomed to a stone that responds,
    They have never had to veil their faces in awe
Of a crater whose blazing fury could not be fixed:
    Adjusted to the local needs of valleys
Where everything can be touched or reached by walking,
    Their eyes have never looked into infinite space

Through the lattice-work of a nomad's comb; born lucky,
    Their legs have never encountered the fungi
And insects of the jungle, the monstrous forms and lives
    With which we have nothing, we like to hope, in common.
So, when one of them goes to the bad, the way his mind works
    Remains comprehensible: to become a pimp
Or deal in fake jewellery or ruin a fine tenor voice
    For effects that bring down the house, could happen to all
But the best and the worst of us . . .
                                        That is why, I suppose,
    The best and worst never stayed here long but sought
Immoderate soils where the beauty was not so external,
    The light less public and the meaning of life
Something more than a mad camp. 'Come!' cried the granite
                                                        wastes,
    'How evasive is your humour, how accidental
Your kindest kiss, how permanent is death.' (Saints-to-be
    Slipped away sighing.) 'Come!' purred the clays and gravels,
'On our plains there is room for armies to drill; rivers
    Wait to be tamed and slaves to construct you a tomb
In the grand manner: soft as the earth is mankind and both
    Need to be altered.' (Intendant Caesars rose and
Left, slamming the door.) But the really reckless were fetched
    By an older colder voice, the oceanic whisper:
'I am the solitude that asks and promises nothing;
    That is how I shall set you free. There is no love;
There are only the various envies, all of them sad.'

They were right, my dear, all those voices were right
And still are: this land is not the sweet home that it looks,
    Nor its peace the historical calm of a site
Where something was settled once and for all: A backward
    And dilapidated province, connected
To the big busy world by a tunnel, with a certain
    Seedy appeal, is that all it is now? Not quite:
It has a worldly duty which in spite of itself
    It does not neglect, but calls into question

All the Great Powers assume; it disturbs our rights. The poet,
    Admired for his earnest habit of calling
The sun the sun, his mind Puzzle, is made uneasy
    By these marble statues which so obviously doubt
His antimythological myth; and these gamins,
    Pursuing the scientist down the tiled colonnade
With such lively offers, rebuke his concern for Nature's
    Remotest aspects: I, too, am reproached, for what
And how much you know. Not to lose time, not to get
                                                    caught,
    Not to be left behind, not, please! to resemble
The beasts who repeat themselves, or a thing like water
    Or stone whose conduct can be predicted, these
Are our Common Prayer, whose greatest comfort is music
    Which can be made anywhere, is invisible,
And does not smell. In so far as we have to look forward
    To death as a fact, no doubt we are right: But if
Sins can be forgiven, if bodies rise from the dead,
    These modifications of matter into
Innocent athletes and gesticulating fountains,
    Made solely for pleasure, make a further point:
The blessed will not care what angle they are regarded from,
    Having nothing to hide. Dear, I know nothing of
Either, but when I try to imagine a faultless love
    Or the life to come, what I hear is the murmur
Of underground streams, what I see is a limestone landscape.

The Shield of Achilles

    She looked over his shoulder
        For vines and olive trees,
    Marble well-governed cities
        And ships upon untamed seas,
    But there on the shining metal
        His hands had put instead
    An artificial wilderness
        And a sky like lead.

A plain without a feature, bare and brown,
  No blade of grass, no sign of neighborhood,
Nothing to eat and nowhere to sit down,
  Yet, congregated on its blankness, stood
  An unintelligible multitude,
A million eyes, a million boots in line,
Without expression, waiting for a sign.

Out of the air a voice without a face
  Proved by statistics that some cause was just
In tones as dry and level as the place:
  No one was cheered and nothing was discussed;
  Column by column in a cloud of dust
They marched away enduring a belief
Whose logic brought them, somewhere else, to grief.

          She looked over his shoulder
              For ritual pieties,
          White flower-garlanded heifers,
              Libation and sacrifice,
          But there on the shining metal
              Where the altar should have been,
          She saw by his flickering forge-light
              Quite another scene.

Barbed wire enclosed an arbitrary spot
  Where bored officials lounged (one cracked a joke)
And sentries sweated for the day was hot:
  A crowd of ordinary decent folk
  Watched from without and neither moved nor spoke
As three pale figures were led forth and bound
To three posts driven upright in the ground.

The mass and majesty of this world, all
   That carries weight and always weighs the same
Lay in the hands of others; they were small
   And could not hope for help and no help came:
   What their foes liked to do was done, their shame
Was all the worst could wish; they lost their pride
And died as men before their bodies died.

      She looked over his shoulder
         For athletes at their games,
      Men and women in a dance
         Moving their sweet limbs
      Quick, quick, to music,
         But there on the shining shield
      His hands had set no dancing-floor
         But a weed-choked field.

A ragged urchin, aimless and alone,
   Loitered about that vacancy; a bird
Flew up to safety from his well-aimed stone:
   That girls are raped, that two boys knife a third,
   Were axioms to him, who'd never heard
Of any world where promises were kept,
Or one could weep because another wept.

      The thin-lipped armorer,
         Hephaestos, hobbled away,
      Thetis of the shining breasts
         Cried out in dismay
      At what the god had wrought
         To please her son, the strong
      Iron-hearted man-slaying Achilles
         Who would not live long.

Mountains

(for Hedwig Petzold)

I know a retired dentist who only paints mountains,
    But the Masters rarely care
That much, who sketch them in beyond a holy face
    Or a highly dangerous chair;
While a normal eye perceives them as a wall
Between worse and better, like a child, scolded in France,
Who wishes he were crying on the Italian side of the Alps:
    Caesar does not rejoice when high ground
        Makes a darker map,
    Nor does Madam. Why should they? A serious being
        Cries out for a gap.

And it is curious how often in steep places
    You meet someone short who frowns,
A type you catch beheading daisies with a stick:
    Small crooks flourish in big towns,
But perfect monsters – remember Dracula –
Are bred on crags in castles. Those unsmiling parties,
Clumping off at dawn in the gear of their mystery
    For points up, are a bit alarming;
        They have the balance, nerve,
    And habit of the Spiritual, but what God
        Does their Order serve?

A civil man is a citizen. Am I
   To see in the Lake District, then,
Another bourgeois invention like the piano?
    Well, I won't. How can I, when
I wish I stood now on a platform at Penrith,
Zurich, or any junction at which you leave the express
For a local that swerves off soon into a cutting? Soon
    Tunnels begin, red farms disappear,
      Hedges turn to walls,
Cows become sheep, you smell peat or pinewood, you hear
    Your first waterfalls,

And what looked like a wall turns out to be a world
    With measurements of its own
And a style of gossip. To manage the Flesh,
    When angels of ice and stone
Stand over her day and night who make it so plain
They detest any kind of growth, does not encourage
Euphemisms for the effort: here wayside crucifixes
    Bear witness to a physical outrage,
      And serenades too
Stick to bare fact: 'O my girl has a goitre,
    I've a hole in my shoe!'

Dour. Still, a fine refuge. That boy behind his goats
    Has the round skull of a clan
That fled with bronze before a tougher metal,
    And that quiet old gentleman
With a cheap room at the Black Eagle used to own
Three papers but is not received in Society now:
These farms can always see a panting government coming;
    I'm nordic myself, but even so
      I'd much rather stay
Where the nearest person who could have me hung is
    Some ridges away.

To be sitting in privacy, like a cat
  On the warm roof of a loft,
Where the high-spirited son of some gloomy tarn
  Comes sprinting down through a green croft,
Bright with flowers laid out in exquisite splodges
Like a Chinese poem, while, near enough, a real darling
Is cooking a delicious lunch, would keep me happy for
    What? Five minutes? For an uncatlike
      Creature who has gone wrong,
  Five minutes on even the nicest mountain
      Are awfully long.

Ave Caesar

No bitterness: our ancestors did it.
They were only ignorant and hopeful, they wanted freedom
but wealth too.
Their children will learn to hope for a Caesar.
Or rather – for we are not aquiline Romans but soft mixed
colonists –
Some kindly Sicilian tyrant who'll keep
Poverty and Carthage off until the Romans arrive.
We are easy to manage, a gregarious people,
Full of sentiment, clever at mechanics, and we love our luxuries.

Shine, Republic

The quality of these trees, green height; of the sky, shining, of
water, a clear flow; of the rock, hardness
And reticence: each is noble in its quality. The love of freedom
has been the quality of Western man.

There is a stubborn torch that flames from Marathon to Concord,
its dangerous beauty binding three ages
Into one time; the waves of barbarism and civilization have
eclipsed but have never quenched it.

For the Greeks the love of beauty, for Rome of ruling; for the
present age the passionate love of discovery;
But in one noble passion we are one; and Washington, Luther,
Tacitus, Aeschylus, one kind of man.

And you, America, that passion made you. You were not born
to prosperity, you were born to love freedom.
You did not say 'en masse,' you said 'independence'. But we
cannot have all the luxuries and freedom also.

Freedom is poor and laborious; that torch is not safe but
    hungry, and often requires blood for its fuel.
You will tame it against it burn too clearly, you will hood it
    like a kept hawk, you will perch it on the wrist of Caesar.

But keep the tradition, conserve the forms, the observances,
    keep the spot sore. Be great, carve deep your heel-
    marks.
The states of the next age will no doubt remember you, and
    edge their love of freedom with contempt of luxury.

Woodrow Wilson

(FEBRUARY, 1924)

It said 'Come home, here is an end, a goal,
Not the one raced for, is it not better indeed? Victory you
    know requires
Force to sustain victory, the burden is never lightened, but
    final defeat
Buys peace: you have praised peace, peace without victory.'

He said 'It seems I am traveling no new way,
But leaving my great work unfinished how can I rest? I
    enjoyed a vision,
Endured betrayal, you must not ask me to endure final
    defeat,
Visionless men, blind hearts, blind mouths, live still.'

It said 'Yet perhaps your vision was less great
Than some you scorned, it has not proved even so
    practicable; Lenin
Enters this pass with less reluctance. As to betrayals: there
    are so many
Betrayals, the Russians and the Germans know.'

He said 'I knew I have enemies, I had not thought
To meet one at this brink: shall not the mocking voices die in
    the grave?'
It said 'They shall. Soon there is silence.' 'I dreamed this
    end,' he said, 'when the prow
Of the long ship leaned against dawn, my people

Applauded me, and the world watched me. Again
I dreamed it at Versailles, the time I sent for the ship, and the
    obstinate foreheads
That shared with me the settlement of the world flinched at
    my threat and yielded.
That is all gone . . . Do I remember this darkness?'

It said 'No man forgets it but a moment.
The darkness before the mother, the depth of the return.' 'I
    thought,' he answered,
'That I was drawn out of this depth to establish the earth on
    peace. My labor
Dies with me, why was I drawn out of this depth?'

It said 'Loyal to your highest, sensitive, brave,
Sanguine, some few ways wise, you and all men are drawn
    out of this depth
Only to be these things you are, as flowers for color, falcons
    for swiftness,
Mountains for mass and quiet. Each for its quality

Is drawn out of this depth. Your tragic quality
Required the huge delusion of some major purpose to
    produce it.
What, that the God of the stars needed your help?' He said
    'This is my last
Worst pain, the bitter enlightenment that buys peace.'

34 Blues

I ain't gonna tell no body
                34 have done for me-e-e
I ain't gonna tell no body what
                   34 have done for me-e-e
Christmas rolled up
          I was broke as I could be

They run me from Will Dockery's
             Willie Brown, how 'bout your jo-o-ob
They run me from Will Dockery's
            Willie Brown, I want your jo-o-ob
        (I wonder what's the matter)
I went out and told Papa Charlie:
      I don't want you hangin' round on my job no more

Well it's down in the country
            it almost make you cry-y-y
Well it's down in the country
            it almost make you cry-y-y
       (my God chillun)
Women and children
        flaggin' freight trains for rides

Herman got a little six Buick
           big six Chevrolet ca-a-ar
Herman got a little six Buick
          little six Chevrolet ca-a-ar
      (My God, what solid power)
And they don't do nothin'
      but follow behind *Holloway papa's plou-ou-ough*

Ah, it may bring sorrow
                        Lord, and it may bring tea-ea-ears
It may bring sorrow
                 Lord, and it may bring tea-ea-ears
Oh Lord, oh Lord
              let me see a brand new year

LOUIS MACNEICE

from Autumn Journal

Conferences, adjournments, ultimatums,
    Flights in the air, castles in the air,
The autopsy of treaties, dynamite under the bridges,
    The end of *laissez faire*.
After the warm days the rain comes pimpling
    The paving stones with white
And with the rain the national conscience, creeping,
    Seeping through the night.
And in the sodden park on Sunday protest
    Meetings assemble not, as so often, now
Merely to advertise some patent panacea
    But simply to avow
The need to hold the ditch; a bare avowal
    That may perhaps imply
Death at the doors in a week but perhaps in the long run
    Exposure of the lie.
Think of a number, double it, treble it, square it,
    And sponge it out
And repeat *ad lib.* and mark the slate with crosses;
    There is no time to doubt
If the puzzle really has an answer. Hitler yells on the wireless,
    The night is damp and still
And I hear dull blows on wood outside my window;
    They are cutting down the trees on Primrose Hill.
The wood is white like the roast flesh of chicken,
    Each tree falling like a closing fan;
No more looking at the view from seats beneath the branches,
    Everything is going to plan;
They want the crest of this hill for anti-aircraft,
    The guns will take the view
And searchlights probe the heavens for bacilli
    With narrow wands of blue.

And the rain came on as I watched the territorials
    Sawing and chopping and pulling on ropes like a team
In a village tug-of-war; and I found my dog had vanished
    And thought 'This is the end of the old régime,'
But found the police had got her at St John's Wood station
    And fetched her in the rain and went for a cup
Of coffee to an all-night shelter and heard a taxi-driver
    Say 'It turns me up
When I see these soldiers in lorries' – rumble of tumbrils
    Drums in the trees
Breaking the eardrums of the ravished dryads –
    It turns me up; a coffee, please.
And as I go out I see a windscreen-wiper
    In an empty car
Wiping away like mad and I feel astounded
    That things have gone so far.
And I come back here to my flat and wonder whether
    From now on I need take
The trouble to go out choosing stuff for curtains
    As I don't know anyone to make
Curtains quickly. Rather one should quickly
    Stop the cracks for gas or dig a trench
And take one's paltry measures against the coming
    Of the unknown Uebermensch.
But one – meaning I – is bored, am bored, the issue
    Involving principle but bound in fact
To squander principle in panic and self-deception –
    Accessories after the act,
So that all we foresee is rivers in spate sprouting
    With drowning hands
And men like dead frogs floating till the rivers
    Lose themselves in the sands.
And we who have been brought up to think of 'Gallant
                                        Belgium'
    As so much blague
Are now preparing again to essay good through evil
    For the sake of Prague;

And must, we suppose, become uncritical, vindictive,
    And must, in order to beat
The enemy, model ourselves upon the enemy,
    A howling radio for our paraclete.
The night continues wet, the axe keeps falling,
    The hill grows bald and bleak
No longer one of the sights of London but maybe
    We shall have fireworks here by this day week.

(VII)

The God of War

I saw the old god of war stand in a bog between chasm and rockface.

He smelled of free beer and carbolic and showed his testicles to adolescents, for he had been rejuvenated by several professors. In a hoarse wolfish voice he declared his love for everything young. Nearby stood a pregnant woman, trembling.

And without shame he talked on and presented himself as a great one for order. And he described how everywhere he put barns in order, by emptying them.

And as one throws crumbs to sparrows, he fed poor people with crusts of bread which he had taken away from poor people.

His voice was now loud, now soft, but always hoarse.

In a loud voice he spoke of great times to come, and in a soft voice he taught the women how to cook crows and seagulls. Meanwhile his back was unquiet, and he kept looking round, as though afraid of being stabbed.

And every five minutes he assured his public that he would take up very little of their time.

from Little Gidding

III

There are three conditions which often look alike
Yet differ completely, flourish in the same hedgerow:
Attachment to self and to things and to persons, detachment
From self and from things and from persons; and, growing
    between them, indifference
Which resembles the others as death resembles life,
Being between two lives – unflowering, between
The live and the dead nettle. This is the use of memory:
For liberation – not less of love but expanding
Of love beyond desire, and so liberation
From the future as well as the past. Thus, love of a country
Begins as attachment to our own field of action
And comes to find that action of little importance
Though never indifferent. History may be servitude,
History may be freedom. See, now they vanish,
The faces and places, with the self which, as it could, loved
    them,
To become renewed, transfigured, in another pattern.
Sin is Behovely, but
All shall be well, and
All manner of thing shall be well.
If I think, again, of this place,
And of people, not wholly commendable,
Of no immediate kin or kindness,
But some of peculiar genius,
All touched by a common genius,
United in the strife which divided them;
If I think of a king at nightfall,
Of three men, and more, on the scaffold
And a few who died forgotten
In other places, here and abroad,

And of one who died blind and quiet
Why should we celebrate
These dead men more than the dying?
It is not to ring the bell backward
Nor is it an incantation
To summon the spectre of a Rose.
We cannot revive old factions
We cannot restore old policies
Or follow an antique drum.
These men, and those who opposed them
And those whom they opposed
Accept the constitution of silence
And are folded in a single party.
Whatever we inherit from the fortunate
We have taken from the defeated
What they had to leave us – a symbol:
A symbol perfected in death.
And all shall be well and
All manner of thing shall be well
By the purification of the motive
In the ground of our beseeching.

(*from* Four Quartets, 'Little Gidding', III)

President Roosevelt

Oh yes
We got Mr. President Roosevelt
Oh yes
    ooooooo
        we got Mr. President Roosevelt
Well you know he gone he gone boys
But his spirit always gonna live on

    President Roosevelt traveled by land
    He traveled by the sea
    He helped the U-nited States boys
    And he also helped Chinee

Oh yes
I *just wanted* President Roosevelt
Well you know he gone he gone sonny boy
Oooo well, but his word would never fail

    Now the rooster told the hens
    Said, When are you hens gonna lay
    Said, No, President Roosevelt's dead
    We ain't got no place to stay

Oh yes
We got Mr. President Roosevelt
Well he gone he gone boy
But his word won't never fail

Well the hen told the rooster
Say, I want you to go crow
Said, No, President Roosevelt's dead, boys
Can't work on the project no more

Oh yes
I'm talking President Roosevelt
Well he gone he gone boys, but I know his
Spirit always gonna live on

(Play it boy)

Well President Roosevelt went to Georgia
And he rid it all 'round and 'round
I *just could see that old pale-horse*
Gonna take the President down

Oh yes
We got Mr. President Roosevelt
Well he gone he gone boys
Oooo well boy the spirit always live on

President Roosevelt traveled by the land
He went across the sea
He helped the Chinee
And also helped me

Oh yes
I *accompanied* President Roosevelt
Well he gone he gone boys, but his
Spirit always gonna live on

Hamlet in Russia, A Soliloquy

'My heart throbbed like a boat on the water.
My oars rested. The willows swayed through the summer,
licking my shoulders, elbows and rowlocks –
wait! this might happen,

when the music brought me the beat,
and the ash-gray water-lilies dragged, and a couple of daisies
blew,
and a hint of blue dotted a point off-shore –
lips to lips, stars to stars!

My sister, life!
the world has too many people for us,
the sycophant, the spineless –
politely, like snakes in the grass, they sting.

My sister!
embrace the sky and Hercules
who holds the world up forever
at ease, perhaps, and sleeps at night

thrilled by the nightingales crying . . .

The boat stops throbbing on the water . . .

The clapping stops. I walk into the lights
as Hamlet, lounge like a student against the door-frame,
and try to catch the far-off dissonance of life –
all that has happened, and must!

From the dark the audience leans its one hammering brow
                                                against me –
ten thousand opera glasses, each set on the tripod!
Abba, Father, all things are possible with thee –
take away this cup!

I love the mulishness of Providence,
I am content to play the one part I was born for . . .
quite another play is running now . . .
take me off the hooks tonight!

The sequence of scenes was well thought out;
the last bow is in the cards, or the stars –
but I am alone, and there is none . . .
All's drowned in the sperm and spittle of the Pharisee –

To live a life is not to cross a field.'

                                     trans. Robert Lowell

'next to of course god america i'

'next to of course god america i
love you land of the pilgrims' and so forth oh
say can you see by the dawn's early my
country 'tis of centuries come and go
and are no more what of it we should worry
in every language even deafanddumb
thy sons acclaim your glorious name by gorry
by jingo by gee by gosh by gum
why talk of beauty what could be more beautiful than these heroic happy dead
who rushed like lions to the roaring slaughter
they did not stop to think they died instead
then shall the voice of liberty be mute?'

He spoke.   And drank rapidly a glass of water

Thanksgiving (1956)

a monstering horror swallows
this unworld me by you
as the god of our fathers' fathers bows
to a which that walks like a who

but the voice-with-a-smile of democracy
announces night & day
'all poor little peoples that want to be free
just trust in the u s a'

suddenly uprose hungary
and she gave a terrible cry
'no slave's unlife shall murder me
for i will freely die'

she cried so high thermopylae
heard her and marathon
and all prehuman history
and finally The UN

'be quiet little hungary
and do as you are bid
a good kind bear is angary
we fear for the quo pro quid'

uncle sam shrugs his pretty
pink shoulders you know how
and he twitches a liberal titty
and lisps 'i'm busy right now'

so rah-rah-rah democracy
let's all be as thankful as hell
and bury the statue of liberty
(because it begins to smell)

For the Union Dead

'RELINQUUNT OMNIA SERVARE REM PUBLICAM'

The old South Boston Aquarium stands
in a Sahara of snow now. Its broken windows are boarded.
The bronze weathervane cod has lost half its scales.
The airy tanks are dry.

Once my nose crawled like a snail on the glass;
my hand tingled
to burst the bubbles
drifting from the noses of the cowed, compliant fish.

My hand draws back. I often sigh still
for the dark downward and vegetating kingdom
of the fish and reptile. One morning last March,
I pressed against the new barbed and galvanized

fence on the Boston Common. Behind their cage,
yellow dinosaur steamshovels were grunting
as they cropped up tons of mush and grass
to gouge their underworld garage.

Parking spaces luxuriate like civic
sandpiles in the heart of Boston.
A girdle of orange, Puritan-pumpkin colored girders
braces the tingling Statehouse,

shaking over the excavations, as it faces Colonel Shaw
and his bell-cheeked Negro infantry
on St Gaudens' shaking Civil War relief,
propped by a plank splint against the garage's earthquake.

Two months after marching through Boston,
half the regiment was dead;
at the dedication,
William James could almost hear the bronze Negroes breathe.

Their monument sticks like a fishbone
in the city's throat.
Its Colonel is as lean
as a compass-needle.

He has an angry wrenlike vigilance,
a greyhound's gentle tautness;
he seems to wince at pleasure,
and suffocate for privacy.

He is out of bounds now. He rejoices in man's lovely,
peculiar power to choose life and die –
when he leads his black soldiers to death,
he cannot bend his back.

On a thousand small town New England greens,
the old white churches hold their air
of sparse, sincere rebellion; frayed flags
quilt the graveyards of the grand Army of the Republic.

The stone statues of the abstract Union Soldier
grow slimmer and younger each year –
wasp-waisted, they doze over muskets
and muse through their sideburns . . .

Shaw's father wanted no monument
except the ditch,
where his son's body was thrown
and lost with his 'niggers'.

The ditch is nearer.
There are no statues for the last war here;
on Boylston Street, a commercial photograph
shows Hiroshima boiling

over a Mosler Safe, the 'Rock of Ages'
that survived the blast. Space is nearer.
When I crouch to my television set,
the drained faces of Negro school-children rise like balloons.

Colonel Shaw
is riding on his bubble,
he waits
for the blesséd break.

The Aquarium is gone. Everywhere,
giant finned cars nose forward like fish;
a savage servility
slides by on grease.

George III

(This . . . is perhaps a translation, because I owe so much to Sherwin's
brilliant *Uncorking Old Sherry*, a life of Richard Brinsley Sheridan.
—R.L.)

Poor George,
afflicted by two Congresses,

ours and his own that regularly
and legally had him flogged –

once young George, who saw
his lost majority of our ancestors

dwindle to a few inglorious Tory refugee
diehards who fled for him to Canada –

to lie relegated to the ash-heap,
unvisited in his bicentennial year –

not a lost cause, but no cause.

In '76, George was still King George,
the one authorized tyrant,

not yet the mad, bad old king,

who whimsically picked the pockets of his page
he'd paid to sleep all day outside his door;

who dressed like a Quaker, who danced a minuet
with his appalled apothecary in Kew Gardens;

who did embroidery with the young court ladies,
and criticized them with suspicious bluntness;

who showed aversion for Queen Charlotte, almost
burned her by holding a candle to her face.

It was his sickness, not lust for dominion
made him piss purple, and aghast

his retinue by formally bowing to an elm,
as if it were the Chinese emissary.

George –

once a reigning monarch like Nixon,
and more exhausting to dethrone . . .

Could Nixon's court,
could Haldeman, Ehrlichman, or Kissinger

blame their king's behavior
on an insane wetnurse?

Tragic buffoonery
was more colorful once;

yet how modern George is,
wandering vacated chambers of his White House,

addressing imaginary congresses,
reviewing imaginary combat troops,

thinking himself dead and ordering black clothes:
in memory of George, for he was a good man.

Old, mad, deaf, half-blind,

he talked for thirty-two hours
on everything, everybody,

read Cervantes and the Bible aloud
simultaneously with shattering rapidity . . .

Quand on s'amuse, que le temps fuit –

in his last lucid moment,
singing a hymn to his harpsichord,

praying God for resignation
in his calamity he could not avert . . .

mercifully unable to hear
his drab tapes play back his own voice to him,

morning, noon, and night.

The United Fruit Co.

When the trumpet sounded, it was
all prepared on the earth,
and Jehovah parceled out the earth
to Coca-Cola, Inc., Anaconda,
Ford Motors, and other entities:
The Fruit Company, Inc.
reserved for itself the most succulent,
the central coast of my own land,
the delicate waist of America.
It rechristened its territories
as the 'Banana Republics'
and over the sleeping dead,
over the restless heroes
who brought about the greatness,
the liberty and the flags,
it established the comic opera:
abolished the independencies,
presented crowns of Caesar,
unsheathed envy, attracted
the dictatorship of the flies,
Trujillo flies, Tacho flies,
Carias flies, Martinez flies,
Ubico flies, damp flies
of modest blood and marmalade,
drunken flies who zoom
over the ordinary graves,
circus flies, wise flies
well trained in tyranny.

Among the bloodthirsty flies
the Fruit Company lands its ships,
taking off the coffee and the fruit;
the treasure of our submerged
territories flows as though
on plates into the ships.

Meanwhile Indians are falling
into the sugared chasms
of the harbors, wrapped
for burial in the mist of the dawn:
a body rolls, a thing
that has no name, a fallen cipher,
a cluster of dead fruit
thrown down on the dump.

trans. Robert Bly

DONALD DAVIE

Remembering the Thirties

I

Hearing one saga, we enact the next.
We please our elders when we sit enthralled;
But then they're puzzled; and at last they're vexed
To have their youth so avidly recalled.

It dawns upon the veterans after all
That what for them were agonies, for us
Are high-brow thrillers, though historical;
And all their feats quite strictly fabulous.

This novel written fifteen years ago,
Set in my boyhood and my boyhood home,
These poems about 'abandoned workings', show
Worlds more remote than Ithaca or Rome.

The Anschluss, Guernica – all the names
At which those poets thrilled or were afraid
For me mean schools and schoolmasters and games;
And in the process some-one is betrayed.

Ourselves perhaps. The Devil for a joke
Might carve his own initials on our desk,
And yet we'd miss the point because he spoke
An idiom too dated, Audenesque.

Ralegh's Guiana also killed his son.
A pretty pickle if we came to see
The tallest story really packed a gun,
The Telemachiad an Odyssey.

II

Even to them the tales were not so true
As not to be ridiculous as well;
The ironmaster met his Waterloo,
But Rider Haggard rode along the fell.

'Leave for Cape Wrath tonight!' They lounged away
On Fleming's trek or Isherwood's ascent.
England expected every man that day
To show his motives were ambivalent.

They played the fool, not to appear as fools
In time's long glass. A deprecating air
Disarmed, they thought, the jeers of later schools;
Yet irony itself is doctrinaire,

And curiously, nothing now betrays
Their type to time's derision like this coy
Insistence on the quizzical, their craze
For showing Hector was a mother's boy.

A neutral tone is nowadays preferred.
And yet it may be better, if we must,
To praise a stance impressive and absurd
Than not to see the hero for the dust.

For courage is the vegetable king,
The sprig of all ontologies, the weed
That beards the slag-heap with his hectoring,
Whose green adventure is to run to seed.

Naturally the Foundation will
Bear Your Expenses

Hurrying to catch my Comet
  One dark November day,
Which soon would snatch me from it
  To the sunshine of Bombay,
I pondering pages Berkeley
  Not three weeks since had heard,
Perceiving Chatto darkly
  Through the mirror of the Third.

Crowds, colourless and careworn,
  Had made my taxi late,
Yet not till I was airborne
  Did I recall the date –
That day when Queen and Minister
  And Band of Guards and all
Still act their solemn-sinister
  Wreath-rubbish in Whitehall.

It used to make me throw up,
  These mawkish nursery games:
O when will England grow up?
  – But I outsoar the Thames,
And dwindle off down Auster
  To greet Professor Lal
(He once met Morgan Forster)
  My contact and my pal.

Homage to a Government

Next year we are to bring the soldiers home
For lack of money, and it is all right.
Places they guarded, or kept orderly,
Must guard themselves, and keep themselves orderly.
We want the money for ourselves at home
Instead of working. And this is all right.

It's hard to say who wanted it to happen,
But now it's been decided nobody minds.
The places are a long way off, not here,
Which is all right, and from what we hear
The soldiers there only made trouble happen.
Next year we shall be easier in our minds.

Next year we shall be living in a country
That brought its soldiers home for lack of money.
The statues will be standing in the same
Tree-muffled squares, and look nearly the same.
Our children will not know it's a different country.
All we can hope to leave them now is money.

                                                        1969

Wilfred Owen's Photographs

When Parnell's Irish in the House
Pressed that the British Navy's cat-
O-nine-tails be abolished, what
Shut against them? It was
Neither Irish nor English nor of that
Decade, but of the species.

Predictably, Parliament
Squared against the motion. As soon
Let the old school tie be rent
Off their necks, and give thanks, as see gone
No shame but a monument –
Trafalgar not better known.

'To discontinue it were as much
As ship not powder and cannonballs
But brandy and women' (Laughter). Hearing which
A witty profound Irishman calls
For a 'cat' into the House, and sits to watch
The gentry fingering its stained tails.

Whereupon . . .
                quietly, unopposed,
The motion was passed.

BROTHER WILL HAIRSTON

Alabama Bus

Stop that Alabama bus   I don't wanna ride
Stop that Alabama bus   I don't wanna ride
Stop that Alabama bus   I don't wanna ride
Lord an Alabama boy   'cause I don't wanna ride

Stop that Alabama bus   I don't wanna ride
Stop that Alabama bus   I don't wanna ride
Stop that Alabama bus   I don't wanna ride
Lord an Alabama boy   'cause I don't wanna ride

Lord, there come a bus don't have no load
You know, they tell me that a human being stepped on board
You know, they tell me that the man stepped on the bus
You know, they tell me that the driver began to fuss
He said, Lookit here, man, you from the Negro race
And don't you know you sitting in the wrong place?
The driver told the man, I know you paid your dime
But if you don't move you gonna pay a fine
The man told the driver, My feets are hurting
The driver told the man to move behind the curtain

Stop that Alabama bus   I don't wanna ride
Stop that Alabama bus   I don't wanna ride
Stop that Alabama bus   I don't wanna ride
Lord an Alabama boy   'cause I don't wanna ride

I wanna tell you 'bout the Reverend Martin Luther King
You know, they tell me that the people began to sing
You know, the man God sent out in the world
You know, they tell me that the man had a mighty nerve
You know, the poor man didn't have a bus to rent
You know, they tell me, Great God, he had *a mighty spent*
And he reminded me of Moses in Israel land
He said, A man ain't nothing but a man
He said, Lookit here, Alabama, don't you see
He says, A all of my people gonna follow me
You know, they tell me Reverend King was very hurt
He says, A all of my people gonna walk to work
They said, Lookit here, boy, you hadn't took a thought
So, don't you know you broke the anti-boycott law
They tell me Reverend King said, Treat us right
You know, in the Second World War my father lost his sight
You know, they tell me Abraham signed the pledge one
                                                          night
He said that all of these men should have their equal rights
You know, they had the trial and Clayton Powell was there
You know, they tell me Clayton Powell asked the world for
                                                          prayer
You know, they sent down there to go his bail
You know they PUT REVEREND KING IN A ALABAMA
                                                          JAIL

Stop that Alabama bus	I don't wanna ride
Stop that Alabama bus	I don't wanna ride
Stop that Alabama bus	I don't wanna ride
Lord an Alabama boy	'cause I don't wanna ride

Stop that Alabama bus	I don't wanna ride
Stop that Alabama bus	I don't wanna ride
Stop that Alabama bus	I don't wanna ride
Lord an Alabama boy	'cause I don't wanna ride

You know, they tell me Reverend King was *a violence 'bide*
A when all the buses passed, and no body will ride
You know, they tell me that the Negroes was ready to go
They had a walked along the streets until their feets was sore
You know, they tell me Reverend King had spreaded the
word
'Bout an Alabama bus ride, so I heard
You know, they spent a lot of money since King go on
You know, in nineteen and twenty-nine that man was born
You know, the five hundred dollars aren't very heavy
You know, the poor man was born the fifteenth of January

Stop that Alabama bus   I don't wanna ride
Stop that Alabama bus   I don't wanna ride
Stop that Alabama bus   I don't wanna ride
Lord an Alabama boy   but I don't wanna ride

ELIZABETH BISHOP

From Trollope's Journal

Winter, 1861

As far as statues go, so far there's not
much choice: they're either Washingtons
or Indians, a whitewashed, stubby lot,
His country's Father or His foster sons.
The White House in a sad, unhealthy spot
just higher than Potomac's swampy brim,
– they say the present President has got
ague or fever in each backwoods limb.
On Sunday afternoon I wandered – rather,
I floundered – out alone. The air was raw
and dark; the marsh half-ice, half-mud. This weather
is normal now: a frost, and then a thaw,
and then a frost. A hunting man, I found
the Pennsylvania Avenue heavy ground . . .
There all around me in the ugly mud
– hoof-pocked, uncultivated – herds of cattle,
numberless, wond'ring steers and oxen, stood:
beef for the Army, after the next battle.
Their legs were caked the color of dried blood;
their horns were wreathed with fog. Poor, starving, dumb
or lowing creatures, never to chew the cud
or fill their maws again! Th'effluvium
made that damned anthrax on my forehead throb.
I called a surgeon in, a young man, but,
with a sore throat himself, he did his job.
We talked about the War, and as he cut
away, he croaked out, 'Sir, I do declare
everyone's sick! The soldiers poison the air.'

ZBIGNIEW HERBERT

Elegy of Fortinbras

for C. M.

Now that we're alone we can talk prince man to man
though you lie on the stairs and see no more than a dead ant
nothing but black sun with broken rays
I could never think of your hands without smiling
and now that they lie on the stone like fallen nests
they are as defenceless as before The end is exactly this
The hands lie apart The sword lies apart The Head apart
and the knight's feet in soft slippers

You will have a soldier's funeral without having been a soldier
the only ritual I am acquainted with a little
There will be no candles no singing only canon-fuses and
                                                    bursts
crepe dragged on the pavement helmets boots artillery horses
                            drums drums I know nothing exquisite
those will be my manoeuvres before I start to rule
one has to take the city by the neck and shake it a bit

Anyhow you had to perish Hamlet you were not for life
you believed in crystal notions not in human clay
always twitching as if asleep you hunted chimeras
wolfishly you crunched the air only to vomit
you knew no human thing you did not know even how to
                                                 breathe

Now you have peace Hamlet you accomplished what you had to
and you have peace The rest is not silence but belongs to me
you chose the easier part an elegant thrust
but what is heroic death compared with eternal watching
with a cold apple in one's hand on a narrow chair
with a view of the ant-hill and the clock's dial

Adieu prince I have tasks a sewer project
and a decree on prostitutes and beggars
I must also elaborate a better system of prisons
since as you justly said Denmark is a prison
I go to my affairs This night is born
a star named Hamlet We shall never meet
what I shall leave will not be worth a tragedy

It is not for us to greet each other or bid farewell we live on
                                                    archipelagos
and that water these words what can they do what can they do
                                                         prince

                              trans. Czesław Miłosz

Pan Cogito's Thoughts on Hell

Contrary to popular belief, the lowest circle of hell is not
inhabited either by despots, matricides or those who are
seekers after flesh. It is a refuge for artists, full of mirrors,
pictures and instruments. To a casual observer, the most
comfortable infernal department without brimstone, tar or
physical torture.

All the year round there are competitions, festivals and
concerts. There is no high season. The season is permanent
and almost absolute. Every quarter new Movements spring
up and nothing, it appears, can arrest the triumphal
procession of the Avantgarde.

Beelzebub loves art. He boasts that his choirs, poets and
painters almost outstrip the celestials. Better art means better
government – that's obvious. Soon they will be able to test
their strengths at the Two Worlds Festival. Then we'll see if
Dante, Fra Angelico and Bach make the grade.

Beelzebub supports art. His artists are guaranteed peace,
good food and total isolation from infernal life.

                              trans. Adam Czerniawski

The Return of the Proconsul

I've decided to return to the emperor's court
once more I shall see if it's possible to live there
I could stay here in this remote province
under the full sweet leaves of the sycamore
and the gentle rule of sickly nepotists

when I return I don't intend to commend myself
I shall applaud in measured portions
smile in ounces frown discreetly
for that they will not give me a golden chain
this iron one will suffice

I've decided to return tomorrow or the day after
I cannot live among vineyards nothing here is mine
trees have no roots houses no foundations the rain is glassy
                                        flowers smell of wax
a dry cloud rattles against the empty sky
so I shall return tomorrow or the day after in any case I shall
                                                                return

I must come to terms with my face again
with my lower lip so it knows how to curb its scorn
with my eyes so they remain ideally empty
and with that miserable chin the hare of my face
which trembles when the chief of guards walks in

of one thing I am sure I will not drink wine with him
when he brings his goblet nearer I will lower my eyes
and pretend I'm picking bits of food from between my teeth
besides the emperor likes courage of convictions
to a certain extent to a certain reasonable extent
he is after all a man like everyone else

and already tired by all those tricks with poison
he cannot drink his fill incessant chess
this left cup is for Drusus from the right one pretend to sip
then drink only water never lose sight of Tacitus
go out into the garden and come back when they've taken
                                        away the corpse

I've decided to return to the emperor's court
yes I hope that things will work out somehow

                                    trans. Czesław Miłosz

The End of a Dynasty

The whole royal family was living in one room at that time.
Outside the windows was a wall, and under the wall, a
dump. There, rats used to bite cats to death. This was not
seen. The windows had been painted over with lime.

When the executioners came, they found an everyday
scene.

His Majesty was improving the regulations of the Holy
Trinity regiment, the occultist Philippe was trying to soothe
the Queen's nerves by suggestion, the Crown Prince, rolled
into a ball, was sleeping in an armchair, and the Grand (and
skinny) Duchesses were singing pious songs and mending
linen.

As for the valet, he stood against a partition and tried to
imitate the tapestry.

                                    trans. Czesław Miłosz

From Mythology

First there was a god of night and tempest, a black idol without eyes, before whom they leaped, naked and smeared with blood. Later on, in the times of the republic, there were many gods with wives, children, creaking beds, and harmlessly exploding thunderbolts. At the end only superstitious neurotics carried in their pockets little statues of salt, representing the god of irony. There was no greater god at that time.

Then came the barbarians. They too valued highly the little god of irony. They would crush it under their heels and add it to their dishes.

trans. Czesław Miłosz

TADEUZ RÓŻEWICZ

Poem of Pathos

They spat on the poet
for centuries
they will be wiping the earth and stars
for centuries
they will be wiping their own faces

A poet buried alive
is like a subterranean river
he preserves within
faces names
hope
and homeland

A deceived poet
hears voices
hears his own voice
looks around
like a man woken
at dawn

But a poet's lie
is multilingual
as monumental
as the Tower of Babel

it is monstrous
and does not die

1967
trans. Adam Czerniawski

Posthumous Rehabilitation

The dead have remembered
our indifference
The dead have remembered
our silence
The dead have remembered
our words

The dead see our snouts
laughing from ear to ear
The dead see
our bodies rubbing against each other
The dead see our hands
poised for applause

The dead read our books
listen to our speeches
delivered so long ago

the dead hear
clucking tongues

The dead scrutinize our lectures
join in previously terminated
discussions

The dead see stadiums
ensembles and choirs declaiming rhythmically

All the living are guilty
little children
who offered bouquets of flowers
are guilty
lovers are guilty
guilty are

guilty are those who ran away
and those that stayed
those who were saying yes
those who said no
and those who said nothing

the dead are taking stock of the living
the dead will not rehabilitate us

1957
trans. Adam Czerniawski

karl heinrich marx

gigantic grandfather
jehovah-bearded
on brown daguerrotypes
i see your face
in the snow-white aura
despotic quarrelsome
and your papers in the linen press:
butcher's bills
inaugural addresses
warrants for your arrest

your massive body
i see in the 'wanted' book
gigantic traitor
displaced person
in tail coat and plastron
consumptive sleepless
your gall-bladder scorched
by heavy cigars
salted gherkins laudanum
and liqueur

i see your house
in the rue d'alliance
dean street grafton terrace
gigantic bourgeois
domestic tyrant
in worn-out slippers:
soot and 'economic shit'
usury 'as usual'
children's coffins
rumours of sordid affairs

no machine-gun
in your prophet's hand:
i see it calmly
in the british museum
under the green lamp
break up your own house
with a terrible patience
gigantic founder
for the sake of other houses
in which you never woke up

gigantic zaddik
i see you betrayed
by your disciples:
only your enemies
remained what they were:
i see your face
on the last picture
of april eighty-two:
an iron mask:
the iron mask of freedom

trans. Michael Hamburger

The Soviet Union

There was that business in Siberia, in '19.
That was disgusting.
My God if John Adams had foreseen that
he would have renounced his immortality.

It was despicable.   My friends, forgive us.
It was done by our fearful invasive fathers.
I have a Russian image: in the Crimea, a train is stalled:
She's in labour, lanterns are swinging,

they couldn't help her.   She hemorrhaged, among the
                                                                    peasants,
grimaced; & went away.
And Nikolay struck down in the advance
seeing the others going on

thought Am I wounded? Maybe I will die!
ME, Nikolay Rostov, whom everybody *loved* so?

You murdered Babel,
we murdered Martin Luther King; redskins, blacks.
You have given a bitter time to Jews.
Maybe one of our Negroes was a Babel.

Trotsky struggled: over the railway system
and which troops were when to be where.
When he addressed the Petrograd Soviet
their vascular systems ran vodka.

Lenin wrote: Stalin is a boor;
& should not continue as Secretary.
Lenin, that great man, dying off there,
with only her (that great woman) to talk to.

Stalin was mad at midnight: & criminal. But that Georgian
                              had high even heroic qualities,
He stayed you through the horrible advance
of the German divisions.   He had faith.
Smolensk; & then in the South.

An Odessa Jew, a bespectacled intellectual small man,
who rode with the revolutionary Cossacks,
was murdered in one of your prisons or your camps.
Man is vicious.   We forgive you.

THOM GUNN

Iron Landscapes
(and the Statue of Liberty)

No trellisses, no vines
        a fire escape
Repeats a bare black Z from tier to tier.
Hard flower, tin scroll embellish this landscape.
Between iron columns I walk toward the pier.

And stand a long time at the end of it
Gazing at iron on the New Jersey side.
A girdered ferry-building opposite,
Displaying the name LACKAWANNA, seems to ride

The turbulent brown-grey waters that intervene:
Cool seething incompletion that I love.
The zigzags come and go, sheen tracking sheen;
And water wrestles with the air above.

But I'm at peace with the iron landscape too,
Hard because buildings must be hard to last
– Block, cylinder, cube, built with their angles true,
A dream of righteous permanence, from the past.

In Nixon's era, decades after the ferry,
The copper embodiment of the pieties
Seems hard, but hard like a revolutionary
With indignation, constant as she is.

From here you can glimpse her downstream, her far charm,
Liberty, tiny woman in the mist
– You cannot see the torch – raising her arm
Lorn, bold, as if saluting with her fist.

Barrow Street Pier, New York
May 1973

SEAMUS HEANEY

Punishment

I can feel the tug
of the halter at the nape
of her neck, the wind
on her naked front.

It blows her nipples
to amber beads,
it shakes the frail rigging
of her ribs.

I can see her drowned
body in the bog,
the weighing stone,
the floating rods and boughs.

Under which at first
she was a barked sapling
that is dug up
oak-bone, brain-firkin:

her shaved head
like a stubble of black corn,
her blindfold a soiled bandage,
her noose a ring

to store
the memories of love.
Little adulteress,
before they punished you

you were flaxen-haired,
undernourished, and your
tar-black face was beautiful.
My poor scapegoat,

I almost love you
but would have cast, I know,
the stones of silence.
I am the artful voyeur

of your brain's exposed
and darkened combs,
your muscles' webbing
and all your numbered bones:

I who have stood dumb
when your betraying sisters,
cauled in tar,
wept by the railings,

who would connive
in civilized outrage
yet understand the exact
and tribal, intimate revenge.

A Constable Calls

His bicycle stood at the window-sill,
The rubber cowl of a mud-splasher
Skirting the front mudguard,
Its fat black handlegrips

Heating in sunlight, the 'spud'
Of the dynamo gleaming and cocked back,
The pedal treads hanging relieved
Of the boot of the law.

His cap was upside down
On the floor, next his chair.
The line of its pressure ran like a bevel
In his slightly sweating hair.

He had unstrapped
The heavy ledger, and my father
Was making tillage returns
In acres, roods, and perches.

Arithmetic and fear.
I sat staring at the polished holster
With its buttoned flap, the braid cord
Looped into the revolver butt.

'Any other root crops?
Mangolds? Marrowstems? Anything like that?'
'No.' But was there not a line
Of turnips where the seed ran out

In the potato field? I assumed
Small guilts and sat
Imagining the black hole in the barracks.
He stood up, shifted the baton-case

Further round on his belt,
Closed the domesday book,
Fitted his cap back with two hands,
And looked at me as he said goodbye.

A shadow bobbed in the window.
He was snapping the carrier spring
Over the ledger. His boot pushed off
And the bicycle ticked, ticked, ticked.

                    (*from* 'Singing School')

Casualty

I

He would drink by himself
And raise a weathered thumb
Towards the high shelf,
Calling another rum
And blackcurrant, without
Having to raise his voice,
Or order a quick stout
By a lifting of the eyes
And a discreet dumb-show
Of pulling off the top;
At closing time would go
In waders and peaked cap
Into the showery dark,
A dole-kept breadwinner
But a natural for work.
I loved his whole manner,
Sure-footed but too sly,
His deadpan sidling tact,
His fisherman's quick eye
And turned observant back.

Incomprehensible
To him, my other life.
Sometimes, on his high stool,
Too busy with his knife
At a tobacco plug
And not meeting my eye,
In the pause after a slug
He mentioned poetry.
We would be on our own
And, always politic
And shy of condescension,

I would manage by some trick
To switch the talk to eels
Or lore of the horse and cart
Or the Provisionals.

But my tentative art
His turned back watches too:
He was blown to bits
Out drinking in a curfew
Others obeyed, three nights
After they shot dead
The thirteen men in Derry.
PARAS THIRTEEN, the walls said,
BOGSIDE NIL. That Wednesday
Everybody held
His breath and trembled.

II

It was a day of cold
Raw silence, wind-blown
Surplice and soutane:
Rained-on, flower-laden
Coffin after coffin
Seemed to float from the door
Of the packed cathedral
Like blossoms on slow water.
The common funeral
Unrolled its swaddling band,
Lapping, tightening
Till we were braced and bound
Like brothers in a ring.

But he would not be held
At home by his own crowd
Whatever threats were phoned,
Whatever black flags waved.
I see him as he turned
In that bombed offending place,
Remorse fused with terror
In his still knowable face,
His cornered outfaced stare
Blinding in the flash.

He had gone miles away
For he drank like a fish
Nightly, naturally
Swimming towards the lure
Of warm lit-up places,
The blurred mesh and murmur
Drifting among glasses
In the gregarious smoke.
How culpable was he
That last night when he broke
Our tribe's complicity?
'Now you're supposed to be
An educated man,'
I hear him say. 'Puzzle me
The right answer to that one.'

III

I missed his funeral,
Those quiet walkers
And sideways talkers
Shoaling out of his lane
To the respectable
Purring of the hearse . . .
They move in equal pace
With the habitual
Slow consolation
Of a dawdling engine,
The line lifted, hand
Over fist, cold sunshine
On the water, the land
Banked under fog: that morning
I was taken in his boat,
The screw purling, turning
Indolent fathoms white,
I tasted freedom with him.
To get out early, haul
Steadily off the bottom,
Dispraise the catch, and smile
As you find a rhythm
Working you, slow mile by mile,
Into your proper haunt
Somewhere, well out, beyond . . .

Dawn-sniffing revenant,
Plodder through midnight rain,
Question me again.

from Station Island

Like a convalescent, I took the hand
stretched down from the jetty, sensed again
an alien comfort as I stepped on ground

to find the helping hand still gripping mine,
fish-cold and bony, but whether to guide
or to be guided I could not be certain

for the tall man in step at my side
seemed blind, though he walked straight as a rush
upon his ash plant, his eyes fixed straight ahead.

Then I knew him in the flesh
out there on the tarmac among the cars,
wintered hard and sharp as a blackthorn bush.

His voice eddying with the vowels of all rivers
came back to me, though he did not speak yet,
a voice like a prosecutor's or a singer's,

cunning, narcotic, mimic, definite
as a steel nib's downstroke, quick and clean,
and suddenly he hit a litter basket

with his stick, saying, 'Your obligation
is not discharged by any common rite.
What you must do must be done on your own

so get back in harness. The main thing is to write
for the joy of it. Cultivate a work-lust
that imagines its haven like your hands at night

dreaming the sun in the sunspot of a breast.
You are fasted now, light-headed, dangerous.
Take off from here. And don't be so earnest,

let others wear the sackcloth and the ashes.
Let go, let fly, forget.
You've listened long enough. Now strike your note.'

It was as if I had stepped free into space
alone with nothing that I had not known
already. Raindrops blew in my face

as I came to. 'Old father, mother's son,
there is a moment in Stephen's diary
for April the thirteenth, a revelation

set among my stars – that one entry
has been a sort of password in my ears,
the collect of a new epiphany,

the Feast of the Holy Tundish.' 'Who cares,'
he jeered, 'any more? The English language
belongs to us. You are raking at dead fires,

a waste of time for somebody your age.
That subject people stuff is a cod's game,
infantile, like your peasant pilgrimage.

You lose more of yourself than you redeem
doing the decent thing. Keep at a tangent.
When they make the circle wide, it's time to swim

out on your own and fill the element
with signatures on your own frequency,
echo soundings, searches, probes, allurements,

elver-gleams in the dark of the whole sea.'
The shower broke in a cloudburst, the tarmac
fumed and sizzled. As he moved off quickly

the downpour loosed its screens round his straight walk.

                                                    (XII)

DEREK MAHON

The Snow Party

for Louis Asekoff

Bashō, coming
To the city of Nagoya,
Is asked to a snow party.

There is a tinkling of china
And tea into china;
There are introductions.

Then everyone
Crowds to the window
To watch the falling snow.

Snow is falling on Nagoya
And farther south
On the tiles of Kyōto.

Eastward, beyond Irago,
It is falling
Like leaves on the cold sea.

Elsewhere they are burning
Witches and heretics
In the boiling squares,

Thousands have died since dawn
In the service
Of barbarous kings;

But there is silence
In the houses of Nagoya
And the hills of Ise.

The Last of the Fire Kings

I want to be
Like the man who descends
At two milk churns

With a bulging
String bag and vanishes
Where the lane turns,

Or the man
Who drops at night
From a moving train

And strikes out over the fields
Where fireflies glow
Not knowing a word of the language.

Either way, I am
Through with history –
Who lives by the sword

Dies by the sword.
Last of the fire kings, I shall
Break with tradition and

Die by my own hand
Rather than perpetuate
The barbarous cycle.

Five years I have reigned
During which time
I have lain awake each night

And prowled by day
In the sacred grove
For fear of the usurper.

Perfecting my cold dream
Of a place out of time,
A palace of porcelain

Where the frugivorous
Inheritors recline
In their rich fabrics
Far from the sea.

But the fire-loving
People, rightly perhaps,
Will not countenance this,

Demanding that I inhabit,
Like them, a world of
Sirens, bin-lids
And bricked-up windows –

Not to release them
From the ancient curse
But to die their creature and be thankful.

A Disused Shed in Co. Wexford

Let them not forget us, the weak souls among the asphodels.
—Seferis, *Mythistorema*

for J. G. Farrell

Even now there are places where a thought might grow –
Peruvian mines, worked out and abandoned
To a slow clock of condensation,
An echo trapped for ever, and a flutter
Of wildflowers in the lift-shaft,
Indian compounds where the wind dances
And a door bangs with diminished confidence,
Lime crevices behind rippling rainbarrels,
Dog corners for bone burials;
And in a disused shed in Co. Wexford,

Deep in the grounds of a burnt-out hotel,
Among the bathtubs and the washbasins
A thousand mushrooms crowd to a keyhole.
This is the one star in their firmament
Or frames a star within a star.
What should they do there but desire?
So many days beyond the rhododendrons
With the world waltzing in its bowl of cloud,
They have learnt patience and silence
Listening to the rooks querulous in the high wood.

They have been waiting for us in a foetor
Of vegetable sweat since civil war days,
Since the gravel-crunching, interminable departure
Of the expropriated mycologist.
He never came back, and light since then
Is a keyhole rusting gently after rain.
Spiders have spun, flies dusted to mildew
And once a day, perhaps, they have heard something –
A trickle of masonry, a shout from the blue
Or a lorry changing gear at the end of the lane.

There have been deaths, the pale flesh flaking
Into the earth that nourished it;
And nightmares, born of these and the grim
Dominion of stale air and rank moisture.
Those nearest the door grow strong –
'Elbow room! Elbow room!'
The rest, dim in a twilight of crumbling
Utensils and broken flower-pots, groaning
For their deliverance, have been so long
Expectant that there is left only the posture.

A half century, without visitors, in the dark –
Poor preparation for the cracking lock
And creak of hinges. Magi, moonmen,
Powdery prisoners of the old regime,
Web-throated, stalked like triffids, racked by drought
And insomnia, only the ghost of a scream
At the flash-bulb firing squad we wake them with
Shows there is life yet in their feverish forms.
Grown beyond nature now, soft food for worms,
They lift frail heads in gravity and good faith.

They are begging us, you see, in their wordless way,
To do something, to speak on their behalf
Or at least not to close the door again.
Lost people of Treblinka and Pompeii!
'Save us, save us,' they seem to say,
'Let the god not abandon us
Who have come so far in darkness and in pain.
We too had our lives to live.
You with your light meter and relaxed itinerary,
Let not our naive labours have been in vain!'

MICHAEL LONGLEY

Wounds

Here are two pictures from my father's head –
I have kept them like secrets until now:
First, the Ulster Division at the Somme
Going over the top with 'Fuck the Pope!'
'No Surrender!': a boy about to die,
Screaming 'Give 'em one for the Shankill!'
'Wilder than Gurkhas' were my father's words
Of admiration and bewilderment.
Next comes the London-Scottish padre
Resettling kilts with his swagger-stick,
With a stylish backhand and a prayer.
Over a landscape of dead buttocks
My father followed him for fifty years.
At last, a belated casualty,
He said – lead traces flaring till they hurt –
'I am dying for King and Country, slowly.'
I touched his hand, his thin head I touched.

Now, with military honours of a kind,
With his badges, his medals like rainbows,
His spinning compass, I bury beside him
Three teenage soldiers, bellies full of
Bullets and Irish beer, their flies undone.
A packet of Woodbines I throw in,
A lucifer, the Sacred Heart of Jesus
Paralysed as heavy guns put out
The night-light in a nursery for ever;
Also a bus-conductor's uniform –
He collapsed beside his carpet-slippers
Without a murmur, shot through the head
By a shivering boy who wandered in
Before they could turn the television down

Or tidy away the supper dishes.
To the children, to a bewildered wife,
I think 'Sorry Missus' was what he said.

DOUGLAS DUNN

Washing the Coins

You'd start at seven, and then you'd bend your back
Until they let you stand up straight, your hands
Pressed on your kidneys as you groaned for lunch,
Thick sandwiches in grease-proofed bundles, piled
Beside the jackets by the hawthorn hedges.
And then you'd bend your little back again
Until they let you stand up straight. Your hands,
On which the earth had dried in layers, itched, itched,
Though worse still was that ache along the tips
Of every picking finger, each broken nail
That scraped the ground for sprawled potatoes
The turning digger churned out of the drills.
Muttering strong Irish men and women worked
Quicker than local boys. You had to watch them.
They had the trick of sideways-bolted spuds
Fast to your ear, and the upset wire basket
That broke your heart but made the Irish laugh.
You moaned, complained, and learned the rules of work.
Your boots, enlarging as the day wore on,
Were weighted by the magnets of the earth,
And rain in the face was also to have
Something in common with bedraggled Irish.
You held your hands into the rain, then watched
Brown water drip along your chilling fingers
Until you saw the colour of your skin
Through rips disfiguring your gloves of mud.
It was the same for everyone. All day
That bead of sweat tickled your smeared nose
And a glance upwards would show you trees and clouds
In turbulent collusions of the sky
With ground and ground with sky, and you portrayed
Among the wretched of the native earth.
Towards the end you felt you understood

The happy rancour of the Irish howkers.
When dusk came down, you stood beside the byre
For the farmer's wife to pay the labour off.
And this is what I remember by the dark
Whitewash of the byre wall among shuffling boots.
She knew me, but she couldn't tell my face
From an Irish boy's, and she apologized
And roughed my hair as into my cupped hands
She poured a dozen pennies of the realm
And placed two florins there, then cupped her hands
Around my hands, like praying together.
It is not good to feel you have no future.
My clotted hands turned coins to muddy copper.
I tumbled all my coins upon our table.
My mother ran a basin of hot water.
We bathed my wages and we scrubbed them clean.
Once all that sediment was washed away,
That residue of field caked on my money,
I filled the basin to its brim with cold;
And when the water settled I could see
Two English kings among their drowned Britannias.

Green Breeks

J. G. Lockhart, Memoirs of Sir Walter Scott,
Macmillan, 1900. Vol. 1, pages 81–5.

Crosscauseway, Bristo Street, and Potterrow,
In Edinburgh, seventeen eighty-three –
     Boys there were poor, their social class was 'low';
     Their futures lay in work or livery.
Sir Walter Scott says they 'inhabited'
These streets they lived on; but, in George's Square,
     'The author's father' – so Sir Walter said –
     Did not 'inhabit' but 'resided' there.
Young Walter and his chums were organized
Into a 'company' or 'regiment'.
     A 'lady of distinction', who despised
     The ragged street-boys from the tenements,
Gave Scott 'a handsome set of colours', which
Made Walter grateful to that Highland bitch
Who'd later 'clear' her kinsmen from her land,
That Duchess-Countess named for Sutherland.

From Potterrow, Crosscauseway, Bristo Street,
The poor boys came to 'bicker' on the Square –
     A military game, if indiscreet –
     To thrash the sons of those 'residing' there.
Offspring of State, Law, Ministry and Bank,
With flag aloft, defended their regime
     Against those 'chiefly of the lower rank',
     Boy-battles at a simplified extreme.
Though vanquished from the subtly written book
That's history, the street-boys often won –
     Scott says they did. Sir Walter undertook
     Average lies in how he wrote it down –
Mendacious annals – that no one should forget
When beggars win, they're in the horsemen's debt;
And only Scott has chronicled their war –
A beaten boy becomes the conqueror.

One of his enemies, says Scott, was both
Ajax and Achilles of the Crosscauseway –
    'The very picture of a youthful Goth' –
    The first to fight and last to run away.
Blue-eyed, with long fair hair, tall, finely made,
That boy-barbarian awed him. Scott could tell
    He and his class-mates mustered to degrade
    This brave, presumptuous, vulgar general.
They called him Green Breeks, this boy whom Scott
                                preserved
As a memento of his opposite
    That, cheating him of what he led and served,
    A novelist could have his way with it.
Scott draws the colour of his hero's eyes,
His shape, his height, but not the boy, who dies
Within the pickle of Scott's quickened prose,
Half-loved by Scott, half-feared, born to oppose.

In one fight, Green Breeks laid his hands upon
Sutherland's 'patrician standard'. Before
    He'd time to win it, he was faced with one
    Too zealous for 'the honour of the Corps'
Who had a hanger or *couteau de chasse*.
For honour, then, that boy cut Green Breeks down.
    To save a flag, the honour of his class,
    He struck him on the head and cut him down.
Imagined horsemen of the old regime
Transformed young Green Breeks to a Dying Gaul –
    A pictured history, the bronze of dream.
    A classic gesture in an urban brawl.
Scott's friend disgraced his 'regiment' and showed
Expedient dragoonship was its code.
Where was nobility? But Scott, you found
Your life's obsession on that cobbled ground.

Scott turned our country round upon its name
And time. Its history obeyed his whip
    When Scott sent out his characters to claim
    Their pedigrees in Green Breeks' leadership.
I do not understand, Scott, what you meant
By your displaced verse-prose 'nobility'
    Unless the tatters of your 'regiment'
    Were patched on Green Breeks, that, for chivalry,
Your heroes might go forth and look the part –
Part man, part prince, part soldier and part God –
    Ridiculous and lacking in support
    As, when they fall, mere modern men applaud.
But Scott, you failed; for where your Green Breeks lives
Is that dark tenement of fugitives
Who, fled from time, have no need to endure
The quicklime of your ordered literature.

Green Breeks did not inform. He kept his pride.
He nursed his lovely grudge and sword-cracked skull
    And took both pain and bribery in his stride.
    They offered cash, 'smart money', to annul
Shame and dishonoured laws. He would not sell
His wound: let them remember it. Scott says
    That childish purse was small – part comical,
    Part serious, the whole antithesis.
They should not meet him face to face, but stood
On dignity and used a go-between,
    Like states, transacting with the multitude,
    Who can negotiate, then intervene
With laws, with cavalry and troops, with style,
With system, representatives and guile,
Who, pompously, can compromise to win,
Pitch coins against a ragged ostentation.

Peasant baroque, like this, its nuts screwed tight
In praise of rabbles and those *sans culottes*,
        Won't change a thing. It whets an appetite,
        Unfankling truths inwoven like a knot.
It gestures like a ghost towards a ghost,
And, bringing Green Breeks back, or trying to,
        It reckons with desire, the human cost
        In losing what was old, and fierce, and true.
What did he do? Where did he live, and die?
That life can be imagined. I let him *be*.
        He is my light, conspirator and spy.
        He is perpetual. He is my country.
He is my people's minds, when they perceive
A native truth persisting in the weave
Of shabby happenings. When they turn their cheeks
The other way, he turns them back, my Green Breeks.

Green Breeks accepted what he asked them give –
A pound of snuff for 'some old woman – aunt,
        Grandmother, or the like,' with whom he lived.
        Kindness, like courtesy, must ever haunt
Love-raddled reminiscence, Walter Scott.
You cannot hide behind mock-epic prose
        Your love of 'haves', amusement at 'have-nots'.
        Between your lines, it's easy to suppose
Deeper affections generate each word
Recalling Green Breeks in your years of fame.
        You drank toasts to his name in Abbotsford,
        Proposed to Green Breeks, not his father's name.
Be not amused, Scott. Go, and give him thanks
He let you patronize his 'lower ranks'.
Go, talk to him, and tell him who you are,
Face to face, at last, Scott; and kiss his scar.

GEOFFREY HILL

Idylls of the King

The pigeon purrs in the wood; the wood has gone;
dark leaves that flick to silver in the gust,
and the marsh-orchids and the heron's nest,
goldgrimy shafts and pillars of the sun.

Weightless magnificence upholds the past.
Cement recesses smell of fur and bone
and berries wrinkle in the badger-run
and wiry heath-fern scatters its fresh rust.

'O clap your hands' so that the dove takes flight,
bursts through the leaves with an untidy sound,
plunges its wings into the green twilight

above this long-sought and forsaken ground,
the half-built ruins of the new estate,
warheads of mushrooms round the filter-pond.

(*from* 'An Apology For The Revival Of
Christian Architecture in England')

TONY HARRISON

On Not Being Milton

for Sergio Vieira & Armando Guebuza (*Frelimo*)

Read and committed to the flames. I call
these sixteen lines that go back to my roots
my *Cahier d'un retour au pays natal*,
my growing black enough to fit my boots.

The stutter of the scold out of the branks
of condescension, class and counter-class
thickens with glottals to a lumpen mass
of Ludding morphemes closing up their ranks.
Each swung cast-iron Enoch of Leeds stress
clangs a forged music on the frames of Art,
the looms of owned language smashed apart!

Three cheers for mute ingloriousness!

Articulation is the tongue-tied's fighting.
In the silence round all poetry we quote
Tidd the Cato Street conspirator who wrote:

Sir, I Ham a very Bad Hand at Righting

note   An 'Enoch' is an iron sledge-hammer used by
the Luddites to smash the frames which were also
made by the same Enoch Taylor of Marsden. The
cry was: Enoch made them. Enoch shall break them!

Anseo

When the Master was calling the roll
At the primary school in Collegelands,
You were meant to call back *Anseo*
And raise your hand
As your name occurred.
Anseo, meaning here, here and now,
All present and correct,
Was the first word of Irish I spoke.
The last name on the ledger
Belonged to Joseph Mary Plunkett Ward
And was followed, as often as not,
By silence, knowing looks,
A nod and a wink, the Master's droll
'And where's our little Ward-of-court?'

I remember the first time he came back
The Master had sent him out
Along the hedges
To weigh up for himself and cut
A stick with which he would be beaten.
After a while, nothing was spoken;
He would arrive as a matter of course
With an ash-plant, a salley-rod.
Or, finally, the hazel-wand
He had whittled down to a whip-lash,
Its twist of red and yellow lacquers
Sanded and polished,
And altogether so delicately wrought
That he had engraved his initials on it.

I last met Joseph Mary Plunkett Ward
In a pub just over the Irish border.
He was living in the open,
In a secret camp
On the other side of the mountain.
He was fighting for Ireland,
Making things happen.
And he told me, Joe Ward,
Of how he had risen through the ranks
To Quartermaster, Commandant:
How every morning at parade
His volunteers would call back *Anseo*
And raise their hands
As their names occurred.

Meeting the British

We met the British in the dead of winter.
The sky was lavender

and the snow lavender-blue.
I could hear, far below,

the sound of two streams coming together
(both were frozen over)

and, no less strange,
myself calling out in French

across that forest-
clearing. Neither General Jeffrey Amherst

nor Colonel Henry Bouquet
could stomach our willow-tobacco.

As for the unusual
scent when the Colonel shook out his hand-

kerchief: *C'est la lavande,*
une fleur mauve comme le ciel.

They gave us six fishhooks
and two blankets embroidered with smallpox.

SEAMUS DEANE

Osip Mandelstam

'The people need poetry.' That voice
That was last heard asking for warm
Clothes and money, also knew the hunger
We all have for the gold light
The goldfinch carries into the air
Like a tang of crushed almonds.

'The Kremlin mountaineer' scaled
The peak of atrocity, seeking
The cold, final barbiturate
Tablet from the Winter God
That would melt in the mouths
He chose to feed. Bukharin,

Our poet's protector, was shot
Along with Yagoda, Rykov and others
Nine months before heart-failure
Silenced the silk-sharp whistle
That haunted the steppes as though
A small shrapnel of birds scattered.

A kerosene flash of music
Leaps from the black earth
Where the anchovied dead of the War
Pale into flammable spirit.
The escheated ground refuses
To fall back in the monster's arms

Because its sons are dead.
Son of Petropolis, tell us how to turn
Into the flash, to lie in the lice-red shirt
On the bank of the Styx and wait
For the Gossamer of Paradise

To spider in our dirt-filled eyes.

evidently chicken town

the fucking cops are fucking keen
to fucking keep it fucking clean
the fucking chief's a fucking swine
who fucking draws the fucking line
at fucking fun and fucking games
the fucking kids he fucking blames
are nowhere to be fucking found
anywhere in chicken town

the fucking scene is fucking sad
the fucking news is fucking bad
the fucking weed is fucking turf
the fucking speed is fucking surf
the fucking folks are fucking daft
don't make me fucking laff
it fucking hurts to look around
everywhere in chicken town

the fucking train is fucking late
you fucking wait you fucking wait
you're fucking lost and fucking found
stuck in fucking chicken town

the fucking view is fucking vile
for fucking miles and fucking miles
the fucking babies fucking cry
the fucking flowers fucking die
the fucking food is fucking muck
the fucking drains are fucking fucked
the colour scheme is fucking brown
everywhere in chicken town

the fucking pubs are fucking dull
the fucking clubs are fucking full
of fucking girls and fucking guys
with fucking murder in their eyes
a fucking bloke is fucking stabbed
waiting for a fucking cab
you fucking stay at fucking home
the fucking neighbours fucking moan
keep the fucking racket down
this is fucking chicken town

the fucking train is fucking late
you fucking wait you fucking wait
you're fucking lost and fucking found
stuck in fucking chicken town

the fucking pies are fucking old
the fucking chips are fucking cold
the fucking beer is fucking flat
the fucking flats have fucking rats
the fucking clocks are fucking wrong
the fucking days are fucking long
it fucking gets you fucking down
evidently chicken town

LINTON KWESI JOHNSON

Di Great Insohreckshan

it woz in April nineteen eighty-wan
doun inna di ghetto af Brixtan
dat di babylan dem cause such a frickshan
an it bring about a great insohreckshan
an it spread all ovah di naeshan
it woz a truly an histarical okayjan

it woz event af di year
an I wish I ad been dere
wen wi run riot all ovah Brixtan
wen wi mash-up plenty police van
wen wi mash-up di wicked wan plan
wen wi mash-up di Swamp Eighty-wan
fi wha?
fi mek di rulah dem andahstan
dat wi naw tek noh more a dem oppreshan

an wen mi check out
di ghetto grapevine
fi fine out all I coulda fine
evry rebel jussa revel in dem story
dem a taak bout di powah an di glory
dem a taak bout di burnin an di lootin
dem a taak bout smashin an di grabbin
dem a tell mi bout di vanquish an di victri

dem seh: di babylan dem went too far
soh wha?
wi ad woz fi bun two kyar
an wan an two innocent get mar
but wha?
noh soh it goh sometime inna war
een star
noh soh it goh sometime inna war?

dem seh: win bun dung di George
wi coulda bun di lanlaad
wi bun dung di George
wi nevah bun di lanlaad
wen wi run riot all ovah Brixtan
wen wi mash-up plenty police van
wen wi mash-up di wicked wan plan
wen wi mash-up di Swamp Eighty-wan

dem seh: wi commandeer kyar
an wi ghaddah aminishan
wi buil wi barricade
an di wicked ketch afraid
wi sen out wi scout
fi goh fine dem whereabout
den wi faam-up wi passi
an wi mek wi raid

now dem run gaan
goh plan countah-hackshan
but di plastic bullit
an di waatah canon
will bring a blam-blam
will bring a blam-blam
nevah mine Scarman
will bring a blam-blam

Swans in flight

It's like violence done to the atmosphere; as if Michelangelo reached out from the stone. And all the swans on the entire continent always take off together, for they are linked by a single signalling circuit. They are circling, and that means that Fortinbras's army is approaching. That Hamlet will be saved and that an extra act will be played. In all translations, in all theatres, behind all curtains and without mercy.

The actors are already growing wings against fate.

Hold out – that's all.

trans. Ewald Osers

Notes

Ugolino   Ugolino was blamed for Pisa's naval defeat by Genoa in 1284 and for the surrender of certain Pisan castles to Florence and Lucca. He intrigued with the Archbishop, who was the Ghibelline leader in Pisa.

from *Piers Plowman*   The cat has generally been taken to represent Edward III.

from *Vox Populi, Vox Dei*   See 'Poems Attributed to Skelton' in *The Poetical Works of John Skelton: With Notes and Some Account of the Author and his Writings* by the Rev. Alexander Dyce, 1833.

The Pillar Perished Is   In this free imitation of Petrarch, Wyatt laments the fall of his patron, Thomas Cromwell, who was executed on 28 July, 1540.

LXXXI   A poem about Queen Elizabeth. *Under a throne*, under a throne's canopy; *The red, and white rose*, roses of Lancaster and York; *Star of the North*, the Pole Star; *true guards*, stars that act as pointers.

XC   *nature*, human nature; *lists to draw*, pleases to pull out of shape, distort.

CI   *of pain*, of painful effort; *nature*, human nature; *set rates*, impose taxes.

To Penshurst   James I tried, by legislation, to make country nobles and gentry live in their country homes instead of succumbing to the pleasures of London, and this was because the social organization of England depended greatly upon regional authority exercised by great families. See Raymond Williams, *The Country and the City*; G. A. E. Parfitt, 'Ethical Thought and Ben Jonson's Poetry', *Studies in English Literature*, vol. IX. Winter 1969, no. 1.

The Hock-Cart   The hock-cart brought the last load of harvest; *maukin*, a pole bound with cloth, used as a scarecrow; *some cross the fill horse*, some bless the horse that draws the cart; *frumenty*, pudding made of milk, wheat and spices; *fans . . . fats*, winnowing-fans . . . vats; *neat*, cattle.

Epitaph on the Earl of Strafford   Thomas Wentworth, 1st Earl of Strafford, was a leading adviser to Charles I during the period preceding the Civil War. Unsuccessful in his attempt to quell the Scottish revolt of 1639–40, he was impeached by Parliament and executed on 12 May, 1641.

On the New Forcers of Conscience under the Long Parliament   In January 1645, Parliament adopted the Directory for Public Worship in place of the Book of Common Prayer. Here Milton attacks the Westminster Assembly's attempt to impose Presbyterianism by force.

On the Detraction which followed upon my Writing Certain Treatises   The treatises referred to in the title are Milton's divorce tracts.

To the Lord General Cromwell   Milton urges Cromwell not to accept a proposal to allow an established church with clergy paid for by the state. This would unite the civil and religious powers ('bind our souls with secular chains') and create a stipendiary clergy ('hireling wolves').

Paradise Lost, II, 226–378.   The phrase 'the sons of Belial' which Milton employs in *P.L.*, I, 501–2, was frequently used to describe cavaliers during the Civil War.

Paradise Lost, VII, 21–39   Here Milton alludes to the persecutions after the Restoration. He was forced to go into hiding while Marvell and other friends 'sought to save him from a revengeful Commons' (William Riley Parker, *Milton: a Biography*).

Paradise Lost, XI, 787–835   An attack on the time-servers in the puritan party (see lines 797–806). Noah, the 'one just man alive', is reminiscent of a second Cromwell. The 'wondrous ark' is the ideal commonwealth.

Paradise Lost, XII, 79–104   Alastair Fowler suggests this passage may recall Milton's regicide tracts.

Paradise Lost, XII, 157–235   The 'river-dragon' (line 192) is Pharaoh whom Milton uses in *De Doctrina* as the classic example of one whose heart was hardened. In *Eikonoklastes* he compares Pharaoh's blindness to that of King Charles.

Paradise Lost, XII, 466–551   A libertarian statement which looks forward to a subsequent revolution which will create a new heaven and earth. This prophecy forms part of the theological paradox of the fortunate fall. In lines 511–22, Milton expounds the central Protestant belief in the supremacy of the individual conscience.

Samson before the Prison in Gaza   Scholars differ as to the date of *Samson Agonistes*. In my view, those who choose the early dating (1647–53) tend to diminish the political significance of the drama. If we accept arguments which place the composition of *Samson Agonistes* during the last years of Milton's life, then it becomes an account both of the failure of the puritan commonwealth and of the persecuted Milton's powerlessness in post-Restoration England. As Christopher Hill shows, the 'idea of Samson as a symbol for the revolutionary cause, and especially for the revolutionary army, would be familiar to seventeenth-century readers'. And in an appendix to *Milton and the English Revolution*, Hill offers detailed and convincing arguments for *Samson Agonistes* being a post-Restoration drama.

The Grasshopper   Sent to Charles Cotton after the execution of Charles I. Don Cameron Allen comments that traditionally the grasshopper 'was a king, an aristocrat, a badge of royalty, a poet; and . . . it was identified with men in political disfavour'. See Don Cameron Allen, 'Richard Lovelace: "The Grasshopper",' *Seventeenth-Century English Poetry: Modern Essays in Criticism*, ed. W. R. Keast.

The Diggers' Song In 1649 there was considerable radical opposition to Oliver Cromwell. On 1 April the Diggers established a community on St George's Hill, a piece of common land near Weybridge in Surrey. The Diggers were harassed by Cromwell's officers and local landlords, and their movement faded out in 1651.

Upon Appleton House For a detailed account of this poem, see Christopher Hill's essay, 'Society and Andrew Marvell', in *Puritanism and Revolution*.

Absalom and Achitophel In 1678, Titus Oates testified before a London magistrate that he possessed evidence of a Jesuit plot to kill Charles II and place his Catholic brother, James, Duke of York, on the throne. The Whig Party, led by Anthony Ashley Cooper, 1st Earl of Shaftesbury, turned the 'Popish Plot' to political advantage and twice introduced, unsuccessfully, a bill to exclude James from the throne. When a new Parliament assembled in March 1681 at Oxford, the Whigs made a third attempt to bring in their exclusion bill, and in the House of Lords Shaftesbury proposed to the King that James Scott, the Duke of Monmouth, Charles's illegitimate son but a Protestant, should be declared his successor. Charles dissolved parliament and popular feeling began to turn against the Whigs.

A Grey Eye Weeping The 'prince who sheltered me' in 'A Time of Change' is Sir Nicholas Brown. Here O'Rahilly inveighs against his son.

Prometheus In 1722, William Wood, an English ironmaster, was granted a patent to coin Irish halfpence. This provoked angry opposition in Ireland. Swift's poem first appeared in 1724.

For A' That and A' That *gowd*, gold; *hoddin*, coarse grey homespun cloth; *birkie*, lively spry fellow; *coof*, clown, lout; *fa'*, lay claim to; *bear the gree*, win first place, come off best.

Charlie He's My Darling Charles Edward Stuart, the Young Pretender, was also known as the 'Young Chevalier' and 'Bonnie Prince Charlie'; *scroggy*, bushy, scrubby.

An Address to the Plebeians *fock*, folk; *geck*, scoff; *feck*, benefit; *thole*, suffer, bear; *jamph*, mock; *brie*, whiskey; *snirt an' snuff*, snigger and sniff; *sair the wyte*, sorely to blame; *buskit*, dressed; *kailyards*, kitchen-gardens; *slee*, wise; *brawlie*, admirably; *speer*, ask; *thrave*, crowd; *ding*, beat.

The File-Hewer's Lamentation *clam*, starve.

Iambes VIII André Chénier attacked the extremes of monarchist reaction and revolutionary terror. He was arrested in March 1794, and executed four months later, a few days before the fall of Robespierre, an event that would have saved him. Chénier's life and poetry are celebrated by Mandelstam in 'Remarks on Chénier'.

Symbolum Freemasonry was a major influence on the American and French revolutions. Although it now has a reactionary influence –

notably within the British police force – it was a radical political philosophy during the 18th century. See Margaret Jacob's study, *The Radical Enlightenment*.

But 'twas a time when Europe was rejoiced 'the very eve/Of that great federal day': 13 July 1790. Wordsworth arrived in France on 10 July 1790. 'The voluntary association of patriots for conference in the clubs, and for action in the National Guard, inspired the Provincial Federations, and culminated in the Parisian Fête of Federation on July 14th, 1790. The idea of celebrating the anniversary of the fall of the Bastille by an armed demonstration of representatives for the new departments was first suggested by the Paris districts, and was enthusiastically taken up in the provinces', J. M. Thompson, *The French Revolution*. See also, *Politics and the Poet: a Study of Wordsworth* by F. M. Todd.

Drone v. Worker   Ebenezer Elliott, the Chartist poet, was the author of *Corn Law Rhymes and Other Poems* (1833).

Gehazi   Gehazi is Rufus Isaacs who was Lord Chief Justice from 1913–21. In 1913, Isaacs and Lloyd George were acquitted of charges of corruption in the Marconi scandal.

The Right Heart in the Wrong Place   From a postcard to Stanislaus Joyce, 27 August 1920. Terence MacSwiney may have been a distant relative of Joyce's. Rumbold is Sir Horace Rumbold, British Minister to Switzerland in 1918, against whom Joyce had a grievance. In *Ulysses* the name 'Rumbold' is given to the hangman-barber in 'Cyclops'.

Voronezh   Written in 1936 after Akhmatova's visit to Mandelstam in Voronezh where he and his wife, Nadezdha, had been exiled. The battle referred to is the Battle of Kulikova Pole (1380) in which the Russians defeated the forces of the Golden Horde, thereby demonstrating the developing independence of the Russian lands from Tartar rule. The apparent optimism of this reference is subtly and obliquely undermined by the fact that historically the victory was of little political consequence. Two years later the Tartars invaded Russia, devastating the lands and looting and burning Moscow.

Last Statement   Mayakovsky committed suicide on 14 April 1930. The poem translated here was found among his papers. He included lines from it in his suicide note.

The Dead Liebknecht   Karl Liebknecht, an outspoken pacifist, was elected to the German Reichstag in 1912. With Rosa Luxemburg, he founded the Spartacus Union. He was killed by counter-revolutionaries in 1919.

Index of poets and works

Index of first lines

Acknowledgements

For permission to reprint copyright material the publishers gratefully acknowledge the following:

Faber & Faber Ltd and Random House Inc. for 'From scars where kestrels hover', 'Letter to Lord Byron', 'O what is that sound', 'Spain 1937', 'Who will endure' from *The English Auden: Poems, Essays and Dramatic Writings 1927–1939* by W. H. Auden and for 'In Praise of Limestone', 'Mountains', 'The Shield of Achilles' from *Collected Poems* by W. H. Auden; Farrar, Straus & Giroux Inc. for 'The Soviet Union' from *Love and Fame* by John Berryman; Farrar, Straus & Giroux Inc. for 'From Trollope's Journal' from *The Complete Poems*, copyright © 1961 by Elizabeth Bishop; Methuen (London) and Methuen Inc. for 'The God of War', trs. Michael Hamburger, from *Poems 1913–1956* by Bertolt Brecht; J. M. Dent and Sons Ltd for 'The Fallen Elm', 'The Flitting' from *The Poems of John Clare*, eds. J. W. and Anne Tibble; Curtis Brown Ltd for 'To the Snipe' from *Selected Poems and Prose of John Clare*, edited by Eric Robinson and Geoffrey Summerfield, copyright © Eric Robinson 1967; Arrow Publications for 'evidently chicken town' from *Ten Years in an Open-Necked Shirt* (1983) by John Cooper Clarke; Grafton Books and Liveright Publishing Corp. for 'next to of course god america i' from *The Complete Poems 1913–1962* by e. e. cummings; Grafton Books and Harcourt Brace Jovanovich Inc. for 'Thanksgiving' from *The Complete Poems 1913–1962* Copyright © 1957 by e. e. cummings; Carcanet Press Ltd for 'Remembering the Thirties' from *Selected Poems*, copyright © 1985 by Donald Davie; The Gallery Press for 'Osip Mandelstam' from *History Lesson* (1983) by Seamus Deane; Faber & Faber Ltd for 'Green Breeks', 'Washing the Coins' from *St Kilda's Parliament* by Douglas Dunn; Faber & Faber Ltd and Harcourt Brace Jovanovich Inc. for 'Little Gidding' (III) from *Four Quartets* in *Collected Poems 1909–1962* by T. S. Eliot; Secker & Warburg Ltd and Atheneum Publishers Inc. for 'karl heinrich marx', trs. Michael Hamburger, from *poems for people who don't read poems* by Hans Magnus Enzensberger; Jonathan Cape Ltd, Holt, Rinehart & Winston Inc., and the Estate of Robert Frost for 'Mending Wall' from *The Poetry of Robert Frost*, ed. Edward Connery Latham; Faber & Faber Ltd and Farrar, Straus & Giroux Inc. for 'Iron Landscapes' from *Jack Straw's Castle*, copyright © 1971, 1973, 1974, 1975, 1976 by Thom Gunn; Mushinsha Ltd for 'Alabama Bus' by Brother Will Hairston from *The Blues Line*, ed. Eric Sackheim; Rex Collings Ltd for 'On Not Being Milton' from *The School of Eloquence* by Tony Harrison; Faber & Faber Ltd and Farrar, Straus & Giroux Inc. for 'Punishment', 'Singing School: 2. A Constable Calls' from *North*, copyright © 1966, 1969, 1972, 1975, 1980 by Seamus Heaney; Faber & Faber Ltd and Farrar, Straus & Giroux Inc. for 'Casualty', 'Ugolino', from *Field Work*, copyright © 1976, 1979 by Seamus Heaney; Faber & Faber Ltd and Farrar, Straus & Giroux Inc. for an excerpt from 'Station Island' (XII) from *Station Island*, copyright © 1985 by Seamus Heaney; Adam Czerniawski and the author for 'Pan Cogito's Thoughts on Hell' by Zbigniew Herbert, translation copyright © Adam Czerniawski; Doubleday & Co., Inc. for 'Elegy of Fortinbras' by Zbigniew Herbert, trs. Czesław Miłosz and first published in *Encounter*, August 1961, copyright © 1961 by Encounter Ltd; Penguin Books Ltd for 'The End of a Dynasty' by Zbigniew Herbert, trs. Czesław Miłosz, translation copyright © 1968 by Czesław Miłosz; the *Observer* for 'From Mythology', 'The Return of the Proconsul' by Zbigniew Herbert, translation copyright © by Czesław Miłosz and first published in the *Observer*, 1962; André Deutsch for 'Idylls of the King' from *Tenebrae* by Geoffrey Hill; Bloodaxe Books Ltd